# THIS EDEN

# THIS EDEN

*Ed O'Loughlin*

riverrun

First published in Great Britain in 2021 by

riverrun

An imprint of

Quercus Editions Limited
Carmelite House
50 Victoria Embankment
London EC4Y 0DZ

An Hachette UK company

A CIP catalogue record for this book is available
from the British Library.

HB ISBN 978 1 52941 285 7
TPB ISBN 978 1 78087 175 2
EBOOK ISBN 978 1 78429 974 3

Typeset in Monotype Fournier by CC Book Production
Printed and bound in Great Britain by Clays Ltd, Elcograf S.p.A.

Papers used by Quercus Editions Ltd are from well-managed forests and other responsible sources.

For Bláthnaid and Iseult, alphabetically.

Mr Bond, they have a saying in Chicago: 'Once is happenstance. Twice is coincidence. The third time it's enemy action.'

— Auric Goldfinger, from *Goldfinger*, by Ian Fleming

# Prologue:

## *Wonderland*

ALICE AND MICHAEL HAD their first date, if you can call it that, at the Museum of Anthropology on the Vancouver campus of the University of British Columbia.

Their first meeting was an accident, as far as we can tell, generated by a random weather event – a light fall of snow. It was the final day of the first semester of their first year, and most of the engineering students had skipped their last class to enjoy the weather. Vancouver is warm, by Canadian standards, and snow doesn't last there. You have to use it while you can.

Fragments of that day – video clips and photos and social media updates – are still posted on various networks. Others, though since taken down, can be seen by those with the right kind of access. Michael didn't have any social media accounts, then or ever, but he later shared the pictures from his phone with Alice, who posted them with hers.

At first, we mostly see the students in a parking lot, grinning, red

Leabharlanna Poiblí Chathair Baile Atha Cliath
Dublin City Public Libraries

faced in the cold. A few, without gloves, have pulled the sleeves of their jackets over their hands; we can infer from this, and from the ice on their clothes, that there have already been snowballs.

Scroll down the timelines, and we see the same students in a different location, sliding on refuse sacks down a short slope towards a line of birch and pine trees. These birches have already shed the new snow, so we know it is already thawing. Beyond the stark trees we see the grey ocean, and a bank of grey cloud that will bring sleet or rain, and in that grey cloud the grey shapes of ships, riding at anchor. The rain has reached those ships, and is already falling on them, all those years ago. To the north, across English Bay, West Vancouver and the mountains are hidden by clouds.

The snow is thin, and the refuse sacks, sliding through it, uncover wide strips of bare grass. No one is wearing waterproof pants. This game won't last long.

Alice Field is in many of these pictures. She is wearing jeans, a red hiking jacket, no hat, no gloves, and canvas shoes that are already soaked. Her hair, which is naturally brown, is worn short and dyed red. She is laughing, but her eyes, which are also brown, never rest on the camera. She is watching the slope as it slides up to meet her, reading its curves. She likes to see a few moves ahead.

Michael Atarian – a dark-haired, slight kid with a shy but stubborn look – is in many of the images created in the parking lot, but in none of those that were posted from the snow slope. It could be that Michael had gone a few yards downhill to take shots of the others, and that the game had to be abandoned, washed out by that

4

cloud we saw over the ocean, that imminent rain in that long ago future, before Michael could have a go himself. Or it could be that Michael didn't like being photographed, and found ways to avoid it, most of the time.

Alice is at or near the centre of most of the pictures taken with Michael's phone. She will notice that, later.

The Museum of Anthropology is a five-minute walk from the place where they went sliding. It would have been the nearest shelter from the sleet and rain about to blow off English Bay. It was there that the last few photos of the afternoon were taken, in the glass Great Hall at the centre of the building, surrounded by cultural artefacts of the indigenous peoples of the Pacific Northwest, such as a frontal pole from a longhouse, a Haida canoe, and a Tsimshian bentwood chest, bright in their colours and lines. In a series of selfies, three other students are packed around Michael, pulling faces. One of these is Alice. The other two students, a boy and a girl, are named in the timelines, but they are of no further interest to us.

The final photograph shows Alice and Michael alone, beside a high window looking over a pond. Rain is streaming down the window, rotting the snow outside. Both are still smiling, but, with the other two gone, there is room in the frame for some daylight between them: alone together, they look awkward. It was probably around this time that Alice suggested coffee in a cafe off the lobby. That's how she remembered it, anyway.

And her memory checks out, in so far as we can check it. Alice Field and Michael Atarian had their first date, if you can call it that, in the University of British Columbia's Museum of Anthropology, on Friday, 21 December of their first year at university.

THEY HAD THEIR SECOND date the evening of the day after the snowfall. They met at an Italian restaurant near her house in Kitsilano, where they shared a large pizza and, having shown their IDs, a bottle of Okanagan red. It seemed to Alice that the rain hadn't stopped since the afternoon before. Water ran down the window next to their table. That's how she remembered it. And it checks out: she was right. It hadn't stopped raining.

Afterwards, they split the bill, went back to her house and opened another bottle of wine, though they didn't really need it. It was clear where this was going. The only question left for Alice was why. They sat together on the living-room couch, facing the TV, though it wasn't on. They talked about lectures, about the weather, about classmates. The important thing was to keep talking until the situation resolved itself. She listened to the rain on the window, looked at the blank TV. She'd done all this before. Why did this time feel different?

She remembered the snowball fight in the parking lot the day before. The students had formed rival skirmish lines, with those who already knew each other a little more likely to choose the same side. Car roofs provided the wet, sticky snow that is perfect for snowballs.

Alice, who had come to the fight alone, had turned to scoop snow from the hood of a Buick when she sensed rather than saw a snowball flying towards her, coming the wrong way, from behind her own lines. She ducked behind the Buick, and when she bobbed up again she saw him: a dark-haired boy, the other side of the car, looking sheepish. She hadn't noticed him in any of their classes. It was like he too had just fallen from the sky.

Hey, she yelled. That's cheating!

It was a bad throw. I wasn't aiming at you.

Yeah? Well, stop hiding back there. If you want to be in this fight you have to pick a side.

Two minutes later, she was reloading again when she felt a snowball hit the back of her knee. She turned. He was standing in the other line of battle, fifteen yards across from her, with another snowball ready to go. This one was also meant for her, but it flew a foot wide.

She hit him on the chest, then turned away to scoop up more snow.

Another snowball flew past her head, a little high this time. She tucked her new snowball in her left armpit, made another, turned to find him. His back was to her as he gathered more snow. This time she hit him on the nape of the neck, where the slush would slide under his collar. The shot was deliberate. She had a good arm.

He turned, gasping from the shock of the ice running down his bare back. It must have felt delicious. She would always remember his face when he saw her, waiting for his full attention, her second snowball ready to go.

He snatched a shot at her, hit her on the shoulder. He seemed shy, but he wasn't the type to give up. Which was probably how, on this couch in Kitsilano, he had just found the courage to take hold of her hand.

Alice was careful not to pack her snowballs too tight. That way, she could go for head shots without doing damage. He had brushed the ice from his eyes and mouth, picked lumps of slush from the front of his collar. Finally, he managed to speak.

You throw like a girl, he said.

Most of the boys she had been with before were athletic types, self-centred and sure, worth dating for their muscles and then getting rid of, if they didn't bail first. They always wanted her to act like a girl, whatever that meant; she didn't care. They were frightened of silences, but expected her to fill them. She liked to be quiet, most of the time. This kid was also quiet, and he didn't seem to mind that they'd both fallen silent on this couch in Kitsilano.

Before this, Alice hadn't really bothered to see herself as pretty. Now, looking into the unlit television, she saw herself and Michael reflected in its screen. She liked to step outside herself, to watch herself from a distance, to be as objective as she could about the subjective. She wondered, watching herself and Michael in that black rectangle, if that first wildly thrown snowball, the one that connected them, had really been random, or if other forces had vectored it in. She decided that if she hadn't sensed it and ducked, it would have hit her. That choice, at least, had been hers. If you want to play this game, you have to pick a side. Reflected in the screen, they looked pretty together. That would do her for now. She kissed him.

*

8

ALICE STILL LIVED IN the house she'd grown up in. It had been built in the 1920s from timber frame and shingle, and was small and warm, clean enough, for the most part, though Alice's parents had a liking for clutter. They'd been renting there for years, from a friend who was, like them, a holdout from the old days, when people without money could still live in Kitsilano. Their rent was a relic of easier times.

The house stood on a corner where two side streets met, with the living room in the angle, so the rain had its pick of two windows to run down. Sometimes, when the wind was right, it could wash down both windows at once. As a little girl, Alice loved to turn out the lights and stand on the arm of the couch in the corner. From there, she could look out each window in turn. She watched the cars on the street, headlights mirrored in wet asphalt. The lit windows of houses shimmered with rain. Sometimes, in winter, when the weather cleared and the moon was bright, the peaks showed white above the trees at the end of the street. Other times, when there was no moon, she could see a few of the brightest stars, shining through the haze of light thrown up by the city.

There was a payphone on the corner, and Alice liked to watch the people who came to use it. She wondered who they were, and why they were making calls on a payphone; even her parents had cell phones by then. Some people stayed a long time inside the box, misting the glass with their breath. Others opened the door, reached in without entering, then wandered away again. Years later, she understood: they were checking the refund slot for lost change, begging alms from a forsaken shrine.

Eventually, her parents would come in and turn the lights back on and carry her off to the room she shared with her big sister. She had everything she wanted: the city and the mountains and the rain on the window. She thought she could never live anywhere else.

ON THEIR FIRST MORNING there together, when the light crept up the walls, Michael noticed a black and white photograph over the bed. It showed two young people with short, spiky hair, and eyeliner, and Dr. Martens boots. They were holding hands, unsmiling. The girl had a torn dress, the boy wore an old army jacket. The girl looked like Alice.

The far wall was taken up by a closet and a bookcase – novels and travel and history and science. The closet was open. He saw men's clothes on hangers. Among them was an old army jacket.

He sat up in the bed.

This is your parents' room.

She pulled him down again.

It's mine, for now.

They aren't coming back today?

They work up in the Territories. They teach high school math. They earn more money up there, and it'll bump up their pensions for when they retire. I'm paying the rent until we've saved enough to buy this place. We have first refusal.

She pushed across him, pinning him down.

What about you?

What about me?

Your parents. Where are they?

So he told her.

A FEW DAYS AFTER his nineteenth birthday, when Michael was finishing high school, his parents were driving to work on the edge of Grande Prairie, Alberta, when a truck full of steel for the McMurray oil sands ran a red light and flattened their car. The driver, who was trying to clear off some mortgage arrears, had exceeded his permissible hours, and fell asleep at the wheel. He went to jail, and his family lost its home, and then fell apart. But that doesn't matter. We've checked the incident from every possible angle and it seems to have been a genuine accident, if accidents are ever really a thing.

Because Michael was past his eighteenth birthday there wasn't much the government could do for him, or to him. But his high school had a contract with a grief counsellor, and the principal sent him to see her. He only went once.

The counsellor's notes for the session are covered by patient confidentiality, but she typed up a transcript at home, then emailed it to her office inbox. Which makes it accessible. It goes like this:

Hi, Mike. Please sit down.

Thanks . . . I prefer to go by Michael.

OK, then: Michael . . . Ms Shevchenko says that your teachers are worried about your reaction to your terrible loss. She says that you went to school the day after the funeral and acted like nothing had happened.

I didn't want to stay at home.

Do you like school?

No.

But you have friends there?

Sure. A few.

Are they being supportive?

I don't really know. I've been kind of avoiding them.

Why?

I don't want to make a big deal of it.

Pause.

OK . . . It says here you have no relatives in Canada. Do you have any family in . . . ? Your parents were from Iran, it says here?

My parents didn't talk about that. They never mentioned any relatives.

So you're alone in the world?

I guess.

I am truly very sorry for you.

Thanks.

Pause.

Were you close to your parents?

I don't know. I guess.

Do you miss them?

Yes.

Pause.

I'm here to help you, Mike, if you'll let me. You've suffered a terrible loss. It helps to talk about these things. It helps to share your feelings with other people.

I don't want to.

Why not?

I don't want to have to think about it.

What's wrong with facing your feelings, Mike?

Part of me is glad that my parents are dead.

You're *glad* that your parents have passed?

They were always scared of something . . . Now that they're gone, I don't have to worry about them. It's like they finally got away.

This grief counsellor wrote *Sociopath?* in her notebook. She had missed the point entirely. Unsure what to do next, she turned to techniques used for drawing out people who are in shock or denial. She didn't think that he was in shock or denial, but the school paid by the hour, so she needed to run down the clock.


THERE WAS A TRUCK, a stop light, a sleep-deprived driver. The truck was hauling twenty tons of steel rods for reinforcing poured concrete. It was moving at fifty miles per hour when it T-boned their pickup. Unlike Michael, they wouldn't have suffered.

As soon as he left early childhood, and could see outside the nest that they had built for him, Michael had started to feel sorry for his parents. He tried to take care of them, their native-born son.

You don't have to live like this, he told them, many times over. You've been in this country for years. I'm a born citizen. There are amnesties and lawyers. You're smart; you shouldn't have to clean washrooms and warehouses, or deliver junk food, or work in the back of greasy spoons. You're not too old to learn better English, get yourselves some education. You need to save money and buy a house, before it's too late for you. There's no future for you, living like kids.

Needling them like this was, among other things, his way of getting back at them for all the questions they wouldn't answer about their past.

His parents never took his advice. Sometimes, at night, through the door of his bedroom, he heard them talking in Farsi, which they wouldn't speak in front of him. It usually meant the same thing: they'd be moving on again, looking for another rental trailer, or short-let apartment, or cash-only job in some northern mining camp, where questions weren't asked, and where housing was part of the deal.

It was in one of these bush camps, he later told Alice, that he'd decided to become an engineer – a civil engineer, someone who moved about all the time, from project to project, but always belonged wherever they were. Someone who built bridges across rivers, bringing new roads to mine camps and oil wells. Solid on the ground, a man who could buy a house for his parents, and maybe someday build a home for himself.

His dad reckoned Michael wasn't good enough at mathematics to get into engineering. His mother thought he would make a good teacher, or maybe a nurse. So when Michael rebelled he became an A student, and scraped into engineering at UBC.

WHEN ALICE WAS A little girl there was always a chess game on the go in the corner of the living room, on a cheap-looking set made of cardboard and plastic.

Alice didn't know the rules of chess, but she noticed that sometimes the pieces were all lined up along opposite ends of the board, and then they would start creeping towards each other, one at a time, over a period of weeks, shifting around the board or retiring to the side of it, like the sin bin in hockey, until one day they would all be back on their start lines, and the battle would begin again.

She never saw her parents go near the chessboard in the living room; they played their own games at the kitchen table, on a magnetised travel set, drinking red wine.

Who was playing this mysterious game? Alice could have asked her parents, but she liked to think that they hadn't noticed the board in the living room, or that they had forgotten about it, or that maybe they couldn't even see it: maybe this game had ghosts for players, or, even better, maybe its pieces had lives of their own, had picked their own fights and were making their own moves. She decided she'd say nothing to anyone, not even to her big sister, Brigid. She would study the problem until she had solved it or it went away.

One day, she was home sick from kindergarten when the mailman came. She sat at the kitchen table, wrapped in her favourite blanket, and watched her father sort through the letters. Among the bills and junk mail was a small, square white envelope, with a British stamp.

There you are, her father said, looking happy.

He opened the envelope. It contained a white card with a few symbols scrawled on it. He pulled a face, then put it in his shirt pocket.

Uh oh, he said to himself. Uh oh.

Alice followed him through to the living room, dragging her blanket across the floor. He stood, looking down at the phantom chessboard, pulling a face. Oh, Alice thought, disappointed. So he can see it too.

Her father moved one of the pieces.

You can't do that!

He looked round at her, puzzled.

What do you mean?

That's not your game! Put it back like it was!

He did.

It *is* my game, though. It's mine, and your mother's.

You play chess in the kitchen. And Sophia's not here.

He pulled the armchair over to the chessboard.

Come sit in my lap.

Reluctantly, she crossed the floor to join him. She knew that by doing so she would lose something precious. He was about to explain the mystery to her. She'd rather have kept things as they were.

You see here, all these white pieces? Your mom and I are white. The black pieces are a friend of ours, one of our old gang. He's doing research at Cambridge, in England. He's just told us his next move.

Her father took the card out of his pocket.

See? It's written here – *P to QB6*.

He moved one of the black pieces, the same one as before.

Pawn to Queen's Bishop Six. Unless your mom can think of something amazing, I think he's going to beat us in the next four moves.

How will you tell him your move, if he's in England?

We'll mail it to him, like he mails his to us. They call it correspondence chess, because you play it by snail mail, one move at a time. It's the most dangerous game in the world.

No it's not.

She tried to wriggle away from him. He knew that she didn't like to be teased. It made her feel hard, and cold, and lonely, and it made her want to hide away. He laughed and kissed her hair.

It's true. More people die playing this game than any other. Even boxing or hockey. Can you guess why?

He had set her a problem. He knew that she loved a puzzle. She thought for a while.

Is it because the games take so long?

I knew that you'd get it. The longer the game, the greater the chance you'll get sick or have an accident before it's over.

So why not send the moves by email? That would be quicker.

He didn't answer for a while, and, though she couldn't see his face, she knew before he spoke that he wouldn't be telling her all of the truth.

We like it like this. It's an old-fashioned way to let our friend know we're here for him. We know that he likes that, to know that we're here.

The game is a message?

Sort of, yeah. But it's also a chess game. And he always wins.

He patted her shoulder.

Get off of me. I'll make us some lunch.

Alice squirmed away from him. Her blanket, dragging behind her, brushed across the little table and pulled the chessboard to the floor. The pieces scattered everywhere, across the wooden floor, under the couch and the armchair, on to the Afghan rug in the middle of the room. She clapped her hands to her mouth, unable to speak.

He put an arm around her, squeezed her.

Don't worry. I can put them all back where they should be. I keep the game in my head.

She wriggled free of him. It would be hard for her father to reach the pieces under the couch. That was one of her secret places; she liked to lie very still there, to watch the rectangle of light that was the rest of the universe, to try to figure it out without being seen.

She slid on her belly and collected the stray pieces.

Here, she said, handing the white ones to her father. These are yours.

He held out his other hand.

I'll need the black ones too.

I'll put them back for your friend, she said.

He watched her replacing the black pieces on the chessboard, each one on the correct square, where the game had left it. When she was finished she looked at him.

Your turn.

He started replacing the white pieces.

Sweetie, he said, it's time we taught you how to play chess.

MICHAEL HAD TO SPEND one last summer alone in Grande Prairie before starting college. He got a job as a pizza delivery driver. It kept him out of the empty apartment at night.

At the end of that last summer, when the lease on the apartment expired, Michael had to move on again. This time, he would be the one to decide where he went. The choice can't have been easy. He'd been accepted by the University of British Columbia's Faculty of Engineering, but why bother with that now? It would cost a lot of money that he didn't have, and he knew he'd struggle with the coursework. Plus, his parents wouldn't be needing that house anymore, would they? Then again, he may have felt that they were watching him. He may have still wanted to prove them both wrong. Love is a difficult habit to break.

Michael packed a suitcase with clothes, and filled a plastic box with computer gear. The rest of the stuff in the apartment – his parents' clothes, the kitchen stuff, a TV, some books written in Farsi, which Michael couldn't read – went to a thrift store. The apartment was furnished. His parents lived light.

Still unsure where he would go next, Michael came back from the thrift store to make one final tour of the empty rooms, hoping that something or someone would say goodbye to him, or offer advice. This was where he'd last seen his parents. There was something new there, something that hadn't been there that morning when he cleared the place out: a sports bag, sitting in the middle of the floor in his parents' bedroom. It contained a large amount of currency in midsize denominations – used, non-sequential bills.

His parents had never had money or friends. He didn't know where this money had come from, but he knew a sign when he saw one. He put the bag in the trunk of his car. He reckoned it might be enough to keep him going all the way through college. You could count that as a blessing. On the other hand, without the money to bind him to the promise that he'd made to himself, and his parents, though they hadn't asked him, to be an engineer, to live a solid life and buy someone or other a house, he might have escaped from this story, if escape is ever really a thing.

Michael left the apartment just as the three of them had found it, two years before: the keys hidden in the fuse box, the front door on the latch.


ALICE ASKED MICHAEL TO move into her house two months after they met. They were young and good-looking and healthy, and they were both really nice people – there was never any doubt about that. Before that, he'd been staying with three other male students he'd found on Craigslist, sharing a dump of an apartment, way out in Burnaby – a long commute and a horrible rent. Alice reckoned that if it didn't work out she could just kick him out again. That's what she wrote in an email to her big sister Brigid, a final year student of

English at McGill, in Montreal. An arrangement made freely could be easily ended. Even the cleverest people believe stupid things.

By then, they had fallen in love with each other, in the way that young people do, the first time they have their own place to themselves. Not much thinking was required. Those first few months they stayed at home a lot. And when their class schedules kept them apart – she would specialise in computers, he was aiming for civil – Alice sometimes sent him photographs of herself, taken at home after he'd left. He had to sit at the back of the class so that no one could see over his shoulder. Later, when he was by himself, he would repay her in writing, by email or text – as we said, he never used social media. He wrote pretty well, considering: he knew to keep it simple and short, and avoid similes, euphemisms and anatomical detail. Alice read, reread and saved his messages for later, waiting for him to come home. But Michael would leave it a day or two and then delete her photos. Or he thought he did: nothing can ever be truly deleted.

It isn't clear to us why he got rid of her photographs. She didn't ask him to, and he doesn't seem to have been prudish. He was, according to the emails that Alice sent her sister, well worth sleeping with, and had earned the intimacy implicit in the photos. Maybe he worried about privacy. He never said.

But Michael would later regret deleting those photographs. We know this because he tried to recover them, and left fingerprints on the servers on which they'd been stored. But those caches had long since been cleared, at least as far as someone like Michael was concerned. If he wanted to see her again, he'd have to make do with his memory, dreams, imagination – analogue tools for seeing our loved ones after we've lost them, if not before.

THE FULL NAME ON Alice's birth certificate was Lydia Alice Field. *Lydia* was a nod by her parents to the punk-art performer Lydia Lunch. *Alice* was just a name that they liked. Her mother's sur-name, listed on the birth certificate, was Kennedy. Sophia Kennedy came from old stock in western Canada, being a descendant of the Saskatchewan-born polar explorer Captain William Kennedy, whose mother was Cree, his father from Orkney. A paternal great-grandfather, Moshé Feld, had fled the Ukrainian pogroms in a round-about direction, crossing Siberia by rail, track and steam-boat, working his passage from Vladivostok to Vancouver. He thought that B.C. was heaven, and he stopped running when he got there; he never went further east than the mountains. Alice never met him, but hoarded this story as personal lore.

At the age of four, Lydia Alice Field read Lewis Carroll for the first time, and decided that she wanted to go by her second given name instead. Her parents went along with this. They figured that any child who could read a book like that at such a young age had the right to be heard. And, as it turned out, the name Alice really suited her. She would spend her life hunting down rabbit holes.

The full name on Michael's Manitoba birth certificate was Mike Daniel Atarian. Most likely, his immigrant parents had wanted him to fit in, so they gave him what they thought were generic Canadian names. In fact, the first name written on the registration form was originally *Jack*, but this was immediately crossed off and replaced with *Mike*. The second given name on the form, Daniel, was left as it was. Maybe the clerk made a little joke to warn them:

Jack Daniel? You sure you want to call him that? Why not Crown Royal?

Five years later, when Michael started kindergarten in Saskatoon, Saskatchewan, the school secretary seems to have assumed that his name had been shortened, because she wrote *Michael* in the register instead of *Mike*. His parents never bothered to correct her. They weren't the sort of people to make a fuss. And so the name stuck in his permanent record.

His father's name, Samvel Atarian, as written on Michael's birth registration, contains the common Armenian and Farsi suffix -ian or -yan, which translates as 'son of'. This suffix can be found in many Christian, Muslim and Jewish names from Persia and its region, so it doesn't tell you much about Michael's father. Likewise, his mother's name on the form, Nadia Jalil, would be unremarkable anywhere in the Muslim and Arabic worlds, and, even so, not all of those who go by the names Nadia or Jalil are Muslims or Arabs. Michael wasn't raised in any religion. His parents never told him who they were before they came to Canada. And the names on his birth certificate were fake.

*

ALICE HAD A STICKER on her laptop that said *This Machine Kills Fascists*. She worked in her old bedroom, which she used as an office, the bed covered with books and other debris. There were posters on the walls for The New Pornographers and The Fall, and photographs of the writers William Gibson, who lived in Kitsilano, and Philip K. Dick, who had attempted to die there. One wall was lined with Ikea tables loaded with monitors and drives and printers and servers, tangled in wires like strangler figs. There was also a chess set with plastic pieces and a folding board, the sort you'd give a child as a stocking filler. This board was a mystery to Michael. Its pieces moved around by their own free will, it seemed to him, but never when he was watching. He never saw Alice go near it. And she never asked him to play her. She must have guessed that he wasn't that good.

Michael was now in a different stream to Alice at college, having barely scraped through his first-year exams. She was in software, he was in civil. But as their second year of college went on, Alice spent less time on campus, more time in her room on her own private business. She had side projects, freelance gigs, invisible friends. Her interests had a lot to do with climate change, and encryption, and the detection of fake news and online malefactors. She was in contact with hacktivists, data campaigners, human rights advocates. They came to her for help.

One day, bringing Alice a coffee, he noticed a new screen saver on her favourite laptop. It showed the winking face of Campbell Fess, billionaire founder and CEO of the tech conglomerate Inscape Technologies, materialising from behind a dissolving Guy Fawkes mask. Fess had commissioned this GIF for his social media profiles. Michael wasn't on social media, but he recognised it anyway. That meme had been everywhere lately.

You hate Campbell Fess, he said to Alice. Why do you want his face as your screen saver?

She closed the lid on her laptop, swivelled to face him.

Because Fess acts like that GIF is a joke, like he's one of us, but it's exactly the opposite. He's saying, You can operate all you like, but people like me always know what you're doing. His face only appears on my screen when I stop working. It tells me it's time to get back in the fight.

What fight is that, Alice?

Against people like Fess. They use their money and tech to sell people lies about race and guns and God and the environment, so they can control them. And they sell them the biggest lie of all, which is that nothing is real or true, so nothing really matters, that things have to be this way, and there's nothing we can do. This planet is our lifeboat, and Fess and his pals are in it with the rest of us, but they're hacking it to pieces and flogging each other the bits. They're selling out their own children. They've gotten so selfish, their own genes can't keep up with them.

Alice became embarrassed by her own sermons if they went on too long. Michael probably thought it was his job to say something to stop her. But he didn't have any real politics of his own. So he teased her instead.

Will you still feel like that when your first start-up goes public?

He *must* have been joking. She told herself that. She knew about jokes. But he must have known how serious she was about the things that she cared about. He should have known; he was one of them. But his parents had taught him to trust nobody and nothing. And Alice didn't know why, then. Michael had said to her, more than once, that we can only rely on ourselves in this life, but she had written that off as some Alberta bullshit.

He doesn't really know me, thought Alice. After that, she rarely talked to him about her other life. It was the first thing that she knew they would not have in common, the end of that time when everything seems possible, when bodies feel endless in each other's arms.

ALICE COULD SEE PAST Michael, now. She tried to make up for this by mothering him. He needed help with his class work. She would re-explain calculus to him at the kitchen table, the one where her parents used to play chess. It took up a lot of her time in the evenings. Often, to make up for this, she would work late in her old bedroom, then smoke hash or weed to help her get to sleep. Sometimes, she'd fall asleep in there, in her old bed. If you had told her, a year before, that they could be in the same house and not sleep together, it would have sounded nuts.

One night, she woke up alone in the small hours, in her old bed, fully dressed. She couldn't remember going to sleep.

There was a sound outside the door. It was what had awoken her. A floorboard creaked as if a weight was lifting off it. She lay there, listening. The sound came again, and again. But the sound had a rhythm. Old timbers were settling. There was no one sneaking about in the hall.

After her first relief, it came to her that she would have liked to hear the bedroom door opening, and see Michael's shadow, tiptoeing in to join her. There would be barely enough room for two in this narrow bed. It would be like the first times, when they'd lain pressed together all night, wasting the space of her parents' king-size mattress. It seemed to her, alone in the dark, that sleeping together in here would feel hot and adolescent. Weren't they adolescents still? It would feel transgressive. They had never done it in her old bed before. They could stifle their noises, pretend that her parents were sleeping next door.

She wondered to what extent her love for Michael – and his love for her, if that's what it was – was bound up with physical warmth, and comfort and shelter: the same things she'd been given, in a different form, by her parents. Would animal warmth be enough to keep them together when there were other things that would pull them apart? She decided, after some thought, staring at the street light in the gap above the blinds, that warmth would be enough for her, for now. Alice was a dreamer, but she was also pragmatic. She got up, took her clothes off, and tiptoed next door.

ONE EVENING, IN THE first semester of their third year at college, Michael cycled home from class, cold and soaked, and found Alice waiting for him with a bottle of wine.

I've decided to drop out of school, she said.

By now, Alice was earning good money by tutoring students in the years above her. Headhunters emailed, even called her on the phone. Still, Michael pretended that he was surprised.

Why?

I've been working on a thing of my own. I didn't tell you about it before because I wasn't sure it could work. Now, I think it can. If you want, you can do it with me.

I'm not like you, Alice. I'll need a degree to get work after college.

Not if you're working for me.

She didn't notice how this stung him. She went on:

I'll handle all the coding and stuff. You'll do what admin there is, and the front and back of house. There won't be much of that, but you'd be very useful. A lot of people in this scene don't like dealing with women.

So I'd be your beard.

You'd be my partner.

Tell me about it, he said at last.

She poured him some wine.

Here's what it is: it's a distributed peer-to-peer cash ledger, a lot like a blockchain, but maintained altruistically, as a co-op, with no coin mining and no environmental cost.

Sorry?

OK . . . It's a new kind of bank. Sort of. But for cash only. It stores all its cash with its customers, and moves it on demand from person to person, without any middleman. Like a dating app for money. Or a crowd-sourced ATM.

I don't get it.

OK . . . Suppose you belong to our network. You've installed our app and paid in a deposit, maybe a few hundred bucks. Later, if you needed some cash, you would order it from our app, just like you'd order pizza or a taxi. Our network would find a member nearby who was holding some cash and wanted to offload it. You'd arrange to meet them somewhere secure. You'd use the app to authenticate the transaction, they'd hand you the cash, then you'd go your own ways.

What's wrong with regular ATMs?

They charge ridiculous fees. And worse than that, they're *watching* us – them and everyone else who has access to their data.

So it's really about secrecy?

It's about freedom. Think about it: you can't get paid anymore, or make most kinds of payments, without going through the servers of a credit card or a bank. Some countries are even talking about banning cash completely, and pushing all payments online. And Silicon Valley wants to take it a step further and launch its own cryptocurrency. OmniCent, they're calling it. Campbell Fess and Inscape are taking the lead, because they dominate fintech. If it works the way I think it would, it could end up replacing all the money in the world.

How is your thing different from that? Or any other cryptocurrency?

It's *totally* different. Mine is based on cash, not control of online data. Cash is our last freedom. Without it, whoever controls the machines controls all the money, and controls all of us. In *The Handmaid's Tale*, they turned women into serfs overnight by transferring all their money into accounts owned by their men. Soon, that won't be fiction: they could switch off anyone they don't like. But as long as there's cash, we still have some wriggle room. We can log off, put our phone in a drawer, take a bus and pay in change, or buy a hot dog from a stand. And we can give a few coins to some poor bastard on East Hastings so they can buy something that's bad for them but they really need. Which is why we'll handle small change too, on principle. The banks won't give you change for a buck anymore. But we will.

Seriously? Who the hell is going to go online to ask a stranger for loonies or quarters?

Maybe someone who's too shy to ask a stranger on the street. Maybe someone who's looking for change for a payphone.

*Pay*phones? Do they still exist?

Sure they do. People just don't notice them anymore because we've all got our own smart phones. But I see them everywhere. They're invisible time machines. Like the Tardis.

How is this going to make us money?

It won't.

What?

It won't make any money. We won't offer loans, or invest the deposits. No interest, no profits, no bank charges, no creation of sketchy new money through reckless lending. It'll be completely frictionless.

How are we supposed to eat, if we're not getting paid?

I can earn enough by freelance coding to keep us both going. We'll keep our names out of it, and when the project is up and running we'll just disappear. Like Satoshi Nakamoto. Or Keyser Söze. No one even needs to know who we are.

You're bullshitting me, aren't you? You're not really going to do this?

I'm calling it Yoyodime. It's a pun — like the Yoyodyne corporation, in Thomas Pynchon.

I haven't read him.

You don't read enough fiction, Michael. You'd be surprised what you could learn.

It's a crazy idea.

You don't want to do it?

Michael had never told Alice about the bag of money on the floor of the empty Alberta apartment. When they'd first met, he told her that he was paying his way through college with compensation from the trucking firm whose driver killed his folks. He must have wanted to seem more substantial than he was. In fact, the insurance wouldn't pay out for his parents because it couldn't find any trace of their legal existence. Michael must not have wanted Alice to know this, or that he had taken that money, not knowing who it really belonged to. To make things worse, the cash hadn't lasted as long as he'd expected; Vancouver was even more expensive than he'd thought. Now it was almost spent, and he still couldn't tell her.

It's different for me, Alice. I'll need a degree to get any kind of real job. Things don't come easy to people like me. Not like for you.

His gesture took in the house, Alice, the wine on the table.

And Alice, hurt again, believed then what she hadn't believed before, that maybe he too could see past the pair of them. She never mentioned Yoyodime to Michael again. Secrets breed secrets.

EVERY SUMMER THEY WOULD get jobs in the Rockies, working in tourist resorts, hiking the trails. For Alice, it wasn't so much for the money as the chance to be outdoors. For Michael, it was both. There was another reason too: summers in Jasper gave them something in common.

A week before the summer vacation in Michael's third year, when he was on campus, sitting an exam, Alice opened a letter addressed to her parents. It was from the estate of the woman who owned the house, telling them that she was dead. The house had already been sold to an overseas property trust that rented out period homes in bijou locations. So much for first refusal.

The letter noted that Alice's family didn't seem to have a formal lease or written agreement with the late owner of the house. It advised them to make contact with the new owners' representatives, details enclosed.

Alice said nothing to Michael, and sent off an email.

Two days later a letter arrived from a company called Mayfield Real Estate Investment Trust, with an address at the office of a big downtown law firm. This letter acknowledged that the Fields seemed to have had an informal arrangement with the previous proprietor, and therefore the new owners were prepared to give them a chance to enter into a new tenancy agreement.

There it was: a first refusal, of sorts.

If they wished to formalise their tenancy, they should please provide the listed documents, guarantees, and deposit, and sign the enclosed lease. Rent had been adjusted in line with the present market rates in Kitsilano, a district considered highly desirable for its bayside location and bohemian history. If this was not satisfactory, they should please get ready to vacate the house.

Alice did some sums in her head, hid the letter.

When Michael came home she was making them dinner. She had opened another bottle of wine. He looked at it, and then at her.

What's wrong?

I can't go to the mountains this summer. I have work to do here.

Seriously? Work? Not your Yoyodime thing, is it? Or some other cause?

No, it's not Yoyodime, or any of my *causes*. I have to take on some more freelance coding. I need the money.

Since when do you give a damn about money?

Since the landlord just raised our rent.

You said the rent hadn't gone up since the nineties.

Now it has.

How much?

She told him his share of it. He looked surprised.

That's not as bad as I would have thought, in this market. But we can't afford it.

I can. I get offers of work all the time.

What about my half? I haven't got that kind of money.

Then just pay what you pay already. I'll make up the difference.

She saw that he was tempted. But he put the temptation away.

I'll pay my full share. But why don't we just move somewhere else? This house is too big for us, anyway. And there are way cheaper places to rent than Kitsilano.

I'm keeping the house for my parents, for when they retire.

Pensioners can't pay that kind of rent either, or those prices.

I'll think of something. Until then, I have to keep up the lease on this house.

MAYBE, IT OCCURRED TO Alice later, it had suited Michael to go to the mountains without her. Maybe they both needed the space and time apart. But he insisted on sending her his share of the rent, all summer long. She couldn't refuse it.

When he came back in the fall for his final year of university he got a job – or rather, work – delivering takeout food on his bicycle, weekends and nights, taking orders from an app that was based in California. He could have used that time better for studying for classes, where he was struggling, but he was determined to pay Alice his full share of the rent.

To go to work, Michael would put on the cheap spandex shirt that the company had sent him after he paid a non-refundable deposit. He would strap the insulated food box, which he'd also had to pay for, to the back of his mountain bike, and then he'd wait for the app on his phone to ping. When it did, he had seconds to bid against other unseen members of the Neighbourhood Delivery Community for the chance to pick up from a nearby joint. If his bid was accepted, the app would monitor his progress with his phone's location services. Each delivery was timed and logged by a database, and an algorithm would send him smiley-faced warnings if it thought he was too slow. But the algorithm had been coded in California, and it didn't seem to know or care about Vancouver conditions, about steep roads, slick with dead leaves and spilled oil, or the insistent rain. He had a couple of falls and collisions that winter, as we can confirm from his medical records. To maintain his performance-related pay rate, he worked most of the way through a dose of the flu, infecting several of his clients. His fitness monitor, which backed his figures up online, tells us that he lost ten pounds. But his tax records show that his earnings, when averaged by the hour, were a good bit less than the minimum wage. The app that he worked for was cashless, and advised its clients not to tip.

At the end of that winter, Alice wrote to her sister that she loved the new tightness in Michael's muscles, but that he was always too tired to be any fun.

MICHAEL'S CHANCE OF BEING a boss engineer, of pouring concrete, and of spanning northern rivers with bridges of steel, standing in mud in a hard hat and work boots, died in his last year of college. He didn't get good grades. His best hope now was to go into the admin end of the trade, work in an office, liaise with subcontractors, do a part-time MBA. But he didn't see that.

You should have gone to business school, Alice thought. Or you should have studied the humanities. You'd have had an easier time at college, and got a better grade on your degree. But she never said that to him. Instead, she watched as he doggedly applied for jobs that he was never going to get, the kind of jobs he had dreamed of. A lot of the students in his year had been hired straight out of college – headhunted, even – but Michael had to fill out forms, tailor his résumé, learn from the web how to fasten a tie – a trick which his father, who'd never worn a tie in his life, hadn't taught him. She watched him leave for the assessments, the group interviews, the one-to-ones, and – if they really wanted to dick him around – the final interview too, with his five original ideas and PowerPoint presentation. Once, he made it all the way through the process and was offered a six-month internship, unpaid. He couldn't afford to take it. Meanwhile, he still went out to race his bike against the algorithm. Even so, some months he needed help with his rent.

Alice said she could afford it. She had taken on a big project, coding from home. Michael, having rejected her Yoyodime proposal, felt too guilty to ask her about this new gig. She worked all hours. He would hear her through the door, typing, and he would knock and open the door to find her sitting at her laptop, the screensaver on, trying to smile at him. Other times, she would be lying on her old bed, staring up at the ceiling, and she wouldn't even see that he was there.

He became jealous of the numbers that competed for her attention. But he couldn't get at the numbers, so he took it out on her instead. They argued. Most nights, now, she worked late in her office, slept in her old bed. They seldom had sex, and they never went out together. She ate at odd hours, ordering in, and bought hash from a dealer who delivered. She would smoke it while he was out.

Alice was now holed up in a cave. She acted like she was frightened of something. Michael must have noticed this. He'd seen fear before, in his parents. And what else could be frightening her, he later told the police, apart from him? He hadn't known it before, but he did have a temper.

MICHAEL WAS WORKING AN afternoon shift, between Christmas and New Year, when the app on his phone pinged. Someone wanted a pizza at a house in Kitsilano. He bid for the gig, then noticed the address.

He put the pizza on the porch, wheeled his bike into the hall, went back and got the pizza. On the door mat lay a small, square, white envelope with Alice's name on it, handwritten, no stamp or address. It was unopened. The morning mail was on the table by the door. There were a number of bills, some junk mail, and a letter, already opened.

Michael looked at the letter. He read it, then read it again.

He picked up the mail and the pizza and went down the hall. He could hear her typing in her office. He opened the door and she stopped.

Alice was sitting by the window. She had activated her screensaver, so that all he could see on her screen was Campbell Fess's winking face. She wore sweatpants and a T-shirt pinpricked with burn holes. He hadn't seen her in daylight for days. Her eyes were bruised. The room smelled of hashish. She looked at him blankly, then she noticed the pizza.

Oh. *You* brought it. Thanks.

He put the box on the unmade bed. There was an overflowing ashtray on the floor.

I saw the letter from the landlord, he said. The one you left out in the hall.

Oh.

Did you *want* me to see it?

No . . . I forgot to put it away. I didn't think you'd be home yet.

He looked at the letter again, made some calculations.

I thought I was paying half the rent here. But according to this, the rent was twice as high as you told me it was. I've only been paying a quarter. You must be paying the rest.

I can afford it.

It says here that they're raising the rent again.

I can afford that too.

Why didn't you tell me how much you were paying?

It's my money. This is my house.

No it's not, Alice. It's their house – he looked at the letter again – the Mayfield Real Estate Investment Trust. They own it, not you.

This is where I grew up.

You said it belonged to one of your parents' hippy friends.

My parents were never hippies . . . She died last year, and her lawyer sold it out from underneath us.

You should have told me that, Alice.

She said nothing. He went on:

We shouldn't have stayed here, paying that kind of rent. We should have moved inland. Somewhere smaller and cheaper.

This isn't about money.

He waved the letter at her.

Of course it's about money, Alice. It's about the *rent*. And you lied to me.

I didn't lie to you. I told you how much rent I wanted you to pay. I never said it was half of the total. You just assumed that.

If this house is so precious, why didn't your parents buy it years ago?

They don't think that way. They left it too long, and then they found out they couldn't afford it. Not with all the offshore money flooding into Vancouver. So I'm going to buy it for them.

How are you going to do that? It must be worth millions.

I'm working on a project for Inscape Technologies.

He stared at her, incredulous.

*Inscape?* You must be joking.

I'm doing some coding for the OmniCent project. I answer directly to Campbell Fess.

You hate Campbell Fess. You hate everything about him.

I don't hate his money.

That's what you hate most of all.

He looked around the room, as if hoping for backup.

Inscape . . . Jesus . . .

He remembered the other letter.

There's another letter for you. Hand-delivered.

He showed her the small, square white envelope, and her expression changed. She took it off him, ripped it open, read. He could see a few scribbled glyphs on a square of white card – numerals and letters.

We can't go on like this, he said.

He had assumed, when he said it, that she'd put up a fight, that he wouldn't have to stand there, just a guy who brought the pizza. But she was staring at the card in her hand. He tried again.

It's four in the afternoon and you're ordering junk food. We never eat together anymore.

She took the card to the chessboard. She reached out for a piece, stopped, let her hand fall to her side.

You might at least have ordered your pizza from a different app, Alice.

He was almost pleading now. But her face was screwed up as she stared at the chessboard. Numbly, she handed him her credit card. He took it from her, looked at it, then tossed it on the bed.

You already paid through the app, remember? . . . Hey, are you listening to me?

She didn't answer. He gave people their food and then went away again. Most of them at least bothered to say thanks.

Don't I get a fucking tip?

But she was looking out the window.

I can't take this anymore. You won't talk to me. You avoid me. You treat me like I'm not here . . . Are you depressed, or something?

Don't shout at me.

I'm not shouting.

But he was.

I'm asking you, she said, just leave me alone for now. We can talk later.

Why? What's the point of talking if you don't tell me the truth? What do I even mean to you? Was I just another project?

What?

Why are we even together, Alice? Did you take me in because I look different from you? Because you wanted to prove that you think people like me belong in *your* country? Because you felt *sorry* for me?

Now, at last, he had her attention.

Is that really what you think of me? Is that who you think we are?

Go fuck yourself, Alice. I'm tired of being patronised. I'm done.

He didn't mean it, of course, even when he said it.

The last he saw of her, as he pedalled away, was her face at the window. He hoped that she'd be crying, and she was. But she wouldn't give him the satisfaction of watching him pretend to leave her. She was looking at the old payphone on the corner of the street.

He worked an extra shift that night, even though it had started raining. He told himself that she would know that he didn't really mean what he'd said. He knew she could be very literal, but she was also fair-minded: she would understand he'd had cause to be upset. They would find a way through this. He'd fired a warning shot, that's all. It was what people did.

When he got in, long after midnight, he thought of knocking on her door. But there was no strip of light beneath it, so he left her to sleep. Things would be better in the morning.

THE FOLLOWING MORNING, SHORTLY after eight, two uniformed constables from Patrol District Four called at an address in Kitsilano. A young man answered the door. He was wrapped in a comforter. The police notes say that he looked tired, as if he hadn't slept well.

The young man confirmed that he was resident at that address and gave his name as Michael Atarian. He confirmed that an Alice Field also lived there, and was sleeping in her room.

Constable Tyrone Chan told Mr Atarian that an unlocked mountain bike had been found that morning on the Lions Gate Bridge. It was registered with the 529 Garage as belonging to Lydia Alice Field, of that address.

Mr Atarian said that Ms Field's bike must have been stolen. He offered to wake her and ask her about it. The constables agreed. They watched him go down the hall and enter a room on the right. Then, without asking for permission, they came into the house and waited inside the door. They had done this sort of job before.

The constables watched Mr Atarian come out of the first room. He was holding a credit card. He went on down the hall, checking each room in turn. The last door on the left was a bathroom. He knocked on the door, said the name Alice, waited a few moments and looked inside. Then he turned around to the constables.

She's not here, he told them, and sat on the floor.

THE LIONS GATE SUSPENSION bridge joins central Vancouver to the North Shore and the mountains beyond. It's a little over one mile long. Two hundred feet beneath it are the First Narrows, where the Burrard Inlet meets the Outer Harbour. The design is similar to that of the Golden Gate Bridge in San Francisco, and it is likewise considered to be beautiful.

In good weather, the traffic cameras on the bridge would show the whole sweep of its three-lane highway, as well as the pedestrian and cycle paths attached either side of it. But it was raining on the night in question, as you'd expect in Vancouver. In the footage which the cops showed to Michael, the raindrops are shooting stars, streaking white across the lenses of the cameras, burning up in the lights from the bridge. The yellow lights along the roadside, and the blue globes on the cables, grow dimmer with distance, then fade from view a hundred yards from the shore, swallowed by the fog and rain that are rolling into Burrard Inlet. The port and the city are lost in this fog. Two hundred feet under the bridge, the tide would, at the time in question, have been ebbing through the First Narrows at almost four knots.

The southern end of Lions Gate Bridge is located in the heights of Stanley Park, a patch of coastal rainforest preserved from the encroaching city. Here, two large stone lions guard the entrance to the bridge, where the approach road curves north through the fir trees and cedars. At 3.11 a.m., a security camera at this end of the bridge sees a figure in a red hooded jacket emerging from a path in the forest, pushing a bicycle.

A car passes, and, when it has gone, the figure crosses the road to access the pedestrian path on the seaward side of the bridge. As the figure passes a security camera, the wind blows back its hood. The image is clear enough, despite the poor light and low resolution. At 3.13 a.m., Lydia Alice Field walked on to the Lions Gate Bridge and vanished in the rain and fog. Michael, watching the footage with the two constables, was able to confirm her identity.

She did not reappear to any of the other cameras which cover both ends of the bridge.

At 5.19 a.m., a police dispatcher received a call from a jogger who had found an unlocked bicycle propped against the railing, three hundred metres out from Stanley Park. Wanting to be helpful, the jogger added that he had looked over the parapet into the Narrows, two hundred feet below, but could see no sign of anyone in the water. By then she was miles away. Strait of Georgia, Salish Sea.

There were interviews, formalities. When they were done, the police thanked Michael for his cooperation and told him they were sorry. They dropped him back to the empty house as the sun was going down. The constables waited at the kerb to make sure he was OK. They noted that he stood for some time on the porch, staring at the door, before he opened it and went inside.

# Part One:

*Valley of Heart's Delight*

MICHAEL ATARIAN DROVE ALL the way from Vancouver to Palo Alto, California without stopping overnight. We know this from location data stripped from his phone. It shows several short breaks at gas stations, and a two-hour halt at a rest stop near Eugene, Oregon, that may have included a nap. It would have been hard for him to drive all that way without sleeping. He was in a bad state before he even set out, leaving right after the memorial service, though Alice's family had asked him to stay.

He may have been reluctant to stop, but he doesn't seem to have been in a hurry. Instead of following Interstate 5 all the way from the border to Oakland, which would have been the quickest route from Vancouver, he turned off at Grants Pass, Oregon, and took Route 101 down the coast, passing through the Redwoods State Park. Maybe he wanted to look at the trees, but if he did, it was through the window of his moving car, the old Subaru station wagon he'd bought with

Alice for trips to the mountains. He passed, again without stopping, through Eureka, Fortuna, Santa Rosa, San Rafael, skirted Sausalito, then halted at the rest stop beside San Francisco Bay.

He stayed at this lookout for a long time, by his standards – almost an hour. There was a washroom and a store there, and he would probably have taken some time to look at the view – Alcatraz and Treasure Island, the Bay Bridge, downtown San Francisco. He was almost at the end of his journey. He needed only to get back in the car and drive across to the Presidio. This route would have taken him to Palo Alto in maybe an hour, if the traffic was good. He did have a smartphone. He could have looked this up.

Instead, Michael doubled back, through San Rafael, then east and south and north again, all the way around San Francisco Bay, via Vallejo, Oakland, Milpitas, Sunnyvale, until he finally reached his destination, Palo Alto. He had driven five hours when one would have done.

Why he did this, we don't know. We don't have the data. The old car had one of those early GPS satnavs that aren't networked online. Alice had bought it, second hand, perhaps for that reason. It could only be hacked by manual means. Maybe Michael had bought an actual paper map in the gift shop at the lookout, and decided to follow that instead, tracing familiar-sounding place names, places that he'd heard about but had never been to. Fremont. Berkeley. Alameda. Or maybe he'd changed his mind at the last minute, decided to go back to Canada, then changed his mind again at San Rafael, tried to turn back, got lost, found himself in Oakland, then missed the

Bay Bridge, and later the Dumbarton Bridge, so that he ended up blundering the long way to Palo Alto, all the way round the South Bay. Or maybe he was deliberately wandering, not using a map or the satnav, and he didn't know how close he'd been to the end of his journey when he baulked at the Golden Gate Bridge.

INSCAPE TECHNOLOGIES IS BASED on the edge of Palo Alto, in a vast, tapering spiral of glass, concrete and steel. The shape of this building represents the eternal whirl of creation and destruction, the Heraclitean fire that inspires Inscape's quest for disruption and rebirth. Or at least, that's what it says on the corporate website. It also says that Campbell Fess, the company's founder, visionary, CEO and largest voting shareholder, sketched the design for this building on the back of a prospectus for his first public share-offering. This is only partially true. Fess had in fact drawn an Escher staircase with a glass dome placed over it, but he couldn't find an architect who could build it for real. The design that emerged from the subsequent compromise is shaped more like a whelk, or a coiled snake, or the sand casts that lugworms excrete on a beach. Fess named his creation The Gyre, because Ouroboros was already being used by a firm in Cupertino, and he'd got mixed up between Hopkins and Yeats. His office was up at the pointy end.

Michael's interview took place one floor below Fess's office. There was only one interviewer, a senior Inscape employee whose name was Barbara Collins. The sign etched on her glass door said,

49

*VP: Special Projects*, but Michael, who was too sleep-deprived to think straight, may have thought she was someone in human resources. Which, in a way, she was.

Barbara Collins was a tall woman, burly but not fat, with a round, smooth face that could be mistaken for motherly. She didn't wear make-up, and her stiff, medium-length black hair, only grey here and there, was usually tied back in a ponytail. At the time of this interview, she was fifty-three years of age, which was old for this industry, but she wore the cargo pants and varsity sweatshirt – in this case, Stanford – that could pass for its uniform.

Barbara Collins did not go to Stanford.

Barb Collins had a reputation for smiling at people in a way that they didn't always like. Did Michael notice? Probably not. He was slumped in his chair, unshaven, wiped out by the drive from Vancouver. He was in the T-shirt and jeans he'd been wearing for three days. He didn't need to put on a show for her. If he wanted the job, it was his.

Barb Collins's notes for Campbell Fess, attached to her covert WAV recording of the interview, say that Michael seemed dazed throughout their talk, staring past her shoulder at the Santa Cruz Mountains. Their conversation, transcribed from her recording, went as follows:

We thought you'd be here a day ago, Mike.

She would definitely have given the smile as she said that.

I'm sorry. It took longer than I thought.

I tried calling you. You didn't pick up.

My phone was off.

Was it?

She was still smiling, most likely.

I didn't know I was supposed to start right away. I don't even know what you want me to do.

Another thing that Barb Collins sometimes did was to lay her head to one side and look sincere and concerned. She would have been doing that now.

Well, obviously, it's because of poor Alice, Mike. Such a terrible loss . . . We'd hoped that you'd both come to Palo Alto when she moved down here full-time, but then . . . So, here *you* are, anyway.

She never told me she was planning to move here. That doesn't sound like her at all.

I guess every home has its secrets.

What did she do for Inscape, Ms Collins?

Please, call me Barb . . . That doesn't matter now, Mike. For now, we just want you to make yourself at home here.

You know I didn't write any of Alice's code?

We know that, Mike. We've seen your grades.

I don't belong here.

Then why did you come?

We can imagine him staring out of the window before he answers. Barb noted that he took his time.

I had to go somewhere. And then you made me that offer. It's a lot of money.

You like the money, do you?

It's not for me . . . I need to buy Alice's house for her family . . . It's the only thing I can do for her, now . . . But I don't think I'm the person you're looking for. If you want to change your mind, that's OK with me.

In her brief for Campbell Fess, Barb Collins noted Michael's honesty, his lack of interest in personal gain. He just wanted to buy a house for somebody else, because he figured he owed it to someone who was dead now, who would never know what he'd done. And yet this kid was willing to walk away from all the cash they were dangling in front of him. You don't often see that, she wrote. On this kind of salary, most people would try to bluff for a few pay cycles before they were found out. He seemed to have integrity. In her view, this made Michael a risky hire. But Fess overruled her. He had other reasons for wanting Michael, but he didn't tell Barb Collins what they were, not then. Fess always said that he liked to compartmentalise.

Don't worry about it, she said. We want to look after you. For Alice's sake.

She would have sounded sincere when she said this.

But what do you want *me* for?

We'll get to that, Mike. Now isn't the time. Have a rest, and look around this wonderful building. I'll have someone show you the ropes. When you're done here today, get yourself settled in your company house.

I get my own *house?*

Sure you do. Right here in Palo Alto. There are execs here who'd kill for the keys to that place.

Then why am *I* getting it?

We'll get to that, Mike. When you're ready.

So, when I feel that I'm ready, I come and find you?

No. When I feel you're ready, I'll come and find *you*.

MICHAEL'S NEW HOUSE WAS a bungalow in the Spanish colonial style, in a new subdivision on the edge of town. It had red roof tiles and cream stucco walls, and there was a shade over the driveway to protect cars from the sun. Out front, a row of newly planted oaks and magnolias, too small to cast shade, divided the lawn from the sidewalk. Inside, flies lay dead on the sills of shuttered windows. Sun slanted through a fanlight over the door.

The front door opened directly into a lounge. Michael stood on the mat, in a haze of floating dust motes, and took in what he could see of the house. The place smelled of spiders and spores. A number of doorways gave off the lounge. At the back, a wire mesh door sieved his view of a porch. The furniture was mostly white, already sagging, made from chipboard with a plastic or wooden veneer. It was the same furniture that he thought he'd left behind with his life in Vancouver.

The house was silent, its air still.

Michael had only taken one bag from the car. Not moving any further into the house, he emptied it on to the door mat, then selected a couple of changes of clothes. He put these back into the empty bag, left the other clothes where they were lying, then went outside again and locked the door. When he got back in his car the engine was still hot. You could hear it ticking all the way across the street.

Michael drove back to the headquarters of Inscape Technologies, left his car in the short-term visitors' parking lot, went into the building, and didn't come out again for a month.

INSCAPE'S HEADQUARTERS GETS ITS famous whorled appearance from the Coil, the external glass corridor, a half section of a tube, that begins at ground level and spirals around the core of the building, ever upward, until it almost, but not quite, reaches the tip.

Designed as an eco-friendly heat-exchange mechanism, and as a passageway and service duct, and also as a gimmick, this award-winning architectural feature is in practice rarely used by anyone but janitors and the occasional self-conscious skater. Most people take the glass elevators from one level to another, shooting through the glass tubes in the yawning central vestibule, bubbles inside a syringe.

In his month wandering alone through the Gyre, Michael spent hours each night in the Coil, walking up and down it until he was tired enough to sleep. Spiralling upward, he would orbit the building's core in ever decreasing circles, the lights of the valley wheeling around him, the intervals shorter the higher he went, then slowly unspooling as he came down again.

For the first few days, he could see their old Subaru in the visitors' parking lot, its windows turning yellow, plastered with parking tickets. After four or five days, a clamp appeared on the front nearside wheel. He stared at it for a long time, from high up in the Coil. He really should do something about that. There was stuff in the trunk from the house in Vancouver. Personal stuff. Alice. He should go pay the parking fines, get an employee's permit. He was entitled to free parking. Two nights later, the car had been towed. It was registered in Alice's name, not his. He guessed that, unclaimed, it would eventually be scrapped or sold.

When the building came back to life in the mornings, Michael, exhausted, would hide in one of the Gyre's quiet spaces, where nap pods were installed to improve employee wellness. He would climb inside one of these coffin-like couches and listen to the voices in the world outside it, the tapping of keyboards, hiss of sneakers on carpet. The sounds of these other unseen lives lulled him.

A hatch in the basement took his laundry and returned it, two hours later, in a crisp cotton bag. There was a gym, sauna, showers, a pool, games rooms, in-house supermarkets and speciality stores, meditation spaces, a cinema, and a chaplaincy hub with links to every religion in a fifty-mile radius. He ate for free from cafeterias serving ethnic and fusion cuisines. All he had to do to access any service in the Gyre for free was to wear his encoded photo ID and wave the company phone that Barb Collins had given him. A near-field wireless application, proprietary to Inscape, verified his identity, logged his movements and approved his requests. His own phone and laptop had been in the trunk of the car.

What did Michael do, when he wasn't walking or sleeping or eating or hiding? He didn't use the gym, or the swimming pool.

The app on his telephone, which told Inscape everywhere he went and everything he ate, every service that he accessed, didn't know where his eyes went when they weren't looking at its screen. Which they almost never were, now. He'd never been one for social media, but, in his previous life, he'd used his phone about as much as anyone else, for news and chat and messaging and entertainment. Sometimes, he even made calls. Now, here, in the Gyre, he neither sent nor read any texts, messages or emails. He never made or took any voice calls. He didn't use the phone's browser to access the Internet. The phone's battery lasted for days between charges. This was automatically flagged as suspicious activity, a sin of omission.

The Gyre doesn't have a library or a bookstore. Michael didn't go to its cinema. He did not, as far as is known, talk to any of the thousands of other Inscape employees who drifted from hot desk to hot desk. His only human interactions were with the subcontracted workers who look after Inscape's talent – the Bengali lady who processed his laundry, the outsourced servers in the various restaurants, humanities graduates, people like that.

How do you get a read on someone who is living so selfishly, so utterly offline? What was Michael looking at, all that time in the Gyre? What was he thinking? What did he *do*?

ON HIS THIRTY-FIRST DAY in the Gyre, Michael did something he hadn't done before. He was sitting in a cafeteria, eating excellent sushi, when he picked up his phone. A few taps on the touch screen opened the settings menu. He located the near-field application that defined his existence at Inscape. His finger hesitated. Then he switched the app to *off*.

Twenty seconds later, an alarm sounded in the cafeteria. The alarm was very loud – a synthesised version of a World War Two klaxon. A light flashed in the ceiling. The doors announced that they were locking automatically. Faces lifted from screens. Eyes almost made contact.

Satisfied, Michael switched the app back on. The alarm fell silent.

Ten minutes later, as he finished the last of the sushi, Barb Collins came for him.

You're ready, she told him. Campbell wants to see you now.


YOU HAVEN'T MET CAMPBELL Fess, but you more or less know him. You know that he went to Stanford, or Caltech, or maybe MIT. At college, he formed a close friendship with another young man with whom he shared a vision, and then a garage, where Inscape was born. You vaguely know that the other guy isn't around anymore. He either got cancer, or Fess bought him out. He may even have killed himself – he was the one who liked Gerard Manley Hopkins.

Hollywood has yet to make a movie about Campbell Fess, but you know what he looks like: a thin, slightly balding but otherwise youthful man in his mid fifties, who wears sweatshirts and blue jeans, and soft leather sandals or black Converse shoes. His hair is short, more grey than black. His eyes are brown, as eyes often are.

What you don't know about Campbell Fess is that he secretly records video and audio of everything that he says or does in his private office, in his various homes, on his Gulfstream jet and aboard both of his yachts. He also monitors, wherever possible, the physical vibrations, temperature changes, gaseous fluctuations, magnetic variations, vital signs and quantum ghosting associated with his existence in this universe.

He does this because he believes that the technologies that already allow several organisations, Inscape among them, to mine your text messages, phone calls, online searches, social media posts, CCTV feeds, medical records, news consumption, shopping lists, criminal record, credit rating, sewage flow, motor traffic data, signal network analysis, GPS coordinates, bank records, battery levels, school reports, biometric traces, baby names and DNA – that enables them to put each and every one of us under the microscope, to fix our activities, beliefs, desires, strengths and weaknesses much better than we know them ourselves – Fess believes that these technologies will soon be merged into a God Algorithm, a technology that will allow those who control the new artificial intelligence (Fess believes that *he'll* control the new artificial intelligence) to reverse-engineer a consciousness from the data it produces. He believes that some day soon, in a decade or two at most, the surging power of artificial intelligence, combined with the processing heft of quantum computing, will make it possible for those who control the technology to encode their own souls and become immortal, to live on as charges in silicon synapses. He believes you can cast a soap bubble in glass.

Why does he believe this? Well, for one thing, Campbell Fess is worth seventy-five billion dollars, minimum, and when you have that much money, it sings to you. It says, If you die, we can no longer be together. If you really love me, you'll find a way to stay. Transhumanism. Post-humanism. Seasteading. Life extension. Cloning. Cryogenics. Fess has bets on all of these escape plans and more. He owns his own submarine, and an island near New Zealand that is partially hollow. He has a half share in a spaceship. There isn't room in it for you.

Of course, Michael wouldn't have known most of this as he sat in Fess's inner office, right at the top of the Gyre. He certainly didn't know that he was being filmed for his part in Fess's biopic.

Fess stood at the window, his back to Michael, staring out across the valley. His lips were pursed, his gaze thoughtful. We know this because there was another camera on a strut above Fess's eyrie, pointing back at the window to cover that angle. It was one of Fess's favourite stances, a look that he wanted to keep.

Eventually, Fess turned, walked back to his chair, sat down, elbows on desk. He steepled his fingers, frowned at Michael through their prism.

I'm glad you came down from Vancouver, Mike. I'm glad to have a chance to say thanks to you in person.

You're welcome, sir . . . Thanks for what?

This is California, Mike. Don't call me sir. Call me Campbell.

Sorry, Campbell.

That's all right, Mike. Barb told you that I had a job for you, right?

Yes, Campbell. But she didn't say what it was.

She doesn't know herself, yet. I like to compartmentalise.

Oh.

What I'm going to tell you now is strictly between me and you. I know I can trust you because of what you've already done for me. You follow?

No.

We can see Michael's face in the camera hidden in a bookcase behind Fess's desk, the one that Fess had installed to capture his rear view. It's clear that Michael doesn't follow at all.

Good, said Fess. I have some sensitive business with someone outside the company. I need you to liaise with them.

Liaise? How?

Fess lowered his hands to the desk, frowning. He was looking past Michael, at the camera in the orchids on the trellis by the wall.

We needn't go into that now. They'll give you the details.

Who will?

No names, Mike. You'll find out when they contact you.

What do they look like?

I don't even know myself, Mike. I don't need to. I've never met them face to face. That's your job. You're my liaison guy. Like I said, I like to compartmentalise.

I don't understand, Campbell.

Fess stood up. He came around the desk to Michael, took him by the elbow, steered him to the elevator.

We know you haven't left the Gyre since you got here, Mike.

Barb says she thinks you've been dealing with some personal stuff. She thinks you feel guilty about your girlfriend. You should never feel guilt, Mike. You did the right thing.

I'm sorry?

Don't be, Mike. It's time to move on. From today, you go home each evening to that house we gave you. That's how my contact will find you. It has to happen outside this building. Do you understand?

Reaching the elevator, Fess shook his hand, released it. The glass door whooshed open.

Thanks again for what you did in Vancouver, Mike. It was the smart move to make, but it can't have been easy.

I don't know what you're talking about, Campbell.

Fess activated the down button with a wave of his hand.

That's really good, Mike. You'll do fine.


AOIFE'S PARENTS HAD CHRISTENED her from a book of Irish-language names, the kind with too many letters that are either silent or make the wrong sound. Like Saoirse, or Sadhbh, or Naoise, or Bláthnaid. Her other given name was Caoilfhionn. There was a good one. Slender and fair.

How does Aoife pronounce her birth names? Lately, it hasn't mattered. Lately, she hasn't been using them much. Today, in Palo Alto, California, Aoife will be Ann, the indefinite article, the most minimal name that there is. She uses it quite often. As for her surname, today she won't need one.

In one respect, she didn't want to be noticed today. In another way, she did. Around her neck was a plain silver chain, dangling a heart-shaped gold pendant in the neck of her light cotton dress. She was wearing more make-up than she would on her own account, but she didn't think she'd overdone it — just a little more liner around her grey eyes. She'd been in this valley for a week already, and reckoned she had a good read on its men, so she had also dyed her chestnut hair blond, to make up for its relative shortness. Waiting in line outside Antonio's Nut House, a regular stop for Inscape's company shuttle, the male engineers glanced at her often.

The Inscape shuttle bus — electric, driverless — turned the corner from Birch Street on to California Avenue and came to a stop. The engineers swarmed to board it. But now Aoife was blocking its door, searching her purse, looking for something that she couldn't find. She gave up, turned sideways, letting them push past her and on to the bus. The bus's door, reading the near-field IDs on their company smartphones, beeped as it let in each one in turn. As Aoife swayed there, trapped between the bus and the scrum, a man pushed past her, a little too close and a little too slowly, trailing a hand across the back of her dress. She lost her balance, leaned briefly against him. He reached the bus door, turned to leer at her, triumphant, but the door beeped a warning and shut in his face. Aoife pushed past him. The door opened for her and then closed again, leaving her groper marooned on the kerb.

Her target, Aoife knew, would have got on the bus at the Gyre. There he was now, two rows from the end, where no one else was sitting, his head against the window, despondent or asleep. She went to the back row of seats and sat in the middle, where she could watch him.

The bus turned on to the Camino Real, driving south, leaving the leafy fringe of Stanford behind it. She took out the phone she had stolen at the bus stop and pretended to look at it; locked by its retinal sensor, it wouldn't open for her anyway. The bus slowed, turned right into a neighbourhood of old ranch-style houses shaded by walnuts and hickory, and stopped. One of the engineers gathered his stuff and waddled down the aisle. The bus returned to the Camino Real.

They were getting close, now. She moved two rows up, sat opposite her mark, her feet in the aisle, turned towards him.

He seemed to be asleep. She could take a closer look. His black hair was longer than it had been in the photographs, and there was a thin beard now too, neglect, not design. His old sneakers were stained, but the sweatshirt and jeans, though tatty and fading, looked as if they'd just been professionally pressed.

She leaned across the aisle and shook his shoulder.

I've a message for you, she said, before he had a chance to fully wake. Keep them off balance, she thought, and they'll fall the way you want them to. That's what McDonnell had taught her in Belfast.

He sat up, groggy.

What?

You were told someone would contact you.

She played with her hair while she waited for him to take in the situation, twisting blond strands round her finger. Textbook stuff, really.

He made the connection at last.

Is this that thing with Inscape? That thing that Campbell—?

No names. Someone wants to meet you.

Who?

You'll find out when you meet him. Do you have any money?

I have cards.

Real money. Cash.

No.

There's a strip mall two blocks north of your house. We just passed it. It has an ATM machine. Wait until it's dark, then walk over there and take out some cash. About two hundred dollars will do it. If it gives you the option, ask for small bills . . . Are you listening?

He was staring at her, face creased in disbelief. Just a little more pressure, in case he recoiled . . . She laid a hand on his bare forearm.

Do you understand?

Yes.

You take out the money. Tomorrow morning at nine you go to the end of your street and wait at the VTA bus stop for a number twenty-two, heading south. Buy a ticket to San Jose. Pay cash. In San Jose, get off at Santa Clara and First. Walk a block south to Second and take a number sixty-eight VTA bus on up the—

Just tell me where I'm going and I can use my phone to tell me the way.

No phones. Don't even look up the route on your phone – not

today, not ever. This trip has to be untraceable. You have to leave your cards and your phone at home tomorrow. I've written the route on this paper for you, see? Don't lose it. You understand me?

Yes.

Good. Take a sixty-eight to Gilroy. Pay cash. When you get to Gilroy, switch to a County Express bus to Hollister. Cash. Hollister is out in the farmlands at the head of the valley. You get off the bus there and find a taxi. You can use the payphone in the courthouse to call one, or there's a limo company over on Fifth. Pay cash. Tell them to take you to up the Santa Ana Valley Road to the junction with Quien Sabe. Get out there. When the taxi is gone, walk for a mile, south, along Santa Anita, to the place where the hills close in either side. There's a fruit store by the road. The meeting is there.

How long is that journey?

There's a lot of bus stops. Three or four hours. Each way.

*What?* Why not just meet here?

The meeting is there.

Can't you give me a ride, then?

No.

I could hire a car.

Without leaving a record? You take the bus, Michael. No one watches the buses.

They were at the corner where his neighbourhood met the Camino Real. The bus slowed for the turn; Michael's phone had already told it where to drop him. As the bus swung ponderously out of its lane, an old lady in a Honda had to swerve to avoid it. She leaned on her horn, lowered her window, uploaded a digit that meant nothing to the bus.

Come on, Aoife said. We have to get off here.

How do you know where I live?

Aoife knew that when you're playing a fish, you don't haul it in at the very first nibble. First, you have to sell it the legend, the one in which it never had a chance of getting off the hook.

Understand this, Michael: we know where everyone lives.

The bus stopped outside his house.

Go on, she said. I'll follow.

When his back was turned, she took out the phone that she'd stolen from the Inscape engineer, wiped it with a tissue, dropped it under the seat. She caught up with Michael at the top of the bus and pressed herself against his back, so the bus would detect only one person leaving. When they were off he turned to her, flustered.

What was that about?

Just be there tomorrow. Fess is paying you plenty.

Will you be there?

She turned, walked away. She hoped he was watching. He called after her.

Hey! What's your name?

Ann, she said, not turning her head.

Ann? That's all?

No. Ann without an E.

*

MICHAEL STEPPED OVER THE clothes that he'd dumped inside the front door a month before. It was time to explore his new home. There were two bedrooms, a bathroom, a lounge, a fully equipped kitchen. A small utility room, just off the kitchen, contained a washing machine and a dryer that he would never have to use, and a Wi-Fi router that blinked in the dark. The lounge had a forty-two-inch smart TV that he fiddled around with and then gave up on. There was an Ikea couch, an Ikea coffee table, two Ikea armchairs and an Ikea bookcase. The bookcase contained mostly dust, but over at one end, huddled together as if for warmth, was a stack of new paperbacks. At the other end of the shelf sat the black plastic cube of a Felix, Inscape's own-brand wireless speaker and digital assistant. But this Felix's duty was ended: someone had smashed it with a hammer, then driven a nail through, just to make sure.

The books must have been a puzzle to Michael. Had they been there when he first came to the house, a month ago, when he'd dumped his stuff and left? He'd only stayed five minutes, and had barely gone inside. Did he now examine the dust on their spines, and compare it to the dust on the bare shelves beneath them? If he didn't, he should have.

What was on that bookshelf?

*The Dispossessed*. Ursula K. Le Guin.

*Solaris*. Stanislaw Lem.

*Player Piano*. Kurt Vonnegut.

*The Crying of Lot 49*. Thomas Pynchon.

*The Drowned World*. J.G. Ballard.

*The Master and Margarita*. Mikhail Bulgakov.

*Parable of the Sower*. Octavia E. Butler.

*Roadside Picnic*. Arkady and Boris Strugatsky.

*Oryx and Crake*. Margaret Atwood.

If someone was sending him a message, or instructions on how to brace for an impact, then subtlety wasn't their thing.

HERE IS MICHAEL, LATER that night, at the strip mall, grey in the lens of the ATM's camera. His face is lit from beneath by the screen. His eyes are just shadows. He must be nervous, because it takes him two goes to put his PIN in correctly. Then, having taken out two hundred dollars, he puts the card back in and takes out one hundred more.

Is he thinking of Alice, and her Yoyodime scheme? There's a payphone in the strip mall, just beside the ATM. Does this payphone remind him of Alice? Is that why he takes out more cash than he'd been told he needed? Something is clearly on his mind, because even after he has his three hundred dollars in his pocket, he puts the card in a third time, re-enters his PIN, and checks his bank balance for the first time in weeks.

Observe his shock. Where did all that money come from? Fess must be paying his wages up front. He takes his card and disappears.

THE SANTA CLARA VALLEY begins in the hills south of Hollister, then falls north-west for thirty miles to San Francisco Bay.

To the west, the Santa Cruz Mountains screen it from Salinas and the coast at Monterey. To the east, the Diablo Range divides it from California's Central Valley.

Once, this was known as the Valley of Heart's Delight, a country of orchards and fruit trees and dairies that exported canned produce all over the world. But then San Francisco metastasised, outgrew its peninsula, pushed south into the valley's mouth. It encysted the ancient redwood tree that the Spanish called El Palo Alto, swallowed the Mission Santa Clara and the pueblo of San Jose. It's still moving today, inching south, up the Guadeloupe valley and the Calaveras Fault, a glacier of concrete and houses, erasing the fruit groves and cornfields and dairies. The leading edge, a grey moraine of industrial parks and transformer stations, has almost reached Gilroy, the garlic city, where Michael will switch to a County Express. No one calls it the Valley of Heart's Delight anymore. They now call it Silicon Valley.

And this too has its beauty, if you know where to look. Consider the cars on the Monterey Road, little worlds that flit past each other, fragile and fearless. See the flowers in a cyclone fence, by the overgrown ditch where a creek that once had names in Ohlone and Spanish now seeps incognito, waiting for someone to name it again. Road signs with place names in a fallen language. Fast-food logos on strip malls, plastic primary colours faded to pastel. *Deal of the Week* boards at the gates of used-car lots. All saying together, This too is beautiful, because this too won't last. Then think of the mountain ranges, east and west, grinding in opposite directions, north and south, a few inches a year, as the coastal faults rip the whole valley in two.

Michael may have noticed this as he headed south on the buses in the early spring sunshine. He may have watched through all the stops between San Jose and Gilroy, seeing school kids and migrant workers come and go from the bus. He may have watched the buildings thin out as he rode south from Gilroy, seen fields of vegetables and wheat, the fruit trees and orchards that Silicon Valley has yet to upgrade. He may have observed the horses and cattle on the green hills that rose over tillage. Or he might have fallen asleep. He might even have brought one or two of those books to read, in his jacket pocket. He hadn't brought a telephone. No one was watching him, and no one talked to him. He had the freedom you earn by taking the bus.

THE COUNTY EXPRESS DROPPED Michael beside a tuxedo rental store, just off Hollister's main square. This was a quiet farming town, with streets of two- and three-storey buildings from early last century, dusty and faded, unaware of their charm. Traffic was light, and the sidewalks were deserted. Michael could have been back on the prairies, except that here it was warmer, a hot wind from the east. Hills appeared in the gaps between buildings. The sky was blue, with fluffy white clouds, and the sun shone down as the sun sometimes does, even in February.

Following his instructions, Michael hired a taxi from the limo company on Fifth Street, half a block from the bus stop. It took him south, out of town, along a narrow farm road, past groves of fruit trees that were not yet in leaf. Neat little farmsteads, half hidden in trees, sat back from the road. The land here was steppe, fields of vegetables and winter wheat with grassy hills above them, closing in on the road as the taxi climbed. A creek ran by the roadside from the head of the valley, shaded with willows and cottonwoods. Lone oaks stood on hillsides, watching Michael pass.

The driver stopped at a junction where three farm roads met.

Santa Anita and Quien Sabe. You sure this is the place? There's nothing out here.

I'm meeting someone.

Michael waited until the driver had gone, then started to walk.

It was early afternoon and the sun was high and hot above the valley. Michael, who hadn't reckoned on such heat so early in the year, hadn't brought a bag or a hat or water, and, having nothing better to do with them, swung his arms as he walked. At intervals, cars and trucks drove past, sweeping the dust from the road with their slipstreams; the dust settled on the shoulder of the road where he walked. It coated his sneakers, made them hiss with each step. When he wiped his forehead, the sweat on his hand was red from the dirt. He could see branches swaying on the oaks on the hillside, but there was no breeze down here.

He walked more than a mile, past the last of the farm houses, and still there was no fruit store. He was becoming frustrated. Why couldn't he have taken the taxi all the way to the meeting, if it really existed? Was this some sort of test?

Then he saw it: an old shack, up ahead, on the right, sagging

by the roadside on a patch of bare dirt. It was shaded by the cottonwoods that grew in the creek bed. Beyond it was an untended
orchard. Closer up, he saw writing: *Casa da Fruta*, in sun-bleached
black stencil, and underneath, hand-painted: *Fresh From the Farm*.

The service hatch was shuttered, its planks furring into splinters
at the ends. Michael stopped, wiped his forehead again. The sun,
now at its highest, threw his shadow a little way north.

A pickup truck went past, moving fast up the valley. He turned
away, screwed his eyes and mouth shut against its dust, and when the
truck had passed he opened his eyes and got a surprise. The hatch
on the fruit stand was open, propped up by a stick.

A man watched him from the darkness inside.

You looking for fruit?

No thanks.

Then why are you standing there?

I came for a walk.

The stranger smiled.

Wait there.

Michael heard a door open – or rather, fall off its hinges – around
the back of the shack. A moment later the stranger appeared. He was
tall and stooped, his hands rammed deep in his pockets. His bony,
sallow-skinned face, close-cropped and balding on top, unshaven
below, so that it seemed to be layered between rashes of stubble,
looked to be somewhere in its early fifties. He wore a business suit
which, though expensive, was now creased and stained, and a pink
shirt with a collar that was grey at the edges. A blue silk tie hung

loose and wrinkled, and his Italian brogues were dusty and scuffed.

The stranger didn't offer his hand.

My name is Towse.

Towse?

Yeah. Like house, with a T. I work for the government. I can't tell you which agency.

The NSA?

Towse shrugged.

Sure. If you like. But I'm on secondment to Inscape. We have mutual interests. Which you already know about. That's why you're here.

I don't have a clue why I'm here.

Towse smiled.

Come with me.

Michael followed him around the back of the shack. Two cane chairs sat either side of an upturned orange crate, on which an eighty-ounce bottle of water, half empty, stewed in the sun. The door of the shack, held partially in place by its lower hinge, leaned against white-painted boards that had long since turned grey. The creek tinkled coolly in its cottonwood shade.

Towse sat, adjusted the knees of his trousers. He waved Michael over to join him. Michael stayed on his feet.

Why should I believe that you really are who you say you are?

You shouldn't. And I didn't.

Michael gestured at the shack.

This is meant to be a government front?

Why not? Ever hear of the United Fruit Company?

Michael heard footsteps and turned. Ann-without-an-E was dressed differently today: sun hat, jeans and a loose cotton shirt. Her hiking shoes and jeans were crusted with mud.

Sorry I'm late, she told Towse. I took a shortcut through that orchard and fell in a ditch.

She jabbed her thumb at Michael.

He's alone. I watched him all the way from where the taxi dropped him.

She spotted the empty chair.

Are you using that?

Before Michael could answer she had already flopped down, stretching her legs out in front of her.

Jesus. My feet are killing me.

She unscrewed the top of the bottle, took a long drink, made a face.

This water's boiling. You should have put the bottle in that stream to keep it cool.

She screwed the top back on the bottle, then remembered Michael.

Did you bring your phone?

No.

Good. There's no cell reception here anyway. That's why we picked this place.

Towse waved at the trees and the mountains.

Plus, there's a really nice view. Paradisiacal. Want some water? We kept some for you.

But Ann-without-an-E cradled the bottle, and didn't look ready to give it up.

No thanks, said Michael.

You sure you don't want some fruit? We've got some in the shack, you know.

It's true, said Ann-without-an-E. It's important to get the details right. We're under deep cover.

She rolled her eyes.

I don't think I want to be here, Michael said.

She smiled up at him, not at all sweetly.

Stick around, Michael. Towse hasn't finished with you.

Towse cleared his throat, got to his feet, took out a pack of cigarettes.

Mind if I smoke? I like to smoke when I make a pitch. It gives my hands something to do. And I like to walk around too – have my chair, by the way; this will take a few minutes. Walking and smoking distracts people, gives them something to look at apart from my face. It makes it harder for them to know if I'm lying.

You're actually telling me that you might be lying to me?

Sure. But only out of courtesy. You should always assume that. Please, sit.

Despite himself, Michael sat down. Towse lit a cigarette and started pacing back and forth, an actor gearing up to deliver a soliloquy.

He stopped, closed his eyes, took a long drag on his cigarette, opened his eyes and started prowling again.

All right. Here it is. I've got it straight, now . . . Have you ever heard of OmniCent, Michael? Do you know how it works?

Sure.

Towse took a pensive drag on his cigarette, looking up at the hills.

OK, then. I'll explain it to you, Michael. OmniCent is a private online currency which Inscape is developing for the world's biggest tech firms and banks. They want their customers to use OmniCent for all their online payments, instead of whatever national currency they have where they live. OmniCent will be what they call a *crypto-currency*, based on a thing called *blockchain technology*. But if it makes it any easier for you, just think of it as special computer money.

I'm a qualified engineer, you know. You don't have to talk down to me.

Towse stopped, took another drag, studied Michael.

I don't? OK . . .

Towse lit another cigarette off his old one, then crushed the butt underfoot. He started pacing again.

Anyhow, some aspects of OmniCent are so sensitive that Fess has set up an elite secret team to develop them off site. Only a couple of dozen people in the world know about it. I'm one. You're another.

But I've never heard of it!

That's the spirit. See, Ann? He's discreet, like Fess said. He'll be perfect.

Michael looked from one to the other.

Perfect for what?

To act as a go-between.

Go-between?

Liaison, said Towse. Contact. Messenger. Courier.

Cut-out, said Ann-without-an-E. Fall guy. Patsy. Chump. Can I have one of those cigarettes, Towse?

I thought you didn't smoke.

I do when I'm bored.

There you go . . . We need a messenger, Michael. Someone exactly like you.

I don't want to be mixed up in anything secret.

Ann-without-an-E exhaled heavily, blowing smoke through pursed lips.

It's too late for that, Michael. You've already been paid.

His bank balance. That made sense, now.

But I don't write code, Michael said. I never have. My last real job was delivering junk food.

We know, said Towse. And you were good at it, Michael. I've seen your stats on the app. You collected promptly and delivered on time. And when there was a problem you didn't give up easily. That's what we need. Someone to deliver, and someone to collect.

Collect what?

Towse grinned.

Great! Then you'll do it! Ann – get the laptop.

She went into the shack, came back with a black nylon shoulder bag.

Here, she said. It's a MacBook. Just like the one you had in Vancouver.

How do you know what I had in Vancouver?

She shrugged. He turned to Towse.

What am I meant to do with it?

Just bring it to work every day. Give it to Barb Collins. She'll pass it to Fess. And when he's done with it, she'll give it back to you. You'll bring it home every evening and Ann will collect it and take it to me. I'll have a look at it, then Ann will give it back to you. Rinse and repeat, until the job is done.

I don't get it.

You don't have to. But I'll tell you anyway. Someone at Inscape has been snooping in the servers of the OmniCent task force. A mole. We need to find out who they are. And whoever they are, they're good at covering their tracks. They've set trip wires that will warn them if anyone comes after them. This laptop will get round that. It will be our Trojan Horse.

I still don't get it.

During the day, Fess will use this computer when he works on the project. That won't look suspicious. He has one just like it. Everyone does. But when he uses it, he'll be importing project data on to its hard drive. The stuff that he wants us to examine. If you take the laptop home, we can search it later, offline, in a sterile environment, without the mole noticing.

Michael looked at the bag. Ann jiggled its strap to make the bait look more tempting.

It sounds to me like *you* could be the ones who are stealing information. You could be setting me up.

Towse turned to Ann.

See, Ann? You were wrong about him. He's not that dumb.

He turned back to Michael.

It does look like we're stealing information, doesn't it? But not in this case. Barb Collins will confirm the arrangement. She's your cut-out with Fess. He told you that in person.

Michael didn't look convinced.

It's too much responsibility. What if someone steals the laptop? What if I leave it on a bus?

They'll never get into it. We have weapons-grade encryption. Quantum based.

The full ride and blow job, said Ann-without-an-E.

And why the hell would I want to do this?

You're being very well paid, she said.

Michael stood, gestured at his clothes, his battered old sneakers.

Do I look like I care about money?

He turned and walked off.

Towse frowned at Ann, then called after Michael.

I heard you want to buy a house in Kitsilano, Michael. They don't come cheap.

Michael stopped, looked at his feet for a while, came back, took the bag from Ann-without-an-E. He wouldn't look at either of them.

Can you give me a lift back to Hollister?

We don't have a car, she said.

How did you get here?

She pointed at her muddy shoes.

Then can't you at least call me an Uber?

No cell phones, remember? And there's no reception up here.

How are you two getting back down the valley?

We're not.

She pointed across the road, towards the Diablo Range. Michael looked for Towse, meaning to appeal to him. But Towse had gone. There was no sign of him anywhere, though Michael could see for a hundred yards up and down the road. He must have snuck into the creek bed, disappeared in the brush.

When he turned back, Ann-without-an-E was skipping over the barbed wire that fenced off the road. He watched her climb the grassy hill towards a sycamore. She stopped and turned.

Hey, she called. If you don't want to walk, you should try hitching.

What?

Hitchhiking. You wait for a car, then stick out your thumb.

I know what it is. Do people still do that?

Beats me, she said, turning. I've never tried.

He watched her climb the hillside, disappear over its crest.

The water bottle sat on the crate, where it had been joined by a string bag of apples and oranges. That part, at least, had been true: there really had been fruit in the fruit stall. He picked up the bottle. It was almost empty, and after he'd drunk what was left he still felt thirsty. He took out an apple and wiped it on his shirt.


MICHAEL'S MOTHER, NADIA, HAD been beautiful in the Iranian way – a slender face, large dark eyes, delicate nose. In the earliest photos we have of her, stolen from the files of the Revolutionary

Guard, we see her in demure post-revolutionary costume – a knee-length *manto*, or raincoat, and a headscarf that didn't quite hide her shiny black hair. She is standing outside a busy cafe near the medical school at Urmia University, north-western Iran, talking to a young man. From their body language, they seem to be flirting. The young man is also very good-looking – dark, as you'd expect. He looks a lot like Michael. He will be Michael's dad.

Samvel is, like Nadia, dressed in middle-class post-revolutionary uniform: in his case, a loose suit, no tie, shirt buttoned to the top. His professor at the Urmia school of physics is devout and pro-government, and his postgraduate students, including Samvel, have to dress in the approved way.

Most of the time, at work, Samvel hides his cheap suit under a lab coat. As a medical student, Nadia wears a lab coat when she follows consultants on hospital rounds. She will later tell a friend, who will eventually betray her, that sometimes, when Samvel's uncle is out of town on business, and Samvel has the apartment to himself, she sneaks into the building, avoiding the concierge, and they make love in all the rooms of the apartment, wearing only their lab coats. It makes class the next day so much more interesting, seeing their fellow students, unwitting, dressed in their clothing of lust.

Years later, in Canadian winters, Nadia will wear a blue cotton parka, its hood trimmed with fake fur, from which, in Michael's earliest memory, her dark eyes look down at him, his hands reaching up to her from his stroller. This, he will tell Alice, is how he would always see Nadia. For him, her eyes would never lose the expression he remembers from that day — or maybe misremembers. Because maybe he was wrong to see her, and Samvel, as eternally lost, confused, vulnerable, in need of someone to look after them. Maybe she is only crying, that day in Red Deer — or it could have been Lethbridge — because it is cold, and her eyes haven't yet got used to prairie winters, if they ever did.

WHEN MICHAEL WAS IN the seventh grade, living in Medicine Hat, Alberta, the school principal asked his parents to come in and see her. They were working that morning, cleaning a meat coldstore that was going out of business, so his mother snuck off to the meeting alone. Michael himself was told nothing about it.

The principal wanted to let his parents know that their son had been showing signs of a possible behavioural disorder. It was probably just a minor case of obsessive compulsion, common enough in children that age. It would most likely clear up with time, but they should look into it, given the chance that a more serious condition — attention deficit disorder, or even mild autism — could be behind it. It was better to nip these things in the bud.

Michael's mother said she didn't understand. What was her son doing wrong? He was never in trouble.

This was true. Michael's parents had taught him to keep his mouth shut, avoid disputes, draw no attention to himself, or them.

The principal noted that Mrs Atarian spoke English well, but with a foreign accent. She also noted that the boy had only been enrolled a few months before. She wrote in her notes: *Culture shock?*

Where, she asked Mrs Atarian, had the family lived before they came to Medicine Hat? A recent move, particularly between countries, could be traumatic for children.

Mrs Atarian said they had moved there from Moose Jaw. Michael was born in Winnipeg and had never left western Canada. What was her son doing wrong?

Michael wouldn't step on the cracks.

In the schoolyard at recess; in the hall going to class; in gym: Michael had developed a morbid fear of standing on the cracks in the paving, in the linoleum floor tiles, in the hardwood floor of the basketball court. Twice, he'd been warned by teachers for reacting aggressively when other students jostled him as they tried to get past, making him step on a crack in the hall. The school had a three-strike policy for violent behaviour. Warning, suspension, expulsion. Better to put him on OCD meds before it came to that.

The principal was then surprised to hear this shy, dark, tired-looking woman, dressed for a cleaning shift, dried dirt on her clothes, explain in detail why she wouldn't put her son on selective serotonin reuptake inhibitors.

She told the principal, in the best English she could manage, that not stepping on the cracks was a harmless superstition or ritualised behaviour that had its roots in a rational fear. Cracks are dangerous. In nature, they hide snakes, poisonous spiders, things that want to be left alone. The cracks in the pavement have the dark fascination of wounds in the flesh or fissures in ice, or the rips in the earth left by sink holes and earthquakes, reminding us that another reality could open and swallow us, or unleash evil forces into our world.

In any case, Mrs Atarian concluded, Michael would probably grow out of it.

Maybe, the principal conceded, Mrs Atarian was right. Maybe it was just a passing behaviour. She would let it slide, for now. It would be unfair to single out Michael for something that many other kids saw as a game.

What game was that? asked Mrs Atarian.

You know, that old skipping game: Step on a crack, break your mom's back. Step on a line, break your dad's spine.

Mrs Atarian said she hadn't heard that one. She was from a different country. She would have a word with Michael when he got home.

Three weeks later, the family moved on again. We can assume, from the lack of any mention of OCD behaviour in his new school's records, that Michael had gotten over the problem, or at least he'd learned to hide it.


MICHAEL WAS ON THE couch the next evening, sunburned and sore from his trip up the valley. He'd ordered pizza from Terún and ate it while reading *Player Piano*. Someone banged on the back door.

Ann-without-an-E stood on the porch. Still holding the door, he looked past her. The yard was surrounded by a seven-foot fence, planks painted white. The gate, which gave on to an alley, was padlocked on the inside – he could see that from the porch. Ann-without-an-E wore a smart blue suit with a pencil skirt and heels. Her tights were unladdered. She was smoking a cigarette.

How did you get into the yard?

Never mind that. Do you have the computer?

Sure. Barb Collins gave it back to me just before I left the office.

She tossed the cigarette, brushed past him into the living room, sniffed the air.

Pizza. Great.

He watched her remove a slice from the box, stepping back as she did so, so that the strings of warm cheese didn't stick to her clothes. Holding it by the crust, she folded it lengthways and bit off half in one go.

You're welcome, he said.

She swallowed, took another bite, raised a hand.

One minute, she said, through a mouthful of pizza.

She took her time, chewing ecstatically, then dropped the crust into the lid of the box.

That's good pizza . . . Did you pay cash or card?

Cash.

Good. You're learning.

She wandered over to the bookshelf, studied the books.

*Oryx and Crake* . . . Have you read it?

I read it on the bus yesterday. I had plenty of time.

She didn't seem to notice the pointed way he said it.

Is it any good?

Yes.

Can I borrow it?

Sure.

She tucked it under her arm, turned back to Michael.

OK. Where is it?

He pointed to the end of the couch, where the laptop sat in its bag.

Ann-without-an-E sat, took out the computer and opened its lid. She kept her knees primly together, half-turned to Michael, so the screen was hidden from him. Taking a little white card from her pocket, she propped it on the couch beside her. Referring to it, as if for instructions, she tapped a few keys, frowned, tapped some more, frowned deeply, then smiled. She took out a flash key, inserted it into the USB port and did some more tapping. Then she took out the key and put it back in her pocket.

That's it, she said, and got up to go.

That's it? You don't want to take the computer away for inspection, like Towse said?

Not tonight. This is sort of a dry run.

So, I give the laptop to Barb again tomorrow?

Sure . . . Do you have a good memory?

We can presume that he did. Apart from Alice, it was mostly rote learning that got him through college.

Why?

She showed him a different card. This one had a number on it.

Memorise this. Then give me the card back. It's my burner phone. So you can reach me in emergencies. But don't call from here, or from your Inscape smartphone. Use a payphone. There's one in that strip mall.

I know. I saw it, two nights ago.

You noticed it, did you? Not bad. Not many people see payphones anymore . . . Remember to keep a few quarters handy. For God's sake, don't pay with a card.

She paused at the screen door, fiddling with it, testing the lock. A thought seemed to strike her.

Oh. If you don't mind, which one is your bathroom?

He pointed, then waited by the screen door to see her out through the back. She was in the bathroom a long time. He became aware of sounds through the door – a tap running loudly and, beneath its white noise, muffled cursing. A few moments later, the toilet flushed. The tap splashed then fell silent. She was smiling blandly when she came out, half-closing the door behind her.

The window catch was broken, but I managed to open it.

It wasn't broken.

Then it is now.

She strolled across the lounge, opened the back door and went on to the porch. Michael walked over to the bathroom door, closed it fully, then followed her out. But Ann-without-an-E was already gone.


THE FOLLOWING MORNING, AOIFE/ANN sat over a plate of huevos rancheros in Taqueria El Grullense, on El Camino Real. She was reading Atwood's *Oryx and Crake*. Her burner phone, set on the table beside her plate, buzzed loudly. She looked at the screen, picked up.

Michael, she said.

She listened for a while, ate some more egg, swallowed.

Don't worry, she said. It was probably just junkies. There's a methadone clinic in that strip mall near your house.

More noise from the phone.

How do I know that? Because I notice things, Michael. Did they make a big mess or take anything else? Apart from the laptop and your phone and your wallet?

A blip from the phone.

If they didn't make a big mess, they were junkies, Michael. Junkies grab the first things of value they see and leg it before they get caught. All they want is a fix, and they won't get one in the police cells. Proper thieves would have taken their time and turned the place over. And you with it.

A longer gap before she spoke again.

They can't get inside that laptop, Michael. We have weapons-grade encryption, remember? If anyone tries to hack into it, it will kill its own hard drive.

She took another forkful of egg, waited for him to finish.

Look, don't worry. It's just a laptop, and last night was a dry run . . . No, we don't need to report it. It would just cause a fuss . . . I'll get you another one. No one else needs to know about it. I'll be there in an hour. OK?


WE DON'T KNOW WHAT Michael did with the rest of that morning. But, at some stage, he calmed down enough to pick up a new book.

Peeping through the back window, Aoife saw he was reading *The Drowned World*. She tapped on the screen door.

Feet shuffled on floorboards. A steel bolt screeched in an aluminium frame. The mesh door shivered open.

You're late. I called you three hours ago.

Shush! Keep it quiet!

She brushed past him into the living room. He stood, staring at her costume. Today, she was wearing military fatigues, bloused boots, a dark blue beret, hair tied in a short pony tail. *U.S. Air Force*, it said on one side of her chest. *Smith*, on the other. There were other patches and badges that meant nothing to Michael. *Oryx and Crake* was in the thigh pocket of her camouflaged pants.

That's not really your uniform, is it?

Fits me, don't it?

She twirled, an excuse to take in the room. He watched her do it.

Yes, he said.

Never mind that. How did they get in?

The front door was open when I woke up.

Did you lock it last night?

Just the regular lock. I didn't use the deadlock.

She approached the front door, ducking to keep out of sight of the windows. Reaching it, she cracked open the door and peeked at the plate of the lock.

I don't see any damage . . . They didn't prise it open with a screwdriver, or anything like that . . .

She tested the door a couple of times, easing it shut and then open again.

It sits loose in the frame. They could have used a credit card or a strip of plastic. Slipped it under the tongue of the lock. Any fool can do that. Which is why you should always use the deadlock, Michael.

He watched her from across the room.

You didn't bring me a new laptop, he said.

She eased the door closed, leaned her back against it and shut her eyes, taking a beat. Then she opened her eyes again.

No, Michael. I did not.

She pointed at the corner.

Go over there. No, not directly. Go around by the wall, and keep clear of the windows. When you get to the corner, lean over just far enough so that you can look across the street. Then tell me what you see.

She closed her eyes again, bowed her head and waited, hearing his feet scuff on bare boards. There was a pause.

There's an SUV parked on the corner. A white Suburban.

Tinted windows, right?

Yes.

Eyes closed, leaning back against the door, she nodded to herself a few times. He watched her slide her back wearily down the door until she was sitting on the floor. Then she turned on to her hands and knees and crawled under the window to join him in the corner. When she stood again her face, lit from the side through the venetian blinds, was a film-noir barcode. She took him by the shoulders. She was as tall as he was. She stared levelly into his eyes.

I'm not going to lie to you, Michael. You're in big trouble. We have to get out of here.

*What?*

The men in that Suburban. They're watching you. We have to go before more of them come.

He pulled himself away from her.

Who are they?

Towse will tell you that. Come on. We'll get out through the back.

He stayed where he was, incredulous.

I'm not going anywhere. I don't know what's going on.

Jesus Christ, Michael. Is it not obvious? It turns out I was wrong about that laptop, OK? It was stolen by pros, serious spooks, and they've already cracked it. They're using its data to hack into some very secret servers, and they've set off alarms from here to the Pentagon. And the agencies think that you're in on it. They think *you're* the inside guy.

What? Why me?

Because you let it happen. You didn't report it when the laptop was stolen.

You told me not to!

I know. I'm sorry. I was wrong. But it's too late to worry about that now. I'm going to take you to Towse.

She sneaked to the back of the room, picked up his empty laptop bag, went over to the bookcase.

But Towse *is* the government. He knows I'm innocent. He'll sort this out.

She swept the remaining books into the bag, stuffed his jacket in after them, talking over her shoulder.

Towse is in the same boat, Michael. He gave you that computer so we could hunt the mole, but now the mole has turned the tables and they're hunting us. This isn't just a massive data breach, it's also a black op. Someone is taking Towse out.

You mean, the mole at Inscape?

For Christ's sake, Michael! Of course I mean the mole at Inscape! In five minutes you're going to have people – not the FBI, not the NSA, but people you've never heard of, and who aren't ever going to tell you who they are – coming in through your windows and doors. You want to wait for them, or you want to come with me? . . . Wait! Listen!

She looked stricken.

They heard a car drive slowly past the house, reach the end of the street, stop.

That's another one, Michael. One parked across the road, now another one taking up position down the street. If we wait any longer, they'll have staked out the alley behind the house. That's our only way out now. We have to go.

This is crazy!

You can stay, if you want, but I wouldn't advise it. You're a foreigner here. You don't have any rights.

I'm Canadian!

So what? You look Middle Eastern, Michael. For people like them, that's not a good look.

Crouching, she made her way to the screen door, opened it a crack and looked into the yard.

I don't see anyone out back. Last chance, Michael. Come with me and meet Towse. He'll figure a way out of this. It's what he does.

Michael turned, cracked the window blind. The white Suburban sat on the corner, the sun gleaming in the black visor of its windshield. You can see all kinds of horrors in a blank gaze like that. It was this that decided him.

Hold on. I'll pack my stuff.

You don't have any stuff, Michael. And we don't have time.

She grabbed his hand, opened the back door and yanked him outside.

The day was warm, the sun shining. Here and there, along the street and across the back alley, people were mowing better-off people's lawns. The houses here were too new to have trees in their backyards. There was no birdsong, and the high timber fence looked blank and forbidding. The yard felt like a cell with no roof.

She had Michael by the hand, but he was a drag on her, in shock. She let go of his hand and punched his shoulder.

Snap out of it, Michael.

Where can we go? I don't even have a passport. It was stolen with my wallet.

Passports won't help us now, Michael.

They reached the back gate, bolted and locked.

Listen, Michael. I don't have time to pick this lock, so I'm going to give you a boost, and then follow you over the fence. That means you go first. OK? If there's anyone waiting out there, put your hands up and tell them not to shoot.

What?

Come on. Let's do this.

When he still didn't move she thumped him in the back.

Come on, Michael!

She cupped her ear.

Oh Jesus! Did you hear that? Someone's banging at the front door!

He came to life, jumped, and grabbed the top of the fence, feet scrambling uselessly on the anti-climb paint. She put her shoulder under his backside and shoved up with all her strength. The fence shook, and he was down the other side, landing with a grunt.

She hung his bag around her shoulders, leaped up, grabbed the top of the fence and pulled herself astride it. Pausing to glance up and down the empty alley, she dropped lightly to the ground, landing where Michael was sprawled in the dirt.

These are yours, she said, dropping the books by his head. You carry them.

You brought them.

We're going to need them, just to pass the time. We've got a lot of travelling to do. And there's no more phones for us. Pick up the books and let's go.

She heard him panting after her.

Where are we going? There're only two roads in and out of this subdivision. Won't they have them both watched?

There are older ways than roads.

The alley, paved with cinders and weeds, led to a gap of blue sky. Reaching the end, Aoife flattened herself against the fence, peeked around the corner.

It's good. Let's go.

The alley had brought them to an unexpected wilderness, a shallow creek, its banks shaded by alders and willows and sycamore. It trickled through stones in long, gentle curves. Butterflies flirted with wildflowers. Midges danced over the stream.

I didn't know this was here, said Michael, impressed. How did you know about it?

The street map. The creek isn't marked, but I knew it was here from the contours. Drainage never lies.

She stepped into the creek bed and splashed downstream, ankle deep in the water. Michael followed her. The banks rose steeply and the trees drew in on either side, screening the creek from the sun. Up ahead, she was almost invisible, the dappled pattern of her uniform blending with the leaves. Michael lost sight of her in the gloom, and bumped into her when she stopped.

Traffic roared past, somewhere close overhead. A concrete culvert, closed by a steel grill, fed the living creek into a storm drain. A gash of bare earth climbed through the bushes, up to a roadside, fifteen feet above. Ann grabbed two handfuls of dry grass, using it to pull herself up from the creek bed.

There should be a bus stop just here, she said.

She reached into her pocket, threw something to him.

Catch.

He didn't. The little cylinder bounced off his palm and into the creek. He fished it out. It was a roll of quarters wrapped in cardboard, already coming apart from the wet.

When the bus comes, she said, you act like you don't know me. Follow me on to it, and follow me off. Nine of those quarters will pay your first bus fare. Keep the rest of them handy. We'll be taking a lot of buses today.

THE LAST OF MANY buses that day dropped them at a Walmart on the edge of Fairfield, California. It was dusk, and they'd been travelling for hours, taking the long way round San Francisco Bay. At the door of the store, Aoife turned and waited for Michael. It seemed that they knew each other again.

Go buy us some snacks, she said. I'm going to call Towse on his burner. He said there should be payphones by those washrooms over there.

When he rejoined her she was done with the phone call.

Towse is sending a car for us. No more buses tonight.

They sat at the far edge of the parking lot, the overflow, where nobody parked, eating potato chips and chocolate, drinking bottled water. The Walmart was built on the edge of the city, nothing east of it but grasslands and the gathering night. The sun, setting behind the Walmart, shone on white crosses in the gloom: a wind farm, becalmed. To the south, there was a line of low hills, wetlands, swamp grass – the northernmost marshes of San Francisco Bay.

The last rays, horizontal, found the Sierra Nevada, a hundred miles to the east, peaks pink with snow.

There was something else too, low in the sky – a bright light, like a star, off to the north. Michael pointed.

What's that?

She watched it grow brighter. There was noise in the sky, echoing off the hills west of Fairfield: the deep moan of jet engines, set for descent. The star became larger, lower, and a shape appeared behind it, an elephantine grey tube with beady black eyes and fat, drooping wings. It sank behind a swell in the ground.

That must be an airport over there, said Michael, watching. Look, there's another one coming in to land behind it.

Aoife took her beret from a thigh pocket and pulled at the hatband, front and back, to get it in shape. She put it on her head, adjusted the angle, stood.

Michael, can you pass me that bag?

He handed it up to her, still watching the sky.

Thanks . . . Can you give me your hand?

What?

I said, can you give me your hand, Michael?

Why do you want my hand?

Because of that.

She was looking at something behind him. He turned to look too. An SUV drove slowly towards them, its headlights on high beam.

Michael raised a hand to shield his eyes. It was another white Chevrolet Suburban, but this one had lights on the roof. The lights were flashing.

Oh God, Michael said.

Aoife took his free hand and squeezed it. He squeezed back. A bracelet locked round his wrist.

She yanked on her end of the handcuffs, experimenting, and nearly pulled him off his feet.

You're under arrest, she told him. I'm escorting you to a military prison. Keep your mouth shut, and do as I say.

THE MILITARY-POLICE TRUCK PULLED up outside a long, low building with a sign that said *Travis Passenger Terminal*. An Air Force officer waited by the glass doors. Aoife saluted him.

Good evening, Major. Thanks for sending your people to give us a ride.

Anything to help, Lieutenant. Colonel Towse said your own transport broke down.

He looked at Michael.

Have you got his documents?

She handed over a sheaf of papers. The major read them, looked at Michael again.

Bring him inside.

Beyond the sliding doors was a small but modern passenger terminal – a waiting area and luggage carousel, with doors leading off it to various boarding gates. A monitor showed flight numbers and the names of Air Force bases. There was also a cafe, the Pacific Gateway Grill, closed for the night.

The major took Michael's papers to a Formica counter marked *Passenger Check-In, Space Available.*

Priority one, he told the two airmen behind it. Get this creep off our base as soon as you can.

They looked at the papers, then at Michael.

A dozen bored passengers, dressed in civilian clothes, were slumped in plastic chairs near the counter. They watched as Aoife led her prisoner to the corner of the room. He was coming out of his stupor.

I need to go to the bathroom, he said.

It was the first time he'd spoken since the betrayal in the parking lot.

Shut up and sit down.

She took out a book. She was reading Le Guin now, *The Dispossessed.*

Michael looked around the waiting room. The other passengers had already forgotten him. They were staring at smartphones and magazines, or numbly at the floor between their feet. He looked at the departures board. The names and the numbers meant nothing to him.

I really need the bathroom.

Keep your voice down . . . You can go on the plane.

Can't I at least have a book to read?

No.

Why not?

Because we're handcuffed together, and it would annoy me whenever you turned the page.

If you don't let me go to the bathroom, or give me something to read, I'll start screaming.

She put her book down, closed her eyes, opened them again.

OK, she said. I'll cuff your hands in front of you, and those airmen over there – she nodded towards the counter – will escort you to the little boys' room. OK?

Sounds good to me.

The only problem is, those men have seen your warrant.

What do you mean?

I'm not sure I'd want them taking me alone into a bathroom. Particularly with my hands cuffed.

What does it say on the warrant, Ann?

It says you're an Air Force deserter. And also, a nonce.

A what?

Christ. Doesn't anyone over here speak English? . . . A paedophile. You molested some Air Force brats on your base, and when their parents found out, you deserted. You're wanted back east for your sex crimes.

No I'm not!

That's what it says on your warrant.

He looked at the men behind the counter. They stared back at him, dead-eyed.

I think I'll hold it until we're on the plane.

That would be best.

He sat quietly for a while, thinking it over. She tried to get back to her reading, but couldn't focus on the words. She was waiting for the penny to drop.

This arrest, he said finally. It's not because of the hacking at Inscape, is it?

She put her book down.

Of course not. It's about getting us on a plane out of California, in a hurry, without going through biometrics or TSA checks, or showing ID, or having to use bank cards. It was Towse's idea.

Where are we going?

New Jersey.

Why?

Towse will tell us when we get there.

Where is he now?

When I phoned him earlier he was in the officer's club. It sounded pretty raucous. He seems to have made friends here.

Is he really a colonel?

They seem to think so.

Right . . . What is this place, anyway?

Travis Air Force Base. This is the Space Availability terminal.

She picked her book up again.

Space Availability?

She put the book down.

Space A: serving and retired US military can hitch free rides on Air Force transport, provided there is space available on the flight. They can only go standby, but it doesn't cost money, and it flies all over the world. The important thing, for us, is Air Force terminals don't have facial-recognition technology or TSA guards or homeland security. Airports do. That's why we're here.

A speaker announced the much-delayed departure of the flight to Pearl Harbor–Hickam. Eighteen seats were available. All passengers would fly, whatever their priority. The other passengers cheered, got up, dragged their baggage with them. Only Aoife and Michael were left in the waiting room. Five minutes later, one of the airmen came for them. They followed him through the terminal, past the carousel, out through a door and on to the apron. The other passengers had formed a line out there, at the steps of a massive grey jet – the same one Michael and Aoife had seen from the Walmart. Michael started towards it. The cuffs brought him up short.

Not that one, said the airman.

He pointed further along the apron, to where a smaller aircraft sat by itself.

Sorry, Lieutenant. But all we've got going east is this Charlie One Thirty. It's not configured for passengers. It'll be a long night.

The cargo ramp yawned for them like the jaw of a whale. The plane's loadmaster, a technical sergeant in flight suit and headphones, watched from the top. From the way she looked at Michael, she had heard about his crimes.

The cargo bay was a cave of green quilted nylon, the deck studded with rollers to ease loading of freight. Someone lay wrapped in a blanket at the front of the cabin, on one of the webbed plastic benches that ran down each side. Whoever they were, they were stinking of whiskey.

The loadmaster closed the ramp, led Aoife and Michael to the bench opposite the sleeper.

Sit here, please.

She picked up a baton, pointed it at Michael.

He has to stay cuffed for the duration, sir, in case he goes nuts, or tries to molest someone.

I really need the washroom, he pleaded. Badly.

Yeah? I'd let you pee yourself, but it would soil my nice clean aircraft . . . There's a urinal back there, by the ramp. But if you try any of your sick crap on my plane, pal, you'll fly the rest of the way hog-tied, face down on the cold steel deck. You understand me?

He nodded, unable to speak. The loadmaster stood back, glaring, while Ann unlocked the handcuffs from her wrist. The loadmaster pointed to a rudimentary urinal, behind a green canvas screen at the rear of the plane. She stood a few feet away, slapping her palm with the baton, while he tried to relieve himself. It took him a while.

Done, he washed his hands with alcohol gel. She followed him back to the bench, reattached the free bracelet of the handcuffs to the steel tube, then went up the ladder that led to the flight deck.

Towse sat up and winked at them.

Hello, people, he said.

Michael tested his handcuff.

Why are you doing this to me, Towse?

This is the only way to fly out of California without leaving a trail. We don't have time to drive.

I meant, why did you have to make me a sex offender? These people really want to hurt me.

Because no one wants to talk to a sex offender. And if there is any talking, I want Ann to be doing it.

She had settled on the bench a few feet from Michael.

Here. You're going to need these.

She tossed him a small plastic box. One handed, he failed to catch it. She unclipped her seat belt, picked up the box and handed it to him.

Earplugs, she said. These planes are very loud.

She watched as he screwed a foam plug into one ear, then tried to insert the other. But his cuffed hand couldn't reach his ear on that side, and he fumbled the plug on to the deck. It rolled out of reach.

Here, she said, let me.

She inserted the ear plug with a surprisingly light touch.

There, she said. Can you hear me?

Not very well.

Good. Now leave me alone.

# Part Two:

## *Vineland*

AOIFE GREW UP ON a small stud farm near Kildare Town in the midlands of Ireland. Her parents, who came from the South Dublin merchant class, loved the country and its wildlife, but its people, not so much. They would have sent Aoife to boarding school in Dublin, but their horses never made money, so they couldn't pay school fees for both of their children. Her older brother was sent to the Jesuits at Clongowes, but Aoife had to go to the convent in the town. Her parents never really forgave her for the loss of caste she had suffered because of her free education, and tried to compensate by preventing her from having close friends; they were worried she might pick up the Kildare accent.

As a little girl, Aoife had too many notions to be truly lonely. She often lay awake in bed, imagining the lives of the people who moved past her house in the night – the headlights sweeping the wall, the clack of trains on the Waterford rail line, planes sighing overhead.

Reading books or watching TV, she measured herself against the characters they showed her. Could she be those people? She thought that she could.

Later, in her teenage years, she learned how to arrange a life that her parents didn't know about. She hid burner phones, permanently on silent, and had a second, secret bicycle that she kept in a hedge, a hundred yards down the road, and that she would use to attend urgent discos and parties, sneaking out of her window when her parents were asleep. She never made a sound, and they never caught her. She had as many friends as she wanted, boyfriends too. Her parents, expecting some pushback against their controls, began to believe she was a little too passive. A bit boring, maybe.

Aoife came to understand that she had a talent for deception. At the age of seventeen, when she was filling out her college application, it occurred to her that she could apply to study theatre. The idea made her dizzy. But her parents had other plans. She did well at school, despite being the youngest girl in her year, but she didn't work hard enough to get into medicine, or veterinary science. Engineering was for boys. There was only one other respectable, ladylike option: Aoife would have to do law.

During freshers' week she joined the college players, and thus fell in with the drama-school crowd. She helped with the sets, took small parts in productions. She didn't tell her parents, or invite them to her plays.

In Aoife's third year of college, there was to be a performance of the latest play by a respected writer-director, and the drama department brought in the playwright herself to oversee the production. Casting wasn't restricted to drama-school students. Aoife put down her name.

The director was impressed by Aoife's audition. But she didn't give Aoife a part in the play.

You're too realistic, the director told her. It's like you're not acting at all. This is theatre. It has to be a little bit showy. You have a real talent, but up on stage, acting like that, you'd just disappear.

AS A LAW STUDENT, Aoife liked to spend time in the courts around Dublin, to observe their theatrics. Towards the end of her final year of college, while classes were out, she spent a few days in the Criminal Courts of Justice, watching a murder trial. The defendant, a vacant young man with short, spiky hair, was accused of fatally stabbing his best friend outside a pub. It was the defendant's case that he had done it by accident, while trying to defend himself against a stranger with a knife who had chased him outside. The defendant said that his best friend had come between him and this stranger, whose existence was never confirmed, and that in his attempt to defend himself he had stabbed his friend by mistake with a broken beer bottle.

The defendant's lawyers argued that the killing was accidental and that their client should have been charged with manslaughter, at worst. The prosecution said that the killing had been deliberate, that jealousy over a young woman, the partner of the dead man and mother of his child, had led to lethal violence.

The third party in this triangle came to court every day. She was a quiet, gentle-faced young woman, who dressed as if she were attending someone else's wedding. She sat there, always alone, gazing fondly at the defendant. When called as a witness, she admitted that she had been living with the victim, but was secretly in love with the man who had killed him. She begged the jury to forgive his crime of passion, so they could be together at last. It must have been an accident, she said. He was a loving soul who would never hurt anyone.

He cried in the dock as she told her story. She was crying too.

The verdict came in: guilty of murder. Aoife, watching the killer's surprise and dismay, lost sight of the young woman. But five minutes later she found her outside, smoking a cigarette, waiting for a taxi on Conyngham Road. Aoife was dressed like a lawyer or a legal clerk, in a dark skirt and jacket, blouse and plain shoes, and she decided to approach the young woman. It would be like a rehearsal for her next role.

Moving to the kerb, pretending to also look for a taxi, she glanced at the young woman, who was smoking fiercely in the other direction.

That was very sad, what happened in there.

The young woman dropped her cigarette, ground it under a white kitten heel, and turned to stare at her.

You mean, the lad who just got done for murder?

Yes.

He's a cunt. I hope he dies in jail.

Aoife, shocked, stood her ground.

But you said you were in love with him!

I did say that, yeah. And the dozy bastard thought I meant it. So did the jury. But I don't want that scumbag near me or the child.

It took a moment for Aoife to put it together.

You stitched him up . . . You wrecked his defence.

He killed my fella because he thought he had a chance with me. No fucking way.

Aoife thought about that.

So why did he believe he had a chance with you? Was there something between the two of you once, that your boyfriend didn't know about?

The young woman studied Aoife, came to a decision.

You're not a lawyer. A brief walks away as soon as it's over – win, lose or draw – to put in for their money.

Your child . . . Was the defendant the real father?

Fuck off.

A taxi took her away.

Aoife watched the people come and go through the doors of the courthouse. She admired the precision of the young woman's performance. The trial had lasted two weeks, a parade of mumbling policemen, timid eyewitnesses, paid medical experts, fawning solicitors, and – lording it over them all – the judge and the barristers, strutting and declaiming in fake Anglo-Irish accents. Only one member of this cast had shown no sign that they were acting. It hadn't been Aoife.

Aoife realised she would not be a lawyer. She would not conveyance property or litigate claims. She wouldn't be a barrister, and spend the rest of her life congratulating herself and her colleagues on second-rate performances.

She needed a greater challenge, higher stakes. The following day, reading the online job ads, she saw that the police force in Northern Ireland was accepting recruits from south of the border. Because of historical imbalances, there would be positive discrimination for people like her, women from nominally Catholic backgrounds.

She had recently discovered the novels of Eoin McNamee, set in troubled Northern Ireland, in which renegade seekers of truth are haunted and broken, doomed to death – or worse, survival – as witnesses to endless and echoing pain. She tried to push them from her mind as she looked at the job ad, to pretend that this was a sober, cold-blooded calculation. She wouldn't want to admit she was looking for romance.

The Troubles were over, pretty much – for the time being at least – and England had not yet gone mad. The border was quiet. But the police in Northern Ireland, though reformed since the old days, were still targets for terrorist splinter groups. If you worked for the police, and these gunmen knew where you lived, they could kill you. That hadn't changed since the Troubles. If she applied, and was accepted, she would have to live furtively, across the northern border, where she wasn't known. She would carry a concealed weapon, and check under her car with a mirror on a stick. And she could tell no one back home what her job was. Her parents least of all.

\*

ONCE AGAIN, AOIFE HAD chosen badly. She didn't belong in a police force. It wasn't so much that she was a woman, a southerner and a nominal Catholic in a mainly male, Ulster and Protestant force. It was more that she disliked the discipline, and was easily bored. She had thought her new job would show her dark secrets. Instead, it gave her the Lisburn Road at closing time, and teenagers on towpaths, wrecked on Bucky and spice. Now, even these low adventures would be taken from her; her superiors had noticed that she had a law degree. Barely out of training, she was taken off real police work, fast-tracked for promotion. She would be streamed into management, starting with a stint in the press office. It would be good for the service to have someone like her to put in the shop window.

Aoife reckoned that if she'd wanted to work in PR she wouldn't have joined a police force. There were easier ways to make money than that. And she definitely didn't want to be put on display.

Anyway, she was tired of the legend she'd created for her parents, the one in which she was a civil servant in London, which explained the UK burner phone she used as a cut-out. Whenever they called her on that number, it went straight to voicemail. She checked that voicemail from her other phones.

It was time to move on, to get serious with her life. Law might not be so bad. Or she could join a circus. Aoife wrote out her resignation, took it into work.

The press office was in the force's HQ on the outskirts of Belfast. She worked in uniform, in an office, with eight other constables, all very nice, who talked about rugby and field hockey, and reality shows that she didn't watch. She had taken up smoking, just to have a good reason for going outside. From then on, she would always associate cigarettes with boredom.

Time for one last smoke, then she'd hand in her letter and give up for good.

The designated smoking area was in a ground-floor porch at the rear of the main building. There were two other people down there, one of whom she'd seen about before. He was an older man, thin, with wiry grey hair and slow, tired eyes. He smelled faintly of whiskey. There, she thought, is my McNamee knight errant.

The other one was younger, tall and good-looking, with a habit of shifting his weight from one foot to the other, like a boxer loosening up. They were dressed in civilian clothes — jeans, casual jackets — like middle-aged dads on their way to a match. When she arrived, they were talking. When they saw her, they stopped. She lit up and looked the other way.

Nice day for it, said the younger of the two.

He had a London accent.

It is, surely.

For reasons unknown to herself, she said it in the Belfast accent. She was pretty fluent. She had a gift.

You work here, do you?

You mean, do I come here often?

She indicated her uniform.

What gave it away?

The cockney laughed.

I'm only trying to make conversation. I'm Cass. Who are you?

Aoife.

Aoife? I don't know that name. Is it spelled E–E–F–A?

What do you care how I spell it? Are we going to be pen pals now?

The older man spoke.

Where are you from, constable?

He had an Ulster accent, a very soft one. Glens of Antrim, somewhere like that.

County Kildare.

A Free Stater? Are you telling me so? I'd have sworn, from your accent, you were Lagan born and bred. Except you hit that vowel in *now* a little too hard.

The end is nigh, she said.

She had finished her cigarette. Time to go. The older man spoke again.

Who's your CO?

Why?

Because I might want to borrow you.

Who are you, so?

My name is McDonnell. And you know who we are.


AOIFE WAS PLAYING A nurse now, with nurse's scrubs and rubber-soled shoes. She lived with a few other young men and women – nurses and teachers – in a rented apartment in County Armagh. The building stood at the entrance to a housing estate, with views of the street and the first row of houses. But the blinds at the front were drawn at all times. Nurses work night shifts. Neighbours noticed how the tenants of that flat came and went at all hours, singly or in pairs. Their faces were constantly changing – young people on temporary contracts, badly paid, no security, who can't stay in the one place for long.

Aoife's briefing had consisted of a drive-by in a Vauxhall with McDonnell and Cass. They showed her the house across the road from the apartment.

That's it. Number eleven.

They kept going, turned the corner. Cass handed her a photograph. It was an elderly man, his face imploded from years of bad living. He stood in the door of a bookmaker's, smoking.

James Brennan, said McDonnell. Also goes by the Irish, Séamus Ó Braonáin. Or, behind his back, Jimmy O'Braindeath. And that's his friends talking. He was never the liveliest company, poor Jimmy.

Who is he?

He's a bomb-maker, said Cass. Provisional IRA. Did ten years in the Maze.

The Provos are on ceasefire, said Aoife. There hasn't been a big bombing for twenty years.

Thank Jimmy for that.

He's an informer?

McDonnell shook his head.

We tried to turn him, back in the old days, when I was in the RUC Special Branch. Nothing doing. He's a staunch soldier of the republic. But he works for MI5, now. He just doesn't know it.

They drove slowly around the town, the windows down, so they could smoke and talk without being overheard.

The dissident republicans want the Troubles back, said McDonnell. They miss the fun and the money. They can do shootings and pipe bombs, and drug dealing and theft and extortion. Diesel laundering, all of that. But they don't know how to make proper bombs anymore. That art is lost to them. Jimmy, on the other hand, is an old-school Provisional craftsman.

But he only works for cash now, said Cass. One of his grandkids needs a drug the NHS won't pay for. Some arsehole in America bought the patent and jacked up the price.

What happens to the bombs he makes?

We watch Jimmy's house to find out who's coming to see him. That way, we know who to lift. Nip it in the bud.

If you lift everyone who comes to see him, won't that give it away?

We make it look like the info comes from other dissidents. Which sometimes gets them shot, which is a terrible shame. But eventually, yeah, they'll think that Jimmy is touting them up.

They'll kill him, Aoife said.

Consider the alternative. Command wires in culverts. Tilt switches under cars.

They pulled up behind the apartment building. Cass handed Aoife a key.

The machines are all set – the bugs and the taps and the cameras. All monitored remotely from Cheltenham. You just have to sit with the blinds drawn and watch the house and the street. Look for the stuff the machines can't pick up.

She got out of the car. McDonnell called after her.

Are you not armed?

She raised her arms and turned a circle in her scrubs.

Where would I hide it?

We'll get you a wee ankle gun, so. If they figure out that Jimmy is watched, they might come looking for the watchers.


THE LANDLORD HAD SET up the bare little flat for maximum profit, regulations be damned. There were two sets of double bunks in each of the two bedrooms, and two more in the living room. Twelve bed spaces in all, and one small kitchen and bathroom. The gas and electricity worked off coin-operated meters that charged the tenants twice as much as the suppliers charged the landlord. When the watchers ran out of coins, which was often, they had to sit in the dark. A sign in every room, put up by the landlord, warned that smoking would lead to loss of deposit. But Aoife smoked anyway. She reckoned that MI5 could afford to lose the money. Plus, they could hardly expect her to smoke outside, could they? And she needed to smoke: if Aoife had thought the press office was boring, nothing had prepared her for life on a stake-out. She had picked the wrong option again.

Business was slow for Jimmy O'Braindeath. His wife had died and he lived alone. In Aoife's first month, working five shifts a week, no one came to see him except his daughter and his grandkids. There were four of them: a nine-year-old, two toddlers and a baby in a pram.

Jimmy went out once a day to visit the shops and the bookmaker. He went on foot. Having placed his bets, he'd walk slowly home again, stopping every fifty yards or so, leaning on walls to get back his breath.

His timing was erratic. If he was out when she called, his daughter would let herself into the house. When he came home the children would mob him, spilling out of the hallway into the garden. He kept sweets for them in his pockets. When the children were visiting, he smoked outside.

BY RIGHTS, THERE SHOULD have been two people on duty at all times, but budgets were low. Aoife was alone, on the fifth week of her secondment, when the blue Ford Focus turned into the estate.

She watched it drive past, turn into a dead end. A minute later it came out again, continued along the street, disappeared from her view. There was nothing unusual in that. People got lost in these housing estates, turned into cul-de-sacs, backtracked.

Aoife went into the kitchen, filled the kettle, put it on the gas ring, went back to her window.

The Ford had returned in her absence. It was pulled over to the kerb, just past her window, directly across from number eleven. It was now facing towards the estate's only exit.

Jimmy was out at the bookies. He'd been gone for a while now.

Aoife leaned forward. From this angle, looking downwards, she could only see the passenger, not the driver. He wore a hooded tracksuit. She couldn't see his face; he was looking away from her, towards number eleven. She could tell that he was plump, and his hair was oily and very short. She picked up the camera and shot a few frames. The long lens showed her the spots on his neck.

She couldn't see the plates on the car.

Jimmy's daughter appeared at the end of the road, pushing the pram. Her husband had gone to England for work, and stopped sending money, and hadn't come back. She always put on smart clothes for the short walk to her Dad's place, shoulders back, forcing the tiredness out of her face. The nine-year-old girl walked by her side, chatting. She was a solemn child, small for her age. Probably the sick one. The two toddlers, boys, ran ahead of their mother, racing each other to their grandfather's house.

Aoife looked at the car again. The spotty young man was still staring away from her. But now he had something bunched on his lap. A blanket. It was a hot August day.

Jimmy's daughter reached the front door of the house, unlocked it, let in a stampede of kids.

Aoife went into the hallway, leaving the door on the latch. Halfway down the emergency stairs was a landing with a window. From there, she could see the Ford's registration. She went back to the apartment and called it in.

Passing the kitchen door, she heard the hiss and tick of the kettle, halfway to the boil.

The door of number eleven opened and the children spilled out again. The toddlers had a football. The nine-year-old was reading a book. Jimmy's daughter appeared and sat on the doorstep, holding the baby, watching the kids.

The traffic department called back. The registration didn't match the car.

Aoife looked down again. The plump man's neck was shiny with sweat. He had opened his window, shifted the blanket. There was something grey underneath it. The long lens on the camera showed her a gun.

Chekov's Law, first corollary. That's what McDonnell called it. They never risk being caught with a weapon unless they really mean to use it.

She called McDonnell on his mobile. As his phone rang, she heard the kettle whistle in the kitchen. It would have to wait.

There's two men sitting in a car with stolen plates outside Jimmy's. One of them has a short.

Where's Jimmy?

At the bookies. He should be back in five or ten minutes.

We can be there in fifteen.

They're going to kill him, aren't they?

We'll catch them before they get away. There's enough time for the cops to put up an outer cordon.

His grandchildren are there in front of the house. And his daughter. They'll see it. Maybe worse.

Stay out of it, Aoife. You're alone. And you're not trained for this.

We can't let this happen.

Yes we can, Aoife. Consider the alternative.

Aoife hung up. She looked around the room. The kettle was screaming now, demanding attention. She tried to block out its sound while she grabbed at ideas.

There was a cheap sofa in the corner, already falling apart. Its cushions hid a German sub-machine gun. The housekeeping gun, Cass had called it. Aoife had qualified on that type of weapon in basic training, with one of the highest scores in her year. She had her concealed carry pistol as well, the tiny semi-automatic that McDonnell had issued her. But it was one thing to shoot at a four-foot paper target, another to aim at a living person and pull the trigger. She couldn't see herself doing that. Nor did she want to be shot at herself. Anyway, those kids on the street had no place in a gunfight.

Consider the alternative . . . McDonnell always said that . . . Non-lethal weapons. Tasers. Tear gas. Clubs. She had nothing like that, and they wouldn't work, anyway. All she had was boiling water, for what little that was worth.

Did she even have that? The kettle was no longer whistling.

The meter had cut off the gas . . .

The elevator was down in the lobby. She couldn't wait for it to come up. She went down the stairs three at a time.

Aoife approached the Ford from behind. She hoped they'd see her coming. It would be a bad idea to startle them.

Excuse me, she called from a distance. Could I borrow your phone?

The passenger turned to stare at her. His face was spotty too. Seen up close, he was very young, little more than a teenager. He was in a flop-sweat, terrified, ready to puke.

He hasn't done this sort of thing before, thought Aoife. He's being pushed into this. This is meant to be his first.

She hadn't done this sort of thing either.

She could see the driver now. He was older, thinner, with a hard, bar-tanned face.

Fuck away off now, he told her. We're busy.

Please, I just need to borrow a mobile. It's an emergency. There's a gas leak in the flats.

Use your own phone.

I couldn't find it. I had to get out in a hurry. I got in from the night shift – she waved at her scrubs – and fell asleep on the couch. When I woke the place was stinking of gas.

We don't have a mobile. Leave us alone.

Either they were smart enough not to bring a phone in the first place, or half-smart enough not to make any calls from what would soon be a crime scene. But they weren't smart enough to give up and drive away, now that someone was talking to them, face to face.

Aoife could see through the car to where the children were playing.

Come on, lads. Please. Everyone has a mobile now. There are kids across the street. There could be an explosion.

I fucking told you. We don't have a phone . . . Why not use that one?

What one?

That payphone. The one over there.

She straightened, looked. There was a phone box twenty feet away.

In all the hours she had spent staring out that window, she must have looked right through it a thousand times and never once noticed it.

Of course the driver would have seen it. Irish gunmen are traditionalists. They like to use payphones for warnings and boasts.

Oh . . . I never noticed that before.

Away off and use it. Don't be bothering us.

She held the door of the box open as she dialled 999. When the call was answered she spoke loudly, as if the phone was on the blink.

I need the gas board. There's a really strong smell of gas in my building . . . No, I don't have their number. Can't you connect me?

She gave the gas board the address, looked back at the car. The two men were watching her. Their windows were open. They still didn't get it. Time to spell it out for them.

And please – she was shouting now – send the police too. They have to get everyone out of the building before someone gets hurt.

There was a short pause, then a muffled commotion inside the Ford. Its engine started and it drove to the entrance of the estate, turned right, picked up speed. A few moments later, Jimmy appeared on the opposite corner. He leaned against a garden wall. She heard his desperate cough.

Across the road, the two little boys were fighting for the football.

Aoife walked back to the apartment and sat on the step in the sun.

McDonnell was first to arrive, with Cass, in their Vauxhall. Armoured Land Rovers followed. Uniformed constables flooded the street.

Aoife stood, stretched, walked to the kerb. She liked the loose, cool feel of the scrubs against her skin. It had been a fine summer, and she'd spent too much of it behind the blinds.

What happened?

They've gone, she said.

McDonnell gestured down the street towards Jimmy, who, seeing what he must have assumed was a raid on his house, was going back the way he'd come, as fast as he could manage.

He'll know that we're watching his house now. So will the lads who wanted to do him. This operation is blown.

Aoife shook her head.

I just reported a gas leak in the flats. If you get the constables here to evacuate the building, and tell the people and the press it's because of a gas leak, no one but us will ever know any different.

Cass and McDonnell looked at each other, then Cass went to talk to the inspector in charge. McDonnell turned back to Aoife.

Have you ever thought about a change of employer?


THE C-130 LANDED IN the early hours to refuel and load freight at Scott Field, Illinois. It took off again and climbed into the dawn. Aoife, who didn't have a phone or a watch, and didn't know what time it was, or even which time zone, felt suspended in the light that streamed through the portholes. Below her was a grid of fields and highways, and the spider web of survey lines, stamped on the earth, ramrod straight, but warped here and there to conform with the enduring facts of hills and creeks and valleys. She could see the shadows of the land's contours in the low slanting sun. You could tame the land and cut the forests, but the drainage never lies.

The plane, and the sun, climbed higher. The perspective foreshortened, shadows declined, until the world through the window, now crusted with snow, seemed flat as a computer screen, nowhere to hide. Towse, across from her, had taken out a laptop to work on, offline. Michael, too, had woken, and was looking down at the landscape.

I'm the one in the air, thought Aoife. I'm the one who moves past while the world tries to sleep.

She took out *Roadside Picnic* and found her page. Stalker. She liked that. She was in that line herself.


IT WAS MORNING WHEN the plane touched down at Maguire–Fort Dix in New Jersey. Towse, who seemed to have VIP status, was allowed to get off before them. The loadmaster stood over Michael, swinging her baton from one hand to the other, while Aoife switched the cuff's bracelet from the bench to her own wrist.

Take good care of him, sir, said the loadmaster. I'm looking forward to reading about the trial.

They emerged into daylight at the end of the ramp. Crossing the

apron, Aoife stumbled, leaned against Michael. It took him a moment
to realise that the handcuffs were gone.

Congratulations, she said. The charges were dropped.

He looked at her sourly, rubbing his wrist.

On what grounds?

On the grounds that you'll be someone else when we walk into
that terminal.

So who will I be?

No one will care. If there is any talking, leave it to me.

There wasn't any talking. They passed uninterrupted through
the long, high hall of the terminal, past benches of hopeful Space-A
passengers, into the cold day beyond.

The gate of the base was a short walk to the north. Nobody
checked them on the way out.

Towse waited in a bus shelter on the tree-lined highway at the edge
of the base. The bench had room for three people, divided into separate
seats by raised metal bars, designed to prevent drunks or homeless people
from stealing a few minutes sleep. Unshaven, sweaty, in his rumpled
suit and tie, Towse looked Chaplinesque to Aoife, a proper tramp, one
from the old days, before homeless people let themselves go.

She sat at the opposite end of the bench. Michael paused, looked
at them both, kept walking.

Towse turned to Aoife.

Can you go after him?

He's no use to us. Can't we just let him go?

No.

Then what do I tell him?

Just enough to make him stay.

Which is all that you ever tell me.

Tell him, if he tries to go it alone, Fess's people will get him.

We told him that the last time. It's not stopping him now.

Then tell him one word. Tell him 'Alice.'

She got to her feet again. Michael, she noticed, was going the wrong way.

THE NUMBER THREE-ONE-SEVEN NEW Jersey Transit bus is a two-hour ride from Fort Dix to Philadelphia. The driver was rude, the bus decrepit. Their feet stuck to the floor as they made their way to the back, where the muffler leaked fumes into the last rows of seats. But the noise from this broken exhaust was a bonus. It meant they could talk freely.

Towse sat in the middle of the back seat. Michael and Aoife were in the next row, on opposite sides of the aisle, turning to face him. This way, they could watch his face as he talked, to try to see if he was lying. Towse couldn't smoke on the bus, or walk around either. For the other two, this was a plus.

Alice, prompted Michael.

She worked with me.

*Alice* worked for the US government?

I didn't say that. I said she worked with *me*. I have my own interests. She was keeping an eye on Campbell Fess for us.

Aoife remembered boozy singalongs in country pubs, back home in Ireland. *Who the fuck is Alice?* She would save that question for a better time.

Michael spoke again.

So it was your fault that Alice started working for Fess.

No. At first, she needed the money. And then she had other ideas. She wanted to adapt Fess's systems for her own use. Turn his own weapons against him. It was her dream project. Yoyodime, she called it. A network for private cash transfers, off grid. Although that would have been just the start of it. It would have gone much deeper than that. She must have told you about it?

Michael looked out the window. Towse watched him, then continued:

So Alice started working for Fess on the OmniCent project. But then she noticed something very strange, and she contacted me about it. I started investigating. But I let Fess think I was working for him. That's always the best way to play it.

Michael looked out the window, buffering. They were passing through the outskirts of Pemberton, New Jersey. It could have been anywhere. Fast-food outlets, signs.

He turned back to Towse.

You're trying to tell me that Alice was the mole at Inscape.

Yes.

But that doesn't make sense. Alice is gone. So who stole the laptop?

Fess. He's trying to cover up what Alice found out. So he staged the theft of that laptop and pinned it on us, to smear me with the agencies.

He must have found out that I was working against him, so he needs
to destroy me. You were collateral damage.

What did she find that could cause all this trouble?

Funny money. That's all I can tell you, for now. We're here in
New Jersey to find out more.

How are we going to do that? asked Aoife.

The usual way. By stealing information.

Michael spoke up.

Why should I believe you, Towse? I lived with Alice for four
years and she never once mentioned you.

We didn't have that kind of friendship . . . I only met her once,
face to face . . . It was on the day she died.


TOWSE SAW HER UNDER the trees, chaining her bicycle. When
he knocked on the window, beads formed in its moisture, racing the
rain drops on the other side. Alice pushed back her hair, wet from
the rain, and looked for the source of the noise. When she saw him
she didn't smile.

She bypassed the counter, where a school tour was buying cookies
and sodas, and sat down across from him. The rain had run off her
waterproof jacket, soaking her jeans and her sneakers. She sat on the
edge of her chair, one knee extended towards the exit, as if she might
take flight at any moment. He thought, We shouldn't be sitting here,
in this window, where anyone can see us and we can't see them, out
there in the rain and the trees.

Why this museum? he asked. It's a long bike ride from town. Are you into anthropology?

You said pick somewhere quiet to meet in an emergency. I like it here, so I picked it. And judging from the card that you left at my house, there's an emergency.

Yes.

Fess knows about me?

He's about to find out. So I'm going to tell him myself, before he does. It will buy me some trust. I can use that against him.

Alice considered that, shrugged.

OK . . . You came to Vancouver to tell me that in person?

I thought we should meet face to face, after all that you've done for us.

Well, now you've met me.

Her eyes, he noticed, were red.

I can get you out of here, he said. You and your boyfriend.

A server took Towse's empty cup. When he was gone, Alice spoke again.

I can't take Michael with me. I don't have the right to hijack his life.

If you leave him behind, he's in danger.

I said, I can't ask him to come with me . . . Not anymore. It wouldn't be fair. But he'll be OK. I have a plan. He doesn't know anything. Once I'm out of the picture, they'll leave him alone.

I wouldn't be so sure.

Then I want you to look after him.

What?

Promise me you'll take care of him.

OK . . . I promise I'll take care of him.

And try and teach him something different. He's a hider. That won't always be enough.

Teach him what?

I'll leave that to you. I never managed it.

I'll see what I can do.

How can I trust you?

I often tell lies, but I always keep promises. And I already promised you, I'll take care of Michael.

Good . . .

She stood, leaning her weight for a moment on the table, eyes closed.

You look tired, he said. Wherever you're going now, I hope you'll be safe.

She smiled at some private joke, one that wasn't very funny.

I will definitely be out of danger. That's for sure.

He reached into his bag, took out a shoebox sealed with Scotch tape.

I brought something for you.

What's that?

It's money. Real money. Canadian and US, small and large bills, non-sequential numbers. And a few rolls of quarters, for payphones and bus fares.

Again, her quantum smile.

I won't need those where I'm going.

Towse watched her gather strength, push herself away from the table.

One last thing, he said. If I need to find you, down the line, there's a system I use. A fallback. It's untraceable. What it is, there's a radio show—

Don't worry about it, she interrupted, turning to go. If I ever need *you*, I'll know how to find you.


THE SECURITY CAMERAS AT Philadelphia's Filbert Street bus station recorded a young Air Force officer going into the ladies' room. The cameras, naturally, didn't work inside. If anyone had checked the tapes, they might have noticed that she never came out again.

The bus journey from Philadelphia to the Port Authority terminal in New York City takes roughly two hours. They sat in the back row together. Aoife – now just another nice-looking kid, a recent postgraduate, maybe, dressed in jeans and a hoodie, too deep in student debt to afford a better ride to her New York adventure – slept the whole way. Sleep seemed to be another one of her powers.

Michael watched Towse work on his computer. He held it with the screen turned so that Michael couldn't see it. Michael pointed to the phone plugged into the laptop, connecting it to the world.

What I don't get, he said, is, if we're so worried about being untraceable, how you think it's safe to use *that*?

A submarine needs a periscope, Towse said. As long as you don't put it up for too long, or too often, you can spy on your enemy but they can't see you.

What do you see now?

They don't know where we are or what we're doing.

Do you?

Towse frowned at the screen. They were almost at Trenton. The bus drove on to a bridge and there was the Delaware, wide and blue on either side. Michael shrank back in his seat.

Well, said Towse, it's time to clear the baffles.

Clear the baffles?

It's submarine jargon. I love that shit. It's the sneakiest form of conventional warfare . . .

Towse unplugged the burner phone from the laptop. Half-standing, he opened the slider at the top of the window and tossed the phone from the bus. It spun over the parapet and into the Delaware.

He sat down again.

That's the last burner I've got, for now. I'll get some fresh phones tonight. The man who we're meeting has a connection.


MICHAEL HAD NEVER BEEN this far east before. The only cities he had known were Calgary, Vancouver, Edmonton, Winnipeg, Saskatoon. He had lived for a month on the edge of San Francisco, but had only seen it once, from across the Golden Gate. Now, he saw castles of glass in the distance, over the strip malls and roofs of New Jersey. Manhattan's windows shone in the sun. Then the

Lincoln Tunnel swallowed the bus, which came back to life in the canyons of Midtown, shafts of perspective supporting the sky. Towse saw the shock of recognition in Michael's face as he took in the dirt and noise and smell of the city where modern cities were invented, capital of the greatest and worst civilisation the world will ever see.

Enjoy it, Towse told him. We're just passing through.

THE CITY OF BAYONNE is a low-rise clump of commerce and housing on the western shore of New York Bay, just south of Jersey City. On the seaward side of Bayonne, you can watch cruise ships dock at the Cape Liberty terminal, or look north to the Manhattan skyline, like the prow of a much vaster ship. Across the harbour are the Brooklyn dockyards, the Bush Terminal, Sunset Park. To the south, tank farms and warehouses, and, on Bergen Point, the Bayonne Bridge, a steel arch across the Kill Van Kull, joining Staten Island to the continent.

For now, though, the bus is dropping our subjects on the west side of Bayonne, facing Newark Bay, in one of those low clapboard districts where unassuming people live mostly quiet lives, backs turned to the glitz of Manhattan.

It was evening, and a few of the cars that went past had their lights on already. Towse led Aoife and Michael two blocks west from the bus stop, to a quiet street of two- and three-storey homes. He stopped outside a little corner bar faced with yellow crazy paving. It had bunker-like windows and an American flag.

This is the place.

The bar was dark inside, an old-guy place, with two old guys drinking in opposite corners. There was baseball on the television, spring training from Florida. A big middle-aged barman, white haired and frowning, looked up from a paperback. He wore a red T-shirt with the name of the bar on the front in peeling white letters. Maybe, Aoife thought, his regulars needed to be reminded where they were. She didn't think that this bar would sell many T-shirts.

The barman put down the book and glared at the strangers.

We don't do food. Or fancy coffee. Or goddamn board games.

Towse rested his hands on the bar.

I'm looking for Tom.

The barkeep stared back at him, unblinking.

Tom never comes here. He thinks it's a dive.

Towse smiled.

In that case, I'll just have a beer.

What kind?

Coors Light.

The bartender stared at Towse, then nodded.

That's the right answer. That's all we got.

He reached under the counter and took out a key that was chained to a large block of wood, the kind they hand out for gas-station washrooms.

Down this street. It's the last trailer on the left. It took some damage from Hurricane Sandy, but the view of Newark Bay kind of makes up for it – if you like cranes, and container ships. Make sure and leave it like you found it.

We will.

The barman took a shopping bag from under the counter.

Here are those burner phones you asked for. They're all clean.

Towse handed him an envelope, led the others outside. Michael turned to him.

That guy in there – he works for you?

He does today.

Who is he?

Aoife took Michael by the elbow, steered him west, down the street.

I'm curious about that myself, Michael. But right now I need the bathroom. And there's no way in hell that I'm going in that bar.

This end of the street consisted of closely packed houses, with steps leading up from pavement to porch. Halfway along, the houses gave out, and they found themselves walking through a quiet little trailer park. Stovepipes smoked. Screen light flickered in windows. Vestigial front yards – window boxes, and little patches of timber-framed dirt – waited for February to give way to spring. An old lady, sitting muffled on a swing set, waved a friendly cigarette at them as they passed.

The last trailer on the left had a dark line on the side that showed where a surge tide had flooded it, though it was jacked up and decked three feet off the ground. Beyond a thin strip of dirt and weeds lay the sheet of Newark Bay. Cranes glided and dipped over giant container ships. A setting sun turned the toxic air red.

The trailer door burped a wet-dog smell. There were three tiny bedrooms, with sheets and blankets and pillowslips folded, military style, into crisp blocks at the foot of each bed. A flush toilet smelled reassuringly of chemicals. The galley was clean, the dishes stowed neatly. A note on the fridge, pinned with a Snoopy magnet, said, *Beer: Help Yourself.*

They took chairs from inside and sat on the deck, all facing the same way, west, drinking the beer and watching the ships. There were aircraft too, transiting Newark International, beyond the pylons and lights of the New Jersey Turnpike. Somewhere close by, maybe in the next trailer, a radio was tuned to country and western, providing human scale – or irony, or counterpoint – to this pastoral of tidewater, concrete and steel. The breeze had died down, and the February evening felt almost mild.

Michael spoke first.

So who is that guy in the bar, and why is he helping us?

Towse lit a cigarette, passed one to Aoife.

The best way to answer that, he said, is to tell you some more about me.

Aoife and Michael looked at each other, sat forward.

Be our guest, Aoife said.

Towse blew out a perfect ring of white smoke.

I don't want to go into too many specifics, but you already know I work in intelligence.

The National Security Agency, prompted Michael.

Yeah. Sure. Them too. But that's only a sideline. What I really do best, what I'm most in demand for, as a sort of consultant, is my work as a gamer.

A gamer?

A war-gamer . . . I model the wars of the future. I detect new threats and think up defences. Predict outcomes. That sort of thing.

Real wars or cyberwars?

It's the same thing, now. Viruses and cyberattacks and hacking and all of the rest of it – psy-ops, election theft, fake news, mass surveillance, truth suppression, asymmetric conflict, gas-lighting. Nowadays, bullets and bombs are only an afterthought.

He jabbed his cigarette at the cranes that lined the docks across the bay.

For instance, that over there is the busiest container port on the east coast of North America. There are tens of thousands of shipping containers stacked in that dockyard at any one time, identified only by digital RFID tags. A cyberattack that erased all those tags would shut down the US economy for weeks. Maybe permanently. And it wouldn't be hard to do. Trillions of dollars worth of tanks and aircraft carriers and missiles and soldiers could be bypassed in an instant. Overrun without a shot being fired. Like the Maginot Line in the Second World War. And it's already happening. They just haven't noticed.

Aoife stared at him, suspicious.

You're not just talking about national security anymore, are you, Towse? When you say *we*, you don't mean the US government? And who is the enemy?

Towse finished his cigarette, tossed it on to the weeds, lit another.

And to make things worse, he continued, ignoring Aoife's questions, the real war is only just starting. The Chinese are using facial recognition to control hundreds of millions of people, in real time. Western governments are starting to do the same. And what the governments don't realise is that the people who build the machines are already more powerful than they are. Inscape is weaponising quantum computing. And the machines will soon be more powerful than the people who built them. And none of these players is on our side.

You sound like Alice.

Thank you, Michael. I admired Alice very much.

Towse got up and walked over to the rail that intervened between the deck and the harbour. He leaned against it, looking away across the water.

But it isn't over yet. You can still run and hide, if you know how. And I do. That's one of the things I built into my war games. Personal cheat codes. Covered lines of retreat. Ways to keep operating while we're being overrun.

You mean, things like Yoyodime?

I'm afraid not, Michael. That died with Alice.

Aoife didn't try to hide her disbelief.

So now you're trying to tell us that the guy in that bar is some kind of *resistance* fighter? He's in the army of shadows?

Sure. Though he probably doesn't know that himself, yet. And so are you, now that you're with me. And Michael too.

I'm not in anyone's army, said Aoife. I tried that sort of thing already.

Michael spoke.

How does that barman fit in, then?

He operates on a number of subterranean levels. For a start, he volunteers as a call screener on an underground radio show. Plus, he's one of a group of people who meet one night a week in a convenience store parking lot to swap second-hand books and bootleg disks, and various types of samizdat. Even better, he's a Deadhead. These are all functioning peer-to-peer off-grid networks. I'm plugged into all of them, and others like them in other places, and I know how to find more when I need them. I can hook into these networks and use them for communications, logistics, even travel, offline and untraceable. No credit cards, no plane tickets, no passports, no computers and no phones.

Aoife had heard enough.

Then what about pizza, Towse? I'm starving. Do you have a way of getting pizza delivered without a credit card or phone?

Sure . . . Go back to the bar and talk to the barman. He'll know a place. Use the bar phone to call them, and have them deliver to you at the bar. Pay cash. Bring it back here. Simple as that.

I'll go, said Michael.

Aoife pushed back her chair.

I'm going too.


THE TV IN THE bar was now showing basketball. Other than this, nothing had changed. The two old guys were still in their lonely corners. The barman glanced up when Michael and Aoife came in, then went back to his book, *At Swim-Two-Birds*. Aoife had read it;

it was a favourite. Maybe, she thought, Towse hadn't been lying about the barman. Maybe there was more to him than showed at first sight.

Still, they had to stand right in front of him before he looked up. Yeah?

We were wondering, said Michael, if you had a phone we can use.

You have to buy a drink first.

Two beers, then.

There's a phone in the basement. Local calls only. It's in the pool room.

There's a pool table down there?

After Hurricane Sandy, there was a pool.

I'll make the call, said Aoife.

She looked at the barman, turned on her smile.

Can you recommend a pizza place?

I order from Rizzo's.

That's the best?

It's the cheapest.

We want the best.

People say Joe's is good.

Then have you got a number for Joe's?

Their card is pinned up by the phone. Joe with an E. Jo without an E is a hooker.

Michael took their beers to a table by the window. He waited, watching cars pass in the street, until she came back from the basement. Aoife stopped by the bar and bought them each a double shot of whiskey.

The pizza will be here in twenty minutes, she said. Drink that. Then it's your turn to get in a round.

Michael had never been much of a drinker, but he did as he was told. Their last meal, hoagie sandwiches, had been hours before, in the Philadelphia bus station. When he came back from his trip to the bar, Aoife emptied her second shot right away, and wasted little more time on her beer.

I'll just get us one more round for the road, she said. Another beer and a chaser. We'll take these last ones nice and slow.

You like to drink.

This isn't drinking, Michael. This is bingeing.

She went to the bar, came back, smiled, clicked his glass.

I don't know who you are, Michael.

I'm sorry?

You. Who are you? We're working together, and I don't even know who you are. Towse didn't tell me.

Michael took a hit on his whiskey. He might have thought this would give him time to think up an answer. It did. But it also gave him more whiskey. He was feeling warm when he spoke.

Didn't you ask Towse who I was?

Professionals don't ask each other questions like that.

But you're asking me.

I don't think you're a professional.

Right . . . Then, did Towse say you weren't supposed to know who I am?

No. The matter never came up. So the way I look at it, it's up to you if you want to tell me about yourself. What I really want to know is this: who is this Alice that you and Towse keep talking about? And what happened to her?

She waited, glass poised, smiling encouragingly.

We were living together . . .

He stopped for a long time, and Aoife, reading the silence, began to regret that she'd asked.

We'd been fighting a lot . . . There was stress about money, and other stuff, about her work for Fess . . . I didn't realise how much trouble she was in, because I didn't talk to her about stuff like that. The stuff she really cared about . . . She jumped off a bridge.

Aoife put down her whiskey, moved her beer beside it so the glasses were kissing. Then she placed her hands, palms down, on the table either side of the drinks, as if completing a rite.

I'm sorry, she said.

She didn't think that she was acting.

Thanks, he said, and leaned back in his chair, looking down at his whiskey.

I'll get us another, she said. A drink for the door.

When she came back both his glasses were empty. He seemed bolder, now.

What about you, Ann? Are you also in the NSA?

Me? No . . . I'm just working with Towse, on this project.

He's paying you?

No. I'm like you. He's helping me out of a mess.

What mess is that?

I really can't tell you.

She thought, I ought to give him something. She felt that she owed him that, after what she'd just done, digging up his dead girlfriend.

Look, my name isn't Ann, OK? It's Aoife.

Is that like E–E–F–A? How do you write that?

You don't. Ever.

Then where do you come from?

If I told you that, I'd have to kill you.

You're an assassin?

She rocked back in her chair.

No! Why would you say that? It's an old saying, a joke. Jesus . . . Do I look like a killer?

I wouldn't know what a killer looks like. But you seem like you would.

Jesus . . . I've made some bad choices, Michael, and I've seen some bad things, but I've never hurt anyone . . . Not directly . . .

She grew quiet. A car pulled up outside the bar. She could see the insulated box on its back seat. She finished her drink.

The pizza guy is here already. I'll handle him. There's a convenience store across the street. Go buy us more whiskey. And get me some cigarettes. Couple of packs.


AOIFE HAD ABANDONED HER career in foreign intelligence after two intense years in unhappy places. Her first and last freelance job, after she quit and came back to London, was run out of a cheap hotel room near Marble Arch. The boss, a stranger to Aoife who called herself Irene, was a sharp-faced woman in late middle age, with giant, owl-like glasses and short, dyed blond hair. She wore a fitted tweed suit and spoke with what she seemed to think was received pronunciation. Upwardly mobile, thought Aoife. Another ex-copper, like me.

It was one of those box-ticking London hotel rooms: a bed, a toilet, and a TV on a bracket, high up one wall. The window gave on to a gloomy brick shaft lined with other blind windows. The bed was scattered with sandwich wrappers and styrofoam cups. There was barely enough space for Aoife, Irene, and the three quiet men with watchful expressions who sat by the door. Aoife didn't know any of these men personally, but she knew what they were. And she had seen what they could do to people. This was one of two reasons why she quit her last job.

The eldest of the three was a small, wiry man with a sun-darkened face and deft, birdlike movements. He sat on the floor, cross-legged, with a PC in his lap, talking into an earpiece. Aoife overheard a soft Scottish accent. The other two, burlier, with heavy, bored faces, sat on chairs inside the door, fiddling with their phones, waiting to go. A sports bag lay on the floor between them. They're the snatch squad, thought Aoife. Gaffer tape, syringes, cable ties, hood. They'll go in last, when all the rest of it is ready.

Irene gave Aoife her briefing.

It's a one-day job. Five grand, cash, paid as soon as it's over.

How did you hear of me?

Willy McDonnell mentioned you. He said you were good. He said Belfast was sorry when you went to work for Six.

I wanted to see the world.

Yeah, well, now that you've seen it, McDonnell says Five would take you back. He told me to tell you that. Me and him were pals in his Branch days. In Belfast and Bessbrook. When it was fun.

Fun for you, maybe, you fucking tourist. But Aoife didn't say that out loud. She needed this gig, having just discovered, on her return from what she'd hoped was her last ever assignment, that her parents had lost all their money, and her money too, the savings she'd been counting on to launch her new life, and which she had given to her father to invest for her. Also, she found it hard to feel too superior. She had come to understand that, like Irene, she was really a tourist herself. That was her other main reason for quitting.

Who's the target?

Irene handed her a photograph. The man in it was youngish, balding on top.

He's a New York banker. Mahmoud Karmi. US-born Palestinian, currently visiting London. He's been secretly shifting large sums of untraceable cash to bank accounts in Kenya. The Americans think that it goes from there to the Islamists in Mombasa. We're going to lift him today, then pass him on to the Yanks, no papers, no warrants. Catch is, he's a US citizen, so he has to disappear without anyone knowing.

What do you need me for?

He's staying in a posh hotel in Marylebone. He'll be leaving it shortly, to walk to an office in Soho. The office is our front. We'll lift him when he gets there. Just in case he does something unexpected, or he twigs that we're on to him, we need someone to stay close to him on the street, without being noticed. That's you.


AOIFE PICKED UP HER mark outside his hotel. He was dressed in a polo shirt, khakis, deck shoes and a light linen jacket, Brooks Brothers or similar. An expensive leather satchel was strapped crossways around his chest, as if he was worried that someone might snatch it.

He walked out of the lobby without looking left or right, nearly colliding with a passer-by. He'd be easy to follow.

Aoife had camouflaged herself for the British high street – Zara and Primark, oversize sunglasses, grey high-top sneakers. A Selfridge bag contained three baseball caps – one blue, one white, one pink – and three light cotton jackets in different styles and colours. If her mark happened to look at her directly, she could drop back a few yards, change shape and colour, then catch up again.

But he walked stiffly and fast, never turning his head. Aoife followed him down Welbeck Street, Henrietta Place, Vere Street, until they reached Oxford Street. There, slowed by the press of shoppers, he stepped into a door and took out a map. It was a tourist map, the kind they leave out in racks in hotel lobbies. Aoife watched his reflection in the a window. The map was shaking in his hand.

He folded the map, stepped off the kerb, then immediately leaped back again, chased by the horn of a bus that was inches from crushing him. But instead of recoiling in shock, he turned and looked about him.

He knows that someone could be following him, Aoife decided. He's been trying to hide that knowledge. But that near miss disinhibited him. He let his fear show.

A pedestrian light turned green and Aoife, hanging back this time, followed him east down Oxford Street, across Regent Street, and then right on to Argyll Street. They were now in Soho, only yards from the destination, a fake brass plate for a fictional law firm. Her job was done once he left the street.

Aoife was slowing, preparing to drop out of the tail, when she saw it happen. There was a postbox on the kerb, a red English pillar box, and as he approached it his hand slipped into his satchel. She saw a white flash as his hand snaked to the postbox. Without breaking stride, he continued on his way. She watched him walk on a few yards, checking the street numbers, until he stopped at a door between two dingy shopfronts. He pressed a buzzer, looked about him. The door opened, and he was gone.

Aoife crossed back over to the postbox. A mail drop. That hadn't been foreseen in her briefing.

The mail compartment was protected by a thick metal door, crusted with many years of coats of red paint. *Royal Mail*, it said on the box. They had the Royal Mail in Northern Ireland too. And she knew how to open its postboxes. She had the tweezers in her purse.

She leaned against the postbox while pretending to search through her shopping bag. Whatever she was looking for in her bag, an observer, if there was one, would have concluded that she couldn't find it, though she gave it plenty of time.

The mail from this box had been recently collected. There were only a few letters lying in the base. The five on top, identical white envelopes, were clearly the ones that she wanted, but she grabbed everything in the box, just to be sure, stuffed it into her carrier bag, closed the door and walked off.

THE SCOTSMAN WAS SITTING on the floor of the hotel room, the PC in his lap, but his colleagues were gone. He seemed relaxed now, uncoiled, his legs no longer crossed but stretched out in front of him. He didn't move them for Aoife. She had to step over him to get to Irene, standing by the blind little window, listening to her phone. She shook her head quickly at Aoife, warning her not to speak, then listened some more, then ended the call.

It's done, Irene told them. We just have to wait a few minutes for the cash to arrive, then we can shut this room down.

There was a problem, said Aoife. But I sorted it.

She took the letters from the bag and handed them to Irene.

Irene shuffled through the letters. The Scotsman came over to join them.

A mail drop, said Irene. Jesus . . . He must have known that we were on to him.

Despite herself, Aoife looked at the envelopes as Irene studied each in turn. They were made from expensive paper, embossed with the name of the Marylebone Hotel. Hand stamped, not franked. The addresses were written in spidery ink:

*The Editor, Private Eye*

*The Editor, Guardian newspapers*

*The Chair, Commons Committee on Intelligence and Security*

*The Commissioner, Metropolitan Police*

*The Director, MI5*

Aoife yawned. She could feel them both watching her.

God, she confided, I'm dying for a cigarette. I always am, after a job. Could I have a crafty one here, while we wait for the cash?

Irene put the envelopes away, picked up her laptop. Turning the screen away from Aoife, she began to tap at it.

You can't smoke in this hotel room. There's a two-hundred-pound fine.

Then I'll just pop outside for a moment. Maybe get a coffee from Pret, while I'm at it. Do you fancy anything?

Irene and the Scotsman looked at each other.

Tea for me, he said. Milk and one sugar.

For the first time, he smiled at her.

Shall I give you the cash?

My treat. Irene?

Irene, typing, didn't look up.

No thanks.

The Scotsman flattened himself against the wall, giving her room to pass. He had remembered his manners. He had also, she noticed, put his ear piece back in.

Once the door closed behind her, she heard him talking quietly and fast. The door was thin. She had to force herself to walk slowly down the corridor, not to break into a run. The hotel was very old, and the emergency stairwell wrapped around the shaft of the single elevator. She went down the stairs two at a time, and every time she passed the door of the lift she pressed the call button; anyone using it to come after her would be stopped at every floor.

AOIFE CROSSED OXFORD STREET, ploughed west through angry shoppers, took the stairs down to Marble Arch Tube. There, in the line for the ticket machine, she slipped her phone into a young woman's handbag. Judging from her sundress and carry-on case, the woman might, with luck, be heading to one of the airports, laying a useful false trail.

Coming up to the street again, on the opposite side, Aoife walked up the Edgware Road. At Edgware Road Tube station, she slipped her Oyster card into a storm drain and bought a day pass from a machine, paying with coins. A Bakerloo train took her to Charing Cross Station, where she cut through Spring Gardens to the Mall. She walked south-west, down the right side of the street, so she could watch, on her left, to see if she was followed. She was not.

From Victoria Station, she took a Southern Rail train as far as Kent House, near the little apartment that she kept in Penge. She didn't think anyone knew about it. She still lived by Northern Ireland rules.

The apartment, rented furnished, held nothing that Aoife cared about, apart from some clothes and some books. She collected her real passport, the Irish one, from a drawer by the bed. The two fake ones were hidden in the crumb tray of a broken toaster. She took those too, putting them in a backpack with the books, some clothes, and a few other basics.

A loose ceiling tile hid the bank notes that she'd stashed for times like this. Pounds, dollars and euros. Cash would pay for a bus ride to Fishguard. It would pay for the ferry to Rosslare in Ireland. Common Travel Area, no formal ID check, no questions asked – so long as you looked white. She could spend some time in the Republic, somewhere nice, out west, in a quiet bed and breakfast. Or she could use one of the back roads that she knew to slip across the border. She didn't want to go back there, but she knew people in the north.

The lobby of her building smelled of chemicals, and was walled on two sides with translucent cubes of green glass. It had always reminded Aoife of an ageing public swimming pool. The lobby contained a rubber plant, a metal table and two fake-leather chairs that no one ever sat in.

Someone was sitting in one of them now.

He looked about fifty, with dark stubble at either end of his long, balding head. He sat back in the chair, a computer open on his lap, hands behind his head. He smiled when he saw her.

Aoife McCoy. You shouldn't have come back here.

American, she thought. Or maybe Canadian.

She slipped off her backpack, holding it left-handed. It was no use as a weapon, but it might do as a shield.

The stranger closed the laptop, stretched and stood. He was rickety and tall, like a badly made scaffold. His business suit and hand-stitched brogues were in need of urgent care.

Aoife sidled away from him, towards the door and the light.

You used to want to be an actor, he said. I have a part for you now.

No thanks. I'm resting.

She reached the door, took the handle. He made no effort to stop her.

Your target wasn't a crook or a terrorist. He was a whistle-blower.

I got that, thanks. Not my problem. Bye-bye.

She turned the door handle.

He's already dead. They killed him to stop him telling what he knows.

Another good reason why it's none of my business . . . How do *you* know all this?

He showed her the computer.

I'm reading their communications. In real time.

She eased the door open. Keep him talking, she thought.

Good with the cyber stuff, are you?

I certainly am. And you're good at the real life. That's why I want you. I'm in need of a burglar. Or, you might say, a familiar. If you work for me, I can keep you alive until we find a way out of this. I have a plan.

No thanks. I'm off. From now on, I'm a one-man band.

She pulled the door open.

You're a loose end, Aoife. The Scotch guy reckons you'll head back to Ireland. He thinks you'll feel safer there. And he knows Ireland very well. Spent a lot of time there, back in the old days. Working both sides of the border.

I know people there. They'll look after me.

He tapped his laptop sadly.

Irene knows those people too. She's a very good liar. You should hear what she's already saying about you.

How do I know you're not working with them? Keeping me talking until someone else gets here?

That's a good question. Tell me this, Aoife: what was in that mail drop?

Mail.

There were five big letters, in hotel envelopes. He wrote them just before he left the hotel and put the stamps on them himself. He didn't trust the desk clerk to mail them for him. They were addressed to—

That doesn't prove anything. Irene could have told you that.

Did you get a look at his handwriting?

What do you mean?

He reached into his jacket, took out a letter, tossed it over. Aoife caught it.

It was a small, square white envelope, containing, she could tell from the feel, a stiff card. It had a UK airmail stamp, cancelled in London a week before. Aoife looked at the handwriting. Spiky but clear. It was the same as the writing on the envelopes that she'd given to Irene.

It's addressed to Professor John Roland, in New York City, said the stranger. It was a distress signal. A rescue call. But he didn't send it in time.

Your name is Roland?

I have a lot of names. You can call me Towse.

NIGHT HAD COME, AND brought an offshore wind with it. They sat outside the trailer, on the deck, so that Towse and Aoife could smoke after they finished the pizza. They looked west, across Newark Bay. Country music played on in the background. It sounded louder, now that the light had faded – plaintive waltzes, sighing steel guitars. A ship thudded past, bound for the yellow lights of Newark harbour. The sky was a dome of dull orange, a chemical haze in the glare of the seaboard. Towse poured them all whiskey, then sat back and sighed.

It's so lovely here, he said, gesturing towards Newark. All that life and hope. It may have got a bit curdled, but life and hope, all the same.

I don't get you, said Michael. What I want to know is, why are we in New Jersey?

To finish what Alice started.

How?

Do you know what a matching engine is?

They didn't.

Do you know what a stock exchange is?

They thought that they did.

OK. That's a start . . . Well, once upon a time, a stock exchange was a trading floor full of fat, shouty people throwing paper in the air. But that was forty years ago. Nowadays, stocks are bought and sold online, by people with computers, and more and more often by the computers themselves, trading by algorithm. The deals are put together in servers owned by the exchanges. These servers are known as matching engines, because they match up the buyers and sellers. Black boxes, some call them. You with me?

They were.

There used to be only a few big stock exchanges around the world, like the NYSE and Hong Kong and London, but now there are dozens in New York alone. And each one has its own matching engine. And almost all of those engines are here, in New Jersey.

Why?

Because of high-frequency computer trading. Online markets move so fast, now, that the speed of light is a factor. You can gain an edge just by being as close to the black box as possible. Millionths of a second are worth billions of dollars. So most of the New York exchanges put their servers just across the Hudson, in New Jersey. It's very close to Wall Street, but the real estate's much cheaper. One of those exchanges belongs to Fess, through a front company. We're here to break into it.

Why would *we* want to do that?

Because, Aoife, this exchange has an even more private exchange nested inside it. It's what's known as a dark pool, a side pot where big players can do deals in secret. The thing that spooked Alice was in Fess's dark pool. She was updating its code to make it OmniCent compatible when she noticed something very strange. To find out exactly what, we have to observe the engine from inside the engine itself, to eliminate the distortions you get from watching from a distance. So we have to break into the server itself, and plug ourselves into it.

Towse took out his laptop, opened the lid and turned it towards Aoife.

This is the data centre where Fess's black box is physically located. It's a bit like a high-tech storage-rental unit – it hosts lots of other fintech servers too. The owners of the building have spent millions on security – key-card access, biometrics, mantrap corridors, the lot. But they hate giving money to actual people, so the only guards on duty at any one time are a couple of illegal immigrants on minimum wage. The local taxpayer stumps up the most for its human security, courtesy of the Bayonne police force.

Aoife looked at the screen.

This info is good. Where did you get it?

From the local taxpayer.

I can't do it alone.

Take Michael.

Aoife looked at Michael. He was nodding off, drowsy from the whiskey.

Why don't *you* come, Towse?

Because we can't run the risk of my face being seen.

Yeah? What about *my* face?

We'll try and keep it out of this. Plus, Fess has never seen you before. Me, he has, but he doesn't know that I'm involved in this yet. Better to keep it that way. He already knows about Michael, so that wouldn't matter. Go on – break a leg.

THE VAN WAS A windowless Dodge, white, an older model, but in perfect condition. Its driver was a woman – thin, short hair, forties, in a green bomber jacket. She stopped beside the trailer, rolled down her window and stared at them, waiting. It was early morning in the trailer park, with no one else around.

Towse spoke first.

How do you want to do this?

When you're done with the van, park it on the street over there, near that bar. Put the key in the glovebox, lock the door with the button, then walk away.

OK.

Do it by this time tomorrow. Otherwise, we have to report the van stolen. We don't want to do that.

Anything else?

Our plates are clean. Keep them that way. If you're doing anything you shouldn't, use your own plates for that.

She got out, gave the key to Michael and walked off, up the street. She wore work jeans and work boots and bounced as she walked, her clothes hiding muscle.

They watched her go.

Who was she?

The beauty of it is, Michael, that even I don't need to know. Go wake up Aoife. It's time to go shopping.


IT WAS LATE EVENING when the van pulled into an industrial park between Bayonne and Jersey City. The sky was bright only in the west. The food trucks had already switched off their cookers, pulled down their shutters, returned to the commissaries where they would clean up, restock and prepare for the morning. Lights went off in office windows, came on in the parking lots. The day declined over courier depots and plant-hire firms, carpet warehouses, wholesale stores for immigrant communities, outlets for factory-damaged electric appliances, African churches, pop-up boutiques, martial-arts dojos, mattress retailers, muffler-repair shops, rental storage units, climbing walls, paint stores and – here and there – the odd vacant unit, marked hopefully *For Rent*, a wallflower waiting to rejoin the dance. And in the trees – young, thin of branch, tender of leaf, so that the sky and the floodlights shone through them – a few lonely male robins sang the evening to rest.

The van turned into the parking lot of Unit 103 Bayonne Enterprise Zone. We can watch it on the CCTV.

Unit 103 is a long, rectangular, windowless building, with blue sheet walls and a roof that bristles with cooling ducts. A cage at one end houses backup generators. The sign on the roof says *Epic NJ5*.

There are two shabby cars parked by the entrance. The van

drives past them, then reverses into a parking space, tail to the wall. It rocks on its springs, people moving inside it. Finally, two white figures get out, lugging a couple of heavy nylon bags. They walk to the door of the building, press the intercom buzzer. This activates a video recording, so we know what the guards saw when they looked at their screen: two hooded people, dressed in white hazmat suits, gas masks hanging loose from their straps, hiding most of their faces apart from their eyes. One of them speaks.

TriState Pest Control, he says. We've come about the ants.

What ants?

The ants in section four of hall two . . . Uh . . . We have to get rid of them before they get into the circuits.

I don't know about any ants. Come back in business hours.

We have to fumigate. We can't do that when there's people around.

On the tape, the first guard can be heard talking to his colleague in Spanish.

Do people even work in there in the daytime? I only ever get night shifts, here.

Beats me. I've only been posted here a couple of times myself. The place is full of, like, computers and stuff. We're not allowed to touch them. That's all I need to know.

The first guard keys the intercom again.

We weren't told you were coming. We can't let you in.

Uh . . . Call your supervisor. They'll know about us.

The guards press the speed dial for their control room in Hoboken. The phone call is answered on the second buzz.

Aardvark Security, said a voice on the line. Hobbes speaking.

Oh . . . Hi, Mr Hobbes . . . I don't think we know each other? . . . This is Gonzales. I'm shift supervisor at . . . I think it's called Epic? It's that big computer place in the Bayonne enterprise park? Some pest-control guys say we're supposed to let them in, but we've got no paperwork. They say you should have it.

Where's that, you say? Let me have a look . . .

You can hear a rustle of papers at the end of the phone line, the tap of a keyboard. There is also what sounds like the clink of ice in a glass, and the distant twang of a lonesome country ballad.

Yeah, said Hobbes. Here it is. Epic. Ants. Fumigation. You can switch off the systems and let them in.

. More rustling of paper.

Oh, and one more thing, Lopes.

Gonzales, sir.

Sure. Gonzales. It says here that the fumigation gas is highly poisonous. You have to stay out of the building until it's done.

We have to watch the cameras, sir.

I'll watch them from here. Go outside and patrol the perimeter until they're finished. And stay out there for two hours after.

The guards buzz the door, then watch the two pest-control operatives bustle past them, their hazmat suits swishing, heads down, as they drag their heavy bags along the floor. They pass through the man-trap doors between the lobby and the climate-controlled server hall. A moment later, they reappear on a different set of cameras, heading down the central aisle. Electric eyes flutter and blink, red and white, in row after row of servers and data storage units, as if sensing the danger as it walks past.

We see the two ghostly figures reach the further end of the hall, where a black metal box, the size of a filing cabinet, stands by itself in a padlocked steel cage. They assemble a tent, a fumigation barrier, over the cage and its black metal obelisk. Zipping their suits and adjusting their gas masks, they go inside the tent. White vapour seeps from under it. Ten minutes later, they're done.

The guards, hanging about in the parking lot, saw them leave the building, dragging their stuff to the van. Then it was gone.

THE VAN PULLED OVER on the Port Jersey breakwater. Aoife and Michael sat for a few moments, looking at the Statue of Liberty, then Aoife got out, took off the false plates and threw them into the harbour. She reattached the real plates with an electric screwdriver, and then they crammed their hazmat suits into the nylon bags, added some rocks from the breakwater, and sent them after the fake plates. They got back in the van and turned west.

You should have done the talking, Michael said.

If they'd heard a woman's voice, they'd have looked a lot closer. Anyway, it was time you did something to earn your keep.

I did the computer stuff.

You plugged in Towse's application and pressed return, like he told you. Anyone could have done that. No offence, but I still don't know why Towse wants you.

Me neither. But here we are.

They were back in Bayonne, driving south on Avenue A, when the first police car overtook them, lights flashing, siren on. Then another, and another.

Neither one spoke. A block from the bar, they could see the street up ahead dammed by police cars, slewed across the junction, lights strobing. Aoife parked by the kerb.

This is where we get out.

What about the van?

We leave it here. Towse's people will find it. If it was up to me, we'd torch it, to destroy any evidence. That's what they do where I come from.

Where *do* you come from?

Never mind. Get out. Take Towse's computer.

She put the key in the glovebox, locked the driver's door with the button, and closed it from the outside.

Put your arm around me.

What?

Put your arm around me. We're going for a stroll.

She grabbed his arm, steered him down Avenue A. There were more cop cars here, and a city ambulance, and yellow tape across the road where a crowd had gathered. A helicopter floated through the bracket of sky at the end of the avenue, its spotlight stabbing the ground. Aoife tightened her arm around Michael's waist, settled her hand on his hip and dragged him towards the police line.

What the hell are you doing?

Aoife turned a loving face up to his, put her mouth to his ear.

Shut up and keep moving. We need to find out what's going on.

They pushed their way to the front of the crowd. There were police cars down by the edge of the water, their beacons splashing red across the trailers in the park. A cordon of unmarked SUVs, parked nose to tail, hid the front of the bar from the onlookers. As they watched, two paramedics appeared from between the SUVs, wheeling a sheet-covered stretcher. They were followed by two men wearing windbreakers that looked like they should have *FBI* on them, but didn't. A Bayonne cop lowered the tape, and the ambulance, hitting its siren, was gone. Aoife tapped the cop on the shoulder.

Hey, officer. What's going on?

She smiled at him. He smiled back, hooked his thumbs in the belt that held his gun and his night stick. He was young, still good-looking, and knew this himself.

The Feds just raided that bar. And that trailer park, down the street there.

Aoife made her eyes round.

Wow . . . The *Feds*? Here? Where I live? . . . Say, who was in that ambulance?

I heard the barman went nuts when they tried to question him. They had to taser him. Several times.

Oh my God! Which Feds are they, exactly? ATF? FBI? DEA? I can't wait to tell the guys at work!

The cop hitched his belt again, looked thoughtful.

I don't know, exactly . . . Dispatch didn't say . . .

Michael grabbed Aoife's arm, yanked her into the crowd. As the people closed around them, he heaved on her arm again, dragging her off balance. Instinctively, she raised her right knee between his legs, felt the breath go out of him. The rubberneckers, ignoring them, left them in their own little pocket of space, between the back of the crowd and the wall of a house. Michael bent double, gasping.

You kicked me!

I was talking to that cop! What the hell is wrong with you?

He straightened, pointed over the heads of the crowd.

Look!

Beyond the police line, by the door to the bar, a woman was giving orders to men in dark suits. She looked like someone's aunt: round of face, slightly rumpled, smiling kindly. Her sweatshirt had a word on it. *Stanford*, it said.

Aoife ducked behind the crowd.

We have to get out of here, fast, Michael. That's Barb Collins, from Inscape.

I know.

No you don't, Michael. You don't know the half of it.


THE DISTANCE FROM BAYONNE, New Jersey to Staten Island, New York is roughly five miles, as the crow flies. But when it's late, and you're on foot, taking the back streets, having to turn away and pretend to be necking when headlights appear, it must feel a lot further.

They didn't speak much. The night seemed to be listening. At

Bergen Point the streets ran together, funnelling them up concrete stilts over oil tanks and houses. The harbour appeared on either side, reflecting the lights of New York and New Jersey.

Bayonne Bridge, lately rebuilt so bigger ships could pass under it, had a new walkway for people, on its harbour side. It hung out over the waters of the Kill Van Kull, 200 feet below. Aoife was too tired to think. It took her some time to realise what crossing this bridge might mean to Michael. We should have gone the other way, she thought. To Jersey City, the Lincoln Tunnel. She had grown unused to sensitive people. Lately, most of the men whom she'd known had been thugs. The only thing she could do for him now, having come this far, was to put herself between him and the drop.

THEY FOUND A GOOD hotel by the Staten Island Expressway. Good, in the sense that it was willing to rent a room, for cash, no ID, to two empty-handed people in the middle of the night.

The room smelled of all the bodily fluids and liquor that had ever been spilled there. They used their quarters to buy chips and bottled water from the machine by the broken elevator, then ate in the room, sitting on plastic chairs either side of the bed. Aoife had her back to the window, expressway lights flaring in its stained curtain. Belfast Rules: never sit with your back to the door.

So, you know about Barb Collins, Michael said.

Towse told me to watch out for her. She's an ex-Oakland vice cop. She had a bad reputation, even for Oakland. Graft, extreme brutality.

Evidence would go missing. Drugs and weapons. A couple of dealers disappeared too, after they said she'd seized more of their product than she turned in as evidence. The FBI was called in, but she's really smart, and she'd worked with Feds a lot, so she knew all their procedures. Then Fess hired her as a special adviser. To work for him on his special projects.

She doesn't look like a cop.

Neither do I. But I used to be one.

Really? . . . Where?

She yawned, despite herself.

Forget it. I shouldn't have said that.

She laid her head back on the sill, closed her eyes for a moment, then opened them; she was scared she might fall asleep.

He spoke again:

What happens next?

I don't know . . .

She forced herself to think through the problem.

I have some cash and a clean passport. I could probably get myself out of this country . . . But I've got no papers for you.

She wondered why she was being level with him. What if he panicked, dragged her down with him? What truth did she owe him? But he seemed a nice guy.

I might be able to sneak back into Canada, he said, after a while. Go to Minnesota, and walk across the border into Manitoba. My parents told me they knew people who'd done that. They said it was easy.

They'd find you and snatch you, even in Canada. I know how they'd do it. I've seen it done.

She yawned again. Why was she trusting him? He was just a mark. Then again, he had managed to get his lines straight, back at the data centre. He seemed to have a stubborn streak. Why else was he still in this game? By now, most civilians would have folded from the stress.

So I'm on my own, he said.

She thought about that, then relented.

Not yet . . . There's a chance that Towse got away. He gave me an emergency fallback, a way to make contact if we got separated.

What's that?

It's a radio show.

A *radio show?*

Sort of a cult thing. That barman works on it, as a call screener. Or he did, before they tased his brains out. It goes out live from New Jersey, one night a week, but only on the Internet. If he's free, Towse will use it to send us a message.

She touched the bedspread, quickly withdrew her hand.

I'm going to sleep on top of the sheets, with my clothes on. You can have the other side, if you want. Though the floor might be cleaner.

THE STATEN ISLAND FERRY docks at the southern tip of Manhattan Island. From there, walking north, you pass through the financial district: Wall Street, Freedom Plaza, all those banks, brokerages, hedge funds and exchanges, stacked in racks of glass and steel, and all the smaller bottom-feeders that scavenge the undertow, sucking in sludgy data, trying to filter it for gold. Phone lines, fibre optics, IR links, satellite dishes, laser comms, microwave links, even – if you know where to look – a few ancient but functioning pneumatic-tube systems, all searching for meaning in the cosmos of money, moving the odds around, hedging the bets. When the aliens make contact, the people on Wall Street will know about it first. They could be talking to them already, in secret, trying to cut themselves a side deal, to short-sell the Earth.

You might wonder, then, whether any of these twitching financial antennae pinged, or bleeped, or traced a zigzag on paper, as Aoife and Michael wandered up Broadway. Did any of them sense the danger that was coiled on the hard drive of Towse's computer, swinging so innocently in its nylon bag? Or did they walk through the beast's lair without being noticed, ghosting through its lattice, fundamental particles too fleeting to detect? Did the beast really not see them? Or did it see them, and say nothing, and choose to let them pass?

THEIR NEXT LODGING WAS in Brighton Beach, in the ghost of a seaside boarding house, a couple of blocks from the sea.

Don't make noise, said the old lady who lurked in the parlour. And let yourselves out when you're done.

Done. They hadn't told her what they would do in the room, but that was her default assumption. They were healthy-looking young people, paying cash, and if Coney Island still had a season, this wasn't it. But, turning the key, Aoife felt suddenly aware of Michael in the hall behind her. She had flirted at him in Palo Alto, but that was strictly operational, one of several lures she had dangled whilst trying to hook him. She didn't even know if that lure had worked. And, of course, she didn't care.

The room smelled of wallpaper paste that had never quite dried in the air from the ocean, but it was otherwise clean, and it had two separate beds, pushed together. Aoife opened the curtains and pushed them apart.

THAT TUESDAY EVENING, THEY bought a second-hand burner phone from a Russian woman in a kiosk, and a pen and a notebook as well. Nine o'clock found them sitting on the kerb on Brighton Beach Avenue, stealing Wi-Fi from a coffee shop. When cars went past, or trains rattled on the elevated tracks, they had to lean together to hear the phone's feeble speaker.

The radio show began cold, at a minute past nine, when the host wandered on-mic and accused his producer of having fiddled with the levels on the sound desk. He fired the producer, played some thrash rock, came back on the mic, rehired the producer, and then gave a ten-minute rant about gas-station sandwiches. A caller rang in to disagree with the host. The host hung up on the caller. The show was already twenty minutes in.

This format doesn't make sense, said Michael. Is there a pattern in this? Is it meant to *mean* something?

Shut up. I'm trying to hear.

Michael got to his feet, eased his knees. A Q train clattered overhead. Aoife sat forward, phone clamped to her ear, and flipped open the notebook.

What is it?

Be quiet!

He sat down again, put his ear to the other side of the phone. The host was playing a record.

A little girl's voice – crackly, mechanical, unsettling, eerie – recited numbers in German.

*Null . . . neun . . . sieben . . . acht . . . null . . . vier . . . neun . . . sieben . . . acht . . . null . . . vier . . . neun . . . vier . . . acht . . .*

Music rose in the background, a fragile tune on an electric organ. A woman, crooning, added her voice to the mix. All the while, in the background, the child continued to call out numbers to the ether: cosmic bingo, or an interstellar distress call.

*Sechs . . . sieben . . . acht . . . neun . . . neun . . .*

The track ended in discord. The host came back on the mic.

That was Stereolab . . . A track called 'Pause'. Off of their album *Transient Random-Noise Bursts with Announcements* . . .

Aoife clicked the little button on her pen, extending the nib. She put it to the notepaper, eyes closed.

What is it? asked Michael.

She shook her head briskly, making a shush with her lips. After a long and bewildering pause, the host spoke again.

That's a song about numbers stations. You know: *numbers stations*. Like, you're listening to the radio, late at night – short-wave radio, if you still got one, which you *should* – and you're spinning the dial – because you have that freedom with a short-wave radio; they don't railroad your choices with digital presets – and the next thing you hear is some strange tinny music, and then some weird robotic voice starts reading out numbers or letters. And then, after a couple of minutes, the music plays again, and that's it for the night.

The host cleared his throat, shuffled some papers, accidentally banged a hand against the microphone.

And what these broadcasts are is this: they are *actual real-life coded messages* to sleeper agents, from spy agencies in places like Russia and Israel and North Korea, and even here in the States. The codes are completely unbreakable, because they change every day. The only catch is, it's one-way traffic. The puppets listen to their master, but they can't answer back . . .

He shuffled some papers, coughed.

Hey, wait a minute . . . *They can't answer back?* I like the sound of that! Maybe I should turn *this* show into a numbers station. We could ditch all the callers and guests, and just read out numbers instead . . . You guys out there would still listen, right? Hey, call-screener – should we turn this show into a numbers station?

Inaudible answer, off-mic.

He says yeah . . . I could just play something short by Guided
By Voices, which is *anything* by Guided By Voices, then read some
numbers. I could go, like, *Oh, one, oh, two, oh*, and then go, like, *Four,
six, three, seven*, and then play the Guided By Voices track again. It
would make as much sense as what we're doing *now* . . . Let's go to
the phones with that as a topic: should the show become a numbers
station? Who's on line one?

Aoife shut off the feed, retracted the nib on her ballpoint.

That was a zip code, she said.


01020-4637 WAS ANOTHER UNIT in another industrial park.
This one was on the outskirts of Springfield, Massachusetts. The bus
dropped them off at the end of the street.

The unit looked much like the one that they had burgled two
days before, except smaller and older, with weeds poking through
the parking lot and discoloured streaks on the walls. A neon sign
above the door showed a bug-eyed alien swinging a bowling ball.
The bowling ball was planet Earth.

Michael squinted at the sign.

*Close Encounters of the Rolling Kind* . . . Are you sure this is it?

It matches the nine-digit zip code.

Inside was the smell of nachos and floor wax, the purr of balls on
lacquered wood, the plink and rattle of scattering pins. It was early
afternoon, a sunny Saturday, and most of the lanes were already
taken. It looked to Aoife like some kind of outing – a church group,

maybe, or a company fun day – families bowling together, no team shirts or colours.

I don't see Towse, said Michael.

I'm hungry. Let's get something to eat.

A counter at the back sold beer and soda and bowling-grade junk food. It appeared to be unmanned. Then Aoife saw the top of a head, covered in one of those catering hairnets, between the bottles of ketchup and mustard lined on the counter. The head was bent forward, as if in prayer.

Excuse me, she said.

The head turned, rose, revealed itself.

Aoife! Michael! You made it. Well done!

Towse put down his book, disappeared, reappeared a moment later, emerging from a door in the wall. He wore the same suit, but it had been cleaned and pressed. The hairnet made him look like an absent-minded surgeon.

Are they still hiring?

Don't be sarcastic, Aoife. I'm just helping out. The owner's having a fundraiser for his faith group, and it's the least I can do, when he's letting me crash here, on the Q.T. . . . Hey, can I get you something to eat? On me?

Two hot dogs, said Michael.

Yeah, said Aoife. Two for me, too. What do you mean, faith group? What are they raising funds for?

Hiroshima Day.

What the hell do they worship? The *Enola Gay*?

They're Raëlians, Aoife. It's a UFO cult, but quite a nice one. Hey —
you got inside Fess's matching engine, right? You got the data I needed?

Yes, said Michael.

He handed Towse the laptop.

Good . . . I knew you'd do it. I'll just go rustle up those hot dogs.
Pull up a stool and we'll talk.

He disappeared behind the counter. They dragged two stools
over and watched him fish franks from grey water.

So this place, said Michael, is some kind of cult temple?

Towse's voice was muffled as he bent to his task.

No. It's a bowling alley. But it belongs to a level-three Raëlian
guide. He's a friend of mine. The congregation likes to come and
roll here. Who doesn't like bowling?

What do Raëlians believe in, apart from UFOs?

They don't believe in God, for a start, which is always interesting
in a religion. They believe that aliens came to earth, thousands of
years ago, and pretended to be angels. All the top angels were really
aliens — Gabriel, Michael, Raphael, Samael. So was Lucifer, of course.
He was the boss alien, although the Raëlians don't know that. He
kept his face out of things. He liked to delegate.

What did these aliens want?

To help out. But they came here, had a look around, and then
decided humans were too stupid to bother with, so they left. But when
they saw the flash from the first atom bomb, they knew that humans
had developed intelligence, so it was time to come back. That's why
Hiroshima Day is the Raëlians' biggest holiday.

Funny definition of intelligence, said Aoife.

Plus, said Michael, the first atom bomb was Los Alamos, not Hiroshima.

Yeah, I know. But don't say that to these guys — you have to respect other people's religion . . . Anyway, today they're raising money for a Hiroshima Day trip to the site of the alien embassy.

The *what?*

The Raëlians want to build an embassy for the aliens. In Jerusalem, of all places. They think it's a city of peace. To make things even trickier, the Raëlian symbol is a swastika merged with a Star of David. There's an innocent explanation for that, apparently, but the Israelis are a little reluctant to take it on board. You can't really blame them . . . Suffice to say, the embassy proposal has run into obstacles.

You don't strike me as religious, said Aoife, but you seem to know an awful lot about religion.

I've made it one of the great studies of my life.

Towse applied onions, ketchup and mustard, and placed the hot-dogs in cardboard trays on the counter.

Help yourselves to beer or soda. I'm going to look at this computer and see what you've got for me. There are some couches over there, in the corner. Take a rest, and later we'll talk.

THEY WERE LULLED BY the drone of the bowling balls, happy voices, waves of pins breaking on a parquet beach. When Aoife awoke, the place was almost silent, almost dark. Over by the opposite

wall, in the only lane that was lit, Towse was bowling by himself.
She watched him roll three strikes in a row, then she shook Michael.
Groggily, they moved towards the light.

Towse, who had just sent another perfect delivery curving
down the lane, was frozen in his release position, one hand raised
before him, palm up, in silent supplication. He ignored them until
the ball struck the left of the frame, converting its spin into lat-
eral fury, turning pins into shrapnel to mow down their friends.
Another strike.

Aoife spoke:

What went wrong in Bayonne, Towse?

He picked up another ball, polished it with his sleeve.

We were raided. They knew we were there.

How did *you* get away? Did someone warn you? And if so, why
didn't you warn us?

No one warned me about anything. It was dumb luck. I went
for a stroll and saw them arriving. That's what really bothers me. I
don't like being in debt to providence . . .

How did they know we were there, then?

Towse stepped up to the lane, swinging the ball.

That's what I want to know. Did either of you make a phone
call, or send an email or whatever? Or did you take money from an
ATM? Anything stupid like that?

He skipped down the parquet, released the ball. Another strike.

It must have been the barman, said Michael. He must have given
us away.

The barman didn't even know who we were. Plus, he's in a coma now because he doesn't like talking to strangers.

Maybe we triggered a silent alarm? When we broke into their matching engine?

Barb Collins was at that bar in Bayonne less than an hour after you left the data centre. San Francisco is five and a half hours flight time from Newark. So they already knew we were in Jersey before you hacked into that matching engine. But they didn't know *why* we were in Jersey. Otherwise, they'd have been waiting for you at the industrial park.

Then they must have picked up our trail online, said Michael. You must have screwed up, Towse. With your burner phones.

I think *you* screwed up, Michael. No offence, but you're our weakest link.

I didn't ask to be here, Towse. You're the one who brought me. I still don't know why.

Aoife found her voice.

I think it was me.

They both turned to look at her.

What did you do?

That night in Bayonne. When we bought the pizza. I used a card to pay for it.

You did *what*?

She found it hard to meet their eyes.

They wouldn't deliver our pizza on the promise of cash. Once they heard the name of the bar, they said I'd have to pay up front before they'd take the order. They said one of the regulars used to order pizza, not pay for it, and then raid the dumpster behind the restaurant.

You, of all people, used a *credit card*?

It was just an odd bit of plastic I picked up somewhere! I keep them for jimmying doors. I didn't even think it would be working, but the system sometimes OKs small payments without bothering to check, so I thought I'd give it a go. But there's no way they could have linked us to that card. It wasn't even mine.

Do you still have it?

Aoife reached into her hip pocket, showed them the card. It was issued by a Canadian bank. Michael stepped closer.

Whose name is on that card, Aoife?

What does that matter?

Whose name, Aoife?

She looked at it.

Some woman called Lydia. Lydia A. Field.


WHEN A BOWLING BALL rolls down the lane, or along the gutter, it is swallowed by the pinsetter, along with any fallen pins, then sent back to the bowler along the return track. But when you throw it with all your force at a mirror, the glass shatters, and the ball falls to the floor, spinning in the shards, until it slows and comes to rest.

Aoife and Towse watched Michael with interest. What would he do next? Would he attack them, or turn and walk out of there, or collapse in tears, or pick up another ball?

He did something else entirely. He began to figure things out.

He turned to Aoife.

You did it. You stole my wallet in Palo Alto, along with that laptop. Alice's old credit card was in my wallet. It was the last thing she ever handed to me. It was *you* who broke into my house.

Aoife tried to look apologetic.

I wouldn't say *broke* in. I left the bathroom window open for myself.

But the front door was open, next morning!

Why climb out through a window when you can walk out the front?

Michael sat down on a return track, working things through.

If *you* stole the laptop, then why were the Feds coming for *me*?

They weren't. Not then, anyway. I sort of made all that up.

But there was a car parked across the road from my house! You showed it to me! Another one drove past us. Someone banged on the door!

I did improv at college, Michael. I was good at it. Cars park outside houses. Cars drive down streets. No one banged on the door. I just told you that to get you moving.

Why the hell would you make all that up?

Because Towse told me to fetch you. And if I'd told you the truth, you wouldn't have come.

Towse, ignoring the signs on the walls, lit a cigarette. He blew a smoke ring at the roof, watched it rise a foot and hover above him.

Fess thought I was selling him government secrets, he said,

smuggled in to him on that laptop. He's interested in some very gnarly stuff. But I'd installed a keylogger on it, so I could read everything that Fess put into it, including his access codes. The simplest tricks fool arrogant people. I needed those codes to break into his matching engine.

Towse reached up, annihilating the smoke ring with a wave of his hand.

We tricked you, Michael. But I had a good reason. I often tell lies, but I never break promises. And I promised Alice I'd look after you. So you had to come along.

Michael said nothing. Aoife spoke next.

So what did you find, Towse? When you used the codes to break into the dark pool?

Do you want me to get technical?

No.

Then it's pretty simple. Fess is using his dark pool to cheat all its clients.

How much?

From the volume of trades that I saw in that sample, I would estimate that Fess is creaming off maybe a hundred million bucks a year from the traders in his dark pool.

Aoife and Michael looked at each other, baffled.

Is that all? That's peanuts to Fess. Why would he go to so much trouble for that?

Because Fess is cursed with the wrong kind of money. He's a victim of the online fintech systems that he's done so much to build.

Every cent that he owns leaves a trace when he moves it. He's bank wealthy, street poor. And right now, Fess needs a lot of street money.

For what?

Towse held his cigarette upright, like an exclamation point, smiling blandly. They waited for him to go on. Michael's patience broke first.

So what is it, Towse? What's Fess's big secret?

What it is, I'm not sure yet. But I do know *where* it is. We have to go and take a look. It's the only way to turn the tables on Fess and get ourselves out of this. Come on – there's just time to hit a book store before we catch the plane.

# Part Three:

## *The Garden*

UGANDA, PEARL OF AFRICA. An equatorial plateau between the Albertine Rift and the Eastern Rift Valley. Birthplace, some say, of humanity. Source, if you like, of the Nile.

The British wanted Uganda so badly that they stole Kenya just to get to it. Uganda was intended to be the halfway point in a chain of roads and rails and inland navigations that would link a continuous band of imperial territory, all the way from Cairo to the Cape of Good Hope.

That didn't happen. The Empire never quite lined up all its tiles from Cape to Cairo, and the Brits were bounced out of Africa after the Second World War. But as far as the average American is concerned, such facts belong to a mythical past, a dreamtime, prehistory. Which might explain why the United States, having learned nothing and forgotten everything, has been secretly building its own African fantasy.

They call it the New Spice Route, a covert chain of logistical bases, airport compounds, supply dumps, surveillance facilities and bush strips, from the Swahili coast to the Atlantic shore. Its waypoints — caravanserais of trucking containers and razor wire and air-conditioned tents — are skeleton-crewed by security contractors, special-forces detachments, surveillance-drone techs and local auxiliaries. The idea is, should the US ever choose to ramp up any given war in Africa, overt or covert, it can quickly reinforce these forward operating bases, rather than keep troops and equipment on site. And some day — not, from the look of it, very far in the future — when the American empire is also a legend of decline, like King Solomon's Mines, or the lost Christian kingdom of the great Prester John, archaeologists will trace its ruin in aerial photos of its overgrown airstrips, buried concrete floor slabs, and the acacias that grow greener over former pit latrines. But for now, burly white men still do weights in moon bases deep in the bush, and Galaxy C-5s thunder skywards from domestic airfields — in this case, Westover Air Reserve Base, near Springfield, Massachusetts — on unlisted flights to Manda Bay in Kenya, Camp Lemonnier in Djibouti, or — in this case, again — to Africa Command's main dark site in Uganda, a fortified compound in Entebbe Airport, on the northern shore of Lake Victoria.

THEIR AIRCRAFT WAS MET by a tall, frowning woman in a polo shirt and chinos. She walked up the ramp, daylight flooding in around her, bringing with her the tang of jet fuel, the hot hyacinth breath of the lake.

Wait in your seats, she told them, and then she guided a blacked-out SUV as it reversed up the ramp and into the cargo bay.

Get in, she said.

The SUV drove them from the plane's hold to the US compound, bypassing immigration. An obese American contractor wearing sweat pants and camouflage, his rifle tricked out with store-bought accessories, waved them through a blast gate that slid shut behind them.

Their guide showed them to a converted shipping container shielded from the sun, and aerial observation, by a camouflage net and a green canvas awning. Sandbagged breastworks protected the door. Its walls were stacked, floor to ceiling, with Meals, Ready-to-Eat and bottles of water.

You sleep here. The dining facility is over there. But if you're too shy for that, help yourself to these Mr Es.

Aoife spoke up:

What if someone here asks us who we are?

They won't. I'm not asking either. Some people told me to help you, and that's good enough for me. The only thing I need to know is how long you're planning to stay.

From tomorrow, said Towse, you won't see us.

I'm not even seeing you now.


THERE ARE A NUMBER of safari lodges in the Budongo Forest Reserve, serving visitors on a range of budgets. The Addison Primate Experience stands apart from them all.

Sited at the remote edge of the forest, where the land falls to Lake Albert in the Western Rift, the lodge is reached, by most of its wealthy guests, via a private dirt airstrip two miles to the east. With a good four-wheel drive vehicle, in the dry season, you can drive from the lodge to the tarred road near Masindi in two or three hours. In a regular vehicle, or when the road washes out in the rains, you might not make it at all.

The remoteness of the camp is inconvenient, but its founder, the famous Kenyan-born adventurer, filmmaker and naturalist, Bill Addison, told the park authorities he would build on this site and no other. It was here, in Budongo, that he proposed to dedicate what time he had left to the study and care of the forest's famous chimpanzees.

The Ugandan park authorities resisted Addison at first, because they thought this remote part of the forest should be left undisturbed. But Addison found ways to make himself agreeable to the presidential palace. The lodge – a large, open-fronted building, its thatched roof held up by beams of mahogany, with cane chairs and tables, a circular bar, the heads of antelope and buffalo mounted on its walls, and separate guest chalets dispersed in the trees – went right where he wanted it, by a fast-moving stream, whose valley, falling off to the west, cut a notch in the forest, showing – in the morning and evening, when the haze briefly cleared – the sheen of Lake Albert, the blue rim of the Rift on the Congolese side.

And there too, hidden away in the trees, a short walk from the lodge, is the Addison Primate Experience research laboratory, a private facility for studying and rehabilitating injured or orphaned chimpanzees, with the ultimate aim of sending them back into the wild. The lab is very well funded. Its donors, whoever they are, are now paying for most of the national park's expenses, including the off-road trucks for its rangers. They seldom now drive them near Addison's lodge.

IT WAS ALREADY EVENING when the hired Landcruiser dropped Michael and Aoife at Addison's lodge, a day's drive from Kampala. The manager, a stocky white Zimbabwean lady called Lynette, wore a Hawaiian shirt that was up for a laugh in a way that her face was definitely not. She took the payment agreed on the phone earlier – walk-in booking, cash only, one day and one night – then showed them to their lodging.

The forest grew close around the camp, and the guest chalets stood in their own private clearings. It was hot and humid, the air composted by the trees. Their bamboo-walled chalet was designed to look rustic, but was very well appointed, with an en-suite bathroom and a ceiling fan and fridge. A mosquito net, tied up for the daytime, hovered over the bed like a Victorian ghost.

The honeymoon suite, said Lynette. We don't get many newly-weds here. Or at least, not on their first time around. Dinner is in one hour, in the boma. Try not to be late.

When she was gone, Michael looked at Aoife.

We're married?

I looked at the brochure before I called in the booking. The honeymoon suite has an extra-large bed. Which is good, because we have to share it. They didn't have any twins left. Believe me, I checked.


TIKI TORCHES, SMOKING TO ward off mosquitos, lit the clearing where dinner was served. A wood fire burned in the central pit. The other guests – elderly Americans and Germans and British, in self-conscious safari clothes bought just for this trip – already occupied their tables.

Come on, muttered Aoife. We'll eat and get out of here, then check out the laboratory when everyone's asleep.

Do you really believe Towse? You think what we find there will solve all our problems?

I don't know. But I know that Towse got us out of the States, no questions asked, which isn't easy. And I like having an ocean between me and Barb Collins. So we'll have to trust him, for now . . . Come on, that corner table is empty. Let's try to eat alone.

But Lynette had other plans.

The newly-weds! You must come eat with Bill, at the top table. He insists. We've chilled the champagne. I say champagne, but it's Méthode Cap Classique. You won't know the difference.

And, watched by the resentful tourists, she led them to the table at the top of the boma, where Bill Addison sat with two younger men.

Addison was a short but heavy man of about seventy years. He wore a bush shirt and trousers, with a thick grey-black beard and long grey-white hair. His face, burned and fissured, had a red, angry tint in the light from the torches. When he saw them he didn't stand up.

The love birds . . .

He stared admiringly at Aoife.

No wonder they're late . . . Come!

He stood, offered Aoife his hand.

Come and sit beside me, my dear. I'll tell you all about our work here. And you – Mark, is it?

John.

John. You sit at the far end, with Lynette.

Waiters fanned out among the tables, bringing wine and food – platters of game meat, and salads and sweet potato, and bowls of mealie pap. The servers wore khaki shirts, with shorts for the men and skirts for the women – the uniform for children in African schools.

The other two men at their table were Americans, late thirties, early forties, with pleasant, bland faces, wearing sweatshirts and jeans. Their names were Kevin and Steve. They said they were geneticists from Berkeley, here to study chimpanzees. Most of the time they sat hunched together, talking quietly, eating quickly, politely declining champagne. After one beer each, they excused themselves. Addison didn't notice. He'd already drunk their share of the champagne and ordered a follow-up bottle of red. Apart from the wine, he was interested only in Aoife.

So, what would you like to see tomorrow, my dear? I can take you out myself. Special game drive. Show you my chimps.

Aoife had worked out her part for the evening.

That would be awesome! I'd be able to tell all my girlfriends I'd been on safari with you! We watch all your shows!

Addison squinted at her.

My shows haven't been on the telly in years.

I meant, on demand. Streaming. We watch your shows online.

Lynette watched Addison top up his own glass.

You should take them out on the *dawn* game drive, Bill, she said. If we all get to bed early – she looked at the glass in his hand – you can show them the chimps yourself.

Addison looked at Aoife, and then at Michael, and then at the quantity of drink on the table. He seemed to be calculating.

Why not? I'm already taking out a few of these bloody Germans, the ones who paid for the premium package. There's room for two more on our Rover. We'll get to bed early. Let's just have one for the road.

I'VE BEEN MARRIED MYSELF, Addison confessed to Aoife, almost an hour later. He was on the whiskey now.

Three times, I've been married. And each time was beautiful. To three beautiful, beautiful ladies. If I had my time again, I would marry each one of them again. In the same order. And I would do it even knowing that, in the end, we would go our separate ways. Everything is eternal, but nothing will last. I learned that in the bush, from Nature herself. Nature is my temple, and my university.

That's so beautiful!

I've lived in the bush for most of my life, in a half-dozen countries, and now I will end my days living here, among my brothers of the forest, the genus of *Pan*. And you know what I have found . . . Rosa, is it?

Rose. What did you find, Bill?

He leaned towards her, close enough for her to smell the whiskey on his breath.

I've discovered this, Rose: Nature wants us to be free.

He held her gaze for a moment, frowning at his own wisdom. Then he placed his hand on hers.

I shall die in this forest. And here, under these trees, I shall be laid to rest. I don't want a grave. I told them that. I said, Just lay me in a clearing, on a nest of leaves and branches, and linger sadly for a while, as the chimpanzees do around the body of a loved one, and then leave me. Nature will reclaim me.

That's so beautiful.

I'm making a film of it, you know. It will be my last.

Please don't say that.

She withdrew her hand, smacked a phantom mosquito, put her hand in her lap. He didn't seem to notice it was gone.

It will be my last film. And my greatest. I'm putting money aside, so they can finish it after I'm gone. Death scene, sky burial, the lot. Then we'll see whose films are outdated.

You're a pioneer, Bill.

My agent is talking to Werner Herzog, to see if he'll do the narration. Maybe even make the final cut. Herzog is an artist. He'd never have worked with Cousteau or Adamson. Or Steve bloody Irwin.

Who even *are* those guys?

Exactly, Rosa! Forgotten, now. Showmen. Oh, look, there's some dolphins over there! Let's jump in with them and film ourselves! Let's bother some fish! . . . Entertainers. Not naturalists, like me.

Science is *so* important to me. I totally believe in it. And you even have your own science centre, right here, in this camp. That is *so* awesome!

Science centre?

Over there, in the trees. Lynette showed us earlier. What does it do?

Oh . . .

He glanced at Lynette, at the end of the table, who was blabbering away to that other stupid kid, Mark, or John, or whoever.

The primate rehab laboratory . . . Well, it's like it sounds. We rehabilitate injured or orphaned chimps. And scientists can come and study them.

What kinds of scientists? I did science at high school.

Top scientists. From America. Like these guys tonight – Kevin and Steve. Genetic biologists. They pay a lot of money for access to our chimps. Because our chimps are pure. Uncontaminated by contact with humanity. They're worth millions, believe me. That's how I'm funding my film.

He lowered his voice.

Some of our chimps have bred in captivity. If anything, it makes them more sexually active. And they also become more nocturnal in their mating. Like people. If you come with me now, I can show you.

His hand reached blindly for hers, failed to find it.

Maybe tomorrow, she said, standing. After the game drive. I'm so looking forward to that. Come on, John. We should get to bed.

A DIM LIGHT FROM the sky seeped through the gaps in the forest canopy, showing no more than the blurs of their faces. Aoife made Michael put one hand on her shoulder, then led him along the path, its stones a pale line in the darkness, to the clearing where the laboratory stood on its own. She moved slowly, sweeping twigs aside with her feet before her weight could snap them. They listened to their own breathing, the whine of mosquitoes, the scuff of their shoes. Leaves and branches brushed past them, releasing a hot musk, fungal spores, and the pollen of night-blooming flowers. Ants stung their ankles, worked their way inside their shoes.

The laboratory wall, appearing abruptly out of the darkness, brought Aoife to a halt. It was another rectangular industrial building, vinyl clad, though much smaller than the one in New Jersey. Her penlight flicked on, found the door. It was steel, held shut by a padlock. A few scratches, then a click, and the creak of metal hinges.

Come on, Aoife whispered. Towse said that whatever's in here, you should see it too.

WHAT LITTLE AIR THERE was inside came from small mesh windows, high up the walls. An ammoniacal stink — a smell like

overcrowded, unwashed bodies, flood-damaged carpet and raw
human sewage – made Michael gag. Aoife shone her flashlight about
them, narrating the scene with its beam.

They were standing in a room, ninety feet long by thirty feet wide,
that took up one end of the building. At the further end was a whitewashed partition with a large double door, and, beyond that, the hum of
refrigeration. Just inside the outer door where they stood, facing them,
was a metal bench scattered with scraps of vegetable and fruit. Rows of
steel cages lined either side of the room, like an old-fashioned jail, with
a stretch of bare concrete down the middle, wide enough to allow safe
passage out of reach of the bars. Dark, viscous fluid, oozing out of the
cages, glinted in the beam of the light. The ooze pooled, stagnant and
stinking, in a gutter that ran down the aisle.

Look.

Aoife's flashlight probed the nearest cage. At first, Michael saw
nothing, just filthy bedding, more excrement than straw. Then a pair
of eyes opened in the beam of light.

Aoife steered Michael down the line of cages, keeping to the
middle of the passage, flicking the torch back and forth.

I count about forty chimps, she said. It's hard to tell, the way
they're lying together. These cages are too small.

Some were caged alone, but most were in groups. A few stared
glumly back at the light. A mother shielded her baby, one hand
over its eyes and the other on one ear. In another cage motherless
infants, clustered together for warmth, slept with the intensity of
exhausted children.

They can't all be orphans or injured, Michael said.

Aoife flicked the beam on ahead. The inmates of these cages looked like chimpanzees at first, except a little larger. Then he got it.

Gorillas! Female gorillas . . . But Addison said they don't have gorillas in this forest.

They don't. They live a long way to the south.

Aoife turned the flashlight to the last cage on the left. Two long, spindly arms were splayed on the straw, crucified by gravity. The face that lifted itself to the light was ugly and wise, fringed with long ginger hair. Two smaller eyes peeped from its armpit.

And they don't have these on this continent at all, Aoife said.

Orang-utans . . . Jesus . . . Are Addison and Fess smuggling endangered apes? For private zoos, or something?

I don't think so. They didn't bring orang-utans all the way to the middle of Africa, just to move them somewhere else. This must be the end of the line.

Aoife opened the door in the whitewashed partition without any difficulty. The small room beyond smelled of diesel and soot. Her flashlight played across breeze-block walls, a concrete floor, another door on the opposite side. In the far corner, a red light was blinking. There was a ticking sound too, loud and steady. Aoife pointed her light.

The flashing light was set in the door of a coffin-like steel box set on a brick bench. A metal flue pipe ran from the box to the ceiling.

Aoife pulled her sleeve over her hand, touched the box. It was warm but not hot, ticking as it cooled. She turned the door handle upwards; it rotated stiffly in steel lugs. Opened, the door released a gust of burned diesel, and something else too – a smell like stripped metal. Aoife shone the torch inside the box. Its floor was heaped with ashes, and a few scorched fragments of bone. White flakes glided through the beam.

What is it? asked Michael.

She looked closer, then turned the bolt home again.

It's a crematorium.

The door in the far wall wasn't locked. Beyond it, tiles gleamed white in the torch beam. Tiles on the walls, tiles on the floor, in the middle of which was a metal-topped table. The whiteness of the tiles matched the coolness of the room, the hum of fridge motors. Glass cabinets lined three of the walls. Inside them, the glint of more glass, of beakers and test tubes and specimen jars. The benches beneath them were sheathed in dull metal.

I guess that part was true, said Michael. This really is a laboratory.

Aoife shone her light on the table in the middle of the room. Its zinc surface sloped gently from its edges down to the centre, where a grill protected the mouth of a drain. Hearing Michael move behind her, she jabbed her torch beam at the door.

I don't see any windows. Close that door and turn the light on. There's a switch over there.

Neon tubes in the ceiling flickered and steadied. They saw themselves reflected in the cabinets, their faces distorted in each vial and beaker, and magnified and dulled in the three stainless-steel doors, each half a metre square, set in a row half way up the far wall. Aoife looked at these doors with a dull sense of dread. I'll get to you later, she thought.

Hey, said Michael, opening a cabinet. Look at this.

The sample jars contained an off-yellow fluid, in which amniotic forms were suspended. Aoife saw tiny bean-like bodies – gill fringed, with curling fingers, winding tails.

The jars in the next cabinet each contained a thick fleshy stump from which twin tubes protruded, ending in a shrunken grey bean. The jars on its lower shelves held soft-shelled eggs, blue veined, floating in pairs in the murky fluid, a coil of grey matter emerging from each, as if they'd been cracked and then partially boiled. Aoife remembered biology at school. We are all descended from tube worms, her teacher had said. Strip us of all our evolutionary accretions, our limbs and brains and organs and bones, and that's what we still are. Tubes for feeding, and for breeding.

The beakers were labelled with stickers, each annotated with handwritten letters and numbers. But some of them – the older ones, she thought, judging from the soupier state of their contents – had a printed identifier in the corner of each label. *RRL*.

Take some photos, she said.

She wanted Michael to be busy.

Towse had bought a camera for them in Kampala, a basic digital SLR. It's mainly a prop, he had said. You're both tourists, remember. But it might also come in handy when you get inside the lab.

Michael shot a few frames of the jars in the cabinets, then lowered the camera.

Hey, there's a PC over there, in the corner. Want me to take a look?

Towse says this place is completely offline and unhackable. No phone, no Internet, no cell reception. That's why he had to send us here in person.

Still, the computer might have some information.

Go ahead, then. See what you get.

Sitting at the PC, his back would be turned to the three stainless-steel doors that were waiting for Aoife.

It wants a password, he said. I'll try *admin*. That sometimes works.

He hit a couple more keys, reached for the mouse.

No good . . . I'll try *password*, this time.

She moved around the metal table and into his blind spot.

The hum of refrigeration was loudest by the three metal doors. She reached for the handle on the first one. It popped open, as if driven by a spring, releasing a trickle of vapour. She waited until it cleared, then pulled out the steel drawer inside it.

The body lay face up, hands joined unnaturally underneath its arched back. Leaning sideways, Aoife saw the ends of the cable tie protruding from livid grooves in its wrists.

The ape's eyes were open, teeth bared, face twisted. Thick black hair concealed any obvious cause of death, but she would have guessed, from the protruding tongue, that it had been strangled.

But what was it? An adult male chimpanzee, or a female gorilla — she couldn't tell which. She was no primatologist, and the most obvious sign of sex was missing, cut away from the lower abdomen, leaving only a cavity, black congealed blood.

*Password* didn't work either, said Michael behind her. Have you any guesses?

No . . . But keep trying.

The next drawer, the middle of the three, opened smoothly.

There had been no need to tie the hands on this one; it was too small to put up a fight. Its infant fur was thin enough for Aoife to see the mark that the ligature had cut into its neck. They could have used a sedative to kill it, put it gently to sleep, but they chose instead to garrotte it . . . They must need the tissue samples to be free of any drugs . . .

This one had also had its sex organs removed.

She wondered if this little one had been the big one's child. Were they mother and son, or father and daughter? Would it have been a kindness for them to die at the same time?

She looked at the third and final door. She'd seen enough already. Why bother to open it? I'm on a hiding to nothing, she thought.

This drawer was well oiled. It slid silently open.

Aoife closed her eyes.

When she was ready, she looked again. She made herself see, thinking in numbed phrases – a language she'd heard from instructors when she was in training. But crime scenes had never been part of her job. She'd seen a lot of dead people, but she'd never had to *look*.

Subject lies on its side, knees raised. Its hands are restrained by cable ties, still attached, which have cut deeply into its wrists as it struggled.

A ligature – likely cause of death – has also left a deep wound, clearly visible in the skin of its neck. Bleeding from these injuries, likely post-mortem, has pooled on the mortuary drawer. It must have been placed in the drawer shortly after its death.

It.

The fact was, Aoife couldn't tell if this African child was a boy or a girl. It too had been mutilated. And it was too young to show any secondary characteristics.

Jesus Christ, said Michael, behind her.

She raised her hand to close the drawer. Then she thought better of it. Towse wanted Michael to see this too. She could see no other reason why Towse had told her to bring him to the laboratory. She could have done all this alone.

That's a *child* . . . A human child.

And yet Aoife was glad there was someone else with her. She had an audience to play to, to keep her to her lines. She slid the drawer all the way open.

Photograph it.

What?

Photograph the body.

She longed for the frame that a camera would place around the subject. But Michael needed it more.

Go on, she said. Photograph it.

The camera had an internal flash built into the top of the viewfinder. It activated automatically in the low light. Aoife let him take several frames – leaning in close, changing angles, his breath catching in his throat – then she gently took the camera from him and checked its screen. They would do.

Are those pictures for the police?

She shut the drawer. He had backed over to the metal-topped table. She was surprised that he hadn't figured out what that was for yet. If he had, she thought, he probably wouldn't be leaning against it.

For Towse. We can't go to the police.

But she's somebody's daughter.

Why, wondered Aoife, does he default to female for a murdered child?

Not necessarily, she said, feeling harsh. There are lots of unwanted kids in this world. If you want to keep a few, you don't even have to cage them. You just have to feed them.

She saw herself in his eyes, and relented.

Look, we have these photographs. Maybe some day we can make proper use of them. But first we have to get out of here.

She used the hem of her T-shirt to wipe any prints from the mortuary doors.

Rub down the computer and anything else she touched. We have to go.

Did you know?

Know what?

What we might find here.

I had no idea.

Towse didn't warn you?

No he did not.

Do you think he knew?

If we get out of here tomorrow, I'll be asking him myself.

You haven't told me where we're going next.

Towse said the plan was need-to-know.

After what we just saw, you don't think I need to know?

He was right, she thought. More than that, he was here.

We get up in the morning and go on their game drive. Then we wait for our driver to come pick us up. We leave, like everything is normal. We have to stay calm.

I'm finding calm difficult.

Consider the alternative.

Where then? Back to Entebbe?

No. You never go out the way you came in. Our driver picks us up after the game drive, takes us back to the highway, then south to Masindi. We pay him off there. Then we double back into the north, taking a bush taxi, long way around. Towse is waiting for us in a big town called Gulu. He knows a way out of here. We have to stick with him.

THE GUESTS ASSEMBLED IN the open-sided lodge in the chill of the dawn. It was still dark. Lynette served them rusks and coffee, then assigned groups to the jeeps that would take them on their game drives. Addison, when he finally showed up, wore the same clothes as the night before, beard matted, eyes bloodshot. He leered queasily at Aoife.

There you are, he said. You look like you've been up all night . . .

He squinted at Michael, who was fiddling with the camera, brought for the sake of appearances.

You probably have . . .

He turned to Lynette.

Who else do we have?

She introduced the Lehmanns and Sauers, and shooed them all out to their open Land Rover. Like all the others, it had been modified for game viewing, its sides and roof removed, the back fitted with padded benches. A Ugandan tracker, perched on a little seat that was welded to the fender, palmed a lit cigarette when Addison appeared.

Aoife and Michael climbed into the rearmost bench and wrapped themselves in the blankets they found there. The Germans, stiff with resentment at the late departure, sat in the two front rows, while Addison got behind the wheel. He checked the load in a rifle that was clamped to the dashboard, tested his handheld radio, then turned blearily to his guests.

What's it going to be this morning, then? Elephants or chimps?

We did the chimps yesterday, said Herr Lehmann. And the day before too. If there is a possibility of elephants, so *late* in the morning, we'd like to see them today, please.

Addison looked at Aoife.

And you two? Elephants or chimps?

Whatever suits.

OK . . . Elephants, then. There's a waterhole out east, and at this time of year they usually stay near it. But the bush there is thick and the ground is pretty broken. If we want to see the elephants, we might have to get out and walk a short way.

The Land Rover swayed and bumped down the track, brushing the branches. Cradled by its suspension, groggy from the long night, Aoife and Michael dozed off at either end of the bench.

IT WAS THE CRACKLE of the radio that woke Aoife. VHF static was an ominous sound in the life she was trying to escape.

The Land Rover had stopped by a clearing in the forest. Addison was listening to his walkie-talkie. Another burst of static, words inaudible to her, and then she heard another sound, swelling in the distance: aeroplane engines.

Addison put down the radio, looked around at his guests.

Sorry, he said. We didn't expect this plane to arrive from Nairobi until later today. But all our other Rovers are being used for game drives, so I need to drop these new guests to the camp.

The Germans muttered together, displeased.

We didn't pay the premium rate to be someone's Uber, Herr Lehmann said.

Ignoring him, Addison let the clutch out, drove into the clearing. There was a bare strip of dirt down its centre, and, at the far end, a windsock. A few antelope, disturbed, trotted off into the forest. Aoife watched a King Air appear, low over the trees. It flared, touched, and taxied back towards the Land Rover. The engines died, the plane's door opened.

A blue sweatshirt in the doorway. *Stanford* printed on it. Barb

Collins from Inscape got out of the aeroplane. The Scotsman from London came after her.

DON'T WORRY ABOUT THOSE two, Addison said. His voice was muffled by the blanket hiding Aoife's face.

You won't wake them now. They must have been up all night. The chimps have nothing to teach them . . . Just take that bench in front of them, and I'll drop you at the lodge.

He must have remembered the Germans.

Sorry, folks. We'll be back on schedule in a few minutes. I'll make it up to you later. I'll take you on an extra special evening drive.

But we are to leave after lunch, Herr Lehmann said.

The engine started, the Land Rover lurched. Aoife wriggled along the bench, keeping under her blanket, and shook Michael. He was somehow still asleep.

Michael, she whispered. *Michael.*

She pinched his forearm.

Huh?

He sat up, brushing off the blanket she'd pulled over their heads. In desperation, she pretended to kiss him, forcing her lips against his, pressing him down on the bench, hiding his face with hers. He started to struggle, shocked. With a free hand, she pulled the blanket back over them, then moved her mouth to Michael's ear.

Michael, she whispered. Shut up and listen. Barb Collins is here.

He stopped struggling.

Here? . . . Where?

In this jeep. Right in front of us. She just got off a plane. She has a man with her. A killer.

Jesus . . . What do we do?

We hide under this blanket until they get out.

For the rest of the game drive?

For the next few minutes. Addison is dropping them back at the lodge. Then we turn around and go look for the elephants.

What if she knows we're here? What if that's why she came?

If that's how it is, we'll find out soon enough.

BUT BARB COLLINS DIDN'T know they were there — not then, anyway. They were left to sleep off their night of passion under their thick woollen blankets, as the sun climbed higher, making them stew. The jeep dropped the new guests at the lodge, turned and started back towards the waterhole. Aoife and Michael threw off the blanket but sat pressed together, whispering lovers.

So who is the other one?

I don't know his name. I met him once before, in London. He's ex-SAS, SBS, something like that. A killer.

We can't go back to that camp. We have to get out of here before they see us.

Shut up. I'm thinking . . . We have a chance, so long as they don't know we're here . . .

The walkie-talkie crackled. Addison picked it up, listened. He slowed the jeep, turned and looked back towards Michael and Aoife, puzzled.

Yes, he said. Yes, they are. Both of them.

The truck moved on. Aoife looked at Michael. Michael looked at her, then he looked at the bush. He threw off the blanket, pointed at the forest.

Hey! An elephant!

Four German heads snapped to the right. Cameras were raised. Binoculars too.

Where?

There! . . . It just moved off into the forest. But I saw it very clearly . . . It was eating a tree.

Addison squinted at him.

I didn't see anything.

It was right there!

I don't think so.

The tracker, perched on the hood of the Land Rover, spoke up for the first time that day.

There are fresh elephant tracks in the road, boss.

If there are elephants here, said Herr Sauer, we want to see them. This is our last chance. We must leave after lunch.

We don't want to go back without seeing elephants, said Frau Lehmann. You have already wasted most of our final game drive. We will be very unhappy.

We will write online reviews, said Frau Sauer.

Addison looked from one to the other, and then he looked at Michael.

All right, he said. We'll take a quick look. But the Land Rover can't go in there. The ground is too broken. We'll have to track it on foot.

He unclamped the rifle from the dashboard and got out. They followed. The tracker pointed to a soft, oval print in the dust. It had gossamer wrinkles, like a fossilised jellyfish. Addison considered it.

OK, he said. The boy may have been right.

Aoife looked at Michael. He shrugged, as if to say, sometimes you get lucky.

We go single file, said Addison. Me and the tracker in front. Be very quiet. An elephant will charge you, if you startle it.

He toted the rifle and set off into the bush, with the tracker beside him. One by one, the Germans followed, until only Aoife and Michael were left standing by the Land Rover. Aoife looked at the keys in the ignition, then at Michael.

Not bad, she said. I think I should drive.


THEIR PEUGEOT BUSH TAXI reached its terminus, the northern city of Gulu, as night fell that same day. Stiff, sun-baked, and battered by two hundred miles of unsurfaced back roads, Aoife and Michael slid down from the sacks of flour and sugar, the bales of cloth and boxes of biscuits, that filled the bed of the old 504 pickup.

Aoife paid off the driver, shook hands with the passengers who had shared their long journey, then considered their position.

They were standing in Gulu's main market. Here, at this soft hour, women sold grilled meat skewered on bicycle spokes; children came back from kiosks with beers for their elders, treats for themselves; drivers made deals under dusty acacias.

And here, right where their truck was unloading, was a bar and hotel, its plaster wall painted with an ad for Nile Special. On the terrace bar, a PA played American country and western, beloved around the Great Lakes of Africa. People were dancing to vintage Kenny Rodgers. And there, also, was Towse, wearing the same bedraggled outfit, sharing a table with three African men in smart suits. He was waving at Aoife to get her attention.

By the time they had pushed their way on to the terrace and through the dancers, Towse's new friends were already gone. Three empty Coke bottles, still wet with condensation, were the only sign they had ever been there.

Michael sat, picked up a cold bottle, rolled it lovingly across his forehead. Towse watched him sympathetically.

Let's get you something to eat and drink. Where did you put your bags?

We had to leave everything, said Aoife, sitting down opposite.

Even the books?

Even the books.

Towse signalled a waiter, turned back to Aoife.

The important thing is that you're here.

Who were those guys you were talking to? Michael asked.

They're Karamojong. A pastoral tribe from the border with Kenya.

They have some interesting religious beliefs. And they're very good at smuggling. They'll get us out of Uganda, no questions asked.

Never mind that, said Aoife. Barb Collins flew into the camp, Towse. While we were there. With that Scotsman from London. If they'd seen us, we'd be dead.

That doesn't surprise me. They were probably bringing more of Fess's laundered cash from London.

Aoife became aware of the fascinated look on Michael's face, watching her from across the table. He hasn't seen me looking this angry before, she thought.

You didn't tell me that Fess was connected to the London thing, Towse. You told me when I joined you that you were getting me away from that.

Jeez. I'd have told you, if you'd asked. I just assumed you'd already figured it out for yourself. It's a no-brainer. Funny money to Africa. Fess.

Aoife looked at her hands for a while. Then she picked up the camera, activated the LED screen, jabbed it towards Towse's face.

Look at these pictures. Then tell me what you see.

She scrolled through the images. Towse looked at them, unblinking.

A waiter appeared, stood over them.

You should try the fried pork, Towse said. It's pretty good. And ask for the Irish potatoes. That means potatoes. If you ask for just potatoes, they give you sweet potatoes.

When the waiter was gone, Aoife put the camera on the table.

Did you know they were strangling children, Towse?

RRL.

*What?*

RRL, on the labels of those jars. It stands for Roodeplaat Research Laboratories. Roodeplaat is in South Africa, near Pretoria. Fess must have got his hands on Project Coast.

What the hell is Project Coast?

It was apartheid's covert chemical and biological warfare pro- gramme. Its most secret component was under development at Roodeplaat. It was a scheme to make sure that white South Africans would become the majority, instead of the blacks. They were looking for an agent that would sterilise black people, but leave white people fertile. They were going to mix it in with the township water supplies, or slip it into vaccines. But apartheid collapsed before they got it to work. All the files and samples disappeared. Until now. Fess must be trying to reboot it.

You sound like a conspiracy nut. An anti-vaxxer.

On the contrary, Aoife. The anti-vaxxers are part of this too. Who do you think stands to gain if regular people stop protecting their kids?

Why don't you tell us who?

People like Fess, Aoife. People who think that regular people with ordinary lives are a species of virus. People who blame the state of the world on overpopulation, instead of stupidity and greed.

You're saying Fess is trying to wipe out his own species, and he's doing it here in Uganda?

No. He's trying to wipe out *most* of his own species. To save the world for people like him, until they can figure out a way to not be people anymore, to turn themselves into machines, or immortals, or whatever. And Fess isn't working alone. There's a bunch of them, trying their luck with a whole bunch of projects. And it's not just the stuff that you've heard about – spaceships and floating cities and private islands and the rest of it. They have other things too. New viruses. Chemical agents. OmniCent. But Project Coast is one of Fess's particular babies. Experimenting on people and apes.

Aoife stared at him, running the combinations.

You already knew what Fess was doing in Uganda, she said.

I suspected. But I needed confirmation. And I needed you to see it too.

Why?

So you'd know how ruthless they are. So you'd know for sure that there's no easy way out of this. Because I want you to stay with me. Because I need your help.

Why?

Towse stubbed out his cigarette, pulled his chair forward, right up to the edge of the table. His two hands, placed on either side of his beer glass, were the hands of a pianist, ready to play.

It all comes down to OmniCent. It's about who's really in charge of it. Fess thinks that it's him and his friends. And I know that it's not.

The waiter came back with their food and their beers. They had to wait until he was gone.

What are you talking about, Towse? Fess has the lead on Omni-Cent. It's not a secret. Everyone knows that.

I didn't tell you before what I'm about to tell you now, because you wouldn't have believed me. But there was something I saw when I ran my diagnostics on Fess's dark pool, back in the US. Alice had seen it too, or at least caught a glimpse of it. But even Fess doesn't know about it.

I don't care about your dark pool, Towse. Why should I listen to you, after you sent us blind into that laboratory? We could have been killed.

Towse carried on, ignoring Aoife.

At first, I only saw what I'd expected to see. The dark pool's regular clients, there to be fleeced, and the usual high-frequency trading bots, taking a skim on their trades. And beneath them were the even faster bots that Fess was using to rig his own casino. Again, what I expected.

Who are you, Towse?

But, barely visible, down in the depths, there was something impossible. Something that traded so quickly that it looked like it wasn't moving at all.

Who do you really work for?

And I was right. It wasn't moving. Its trades were instantaneous.

Aoife gave up.

What does that mean, Towse?

Deep down in the dark pool, the money is trading with itself. It's going where it wants to.

I said, what does that mean?

He laced his fingers together and laid his hands on the table, looking down at them as if in prayer.

It means the money is alive.

THE KARAMOJONG PEOPLE OF eastern Uganda believed, before the missionaries got to them, that God had given them all the cattle in the world. So when they rustled from neighbouring peoples, as they religiously did, it didn't count as stealing. They were taking back what was already theirs.

Who spoke to the Karamojong, in their centuries of wandering, after their ancestors trekked out of Ethiopia, driving their cows into the Turkana, then onward across the Rift Valley, up over its rim, into the region that we now call Uganda? Who told the Karamojong that the world's cattle, which they worshipped then as we now worship money, were their birthright alone?

Was this that voice's only dispensation, or has it cut deals with other people since? Has it refined that idea? Who told Fess and his friends that they should own all the wealth in the world?

Who indeed? We'll get to that in a minute. For now, let us only say this: the Karamojong got off lightly when they were merely cursed with cattle.

*Ophiocordyceps unilateralis* is a fungus that infects carpenter ants in tropical forests. Its spores burrow into the nervous system of a healthy ant and turn it into a zombie, forcing it to wander away from its colony, to the humid forest-floor environments where the fungus can thrive. There, the fungus forces the ant to bite into a leaf vein and hang by its mandibles, while the fungus eats it alive. When the ant is dead, an obscene fruiting body, a glistening tube, longer than the ant itself, grows from its head, swells, lengthens and bursts, spurting a cloud of infective spores.

Ants are primitive creatures, of course, with simple nervous systems. Not like us mammals.

*Toxoplasma gondii* is a single-cell organism that can reproduce sexually only in felines. But it can multiply asexually in most other mammals and birds, spreading itself in their food or water, or by sexual contact, or from mother to infant. When rodents are infected they lose their innate fear of cats. The cats eat the rodents. *Toxoplasma* wins.

Approximately two billion people around the world are infected with *Toxoplasma gondii*. It usually goes unnoticed, but is statistically associated with increased aggression, selfishness, jealousy, and auto-destructive behaviour. There is a high incidence in people who describe themselves as entrepreneurs and risk takers, and in drivers involved in fatal crashes.

Most people contract *Toxoplasma gondii* from contact with cats or their faeces. But French scientists demonstrated in the 1960s that it could also be spread to humans in food. The scientists determined this by feeding portions of undercooked meat to their test subjects. Their test subjects were orphans in a Paris home. We don't know if the scientists ever tested themselves for *Toxoplasma gondii*.

Microscopic organisms in the human gut produce neuro-transmitters that can modify human emotions, make people feel depressed, or happy, or hungry, or gregarious. They speed us up and slow us down, direct our footsteps, make us crave certain foods that the organisms favour. Are they hitchers or hijackers? Who's in control?

In the early years of the AIDS epidemic, after the link to the human immunodeficiency virus was shown, it was assumed that if you had HIV it would kill you. Then, as time passed and many infected people survived, a new realisation took hold. You could live indefinitely with HIV, so long as you suppressed the degree of infection, lived as healthily as possible, took retroviral drugs. HIV was only lethal when the virus was present in sufficient numbers to swarm the immune system, overrun its defences, batter holes in cell walls to let in other afflictions. Patients with low viral loads were not only healthier themselves, but also much less infectious to others.

The more of the virus you had, the more lethal it was, to you and to others.

A virus is a genetic package in a protein envelope. It doesn't eat or grow or move, and can only reproduce by tricking a host into copying its genes. Genes are information, encoded as strings of DNA or RNA. A virus exists only to replicate this information. A virus, Towse told Aoife and Michael that night in Gulu, whether computer, organic, or meme, is really just an unhealthy idea.

*

WAITERS LOITERED ON THE edge of the terrace, noisily stacking the chairs. The music and dancers were gone. The coloured lights, strung on poles above the dance floor, had been disconnected. Flames guttered in the unlit market, itinerant traders cooking a meal before settling down for the night.

Towse, having mesmerised Aoife and Michael with his set-ups and feints, his flickering vistas, had revealed his prestige. When he opened his hands, looking up at his companions, Aoife half-expected them to release a dove.

So that's what Alice saw in the dark pool. The money's alive. It's a new kind of organism. A global online virus. A multi-cellular meme.

That's insane.

It's the conclusion that fits the observed phenomena.

Michael spoke up:

Assuming it's alive, is it sentient?

Define 'sentient'.

Does it know what it wants?

It wants to be with other money. And to propagate itself. So it infects vulnerable hosts, and drives them away from the rest of humanity. The more money they have, the sicker they get. At an advanced stage of infection, they no longer behave like humans at all. It makes them think that they're gods. And they start shedding money, through their lawyers and politicians and journalists, to poison herd resistance. The money is used to persuade people that nothing matters, nothing is real, things have to be the way that they are, that money is the only real power and that you can't do anything about it. If you have a problem in your life, blame it on blacks or women or Muslims or gays or whoever. Never the money.

If you're right, said Aoife, and you can't be, how would something like this evolve?

I'm not sure. But think about this: what if a non-human super intelligence already existed, but it was too smart to show itself? What if it was manifesting itself as money, to soften us up, until it was ready to destroy us by some other means, like a war, or a famine, or a virus? Or even a meme?

Neither Aoife nor Michael could speak. Towse was proud of being a liar, but that didn't mean they could trust him to be lying now.

You're saying our machines could be doing this?

That's the most likely hypothesis. I did some simulations, ran lots of projections. There was only one other possibility that really leaped out at me, though it was kind of remote. My Raëlian friends got me thinking . . . What if money is some kind of alien probe?

*Aliens?*

No, really, Aoife. Aliens. What if these aliens are looking for new planets to colonise, so they send a cloud of memetic ideation on ahead of them, at light speed or faster, while they follow more slowly in colony ships? By the time their ships get here, their terra-forming device, which is money, will have altered the planet to make it suitable for them. Judging from what we're seeing with climate change, they would probably be reptilian. They want a world that is hot and humid and mostly underwater.

*The Drowned World*, said Michael. Now I get it. You put those books in my house at Palo Alto.

I got Aoife to do it. I was trying to loosen you up. You're so fucking uptight, Michael. Alice was right about you.

Never mind that, said Aoife. The great thing about your stories, Towse, is there's never any way to prove or disprove them.

You're wrong, Aoife. There's one sure way to find out if something is alive or not.

And what's that, Towse?

I'm going to try to kill it, then see what it does.


TOWSE HAD ONLY TAKEN two rooms in the hotel. One was for him, the other for Aoife and Michael. He seemed to take it for granted that, having been forced to share before, along the road, they'd continue to do so.

Aoife could have demanded a room to herself, but she'd decided that she felt sorry for Michael. No one should have to share with Towse. There was something uncanny about him. What if you opened your eyes in the night, and he wasn't in the room with you, and you blinked, and then he was? Compared to Towse, she and Michael belonged to a similar order of being. It almost felt like they were colleagues. He was starting to come good.

The room had whitewashed walls and a red tile floor; it was clean, but with rust stains in the shower and sink of the small en suite bathroom. There was no glass in the window, only torn wire mesh.

Mosquitoes bided their time on the ceiling. There was only one bed.

Neither of them said anything. They may have been too tired to talk. Aoife took off her shoes, stood on the bed and killed all the mosquitoes she could reach with the Gideon Bible. Michael blocked the torn window mesh with a towel from the bathroom. That would have to do for now. She'd get some chloroquine tomorrow, for both of them, just in case.

Aoife showered and then, having no luggage, got dressed again in her T-shirt and jeans. As Michael took his turn in the shower, she switched off the light and lay along one edge of the bed.

It was the small hours now, and the market was quiet. Aoife felt Michael settling beside her, their bodies held stiffly apart, despite the gravitational pull of the saggy old mattress. She wondered if he was dressed too. She hadn't opened her eyes when he came out of the bathroom.

His breathing was shallow. She could smell the nicotine on her own breath. She was already sweating. At last, he spoke.

Do you believe him?

I don't know.

Everything he told us is crazy.

So is everything that's happened.

We still don't even know who he is. No matter how many times we ask, he always deflects.

He's like a magician. He makes you look in the wrong place.

Michael shifted his weight, and the mattress shook. He was sweating again too. They lay in their mingled scent.

Are we going to stay with him?

*We*, Aoife noted. Since when was that the default?

Consider the alternative, she said. He's kept us a step ahead of Fess and Barb Collins, and whatever Feds they have on our tail. He knows how to get us out of Uganda. We don't. So I'm going to stick with him, for now.

Until when?

Aoife thought about that. She assumed that Towse would keep opening one Russian doll after another, that his fan dance would never end.

It's too hot in this room, she said.

She swung her legs over the side of the bed, stood with her back to it, took off her jeans. She lay back down, restoring the original distance between them. The equatorial night, close and still, did nothing to cool her. She wanted to spread herself out to it, but there wasn't room.

It was a while before Michael spoke again.

I don't know why Towse wants me. I know what *you* do for him.

And what's that?

Lots of things . . . For one thing, you got me into this.

Was he talking about *that*? The summer dress she'd worn the day she first approached him, the tailored uniform, cut to look good? The way that she'd ruthlessly negged him at first, a trick that worked better on men than on women? How far did he think all those ploys really went?

She had slept with colleagues a couple of times, on the road, and one or two strangers, as physical facts, fellow travellers, interchangeable.

But Michael was a mark, not a colleague or a stranger. She'd always felt sorry for the marks that she followed, whose houses she bugged and whose secrets she stole. To do these jobs properly, she had to predict their likely movements, which meant she had to consider their motives, to understand them as people, to rehearse their roles. This was one of the ways that the job had destroyed her. And Towse had only made things worse: he hadn't told her about Alice when he sent her to lure Michael. This time, she hadn't been ready for the role she was playing. It hadn't been fair on Michael. It hadn't been fair on her, either.

I don't know why Towse wants you, she said. But he must have something planned. I feel like he's pulling strings that I don't even know about. Everything he does is worked out in advance.

Predetermined, said Michael.

He shifted his weight, and the old mattress narrowed the distance between them. They both lay with their arms folded behind their heads, to stop their elbows from brushing in the middle of the bed.

We could fight it, she said, but it seems like there's no point.

She closed her eyes, yawned, gasped a lungful of warm air.

She took her arms from behind her head and stretched them in front of her, pale against the paler ceiling. Then she turned on her side and faced him.

Michael, she said.

After a while he turned and faced her.

It's OK, she said.

What is?

She crooked her left thigh and laid it over his knee, feeling sweat-softened denim, coarse on her skin.

His arm came around, rested on the small of her back.

I shouldn't, he said.

She lifted her head, laid it carefully in the curve of his bicep. The sleeve of his T-shirt had ridden up; his arm there was bare. She wanted to lick it, to taste the salt. We exude things, she thought, because we are mammals.

This is different, she said.

But she thought, after they were finished, as he lay beside her, maybe already sleeping, that they'd both been so gentle. It made her feel guilty, which she hadn't expected. Maybe, she told herself, it was because they were tired. Or maybe it was Alice he'd held in the dark. And so what if it was? She told herself, fiercely, that she owed him that much.

# Part Four:

## *Milk and Honey*

THE TRAILS THAT BROUGHT the Karamojong to Uganda have existed for longer than mankind itself. They still exist today, if only for the Karamojong, smuggling cattle and guns from the Kenyan frontier.

Picture two deep ruts in the sand and the gravel, snaking through the dry thorn bush where humanity was born. They pass north of the forests of Mount Moroto, curve to the east through a notch in the escarpment, and then – if the pass isn't washed out by rain or blocked by fresh rockfalls – plunge down to the floor of the Eastern Rift Valley.

There are no signposts to mark the border with Kenya, no customs, no garrison, not even a couple of bored policemen with a string across the road. Outsiders rarely cross here, and those who do are expected to present their passports at the nearest police post. If you don't have a passport, you don't have this problem.

*

EARLY EACH MORNING, A few dozen Toyota pickups appear beside
the runway at Wilson Airport, a rustic airstrip on the edge of Nairobi.
Their cargo, sacks of green leaves, is tossed into a line-up of old
twin-prop aircraft with expired markings, and sometimes no markings
at all. The planes take off, turn north. Khat, a herbal amphetamine
grown in the Kenyan highlands, begins losing its potency as soon
as it is harvested. It has to reach its Somali markets on the same day
that it's picked.

THEIR BOAT HAD BEEN built for somebody's navy in some long-ago
great power war. It was steel, slab sided, with an open-decked hull.
The bow was a flat armoured ramp, designed to be lowered to let
troops storm ashore, but it had rusted shut a long time ago, and was
now bulling north through a steep and nasty cross-sea, hugging the
Red Sea's African shore.

The boat was fast, but its bottom, flat and shallow, wasn't designed
for long ocean voyages. Two eyes, painted for luck either side of the
bow ramp, washed themselves, turn by turn, with each gut-heaving
pitch and roll.

Aoife leaned over the rail outside the wheelhouse. The fumes
from the old petrol engine added to her nausea. And when the wind
dropped, or backed into the north, the stench from the cargo made
life even worse. Dozens of camels, legs lashed beneath them, filled
the bed of the boat, roaring and spitting and shitting and puking.

When she could look up, every now and then, she would fix

her eyes on the hills to the west, shimmering red. They were half a day out of Berbera, where their khat flight had landed. That must be Eritrea off to port, she thought. Or maybe Sudan. If she could only focus on the hills, level her world on them, she might forget to be seasick. Poor Michael lay flat in the scuppers beside her, too far gone to lift his head.

The door of the wheelhouse opened and Towse came out. He lit his cigarette, smiled.

Aoife managed to speak:

You couldn't get us a better boat than this?

This boat is perfect. There's a line of reefs along the Saudi shore. A boat with a deeper draft wouldn't get over them.

Why Saudi Arabia?

He waved a hand at the cargo.

Camels are Somalia's main export. And Saudi Arabia is the biggest market – especially during the hajj, for their milk and their meat. But camels can spread a coronavirus. Middle East Respiratory Syndrome. It kills one in three people who get it. So now the Saudi market is strictly controlled. Which pushes up the price of camels.

We're smuggling cheap camels, that could kill lots of people?

Our Somali skipper is. He doesn't want to, but he has no choice. He used to make a decent living as a pirate, but the western insurance firms priced him out of the game. They kept raising the kickbacks they charge on each ransom, until they'd squeezed out his margins. Now he has to flog camels instead.

Too bad. Why do *we* want to go to Saudi?

We don't. We want to go to Jordan. But if we land in Saudi, our skipper's clients will sneak us across to Aqaba at night. They're Bedouin. Howeitat, in fact. Very traditional people. They don't believe in viruses or borders. In the desert, they still go where they want.

Why do you always have to drip-feed us your plans, Towse?

Because I don't think you'd like them.


A WHEEL STRUCK A pothole, Aoife's head smacked the window, and she woke to the onrushing night. Her neck ached. She straightened it, shook her head, looked around her. Michael had toppled over sideways in his sleep. His head, lolling as the old Mercedes swept through long, fast curves, rested on her thigh. Towse, up front with the driver, peered up to the right. There was a glow on his face from outside the car. He turned to look back at her.

Moonrise. Now you'll see something.

Silver light softened the glare of the headlamps, showed her a slope of grey scree and loose boulders. Another rift valley – or was it the same one, extending infinitely? – and another volcanic escarpment. But here it was grassless, treeless, forgotten by time. She looked to the left, across Michael's sleeping body, and saw moonlight on water, dancing away from her, then a further escarpment – another line of futile, ageless mountains, grey in the moonlight, marching in parallel.

Salt flats reached out to the edge of the water, cracked, pocked with sinkholes, hinting at ancient corruption below. Her window let in the smell of old soap, caked in a plug hole.

That's the Dead Sea!

If you'd slept any longer you'd have missed it. We're almost past its northern end already.

She'd been through Jordan several times, to get to other places, but she'd never been down to this valley before. There was only one other place you could go to, from here, and she'd never worked there. It was out of bounds.

Over there, she said. That's Israel.

Actually, it's the West Bank. Occupied Palestinian Territories. But it comes to the same thing, as far as we're concerned. We have to go through Israeli security to get there.

Seriously? We're going there? The Americans are after us. The Israelis work with them.

They do when it suits them. Sometimes, they don't. And I have to go to Jerusalem, to pick something up.

You're with the Israelis, too?

That's a complicated question. But they'll take us in tonight. I have an old friend waiting for me.

I don't doubt they'll take us in, Towse. Getting out again is the problem.

They had reached the lowest point on earth, where the Jordan dribbles, polluted, into the Dead Sea. Here, where farming was born and our Golden Age ended, water stolen from the river drags a ten-thousandth crop from exhausted soil: date palms, dusty citrus, fields of sad onions.

Towse pointed out landmarks in the bright moonlight.

Those lights in the valley ahead of us, off to the left – that's
Jericho, the oldest city in the world . . . And beyond it – that mountain – that's the Mount of Temptation. That's where Satan tried to
get Jesus to defect.

He shook his head.

Now *that* was a fucked-up recruitment. You *never* lead off with
the bribe . . .

There was a junction, a road block, men in camouflage uniforms.
A Humvee sat under an awning, a soldier pointing the machine gun
mounted on its cab.

Another soldier appeared at the driver's window, and one beside
Towse. They shone lights on Aoife, on Towse, on Michael, who
woke. The driver spoke to the soldiers in Arabic. A radio crackled,
the men waved them on.

The Mercedes turned west, off the main highway. There were no
fields here, or fruit trees, just desert scrub, barbed wire, and signs, in
English and Arabic, warning of mines. The car drove under a steel
arch and passed, without slowing, a low, brightly lit terminal building.
Ahead, a line of lamps showed a narrow two-lane blacktop, curving
west through the brush of this forsaken plain. Another Humvee
pulled off the road in front of them, letting them pass. Their car
slowed, stopped.

This is where we get out, Towse said.

The driver pulled a U-turn, drove back the way he'd come.

They were standing on a flat concrete bridge, floodlit from either
end. Before them was a heavy steel gate, concrete blast walls, a

watchtower, and then heaps of broken ground, miniature mesas, the badlands of the valley floor. Beneath the bridge, a stream flowed listless between bullrushes and reeds. It had an estuary smell.

Towse pointed over the parapet.

The River Jordan. The spring where John baptised Jesus is right over there.

He tapped the iron railing.

Allenby Bridge. It closes at night. Best time to cross.

The metal gate slid open and a jeep drove out to meet them. The jeep was brown, armoured, empty apart from the driver. He was balding, like Towse, but short and plump, and when he opened his door, Aoife saw that he wore jeans and sneakers and a grey puffer jacket. She also saw the carbine cradled in his lap. He looked at her and at Michael, then at Towse.

You didn't tell me you had people with you.

He spoke English well, though with an accent.

You can swing it for me, said Towse. I found that thing for you. Remember?

The man jerked a thumb.

OK. Get in. But I don't want any introductions.

Towse opened the back door, showed Aoife and Michael into the jeep. Then he got in the front, turned back to them.

This is Captain Jones, by the way. Jones – meet Rose and John.

The driver, who'd been letting the clutch out, put his foot down again.

Go fuck yourself, Tavass.

Towse grinned at Aoife and Michael.

Tavass is just a nom de guerre, he said.

So is Jones, said their driver. And I'm not a captain anymore, either. I've been promoted.

I know, said Towse. Thanks to me.



JERUSALEM, A SMALL AND unimportant town in every way but one, sits in a notch in the hills between the sea and the Jordan. To the east of the Old City, screening it from the dawn, is the high stony ridge that is called, in many different languages, the Mount of Olives. A neck of land connects it to an even higher northern spur, known for thousands of years – in Canaanite, Hebrew, Coptic, Aramaic, Persian, Greek, Latin, Arabic, Frankish, Turkish and English – by some variation on the same meaning: lookout mountain. In English, we call it Mount Scopus. The Egyptians and Persians camped on its summit, and the Romans and Arabs and Crusaders and Turks, then Allenby's army and the Zionist Haganah, to mention a few.

Let's approach Mount Scopus from the east, climbing from the Jordan valley, in a taxi that is driven by a man who is not a taxi driver, whose real name we don't want to know, and who has tucked his M4 carbine between his knee and the door. Let's watch, red in the dawn, the rocky hills on either side of us, the Judaean Desert, God's abandoned building site, ugly as mine spoil, with stony tracks to the left and right, disappearing into badlands of hillocks and ravines, leading to military firing ranges, to Bedouin villages condemned to demolition, and to hilltop trailers from which the latest brood of cyclical fanatics, like the zealots and anchorites and stylites who preceded them, look down on the world in fear and contempt.

Now the summit of Mount Scopus looms over our taxi. From its crest, Ofrit Camp, an Israeli army listening post, squints into the dawn with its parabolic dishes, towards Jordan, Syria, Iraq and, beyond that, Iran. For twenty years after 1948 the summit of Mount Scopus, containing the Hebrew University and the Hadassah Hospital, was a besieged Israeli enclave in Jordanian-held territory. After the 1967 war, when Israel seized everything west of the Jordan, it built Ofrit Camp outside the boundary of that former enclave, in what was now the occupied West Bank. Jerusalem itself, then and now, is a disputed city under international law, officially belonging to no one, yet. So Ofrit is nested in several ambiguities, not entirely anywhere, a black hole on the hillside, sucking in data, emitting no light. Its military staff handles cyberwar, signals intelligence, online surveillance, stuff like that. There are other people on site too, unacknowledged – American staffers from the No Such Agency, the Never Say Anything, the Maryland Corporation. They, more than anyone, aren't really here.

Look up at Ofrit's eyes and ears, at those graceful steel bowls in which dawn is reflected, at gantries and antennae, black against the morning sky. And now our taxi disappears into the road tunnel, brightly lit, that takes Route 1 under Mount Scopus. When it emerges, two minutes later, we're in modern Jerusalem, with its early-morning cars.

\*

I'LL HAVE TO LET you out here, said the man who wasn't a captain and wasn't called Jones. I'll get the thing from Ofrit and come back for you.

They were on the southernmost curve of the road that loops around the top of Mount Scopus. To the north rose a sheer retaining wall, and, above that again, the yellow stone blocks of the Hebrew University. To the south, a stand of conifers and bay trees, grit scattered with pine cones, and then the steep drop into Wadi al-Joz.

Pull over, said Towse. We'll wait for you here.

Jones reached into the glovebox, pulled out an ID attached to a lanyard, hung it round his neck. He left the back, which was blank, facing outward.

I'll be about twenty minutes.

They stood, orphaned, in the fresh morning air. It was the first time in days that Aoife had felt cold. She rather liked it. Towse led them across the pavement, through a gap in a low wall and into the trees, where it smelled of pine needles and rosemary. The hillside fell away before them. The Old City of Jerusalem was spread out below.

Who is that guy, Towse?

Someone who owes me a favour. I helped him find something that he'd lost.

Towse smirked to himself, then recalled where he was.

That doesn't matter. While we're up here, let me show you the view.

Towse waved his left arm.

Over there is the famous Mount of Olives. Those white arches you see are the Mormon University. The Mormons get to have a whole college in Jerusalem, but my Raëlian pals can't have one little alien embassy. Fucking Abrahamic bias . . . I wouldn't mind, but Abraham was an alien too . . .

He moved his hand to the right.

Over there, that tower on the hill is the Chapel of the Ascension. That's the exact spot where Jesus ascended into heaven. Assuming that Jesus was Russian Orthodox . . .

He lit a cigarette, puffed, exhaled, coughed, recommenced. He sounded bored.

Beyond that is the Jewish cemetery on the Mount of Olives. If you can get yourself a grave there, you have a ringside seat at doomsday. Because down there, beneath the cemetery, between the Mount of Olives and the Old City, is the Valley of Jehoshaphat. That's where God will assemble and judge all the nations of the earth. Good luck with that, nations of the earth.

He moved his hand south.

That big yellow thing is the Temple Mount, the Dome of the Rock, Mosque of Omar, Haram esh-Sharif, whatever you want to call it yourself. The Western Wall is beyond it, but you can't see it from here. Then there's the Church of the Holy Sepulchre, which they'll tell you is built on the hill of Golgotha. And that, down there, is the Damascus Gate – I like the Damascus Gate, because it really is a gate, and it does face Damascus . . . Beyond the Old City, in that falling ground, is the Wadi Nar, the valley of fire. It runs east, past Bethlehem, down to the Dead Sea. And just down there to the right, where that tram is running, is the old Green Line between East and West Jerusalem. The Green Line doesn't exist anymore. Unless you happen to be an Arab.

You don't seem to like this place much, said Michael.

I spent a lot of time here.

He pointed at the road beside them. Cars sighed past at intervals – early birds, heading to work.

This road, here, is called Martin Buber Street. Buber was an existentialist philosopher. But a religious existentialist, not the fun kind. He used to teach here.

Are *you* the fun kind of existentialist, Towse?

I'd like to think so, Aoife.

He pointed at the sheer, fortress-like buildings of the university.

I used to do research here, if that's what you can call it. For my war games. I worked mostly in the university, but I also had an arrangement with the Israeli army. Sometimes I'd pop across the road to Ofrit, to use their mainframes. And sometimes I'd go for walks around Mount Scopus, to remind myself what the world looks like in analogue.

He raised two fingers.

I used to walk around Mount Scopus twice, a mile and a half in each direction. Ideally, I'd have preferred to go around three times – I don't like even numbers – but twice one-point-five is three miles, and that's an odd number, and also a good distance to walk. It took me an hour. I don't like to walk fast . . .

You don't seem to like to do anything fast, Towse.

One time, my head was particularly fuzzy. I'd been up here on the mountain for seven days straight, working on an especially difficult problem. Free will, as it happens. I needed a break. So I walked twice around the mountain. But this time I didn't stop at two laps – because my answer had just come to me, on the second lap. And I'd also just realised that I was going to leave this city. I'd learned all I could from Jerusalem. So I decided to walk round again, for one last look at the view. Three times around Mount Scopus. I didn't think I'd ever be back.

He pulled a face.

Providence has decided otherwise. I fucking hate providence . . . Anyway, the third time, when I got back here, there was someone waiting for me, right here, sitting on my favourite rock.

Jesus Christ, Towse. Just tell us who it was.

He was a young guy, early thirties, in civilian clothes. He said he was American, like me.

So you really *are* American?

Of course I'm American! . . . As well as all the other things. Who the fuck wouldn't be American? . . . Anyway, his name was Campbell Fess.

He left the name hanging there. It was Aoife who spoke next.

*Fess* worked for Israeli intelligence? It doesn't say *that* on his résumé.

He didn't. He worked for the National Security Agency. It doesn't say that on anyone's résumé . . . He'd just been sent here from Maryland to work on a joint project. Very, very secret. And he wanted my help.

How did he know who you were?

I had a reputation.

I'll bet you're not going to tell us what that project was.

Wrong again, Aoife. You ever hear of Stuxnet?

Michael spoke up:

It's a computer virus that the Americans and Israelis made between them. We were taught about it in university. It attacked the computer systems for Iran's nuclear programme. The Iranians had built centrifuges for refining uranium, potentially to weapons grade. Stuxnet made the centrifuges run at uneven speeds, until the stresses tore them apart.

Correct, said Towse. Stuxnet was derived from the project that Fess came here to work on. He was part of the NSA's joint cyberwar team with the Israelis, although he wasn't particularly high in the pecking order. More of a gopher for the real engineers. But he'd heard I'd written some personal spyware that I was using for my war games. Sneak and peek stuff. He figured that if he could get access to my code, it could take him to the top.

You didn't help him, did you?

We shook hands on it, right here.

But what was in it for you?

Nothing, really . . . I just wanted to see what would happen next. You have to dabble in empiricism, every now and then, if you want to stay in touch with reality. I still believe there's a reality, by the way. I'm very old-fashioned like that.

What about the truth, Towse? Do you believe in that?

Of course I do, Aoife! I may tell lots of lies, but I know when I'm doing it . . . Anyway, Fess asked me if he could use my stuff, just for surveillance. No one would get hurt. No innocent victims. And he wouldn't share it. It would just be between us.

Aoife and Michael looked at each other.

You didn't actually believe him, did you?

Fuck no. I figured he'd break his word, first chance he got.

And yet you let him do it?

I had to give him the chance. I'd just decided that I believe in free will.

Wow . . . So, what happened then?

With a lot of help from the Israelis, he began modifying one of my tools to take a weaponised payload. It eventually became Stuxnet. The rest of my stuff he kept for himself. It's what made him who he is.

He ripped you off.

Not really. I wasn't going to use it. I don't care about money.

Jesus . . . What did you do next?

Like I said, I left Jerusalem. Too many religions in too small a place. I wanted to go somewhere more innocent. Where everyone worships at the same shrine. So I went to work in Wall Street as a quantitative analyst.

You just said you didn't care about money!

I don't, Michael. But I crave information, and Wall Street gives its quants all the data in the world.

So that explains the suit, said Aoife.

I was wearing it the day Alice sent me her first chunk of raw data from Inscape's dark pool. Three hours later, a bunch of vans pulled up outside my hedge fund. Blacked-out windows. Maryland plates. My own goddamn people. I saw them a mile away. Lucky for me, I was coming back from a stroll. Providence again. So I turned and ran, and I've been running ever since . . . Look, here comes our friend.

The white taxi pulled up beside them.

Get in, said the man who wasn't called Jones. I'll take you somewhere to rest and clean up. I can give you a few hours, then we have to move on.

You got it? asked Towse.

Not Jones handed him a thumb drive.


THE TAXI LEFT JERUSALEM in the early hours of the morning, descending a steep, narrow road through round, stony hills, past olive groves and pine woods, down to the coastal plain.

It drove, without stopping, through a military checkpoint; Aoife guessed that they had re-entered the West Bank. She sat in the back, her head resting on the window pane, and saw, at intervals, the concrete obstacles that denied the use of this road to the villagers on whose land it was built. Old Mercedes taxis, yellow, with green Palestinian plates, waited for custom beyond bulldozed barricades, sidelights glowing in the mist. Men stood in groups by the roadside, smoking, hoping for a day's illegal labour in the cities of the coast.

The car slowed, stopped. A torch shone in Aoife's face. She glimpsed sandbags, a parked jeep, concrete bollards, the dark green uniforms of the border police. The torch beam found Michael. An angry voice spoke in the dark. Not Jones rolled down his window, answered the border policeman in Hebrew.

Towse turned to Michael.

He reckons you look like an Arab. This road's in the West Bank, but Palestinians aren't allowed to use it. He's saying he wants to see your ID.

You know I don't have one.

Not Jones was talking again. He opened the glovebox, took out three passports, gave them to the border policeman. Then he reached inside his shirt, fished out his lanyard. The passports, unopened, came back through the window. The policeman waved them on. Towse handed the three passports into the back.

This is who we are now.

Michael saw harps on the front of the passports. He opened his.

We're Irish now? My name is Sean Sherrard?

Irish passports are popular with criminals and spooks. Good for getting into Britain, good for travelling in Europe. Mossad has a bank of stolen Irish identities. They won't miss these three.

The car passed a sign with the outline of a plane on it.

We're going to the airport?

Not Jones laughed.

Ben Gurion? You must be joking. That's the most closely watched place on earth.

So where are we going, then?

To the second most closely—

To Egypt, said Towse. We'll be in Alexandria tomorrow night.

NOT JONES DROPPED THEM at an all-night petrol station and drove off in his taxi. They bought coffee and doughnuts, and ate them outside in the cold. There was a heavy fog, a smell of the sea. Young army conscripts, off duty, sat on benches on the forecourt, drank coffee and smoked, looking at their phones, too cold and too tired to talk. The fog drifted through the arc lights that corralled the darkness, a theatrical flourish that Aoife quite liked. When Not Jones came back, he was in another military jeep, driven by a much larger man in a green army parka, no beret or hat. He had the face of a boxer who takes a lot of punches just to tire out his foe. Aoife recognised the type. They work in soundproof basements, in cells with doors that lock from the inside.

Towse looked at this ugly giant, didn't offer his hand.

Abu Isa. You're still working in the zone, then.

He's getting you across the fence, said Not Jones. That's one of the things he still does.

There wasn't much room for three in the back of the jeep. It bounced and rocked, in the dark and the fog, down a farm road, unpaved, through fields of winter wheat. Another checkpoint, a cluster of houses and farm buildings, unlit, in trees to the left, then a glow in the fog up ahead. The jeep stopped.

Here, said the driver.

He switched off the engine, killed the lights. They got out, felt their shoes crunch on gravel. A mound of bulldozed dirt blocked the track. Beyond it was a line of lights attached to wooden poles, dimmed by the fog.

Abu Isa took a rifle from somewhere at his feet and led the way across the berm. There was a bare strip of sand. Lamplight shone in the droplets condensed on the strands of an eight-foot electrified fence. The top of the fence, coiled with razors, bent out into the fog. A scrap of red cotton hung from one barb.

Abu Isa walked towards the rag. They followed. The ground was smooth sand, scored with shallow grooves parallel to the fence. The border patrols must drag a chain behind their jeeps, thought Aoife, so intruders' footsteps will leave a tell-tale trail.

Abu Isa arrived at the scrap of cotton, reached up with both hands. The razor wire came apart easily, already cut. He pulled the coils aside, turned back to them, waiting.

Not Jones looked at his watch.

You have three minutes. Then the fence goes live again. That's all I can do for you. And Tavass – we're even, now. I don't want to hear about that washing machine again.

OK. We're even . . . Abu Isa – please, give me a leg-up.

Towse went over the wire, dropped, swore. Aoife followed unaided, then stopped, waiting for Michael. Towse had already moved away into the fog. Michael landed beside her. When she looked back, Not Jones and his sidekick had gone. The wire was back as it had been before, but the red shred of cotton was no longer there. Beyond the fence, in the east, the sky was turning pale.

Come on, whispered Towse, somewhere in front of them. The sun will be up soon. And these coastal fogs can lift pretty quick.

They stumbled on a few yards and found Towse, leaning against the shattered trunk of an olive tree. The soil here had once been tilled, but now it was abandoned to weeds and windblown garbage. The fog was thinning. Aoife could see shapes in the west, broken buildings adrift in the mist. A shattered streetscape, a blacked-out city, crafted by bombardment. Now she knew where they were.

That's Gaza City! Are you crazy, Towse?

No.

You said we were going to Egypt!

We are — via the Gaza Strip.

If the Israelis see us sneaking around their fence, they'll blow us to froth! And what about the locals? Hamas? What if they find us first?

Keep your voice down. Look — someone's coming.

A pair of headlights detached themselves from the rubble at the edge of the city, a couple of kilometres away, drove towards them, stopped. The lights went out, came on again, repeated their signal twice more. Towse took out a flashlight, returned the signal. Aoife watched him, aghast.

Who the hell is that?

Hamas.

Aoife grabbed Michael's arm, pulled him back towards the fence. Come on, Michael. We'll take our chances with the Israelis.

Towse called after them.

That window's already closed, Aoife. Touch that fence and you'll light up the surveillance screens. You know what that means.

At least it would be quick.

These guys are *Hamas*, Aoife. Not Al-Qaeda or ISIS. Say what you like about your old-school Muslim Brotherhood, they know how to network. And they usually stick to their deals.

He set off towards the headlights.

Come on. It's twenty miles to the Egyptian border at Rafah. I've booked us a tunnel, and paid off the Egyptians, but it's better to go before it's full light.

WHAT IS RESUMED IN the word Alexandria? It's a duller city now than it was in Durrell's time. Then, its thousand dust-blown streets were home to five races, five languages, a dozen creeds. Five fleets rode at anchor in its greasy harbour. If the old Alex could not, in the end, hide Justine and Darley (except, alas, from each other), can this new one yet shelter two uncertain lovers? Its population has grown since that war in the desert, but the Turks are gone, and the Jews and Circassians, the Venetian merchants, the British and French, and little remains of that Levantine ferment, the winepress of love.

We did not, you may have noticed, include the Greeks in that list of post-war departures. The Greeks, who built this city in the first place, maintain a bridgehead, a strategic outpost, on the beach in the old harbour, the place where their forebears first came ashore.

There, the Greek Club of Alexandria takes a long view of history. Its terrace bar looks, to the east, over the Citadel of Qaitbay, where the Pharos lighthouse once stood, and across the eastern harbour, where several older Alexandrias, drowned by earthquakes and erosion, lie buried in the silt. To the south, Cavafy's city still crowds the corniche, its spidery buildings, concrete colonial, held together by grime, the soot from a million deadbeat carburettors. To the west is the Alexandria sailing club, and a flotilla of fishing skiffs and pleasure craft, their numbers diminished in this late winter season, bobbing in the slop from the gusting northwester, that cold visitor from Europe, that sends Vs of unrest through the gaps in the mole, and drives the rain and the spray that beat on the windows, there at the back of the Greek Club, where, in lazier times, members could sleep off their lunches in rooms that faced northward, towards the home islands, but which are now shut away, used mainly for storage.

Except for this one room, under the roof of the square, yellow building, its window obscured by the brutalist colonnade. Reached by a stair full of junk and old furniture, this room – red tiled floor, whitewashed plaster, high stucco ceiling, with a rotary fan that doesn't work, but isn't needed in this winter weather – is empty apart from three metal beds. Two, unmade, have been pushed together in one corner, away from the draughts that gust through loose windows. The other bed, with sheets but no blankets, stands by itself against the far wall. Towse hasn't used it. He's been gone for three days, leaving Aoife and Michael alone in this hideout, where they wait for him together, with a broken metal dining chair, scavenged from the hallway, jammed under the door handle. They don't know when Towse will come back, or when the Greek concierge, who wears a black dress but is, disappointingly, neither old nor disapproving, will sneak them their next meal. And they don't want to be interrupted when they are distracted.

This time, it had been Michael's idea, more or less. Until then, neither had mentioned what had happened between them in Gulu, and Aoife for one would have left it at that. She hadn't known, until it happened, that she'd wanted it to happen, but it seemed to her that she had, and she wasn't going to let herself feel bad about it afterwards. She liked to think she was pragmatic; it had been good for her at the time, and he'd seemed to enjoy it. And if he felt any guilt, on his own account, or because of Alice, he had the manners not to let it show. Aoife admired that. She had manners of her own.

But Towse had left them at the door of this room, the evening they arrived in Alexandria, saying he had business in the city, and might not be back until the next day, or the day after, and Aoife, who had gone to look out of the window, across the breakwater to the wild sea beyond, silver and pink in the storm and the sunset, had been startled by a scraping sound behind her, metal on tiles. Turning, she saw Michael in the middle of the room, caught in the act of pushing the centre-most bed, as if testing its weight. It must have been lighter than he'd thought, and skidded loudly across the tiles. He straightened slowly, looking back at her. It was the first time they'd been left alone together, in private, since that night in Uganda. Funny, she'd thought. He doesn't seem embarrassed. Or expectant. But he's right; there would be no alcohol to ease a second transition, no adrenaline, no exhaustion, no easy words. They only had the light from the sunset, which picked out his face but left hers in shadow. If they were going to do this again, it would have to be matter-of-fact.

Go on, Aoife said. Push it against that bed in that corner . . . We could be here for a while.

And she had crossed the room to join him.

Towse, wherever he is, has since sent them some books – stolen, he claimed in a note, from the club's informal library. But Aoife has reason to doubt this. Towse was too on the nose with his choices, as if he'd found his books with a search engine, based on their subjects, but hadn't read them himself. Lawrence Durrell was a bit bloody obvious . . . Next, *Slow Learner*, paired with an 1899 Baedeker guide to Egypt. Towse must have looked up Alexandria on one of his burner phones, or the catalogue of some bookstore, and these titles had come up. Maybe he didn't understand, as Aoife did, that fictions are also a kind of war game, models that run in the mind of the reader, designed to compute not so much what might happen as how it might feel.

Then again, maybe he did understand that. The edition of the *Alexandria Quartet* that he gave them contained all four books in one volume. So they had to take it in turns to read *Justine* to each other, lying together on the two kissing beds. It was another way to pass the time.

Towse had never asked them to shake hands with him. No spitting in palms, no devil's bargain. He was fair to them like that, careful to leave them their freedom. But it was only their freedom from him, and not from each other.

The room was unheated. On their third night together, the coldest one yet, they took the blankets from Towse's bed and added them to their own, laying them sidewise, to cover the gaps between the two beds, sharing their warmth. The wind, unabated, tugged at windows, uncurtained, which let in light from the cars that passed on the breakwater. The lights rose and fell like waves, high on the wall. If only, thought Aoife, there was still a lighthouse. How unlike Towse, who had conjured this scene for them, not to have thought of a pharos, here, of all places.

Beside her, Michael reached to the floor, retrieved a pack of cigarettes. He was smoking now, too, though he said he disliked it.

He took out two cigarettes, passed one to her, picked up a lighter. His other arm was around her bare shoulders, keeping them warm.

I want to give Towse the slip, he said.

Why?

She did too. But she wanted to hear him say it.

I still don't know who he is. And I still don't know what he wants from me.

She turned to him, slid a leg over his. Her movement disturbed the carefully nested blankets, letting in cold air. She shivered against him.

I don't know why he wants you either.

Don't you?

She slid her leg off him.

What do you mean by that?

He sent you to get me, in Palo Alto. I don't believe his story about promising Alice to take care of me.

I don't know any more than you do, Michael.

You know who you really are. I don't. You never told me. You said it would be unprofessional.

She smoked for a while, staring up at the ceiling, at the lights from the passing traffic. She had done this as a girl, in the deep Irish countryside. There, the lights came less often. She had always been alone.

She tossed the stub of her cigarette at the ashtray. This time, she missed.

My name is Aoife Caoilfhionn McCoy. I grew up near a small country town in Ireland. Kildare. After college, I joined the police. But not the police in the south, where I come from. The police in Northern Ireland. It's different up there. They still have terrorists. Not like before, in the Troubles, but plenty of gangsters and wannabes. If you're police, and they find out who you are, they might come after you where you live. So I kept my job secret from my friends in the south. Even from my parents. They wouldn't have approved, anyway. They never did . . . I suppose the secrecy was part of the adventure for me. And not long after I joined the police I got headhunted by intelligence. I had a gift, apparently. I thought, this probably isn't for me, and I'm not even British, but I'll do a couple of years, have some adventures, see some stuff that most people don't see, then leave, go back to a normal life.

Did you?

What?

Leave.

I'm here now, amn't I?

How do I know you're not still working for the British government? One of their agencies?

I used to. But I promise you, I don't now.

I promise you. That's what Towse always says. How do I know you're not with me for his sake, to keep me around?

She pulled away from him, wrapped her own blanket around her.

You don't. The same way that I don't know if you're thinking of Alice while you're fucking me.

I wouldn't do that.

And I wouldn't care.

Michael said nothing for a while. Finally, he spoke again:

I'm sorry.

She didn't answer. Michael tried to change the subject.

My guess is he's taking us to Europe. Irish passports are EU passports. Once you're in, you can go wherever you like.

No shit, Michael. That's really clever of you.

He tried again.

If we were in Europe, we wouldn't need Towse anymore. We could strike out for ourselves.

That's right, Michael. We could do that . . . I could go one way, and you could go the other.

It was his turn to fall silent. After a while, he leaned out of the bed, picked up the pack of cigarettes. He offered her one. She shook her head.

For someone who doesn't smoke, she said, you're smoking a lot.

He put a cigarette in his mouth and lit it, lay back on the pillow.

I don't like the taste, he said. But if I smoke them myself, I won't taste them off you.

She had to flip that around in her head a couple of times before she could see it clearly. Then, carefully, so as not to dislodge the blankets, she slid across the draughty gap between the beds. She arranged herself, prone, along the length of his body, tucked the blanket in around them. When she raised her head, their bodies were pushed even closer together. He was looking up at her. But is it too close for him to focus on my face, she wondered? Could I be someone else?

She straddled him, sat back, letting the blankets fall away. She didn't care about the cold. She wanted him to see her clearly.

Give me a drag on that, she said.


THEY WERE AWAKE, ONLY just, tangled together, when they heard something bang in the stairwell, a curse, feet shuffling, then a knock at the door. Someone tried the handle before either could answer. Checked by the chair wedged underneath, the lever went back to horizontal, then jiggled furiously. The chair, dislodged, tipped backwards on the floor. The door, bursting open, sent it sliding across the tiles.

You really thought that old trick would keep someone out?

They didn't bother to rearrange themselves. Towse seemed to take them for granted, just as they were.

We didn't know if you'd knock, said Aoife.

I did knock. What am I, some kind of savage?

We also didn't know if you'd wait for an answer. We do now.

Yeah? Well, that's because I'm in a hurry. Get dressed. We're moving on tonight. I've found us a boat.

He was still in the same old suit. But now it was soaked, stinking of salt water. His shoes were caked in wet sand.

It's blowing a storm out there, Towse.

So no one will see us.

It's three in the morning.

Best time to leave.

We're not getting into another stinking barge with you, said Michael. We nearly died last time.

Here.

Towse tossed a box on the bed.

Dramamine. But I don't think you're going to need it. I got us a pretty sweet ride, this time. And it's only a short row offshore.

# Part Five:

*Wine Dark Sea*

THEIR NEW BOAT WAS a hundred-foot luxury motor yacht, with the name *Penelope* painted on the stern. The Egyptian flag flew on the ensign-staff, but the crew spoke to Towse, and each other, in Russian, Ukrainian, something Slavic like that. They didn't talk to Aoife or Michael at all.

The skipper was the youngest of the three crew men, with bright blond hair and rather more muscle than his job would seem to require. He gave Aoife and Michael a stateroom with a vast double bed. There was also a Jacuzzi – though empty, and covered – and a large en-suite bathroom with gold fittings and taps. Two lines of paintings – expensively abstract – lined either wall, matching the scheme of eggshell and blue. It had a cold look, but was heated, so they took off their wet clothes and got into bed. Towse was right: the boat was well stabilised, and, after some pitching and rolling at the mouth of the harbour, the engine note deepened and the boat levelled out. But by then, too tired to care, Aoife and Michael were already asleep.

THE STORM BLEW ITSELF out the first morning, and from then on they motored westward through bright windy days and cold moonless nights. Towse was always on the bridge, his laptop plugged into the satellite system. He nested in a corner, where a GPS repeater showed their progress across the Mediterranean.

The skipper and his two crew took turns at the wheel, watching the machine that did the real steering, that laid a white carpet, ruler straight, behind the boat. They passed tanker ships and container vessels, whose bow waves sent them pitching and bobbing, and they saw fishing fleets at night, lights mirrored in black water, but never any land. The sky hung, equidistant, its horizons unbroken. Three days and nights, born in their wake, passed smoothly along the length of the hull before drowning themselves in the west. Cut off from the world for weeks already, deprived of news and everyday lives, Aoife and Michael allowed their timeline to slide.

The boat had a well-equipped galley with hardly any food in it. The Russians, Ukrainians, whoever they were, had stocked one of the freezers with hamburgers, fish sticks, shrimp and oven chips. A fridge contained two cases of beer, three cases of vodka, and a couple of cucumbers, dissolving to slime. On the second day, Aoife counted the bottles of vodka and decided the crew wouldn't miss one or two. If they did, she was prepared to stand over her crime. She had run out of cigarettes, and she had to fill the void with other compulsive behaviours, most of them with Michael. It was something to do when not walking the deck.

ON THE MORNING OF the fourth day, climbing up to the bridge, Aoife felt the wind move on to her left cheek. The boat wallowed in a cross sea, climbed out, found its footing again. She opened the door to the bridge.

We've just turned north, she said to Towse.

He pointed at the GPS repeater. Bright contours of land filled the edge of the screen.

Sardinia, he said. We'll skirt it today, then on past Corsica.

So we're going to France.

Antibes.

Isn't it out of season?

Our skipper has business there.

What is his business?

He's a smuggler.

Guns, people or drugs?

Boats.

A shadow moved past the window. Michael stood out on the bridge wing, looking out to sea. He might come in at any moment. Aoife decided to press Towse while they were alone. He might still think that Aoife was on his side, not Michael's.

What do we do when we get to France?

What you and Michael were planning to do. We split up.

You were listening to us. Back in Alexandria.

No. I saw it coming. It's an obvious play.

Is that what you planned, then? You drag us halfway round the planet, just to dump us in Europe?

I'm not dumping you. I'm giving you a chance to decide for yourselves if you want to stick with me. In Europe, you'll be fine without me, so you'll have a choice. Like I said before, I believe in free will.

You won't even tell us your plans.

That thumb drive that we picked up in Jerusalem. It contains a weapon. If money is a virus, then a virus can destroy it. And as it happens, the best place to launch my attack is in Dublin. Which is your old town.

She thought back to their first meeting in London, the day she'd been tricked into helping to abduct the whistle-blower. How had she not seen this before?

I don't know how you did it, she said, stepping closer to him, but it was you who got Irene to hire me. You were already watching me. You dragged me into this on purpose.

I needed your help. I heard you were good. And you know your way around Ireland.

I was happy before this, Towse. I had my own life.

You weren't and you didn't.

Go fuck yourself, Towse. I won't do anything more for you.

He gestured at the window.

What if Michael wants to come with me?

He's the one who wanted to give you the slip. He said it before I did.

Really? . . . Good. He's learning.

The door opened. Michael came in.

We've changed course, he said. We're sailing north.

To France, Towse told him. And when we get there, we'll split up.

Michael looked at Aoife.

I trusted you. You shouldn't have told him.

I didn't. He guessed.

We're going to split up, continued Towse. I have things I need to do on my own for a few days. If you want, you can rejoin me later. In Dublin. Separately or together, that's up to you. But first, let me buy you dinner in Antibes. I promise you, Michael, it'll be worth your while.


THEY ARRIVED IN ANTIBES late on a blustery evening, berthing under the bastions of the Fort Carré. The Port Vauban marina was, as Aoife had guessed, very out of season. Boats too big to haul out for the winter, which was most of them, were made fast to pontoons, their windows and hatches shrouded in canvas, decks caked in red mud from the last Saharan dust storm. The police and customs, having little else to do at this time of year, boarded their boat as soon as it docked, searched it thoroughly, looked at their passports, then let them ashore. Some of the officials wore medical face masks, which made no sense to Michael or Aoife, unless they were frightened of African dust.

A taxi drove them to a cafe on the edge of town. It was out by the autoroute, where the Esterel ridge rises over the coast. When the wind dropped, which wasn't often, they could hear cars and trucks moaning past in the night.

The cafe, set at the corner of a street of shabby houses, didn't look much from the outside. From the inside, not much more. The decor was dingy generic Mediterranean – chequered tablecloths, red velour walls, sentimental landscapes. A fishing net, full of champagne corks that had surely not been popped in a cheap joint like this, hung over a bar stocked with sad, dusty bottles. There were no other customers: the place appeared to be closed for the winter.

Their waiter, a small, brisk man in his sixties, seemed to be the owner as well. He showed them a booth, gave them three tumblers and a red vin de table, and disappeared into the kitchen.

I thought you were treating us, said Aoife. Why this dump?

The owner used to be in the French Foreign Legion. They have their own thing.

The owner came back from the kitchen, balancing three plates. He swept them on to the table with a flourish of contempt.

Egg, beans, sausage and chips.

He spoke English with a strong German accent. Aoife and Michael looked at their food.

Don't you have anything else? asked Aoife. We've been eating crap for a week.

That's what all the English ask for: egg, beans, sausage and chips.

We're not English, said Michael.

My passport says I'm French. You're English tonight.

The owner cocked his head towards the bar.

You want more wine, help yourselves.

He went back into the kitchen. The food wasn't good, but they ate it all anyway. The bottle was emptied, another one opened. Towse pushed his plate away, took out his cigarettes. A sign on the wall said *Défense de Fumer*, but none of them had admitted to knowing any French. Besides, cigarillo smoke seeped under the door from the kitchen, where a soccer game played, too loud, on TV.

Our friend in there, began Towse, is holding some cash for me. I'll give you a share and then we'll split up. But before we do – he raised his glass – I have to thank you both for all that you've done for me. A toast: until we meet again.

He held his glass out to them, expectant. Michael sat back, saying nothing. Aoife sipped, put her own glass back down.

You still want something from us, she said. Why don't you just tell us what it is?

Towse studied the chequered tablecloth. It resembled a chessboard, except with red and white squares. He moved his glass carefully into a white square.

We split up tonight, he repeated. I'm getting a ride to where I have to go next. Tomorrow, you can go your own way. Alone or together, that's up to you. But I'm going on to Ireland. If you want to help me finish this, meet me in Dublin. You have until Friday next week. March 13th. That's when I have to do it.

Why would we want to help you? Michael asked.

Towse struck a match. Here it comes, thought Aoife.

Let me tell you a story, Towse said.

SAMVEL AND NADIA WERE lying together, naked apart from their lab coats, in his uncle's apartment in Urmia, north-western Iran, when the men from the ministry came.

If Nadia had not been there, at that particular time, on that particular afternoon, maybe she would never have been in this story. Left to themselves, she and Samvel would probably have continued their thing a while longer, grown bored with each other, had a row and moved on. They had, as far as we can tell from the interrogations of their friends, no plans at that point to get married. They were in love, of course, but they were also young. They came from different backgrounds, were different people, going different places. Life is crowded at that age. It's easy, then, to lose sight of good people. It's only much later that you start seeing them again, glimpses of faces in other crowds, or on ceilings at night, still the same age as when you were with them.

So most likely, Nadia and Samvel would have slowly grown apart, then gone different places in search of their lives. Most likely, Michael would not have been born.

But Nadia happened to be there when the men from the Ministry of Intelligence came. So she was also arrested and taken to a basement cell, where she, like Samvel, in a cell just down the corridor, was beaten and tortured. She, like him, quickly confessed to all the charges laid against her, whatever they might be.

During this time they were held apart. They were each told how their lover was ratting them out for terrible treasons, and they were each invited to reciprocate, which they both did. But, though they did their best to please their torturers, neither could reveal any useful new information. Their interrogators put this down to their loyalty to the foreign agency they worked for. There was no chance that they were innocent, that they knew nothing at all.

Nadia didn't know anything, of course. Neither did Samvel. Their innocence was so complete that it confirmed suspicions. So there was little surprise at the ministry, or the Revolutionary Guard, when, a year after their old lives had ended, an overseas go-between made contact with an offer. An Iranian asset had been caught doing something he shouldn't in Britain. Perhaps the ministry would like to swap him for a certain pair of jailed American agents? You've squeezed everything out of them. We're finished with your guy. Now that we're both done, let's look after our people.

They didn't recognise each other at first, in the back of that windowless van, bumping through the valleys of the Zagros Mountains, where Nadia was born, through the poplars and aspens which she couldn't see now, and would never see again. And even when they each realised the identity of that other prisoner, beaten and starved, they hid at opposite ends of the van, keeping their escorts between them. They weren't the same careless people who'd made love in white coats on hot afternoons. They'd been driven a long way inside themselves, acquired the instinct to hide. Anything you said would be used, horribly, against you. Better to never talk to anyone again.

And each of them was reasonably sure of only two things: that they'd done nothing to deserve this thing that had happened, and that it must therefore be the other one's fault.

So they said nothing to each other, or to anyone else, when they were taken from the van and found themselves, blinking, on the side of a mountain, brown rocks, green grass, streaks of melting snow. The van had stopped on a rough track, just short of a ridge line. Up on the ridge was an American pickup with Iraqi plates. Beside it, armed men wore camouflage and Kurdish scarves, but none of them was a Kurd.

Nadia and Samvel were ordered to walk towards these strangers. They went slowly, heads bowed, not daring to look up, not wanting to look back.

The extraction team drove them to the airport at Erbil, in Iraqi Kurdistan, and put them on a military transport. No one bothered to talk to them. They were treated like freight.

It became clear to them, once they reached America, that they were to act as if they were still a couple, however they felt about that themselves. At their point of arrival, a military base the name of which they never knew, they were given a room with one bed to share. Both slept on the floor, in opposite corners. It was what they'd been used to in jail. Their new papers, the names assigned to them, assumed that they were man and wife. They were given new clothes, some money, a few lessons in basic English, and then flown to Minnesota. There, they were told to live quietly, keep to themselves. Iran has a long reach, they were told, incorrectly. If you tell anyone your story, they can find you, even here.

They were left there, alone together, in a flat winter waste. They didn't even know which agency owned them. They hadn't been debriefed. No one cared what they knew, or didn't know, and no one cared what they did with the rest of their lives, so long as they did it in secret. What choice did they have but to stay together, however much they hated each other at first?

Their new home was a trailer on the edge of a small town in the heart of the prairie. They looked at the flat horizon, saw their deaths in the snow. Anything could happen to them here, and who would know or care? They were to sit here and wait, but wait for what?

On their third night in their new home they left their fake IDs on the kitchenette table and walked out into a blizzard. They didn't have a car, or winter coats or shoes. It was presumed that they hadn't got far.

WHY THEM?

Michael stared at the cigarette held in his hand. The tip had almost burned down to his knuckles. Towse took the cigarette, stubbed it out.

Stuxnet. To see if it would work, they had to introduce a test version into Iran's nuclear systems, a dummy run. But this was back in the nineties, so it had to be done manually. Your father's physics lab was thought to be a weak point in the Iranian network. But the Iranians still detected the attack.

You're saying my parents were foreign agents.

No. But your father's supervisor was. He liked money and underage boys, so he was easily recruited. But when that first scouting attack was detected, Fess needed to protect his agent for a second try.

So they pinned it on my father.

Your father's supervisor chose him. He knew about his affair with your mother. It offended his principles.

You said he was a paedophile.

Sure, but he was very devout. And he didn't like people from other religions. Your father was an Armenian Christian.

A Christian who was having an affair with a Muslim?

Your mother wasn't Muslim either. She was a Yazidi.

What's that?

An ancient people from the Zagros. Some call them devil worshippers, although they worship the same god as everyone else. But they venerate one of his angels above all the others. Melek Taus — the Peacock Angel. The only one with the guts to say no to an absurd command.

Beyond the kitchen door, someone scored a goal in the televised football game. The ex-legionnaire spat bitter words in German. Finally, Michael looked up.

Why do you care what happened to my family?

Towse moved his wine glass to a red square on the table.

Fess promised me that no innocent people would be hurt. That was the deal. But your parents were hurt. They were innocent. And I always collect on a deal.

Your stories keep changing, Towse. I thought I was dragged into this because of Alice. Now you say it's because of my parents?

That's the problem, Michael. It's both.


YOU CAN'T DIE ON a public street in Canada and not come to all sorts of attention. Particularly when the police realise that nobody knows who you are. They circulate fingerprints, photographs. Appeals are sent out on the Interpol network. And so, twenty years after they disappeared in a Minnesota blizzard, Nadia and Samvel reappeared on the radar. Not that anyone cared by then. They'd long since served their diversionary purpose. Their death was an accident. The world had moved on.

But they also had a son, just graduating high school. Should they pick him up, see what he knew?

Better to let things stay as they were. From what the RCMP said in their case notes, the kid didn't know who his parents were either. Tipping him off could only bring trouble.


THAT MONEY IN THAT bag, said Michael. The one in Grande Prairie. That was from you.

I felt some responsibility for you, if only second-hand. I paid it off.

But then, years later, your name popped up again. Only now you were living with someone else I knew.

Alice.

Her parents were part of my first private network. Cryptographers and math geeks. Anarchists, a lot of them. We sent messages by snail mail, disguised as moves in correspondence chess. Years later, Alice got in touch with me herself about her own big idea. Yoyodime. It was going to be the antidote to OmniCent, hidden inside it. It was like she was deliberately designing the flaw in the Death Star. But she never got to finish it . . .

He looked at Michael. Michael said nothing. Towse continued:

Anyway . . . she contacted me to say she was worried for herself and her boyfriend. She mentioned your name. And that's when my warning lights started to flash.

It was just a coincidence, Towse.

It wasn't just *one* coincidence, Aoife. It was a bunch of them. Michael was living with Alice. Alice was working for Fess — Fess, who ratted out Michael's parents. And I was connected to all of them separately. There's an old rule of thumb in intelligence: once is happenstance; twice is coincidence; three times or more, it's enemy action.

I've heard that before.

Ian Fleming used it in one of his Bond novels. *Goldfinger*. And Fleming knew what he was talking about. He was in British intelligence during the war. He'd worked in Room 39 at the Admiralty, which was naval intelligence, and Room 40, next door, was the birthplace of signals intelligence, electronic surveillance, electric computers – all the shit that we're living with now.

What about Room 38?

Towse shot up in his chair.

Who told you about Room 38, Aoife?

She hadn't seen Towse look flustered before.

I was joking. I made it up. You were banging on about Room 39, Room 40, Room whatever.

Don't ever joke about Room 38.

He subsided in his chair.

Anyway, third time, it's enemy action. But who was under attack? Me? And who was the attacker? I had no clue. And I hate that.

It was the money, said Michael. It's alive. You already told us that one.

Towse pushed back his chair, went over to the bar, returned with another bottle of wine. He put it down and started walking back and forth.

On one level, yes. But can money shape coincidence? Can it breathe life into matter and move it around? Can it make people fall in love, and raise children, and build a whole world for them? People were doing that long before money showed up. That's what history and science tell us . . . If history and science are real.

There it is, said Aoife heavily. I've been waiting for that one. Metaphysics 101.

Don't mock. You must have heard of the simulation hypothesis? What if we're just software and the universe is a supercomputer?

According to the simulation theory, most of the glitches in our reality —
like crazy coincidences, and dumb luck, and crushing irony, and déjà
vu — are caused by the game looping back on itself, to save on storage
and processing power. That's what Alice thought she saw when she
looked into OmniCent: that money is the source code that powers our
game, a binary based on have and have not, instead of ones and zeros.
I think she couldn't live with that idea. She'd always thought she was
a player, not somebody's bot. She always needed the world to be real.

Michael was silent.

That's all very well, Aoife said. But we want out.

Don't you want to have free will, Aoife?

I want to have the quiet life. Right now, that seems crazy enough.

Towse stopped pacing.

It's not, he said. You could hitchhike from here into Italy, or
Spain. People still hitch in France, you know. You could stay off the
grid, pay for everything in cash. No one will find you. And it won't
be long before they stop looking.

Fess won't give up that easily.

Fess will stop if he catches me. Or if I stop him. One way or the
other, this will end soon. In Dublin, of all the dumb places. That's
where I make my move against OmniCent. It launches next Friday,
in secret, and that's when it will be vulnerable, before it metastasises.
But my odds are much better if I have your help.

Aoife and Michael looked at each other.

It seems to me, said Aoife, that we'd be safer without you. We'll
take our chances on the road.

Alone or together?

They looked at each other again.

Together, said Aoife.

Together? . . . Well, that's something, at least . . .

Towse tore a strip from his cigarette pack, wrote down a number.

That's my contact in Ireland. It's a landline. You might have to call it a few times before someone answers.

We won't be doing that, said Aoife.

But she took the number anyway.

Towse lurched towards the kitchen. Beyond its door, the soccer match had reached a crescendo, the kind of noise you only hear when there's a sending off, or a riot, or a perverse decision by the referee. Towse reached the door, turned back to them.

There's a room for you out back. I left your money there, and some clothes and gear that will suit you for the road. If you change your mind, I'll be in Dublin on Friday next week. That's when I'm going to find out if I'm right about the money. That's when I attack. It has to be there, and then.

We won't be there, said Michael.

Friday next week. Good luck, if such a thing exists.


THE FOLLOWING DAY, THE wind had grown stronger and now carried rain. Aoife and Michael sat on their packs in a petrol-station forecourt on the edge of Golfe-Juan. They were dressed in jeans, scuffed boots, old army jackets – the gear that Towse had arranged for them, to fit their new legend, travelling drop-outs, *sans toit ni loi*. They looked a lot like Alice's parents, in that photo over the bed in Vancouver.

They had bought food in the petrol-station kiosk — a baguette and cheese and ham. Michael was trying to build them a sandwich.

Towse said we should go to Italy or Spain.

Then we go north, said Aoife. To Copenhagen, I think.

Why there?

We'd fit in without being noticed. We could find somewhere there to stay for a bit. Somewhere indoors, until the weather gets warmer.

Paris is on the way. I've never been there.

I have. Too many watchers.

Oh.

She relented.

I suppose it *is* on the way.

She watched him gluing the ham to the bread with smeared Vache Qui Rit, to hold it down in the wind. He spoke again, without looking up from his work.

I've been thinking, Aoife . . . Maybe we shouldn't be doing this.

What?

Maybe we should split up.

Aoife hadn't seen this coming, even though she'd been thinking it herself. Alice, she thought. He hides his guilt well.

Why do you say that, Michael?

Maybe we'd be safer if we went our own ways . . . I'd be all right. I could manage by myself.

Could you?

He looked up at her.

Yes I could, Aoife . . . I learned a few tricks from my parents, you know. I didn't know why we had to live under the radar, but I know how we did it. It's not that hard.

He went back to making the sandwich. And Aoife thought, maybe he's telling the truth. Maybe he does have some game in him. Maybe I should let him go. It was true that if they split up they'd both be harder to track. And she was pretty sure that no one would catch her, if she wasn't encumbered. What Michael was saying made logical sense, especially for Aoife.

And yet she found she didn't want to do it. Not just yet. I must be feeling guilty too, she told herself. I shouldn't have dragged him into this mess, way back in Palo Alto. And I shouldn't have come between him and his Alice. That was low, even if I was just trying to be kind. I should look after him for a little while longer, to make it up to him. He won't know that's why I'm doing it. But it will be.

Aoife considered the immediate problem, came up with a half-lie to solve it.

We can't split up, Michael. I need you.

He was peeling another slice of ham from the packet.

What?

I need you to stay with me. It's not safe for me to travel alone.

I'm pretty sure you could handle yourself.

Maybe. But the secret of defending yourself is not to have to do it in the first place. Travelling alone, looking like this, I'd attract all kinds of creeps. Especially policemen. I'd look a lot less vulnerable as half of a couple. Men would leave me alone.

So you really think we should stay together?

Sure . . . At least for now, until things die down. Then we can go our own ways.

The sandwich was finished, Without saying anything, he tore the baguette in two and handed her half. This breaking of bread was, she realised, their first meal alone together as acknowledged partners. Though what kind of partners, she wasn't sure.

It started to rain properly, slanting out of the north, and Aoife wrapped them both in the old shelter-half that she had for a poncho. The rain pattered on its canvas with a comforting sound.

I get the feeling, said Michael, that Towse isn't finished with us.

We won't make it easy for him . . . The direct road north is through Grenoble. That's how Napoleon went, on his way to Waterloo. So we won't go that way.

Michael took out a map, unfolded it awkwardly. We don't do maps anymore, do we? thought Aoife. We're too used to our phones.

There's another road that goes west and then north, he said. It runs along the Rhône river . . . The N7, it's called.

She took the map from him.

The N7? Really? Is that what they call it?

What's the big deal about that?

I grew up near an N7.

Just another coincidence.

I hope so . . . It's the road we have to take.


AOIFE HAD AN EARLY memory of a line of people, spaced politely apart, by a stand of dark firs on the western edge of Dublin. Newlands Cross. It was where the city began and the N7 ended. The people had cardboard signs for Cork, Kerry and Limerick. Some were young women, travelling alone. One day, when she was much older, passing that same crossroads, she remembered that hitchers had been a thing once, a long time ago, but now they were gone.

Why had people stopped hitching? Why was it no longer done, to ask a stranger to give you a lift, when they were already going your way? Stories of murder and rape, or of drivers ruined by false accusations? Cheaper bus fares? Mobile phones? Ride-share apps? Harder hearts? How had the change revealed itself to those on the roadside? The waits must have grown longer and longer. Who was the last hitcher, and where had they gone? Had they given up and walked off, or waited there stubbornly, for the last free ride to the end of the road?

In France, her new world was chopped into segments that ran at different speeds – the pulse that raced as an approaching car slowed, the smooth rush of the journey, the feeling of loss at the end of the ride, and then, most likely, the long slow trudge through some small town to the next good place for hitching, leaning into their shoulder straps, shopping for food at roadside convenience stores, eating in parking lots, in forgotten corners, then taking out the cardboard sign that said *Paris*, with the flowers that Aoife had drawn in coloured marker, and toeing the white line again.

Golfe-Juan. Fréjus. Aix-en-Provence. She watched the cars and trucks escape the gravity wells of the towns, gathering speed, reeling in the worlds they were bound for, mysteries round the next bend in the road. She didn't mind when they didn't stop for her and for Michael. Everyone has their own mission. Hers was to stand in the cold wind and smile.

Her French was only fair, and Michael's was worse. But no one seemed to mind. Most drivers were happy to sit there in silence. Were they doing this out of mere kindness?

At Avignon, they slept in a park by the river, at the end of the broken bridge. They unrolled their sleeping bags but left them unzipped, their tent unpitched, in case someone attacked them while they slept. In the cold early hours, the sprinklers, activated by a timer, chased them out of the park, into the town centre, where they bought coffee from an all-night cafe and waited until it was light enough to move on.

Their last ride that day left them outside a small village. It was already dark, and they sensed, rather than saw, the Rhône, which they'd followed all afternoon, in the valley beneath them. The wind was funnelled by high ground on either side. They climbed over the metal barrier between the road and the river, slid down a steep slope, found a stretch of flat grass wide enough for their tent. Sometime in the night the wind dropped away and Aoife, waking, became aware of a new sound, a low, steady moan. It seemed to rise from the ground. She turned on her side, watched Michael sleeping beside her. We are wild here, she thought.

The following morning, waking first, she wandered around a bend in the slope and found the source of the sound: concrete cooling towers, pylons, transformers and sluice gates, canalising the grey river. A nuclear power station, sucking in water to cool its reactors. It powers the grid, she thought. They had just slept – and more than that – for free, on a piece of land beside it, an offcut of nobody's property between the river and the road, hidden from the world, too narrow to farm, too steep to develop, where she now saw wild flowers that grew through the grass. She was cold, a little hungry, alone above this famous river she had only known from maps. To be this free, she thought, we only have to keep moving.

I can see you, she told the power plant, but you can't see me.

THE FOLLOWING EVENING BROUGHT them to Nevers. Their driver, who lived in the town, dropped them on the old bridge.

I could take you to the northern edge of town, she said, but you won't get a lift there. It's too late in the evening. You should stay here tonight, or catch a late train into Paris.

She was a retired teacher. She said she gave lifts to young people because she missed looking after other people's kids. She offered to help with their train fare. But money wasn't their problem. Towse had been very generous.

The Loire at Nevers is shallow and wide, streaked with yellow sandbanks. The piers of the old stone bridge were built on the edge of a weir. Aoife and Michael leaned over the parapet, lit cigarettes, and watched the foam from the weir dissolve in the water, fading away like their smoke.

You want to stay here for the night, said Michael, or get a train for the last stretch, into the city?

She knew he would like to see Paris, but she dreaded the mass of it. She didn't want to get drawn into stone canyons, concrete underpasses, hostile cops and watchful suburbs.

What do you think?

We should stay here, he said. Find somewhere to sleep in that park, over there. It's a bad idea to arrive late at night at a big city station. There are cameras. And people follow you outside.

Were these, she wondered, the fairy tales on which his parents had raised him? Were stations and back streets his haunted forests?

OK, she said.

But he looked disappointed. A horn beeped behind them.

A Renault estate car had stopped on the bridge. The driver, leaning out his window, was a man of about sixty with a heavy grey beard. He called to them in French.

Hey! I'm going to Paris. I can take you, if you want.

Aoife looked at Michael.

Did you stick your thumb out, just now?

No. Did you?

No . . .

The Renault, engine idling, blocked the bridge's northbound lane. Another car swerved to pass it, its driver leaning on the horn.

If you want to come, come now, called the bearded man. I can't stop here.

They looked at each other again.

Looks like we're going to Paris tonight, said Michael. It is written.

Nothing is written, said Aoife.

But she was beginning to worry that maybe it was.

THE DRIVER WAS CALLED Didier. He wore a Phish T-shirt and he chain-smoked Camel cigarettes. Once he heard them talk French, he insisted on English. He spoke it well – if anything, too fast, swallowing his sentences, tailing off at times into nervous giggles. They drove through the old stone heart of Nevers to the retail lots and commerce on the northern edge of town.

We'll have to take the autoroute from here, Didier told them. I prefer the N7, but I need to reach Paris by midnight. Don't worry, though. I've put the spray on.

Spray?

*Laque.* Hairspray. On the registration plates. So the bastards can't read the number. People like us need to mind our privacy.

Aoife wondered what he meant by 'people like us'. Who, for that matter, was Didier? She knew about the hairspray trick. You put it on licence plates so cameras couldn't read them. She also knew that the trick didn't work.

The car drove on to the autoroute for the last stretch to Paris. They were in the countryside again, amid woodlands and corn fields. Inside, the car was lit only by the rise and fall of passing headlights, the glow of the dashboard. Aoife, who was sitting in the back, was able to look around the interior. Behind her seat, a blanket hid the contents of the rear of the estate car. She yawned, stretched, and, snaking a hand back, pulled aside a corner of the blanket. A truck, overtaking, flooded the car with its lights.

Yellowing varnish. Red, pointy hats. Sculpted grey beards. Patient hands, crossed on round bellies, or clutching rods that had never bent for a fish.

The back of the car was packed with garden gnomes, of varying designs and sizes, both wooden and plastic, most of them old and some badly weathered. They were arranged upright together, parade formation, all facing the front.

Aoife pulled the blanket back into position, yawned again. She prodded the back of Michael's seat with her toe.

So Didier, she said loudly. Do you live in Paris?

Nah. I'm from Lyons. I fucking hate Paris. I'm only going there to meet up with some friends. We're on a sort of a mission. But I can't really talk about it. It's kind of confidential . . .

He giggled, then trailed off.

I see . . . said Aoife. Tell me this, have you by any chance ever met a guy who calls himself Towse? Tall, thin guy? American? Wears an old business suit?

Didier turned, took a good look at her. Then he looked at Michael, then back at the road.

No, he said thoughtfully. No. I can't say I have.

After that, he stopped talking.

THEY REACHÈD THE OUTSKIRTS of Paris a little before midnight. Aoife watched Michael, watching the edgelands move past in the night. Factories. Truck depots. Supermarket islands in acres of asphalt. Floodlit boxes of glass and aluminium, abandoned until day. Were they back in New Jersey? Had their journey been rewired, in the quantum uncertainty of a highway at night, transposing them to yet another of these discs of hope and commerce, some other city on some other world?

The road rose up on concrete stilts. Now there were human streets below them, apartment buildings, corner cafes, advertisements in French. Cars waited at stop lights. Kids stood on street corners, stamping in the cold. Still in France, then. Would this journey confirm for Michael the existence of Paris, the Eiffel Tower, all those other myths?

Didier reached the Boulevard Périphérique, turned on to its eastbound lane.

I'm getting off at Bercy, he said. On the river. There's a Métro station there that can take you where you want.

They reached the Seine a few miles upstream from the city. Beneath a bridge was fast-running water, stone embankments lined

with barges, a depot for gravel and sand. Ahead, a shopping mall
stood in a tangle of slip roads, the exposed guts of the town. Didier's
car left the Périphérique, descended an off-ramp and stopped on the
embankment beside the Seine.

I have to let you out here, said Didier. The Métro is over there,
beyond that next bridge.

Michael shook hands with him. Aoife paused in the door, holding
it open. It was safe to ask now. But she couldn't think of the French
word for gnome.

What are you doing with them, with the little men in the back?

*Les nains?* The gnomes? You saw them?

Didier pointed.

Look over there.

There was a small green space by the embankment, a scrap of
nature marooned between the footpath and an underpass. A single
tree, a small oak, grew in the middle.

Underneath it, in cheap nylon sleeping bags, bodies lay on sheets
of flattened cardboard. A woman and three young children, pressed
close about her, borrowing heat. The children slept, but the mother
was awake, looking at a smartphone. Its light showed them her face.
Aoife could see her breath in the air.

Refugees, said Didier. They came west in boats, to escape from
the wars that we started.

He jabbed his thumb at the back of his car.

Tomorrow morning, my little friends here will also go west. They
are refugees from human servitude. We will put them in a boat that

leaks, and float it downstream through the centre of Paris. I don't know how far they'll get. But at least they'll have a chance to find safety and freedom.

I see, said Aoife. Good luck.

She saluted him, military fashion. They watched him drive off.

The Garden Gnome Liberation Front, said Michael, impressed. I read about them years ago. I thought they'd disbanded.

So did I. It looks like they're back.


THE HOUSEBOAT WAS A converted barge, moored at a pontoon in Bercy marina. Padlocks told Aoife that its owners weren't home. That was unlikely to change at this hour. She and Michael would be safe here, for one night at least.

A propane heater drove the cold and damp from the bare little cabin, and the electric shower gave hot water straight away. Michael went first. When Aoife came out of the shower, he was undressed, airing the mattress in front of the heater. They found ways to warm themselves until it was dry.

Afterwards, she craved a cigarette. But it would be rude to smoke inside this stolen refuge. Michael, lying beside her, was already asleep.

It was two in the morning, a weeknight in early spring, and the embankment was deserted. The few cars that passed on the boulevard, out of sight, overhead, seemed romantic and lost. She trailed her finger along the railing by the river and felt the sting of late frost. It reminded her of childhood and home, cold nights in winter, hard stars in the sky. There were no stars here, only the haze of light from the city.

Her feet carried her eastward, back along the embankment, to the spot where Didier had dropped them. She stopped by the oak tree, where the family slept.

The woman now lay on her side, spooning a daughter. Her headscarf, pulled around to the front, hid her eyes from the lights that burned on the embankment. One hand, trailing over the girl, still held her phone.

Even refugees have phones now. Even fugitives can network. No need for secret messages, gypsy codes, the signs that tramps used to scratch on door frames and gate posts. *Gives food but not money. Angry dog here.*

The children lay beside their mother, confined in their sleeping bags, faces buried inside.

It would be easy to hurt them or rob them, thought Aoife. Who would they complain to? No one wants them here.

The youngest child whimpered, wriggled, and the woman hugged her tighter, still sleeping. Her hand moved away from the phone, leaving it exposed, there for the taking.

It's a burner phone, thought Aoife. Bound to be. A cheap phone, bought locally, with whatever money this woman had hidden about her, or could beg, so she could cling to the scraps of her life. Who does she reach for? Is the children's father alive? Did he disappear into a prison? Is her family in Aleppo or Raqqa or Damascus, or in a camp in Jordan, Turkey or Lebanon? Aoife knew some of these camps first-hand . . . Are her people scattered along the road she has travelled, or is she lost to them for good?

It was many weeks, now, since Aoife had called her British burner phone, the mailbox she used as a cut-out for her parents. She hadn't even seen the news, lately. Never before had she been out of touch for so long. But she'd had no way to call them, on the long road behind her, with no laptop or phone. France still had hitchhiking, but it had recently removed the last of its payphones. A driver had told them this, when they were hitching near Aix-en-Provence. *Supprimer*, that was the verb he'd used. France had suppressed the last of its payphones.

She stepped on to the grass. None of the sleepers moved. Watching her feet, she circled around them. The phone lay loose by the woman's fingers, on the exposed corner of a sheet of flattened cardboard. *Amazon*, the cardboard said.

Aoife stooped, picked up the sleeping woman's phone, put it in her pocket. Then she took out a thick roll of euros and placed it between the woman and her daughter. A short way downstream, when she was out of earshot, she leaned her back against the balustrade and turned on the phone. No password. Just a burner, then, its screen scratched and cracked.

She had five voice messages in her mailbox, all from the past four days. Her mother's voice, increasingly anxious:

Aoife. It's your mother. Please call me as soon as you can.

Aoife. It's your mother. Please call me as soon as you get this.

Aoife. Your father's not well. Call me as soon as you can.

Aoife. Where are you? Your father's in hospital.

Aoife. You have to come home. Your father wants to see you before it's too late. The hospital has discharged him. Please, please give me a call.

She shut off the stolen phone and turned, so that her elbows rested on the rail. The river flowed past, just beneath her. The lights of the city shone in its water. She no longer felt the cold.

Across the river, beyond the moored barges, surrounded by modern glass and steel boxes, she noticed an odd-looking building. It was much older than its neighbours, maybe late nineteenth century, made of riveted steel and ornamental brickwork, with a tall red-brick chimney. The whimsical arrangement of its windows – some squared, some curved – gave it a playful art-nouveau appearance. There was a sign on the front, worked into the brickwork: *Distribution d'air comprimé. SUDAC.*

Compressed-air network? Why would they have needed compressed air in Paris, back in the old days?

Then she remembered. The pneumatic post. Miles of airtight tubes, running through catacombs and storm drains and Métros. Sealed metal canisters – containing urgent messages, documents, cash money – blown through these tubes, all around the city, by bursts of compressed air. She had learned about this system as a child, seen it in black and white on a colour television. Her father had been watching with her, that day – the memory stabbed her. He had told her how, when he was a boy, he'd seen pneumatic tubes in a department store in London, shuttling payments and change between clerks and cashiers. He said it was one of his earliest memories. It might already be lost forever. She felt her world sway.

Aoife wondered if Towse, or something else, had wanted her to stand here and notice this ghost of an older way of doing things. She wondered if any pneumatic tubes were still in operation, here in Paris, or anywhere else in the world. Did money and words, invested in paper, still flit in secret beneath city streets, down in the dark, where no one could catch them?

She reckoned she could be in Ireland in less than two days, travelling by boat from Cherbourg to Dublin. Flying was out of the question.

Towse, too, would be in Dublin.

She looked again at the old compressed-air plant. It seemed to her brighter, more electric, than the modern buildings around it, even though it was dark and their windows shone with light. It looked as if it would dissolve into sparkles if you touched it, revealing its secret, a shortcut to the next level of this game, some other Eden in some other multiverse. Maybe Towse was right to worry about the simulation hypothesis. Maybe nothing she could see was real. Was someone, or something, reeling her in? Was it Towse?

You have to carry on, she told herself. You have to live by the old rules of thumb. Reality is whatever smacks you in the face if you walk around with your eyes closed. Her first job, in this heuristic now, was to get rid of the stolen phone. At any level of reality, it was compromised. Once you picked up a phone, punched a number, the shockwaves spread outwards, alerting the sharks. Protocol demanded that she toss it into the nearest body of deep water. She had paid the refugee woman for it, many times over, with that fat roll of fifties. It was time to pick her spot, as far out as she could. She turned it over in her hand, bracing for the throw. And then she saw the sticker on the back.

It was a sticker of a pretty cartoon princess. Aoife recognised her as a character from the movie *Frozen*, though she didn't know which one. The name was printed on the bottom of the sticker, but Aoife couldn't read it. It was in Arabic script.

The colours were faded, the paper scratched and scored, and part of the sticker had come away, leaving its glue on the plastic.

Aoife looked at the smiling face of the strong, brave young princess, and calculated the damage that she had done.

Not just a burner phone, then. Not bought locally. This phone had come on the long road from Syria, treasured all the way. A long way back, in a peaceful moment, a little girl had put a favourite sticker on her mother's phone. She had done this as a gift.

Aoife herself knew only six phone numbers by heart, and three of them no longer worked. How many numbers did this refugee carry around in her head? How many more were stored only in this telephone? Sisters, cousins, friends, strewn around the world.

Protocol demanded. Consider the alternative. This phone was now toxic, to the refugees as well. Aoife drew her arm back and threw it into the Seine.

\*

I HAVE TO GO home to Ireland, she told Michael. I have to leave right away.

There were yellow flowers on the nylon curtain, pulled across the little round window over the bed. They shone with the morning. She wished they could stay here for just one day more.

Towse?

He almost sneered when he said it.

She stood in the door.

No. My parents.

Parents?

My father. He's very sick.

He rubbed his face, as if trying to wake it.

So you have parents now.

Of course I have parents, I . . .

She stopped.

Tell me about them, he said. You know about mine.

OK . . . My parents are from Dublin. Not from the country, which is where I grew up. They met in London, when he was working as a banker in the City. He made a lot of money. My mother loves thoroughbred horses. They cost a lot of money. So he retired early and they moved to Kildare, where there are lots of horses. But the people in Kildare don't sell their good horses to blow-ins from Dublin or London, or pay them to train them. So my parents don't have any horses now, or any money. When I was planning to quit my old life, I gave them my savings to invest for me. They invested them in horses. I suppose they meant well, at the time.

Behind her, in the boat's little kitchen, she could hear the kettle she'd lit earlier. It was starting to sing. That again.

This is just another one of Towse's tricks, isn't it?

If it is, I'm not in on it. I got a message. My father is sick.

How did they send you a message when you don't have a phone?

He wants to believe me, she thought, but even the truth makes me look guilty. The kettle was screaming. She slumped back against the wall.

I went out for a smoke last night. I stole a cell phone from those refugees. I called a voicemail that I use as a cut-out. My mother had left me messages.

She wondered how long that kettle could scream before it evaporated all its water, before the bottom turned red, then melted into the propane.

You could be making all that up, he said.

That's right. I could.

You could be making it up to lure me to Ireland, because that's where Towse wants me.

That's possible. But it isn't true.

Or you could be making it up as an excuse to get rid of me.

If I wanted to ditch you, Michael, I wouldn't bother with excuses. You'd turn around and I'd be gone.

He nodded, continued:

Or the message could be real, but it could be a trap. For one or for both of us.

The message is for me, Michael, not for you.

Maybe they think I'd come with you.

I won't let you. You're safer here. But I have to do this. I have to go to Ireland, to find out for certain. He's my Dad.

I'm coming with you, Aoife.

No you're not. I don't want you to.

She wondered why she was lying, to herself and to him. But there was no time for that now. It was a moot question. The blunt fact remained, that there was no point in both of them walking into an ambush, if that's what it was.

You can't come with me, Michael. I have to do this alone. This is where we say goodbye.

So, like, we'll always have Paris?

I'm going home, Michael. I don't need you anymore. That's all there is to it. Goodbye.

He folded his arms.

I didn't say I was going to Ireland for you, Aoife. I'm going for Towse.

*Towse?*

He said he needed help with his end-game in Dublin.

Why the hell would you want to help him, after all he's done to you?

Because of last night. Because of Didier, and those refugees.

What?

Those gnomes have got me thinking.

Those words have never been said together before. What the hell do you mean?

I mean, maybe it's time I got in a fight.

Bullshit, thought Aoife. Why can't he look me in the eye while he says that? Why does he really want to come to Ireland? For his parents? For Alice? But vengeance is violence, and he was not the violent type.

The kettle was still screaming. She turned on her heel, stopped, turned back to him.

Come if you want, then, she said. I can't stop you. But keep me out of Towse's thing, whatever it is. I don't want to have anything to do with it. You shouldn't either. That guy will get you killed.

# Part Six:

*Tír na nÓg*

CHERBOURG TO DUBLIN WAS an eighteen-hour crossing. English Channel, Irish Sea. They paid cash for their tickets, and some extra for a cabin, where, without any discussion, they slept in separate bunks. In the morning they went on deck to watch Ireland on the port side, sliding into the south. It was a blustery day, wind and rain from the west, and hills hardened and softened in the gaps between squalls. Michael had no names to put on anything he saw, so he thought of ones that he already knew: English Bay, Strait of Georgia, Juan de Fuca, Salish Sea. These hills were also livid and green, and the rain here was warm. Snow would be wet, like the snow in Vancouver. It wouldn't last long.

Aoife, who had begun to talk again, a little, showed him a lighthouse that rose sheer from the sea. Kish, she told him. This wasn't Vancouver. Alice had never lived here, and he wasn't going home.

Aoife showed him some hills.

Wicklow, she said. Soon we'll see Dublin. It's around that next point.

Is that where your parents live?

It's where they live now.

Do you want me to go with you?

She remembered her childhood, cold stares at her friends.

No.

She saw his reaction. It's not like that, she thought. But she couldn't say it aloud.

It's not safe, she told him. I have to go alone. I'll come and find you later.

What would I do if I waited for you?

I don't know . . . We can find you a bed and breakfast, one of the quiet ones near Connolly Station. You should be safe there. You can go to the museums. Take a bus trip around the city. Do whatever you do on a foreign vacation.

I've never been on a foreign vacation.

She reached over, squeezed his arm for a moment. But the touch felt insincere to both of them. They had spent nights together, but by daylight they were spies.

The ship turned west and entered a bay. Strobe lights flashed red on two high brick chimneys. Homely little houses lined the shore. No glass and steel towers, no marshalling yards, no silos or mountains of sulphur, no Vancouver, just the fringes of a town that, to Michael, looked like nothing but fringes. Channel markers, sea walls, a river mouth, cranes. The ferry sidled up to the dock, acres of concrete, where cars and trucks waited for the return sailing. The wind was up, and flurries of drizzle brushed the shine from the water. So this is Dublin, thought Michael. He looked at Aoife, leaning at the rail beside him, watching the ship dock. She had seemed so exotic, when he first met her, yet even she had a family, and a place where she belonged.

There was a payphone in the ferry terminal, in a corner by itself. It had a slot for coins and another for plastic. Michael stopped in front of it.

Give me Towse's number.

You're not really going through with this, are you Michael? He'll only bring you trouble.

Stop playing games, Aoife. It's why you brought me here, right?

No. And you're the one who's playing games now. You don't have to help Towse just to prove a point to me.

Give me his number, and let's get this over with.

Listen: I *can't* go with you to meet Towse now. I have to go see my father right away. He's sick. I could already be too late.

Then I'll go without you. I guess that's part of Towse's plan too.

I really doubt that.

Screw you, Aoife.

I've no right to stop you, Michael. But wait for me, please. I'll go see my father and then I'll come and help you.

What day is it?

It's Friday.

Then it has to be now.

Michael had never used a payphone before. He tried the number three times before Aoife, relenting, told him not to put the Dublin 01 area code in front of the number. This time the call went through; it rang out, unanswered.

There's no one there, said Aoife. Forget about Towse. Come with me.

He turned away from her, dialled again. She watched him, helpless.

I have to go now, Michael. I can't wait anymore . . . If you won't come with me, let me give you my parents' phone number. If you change your mind, you can call me there.

She wrote the number on a leaflet she took from a stack on the counter – something about a virus, and quarantine, and reporting symptoms.

I have to go now, she said. I hope that Towse never answers.

But when she was gone, on the third try, he did.


AFTER AOIFE'S PARENTS HAD burned through the last of her father's banking money, and all of Aoife's savings, and their stud farm in Kildare finally went broke, they moved to a small apartment beside the River Tolka, on what was, for them, the wrong side of Dublin. Aoife made the taxi driver go two hundred yards past the entrance before she got out, then walked back to the pub opposite the apartment. She went in, used the bathroom, came out again, smoked a cigarette in the doorway. It gave her a chance to check out the flats.

She could see no sign of danger. The complex had been built in the 1970s, and mature trees filled the gaps between the red-brick units. They were coming into leaf; spring always came earlier in Dublin than it did in Kildare, only forty miles inland.

It made no sense to her that her parents were here now, in the city. She had stayed with them in their new flat last Christmas, sleeping in the spare room. There was always fake jollity, a feeling of silence interrupted. In the countryside, there had been something to look at outside the window, the sound of horses and tractors, work to be done in the stables. Here, there was the television, which they left on all day, the volume up loud. They had a balcony, a view across the river to the Botanic Gardens, but Aoife knew that her mother rarely looked out.

She took the lift to the third floor, confronted the door of her parents' apartment. She had to get ready for what lay beyond it, down the hall, in the larger of the two bedrooms. She pictured a bedside, a nurse, her father's two sisters, her brother in a chair, reading a book. Maybe there'd be a priest – her father wasn't religious, and neither were his sisters, but they liked to pretend they came from old money, that they were a family which did things in a certain way. It had hurt them to have to send Aoife to a school that didn't charge for the privilege. But there had been the cost of running the stables, of all the plans that had never quite come off.

The plans. She felt like crying. She remembered how, when she was small, her father had decided to lay out a tennis court on the lawn, which was certainly big enough: they basically lived in a field. We're going to have tennis, she had told the other girls in school. Her dad had driven the posts in, then, distracted by something else, had never marked the lines out, or strung up a net. We're going to have a tennis court. She'd forgotten about that. But the little girl who hid inside her, under all those years of accretion, still believed that there would be a tennis court, and she would continue to believe it until the man who had mentioned it, all those years ago, finished the job or formally renounced it. He was behind this door, now. He was dying, if not dead.

Had she made it in time? She put her ear to the door, closed her eyes, listened for clues. Somewhere inside was a murmur of voices. It could be people talking, or it could be the television, in the corner of the living room, her mother's daytime shows.

Aoife knocked on the door.

The voices stopped. Quick footsteps in the hall. Aoife got ready for the worst thing she could think of. Her mother would open the door, tell her that she was too late, that he had died asking for her, and then close the door again, leaving her outside. She knew her mother wouldn't do that, but she needed to punish herself by experiencing it now. Whatever happened next, when the door opened, she reckoned she'd deserve it.

The door opened.

Aoife?

Her father was dressed for the street, except wearing slippers. He looked perfectly healthy.

*Dad?*

\*

THE CROSS GUNS BRIDGE, said the bus driver. You get off here.

His voice was muffled by a medical face mask, though the air outside seemed fine to Michael. He'd seen a lot of those masks since arriving in Dublin. Were Irish people given to hypochondria, or were they deeply withdrawn? All that Michael thought he knew about the Itish was that they liked to drink.

Michael got off the bus and looked around him. The rain had cleared, a spring sun was shining, but it felt to him like the day should be grey. A busy road, red-brick terraced two-storey houses. A fish and chip shop, closed. A hardware store, open. A sign, painted on a corner, that said *Bang Bang*. He was only a mile or so from where he had boarded this bus, and already it felt like the city was behind him. Was this how suburbs worked, in Ireland? To him, the houses here looked tired and small. They told him about old people, yellowing doilies and antimacassars, about clocks that ticked slowly, dust and sad memories. Where he came from, they bulldozed old houses to put new things on top of them, to tamp down the ghosts. They exorcised the past with money, which was why they always needed more and more of it. Here, it looked as if at some point they had just given up, stopped, turned to face what they should run from. Maybe they were on to something, after all.

Michael turned, followed the bus as it drove up the road. Pub on the right, closed. Office building on the left, vacant. And now a narrow canal, running east–west under the road, and a bridge with a green iron balustrade, water foaming through the sluices of a lock. He considered this canal bridge before he crossed it: it was mercifully low, not quite twenty feet wide. Having crossed, he turned left, past a furniture sales room, on to a towpath that led into the west.

The canal broadened here to form a small basin or harbour, a switching point, from the days when summit canals were the hottest thing in technology. A tall, stone-fronted warehouse, converted into apartments, stood reflected in the water. Beyond it rose a derelict grain elevator, a cluster of grey concrete cylinders. This elevator was small, not like the timber cathedrals of his prairies, but it was still the tallest building in the area. Beyond this, the canal narrowed again, and the towpath climbed to another, higher lock.

This was definitely the place, just like Towse had described it. Where was Towse?

Someone had climbed to the top of the old grain elevator and painted the word *Thirst* there, but it was now partly hidden by a coat of whitewash. Traffic hissed on the bridge like radio static. To his right, a spiked metal fence was woven with nettles and elders and the papery white flowers of bindweed. He thought of the edges of all the small towns that he'd passed through down the years. If this were the prairies, there would also be a railroad, boxcars left standing in switchyards and sidings, frozen in the act of passing through. And there it was – the singing of rails, the sound of a train's horn, invisible but only yards away. Somewhere close by, just beyond that steel fence with its curtain of bindweed, a railway was hidden inside a deep cutting.

You could adjust the colour palette, switch out a few details and vary the difficulty setting, but every level of this game was pretty much the same.

When the train was gone, the towpath returned to the quiet of midday. Except now, having wandered on a few more yards, he could hear voices. Beyond the fence, men were laughing.

As he watched, the lower section of the fence swivelled outward and upward, like an overgrown cat flap. A man crawled out from under it, on his knees and one hand. The other hand held a can of strong cider. He was dirty, unshaven, clothes shapeless and greasy. Michael couldn't see his face, but he recognised what had once been a well-tailored suit.

He's lost it, thought Michael. I should pretend I don't see him, just keep walking along this canal. It has to go somewhere.

Towse turned his head quickly, as if he'd overheard the words that Michael hadn't spoken. His face was dirty. There were bruises on his left eye and cheek.

Michael! There you are! I was just coming to look for you. But Wojciech was telling us a very funny story, and I didn't want to interrupt.

Wojciech?

Come on, through here.

Towse lifted the fence for him, smiling encouragingly.

Michael stood his ground.

What happened to you, Towse?

What do you mean?

You look like you've been beaten up. It's the middle of the day and you're already drinking.

Towse raised the can of cider in a toast.

When in Rome.

He took a swig, shuddered, staring past Michael, back towards the bridge.

Where's Aoife? Don't tell me she's not here.

AOIFE'S FATHER HAD A newspaper in one hand. The other held the front door, as if he wasn't sure whether he should let in his only daughter. I'm in trouble, she found herself thinking. She shrank into the old defensiveness, felt that familiar urge to be anywhere else. That kid never goes away. She's still hiding inside me.

You're looking well, she said.

So are you.

He hugged her awkwardly.

Mum told me you were sick, Dad.

He didn't release her. She couldn't see his face.

You should have been here days ago, he said.

You obviously got better.

Pulling away, he looked at his slippers, the door handle, then last of all, her face.

Your mother's in the living room. She'll tell you all about it. We were just making tea. I'll go and get it.

He stood back, letting her pass. The hallway, with no window to the outside, was narrow and dark. The walls were lined with photos and etchings of famous horses, and jolly prints of Edwardian hunting scenes. *View Halloo. The Stirrup Cup.* They had brought them from the old house, where the walls had more space for them, and where there were living horses outside in the yard. These pictures had always depressed her. The horses they showed her were dead.

Go ahead, said her father, and opened the living-room door.

She stepped inside, saw her mother in her armchair, and then the door clicked shut behind her.

Her mother wasn't alone. There was a woman sitting on the couch with her back to the balcony, her face obscured by the daylight behind her. Aoife sensed someone else too, in the corner, behind the door, hidden from her as she entered the room.

Her eyes found the mirror over the hearth. It was the Scotsman, Fess's enforcer, from London and Uganda. He was dressed in a plain dark suit and tie, smiling unctuously, an undertaker who's turned up a little too soon. He wasn't looking at Aoife but at her mother, his face full of sympathy. Then his eyes flicked to the mirror, saw Aoife watching him. He winked.

The woman stood up from the couch. Aoife saw a business skirt and blazer, a blouse fastened to the throat, round owlish glasses, the smile of a HR manager who's just popped by your desk. She'd last seen that face in a London hotel room.

Hello, Aoife, said Irene. We're here to help.

Aoife's mother, still sitting, folded her arms and looked at her daughter, sad, disappointed.

There's no point being angry at us, Aoife. And there's no point denying things. We already know.

Aoife took a step into the room, buying herself another arm's length

from the thug in the corner. The room was full of potential weapons —
ornamental pokers, her mother's old showjumping trophies, brass shell
cases from Kildare's old artillery barracks — but she knew what men
like the Scotsman could do. For now, it was better to talk.

Know what, Mum?

Sit down, dear. Ronan — her mother raised her voice — where's
that tea?

Her father's voice carried from the kitchen.

Coming, Fiona. Do you want biscuits too?

Yes, said Aoife's mother. I think biscuits are called for. If we have
any left. We've been waiting for you for days . . .

And she gave her only daughter another sad look.

Aoife sat on the couch, her back to the balcony. How long would
it take her to open the catch on its door? How far was the drop to
the bushes below?

She mirrored her mother's unhappy expression. It was, she realised, depressingly easy for her to do. Will I grow to be like her?

Dad wasn't sick at all, she said. You lied to me.

It was for your own good. We had to bring you back here. So
you can get the help you need.

Irene stepped over to the fireplace, behind Aoife's mother. The
Scotsman left his corner and also stood behind Fiona. Oblivious,
Aoife's mother kept talking.

These people told us everything, Aoife. And we checked it for
ourselves. We called the Home Office in London. They've never
even heard of you. You've been living a lie.

Aoife, looking past her mother, watched as the Scotsman lifted the hem of his jacket. The grip of a pistol showed over his belt. He patted the pistol with his free hand. Irene extended her right arm, thumb cocked, two fingers pointing at the back of Fiona's head. Her thumb shot forward. Pow, she mouthed silently. Then she raised a finger to her lips, mimed *shush*.

Aoife nodded. Her mother, seeing Aoife nod, relaxed into her chair.

I'm so glad you see it our way, Aoife. We love you very much. We had to do whatever we could to save you.

Save me?

From the cult.

The *cult*?

Irene contacted us a week ago. She told us all about it. She said you were in one of those fake religions where everyone . . . where they all . . . Well, you don't need me to tell you what you all get up to. Irene and Mr Stewart here are professional cult busters. They rescue people from fake religions, deprogramme them and return them to their families. We had to play a trick on you to get you to come back to us.

You told me Dad was dying. That's some trick, Mum.

We had to hope that you still had some human feelings for us, that the cult hadn't totally brainwashed you yet. I'm sorry, Aoife. But we'd do it again, if we had to.

Her mother stood, held out her arms, inviting a hug. There were tears in her eyes.

Because it worked! Here you are!

Aoife stayed in her seat. I should be screaming, she thought, looking up at her mother. Instead, I'm sulking. It never goes away.

There was a clatter in the hall. The Scotsman went over and opened the door, letting Aoife's father in. He set his tray on the coffee table, looked at his wife.

You've had that little chat with her?

Yes, said his wife, looking away from him.

About that whole . . . ?

Yes.

He looked relieved.

Well, that's good then. I'm glad that's all settled.

He turned away, poured tea into cups.

Milk and one sugar for you, Andrew . . . Milk no sugar for you, Irene. Usual for you, Fiona, darling . . . And you, Aoife? How do you take your tea?

Milk no sugar. Like always.

The Scotsman sat beside Aoife on the couch. Irene continued to stand by the fireplace; she took a sip from her tea, put it down again.

I think, she said, looking around the room, that this intervention can begin?

She turned to Aoife, face serious and kind.

The first thing you have to understand, Aoife — and it may be hard for you to believe, after the depths you've sunk to — is that it's still possible for other people to love you, and for you to love them. I think this intervention is already helping you to see that. You still have some love for your father, otherwise you wouldn't have come back here. You've already felt the pain of thinking you might lose him. You know how that would feel for real. You understand?

I get you, said Aoife.

She took a sip of tea. It was warm but not hot. Her father was a city boy, who had never learned to scald the pot before putting the tea in. No point hurling this slop into somebody's eyes . . .

Irene put on a sad face.

And imagine, Aoife, how your parents might feel if they lost *you*. Imagine them – for instance – watching their only daughter dying in front of them. No parent should have to see their child die. It's against the natural order. Imagine your parents seeing you pass, knowing that they were soon about to pass too, perhaps in considerable pain.

Aoife's mother looked into her teacup. She sniffed, long and loud. Irene put a hand on her shoulder, squeezed.

Don't worry, Fiona. I'm only saying these things to establish a connection with Aoife. An understanding . . . You do understand what I'm saying to you, don't you, Aoife?

Yep.

Good. We need to know that you're going to work with us. For your own sake. And for theirs.

They have nothing to do with it.

Fiona sniffed again, less loudly, and shot another sad glance at her daughter.

I don't know where we went wrong, she said.

Don't blame yourself, Fiona, said Irene. Now, if you don't

mind, we need a quick chat with Aoife alone, to establish some ground rules. Would you mind waiting here, while we talk in the hall?

Be our guests, said Aoife's father.

Irene went first, with Aoife following. She didn't have to look around to know that the Scotsman was close behind her. They had her snookered. The door clicked shut. The hallway was dark. Aoife turned and faced them.

You don't have to hurt them. I haven't told anyone about that banker in London. It's none of my business.

Irene shook her head in mock disbelief.

You want to pretend that this is about *London*? We know you're in a lot deeper than that, my girl. You were snooping around in that lab, in Uganda.

Keep bluffing, thought Aoife.

No I wasn't.

You forgot to shut down the computer. Those Berkeley scientists knew straight away that someone had been snooping in there. And those guys are geneticists. After you took off in that jeep, they took DNA samples from the bags in your room. We got no match at all for your friend – he's like a ghost. But your name came up straight away. Your mum's been sending her spit to the free genealogy sites.

She thinks she's descended from Mary Queen of Scots.

We got quite the shock, seeing your name pop out of the database. We didn't realise you were a plant, when we'd hired you for that job in London.

I didn't know either. But that doesn't matter now. What do you want?

Irene looked at the Scotsman.

She's a good girl, she said. She knows when she's beaten. You can't always count on that, with the Irish . . . The first thing you need to understand, dear, is that we don't care about you. It's not you that we want. It's your boss.

And Aoife, looking meek, thought, I can't believe she said that to me. What an insult to my professionalism. Does she think I haven't heard that before? I know it's not me that you really want. But I also know that you're going to do me anyway.

We only want your boss, Aoife. Where is he?

Towse. Where was Towse? Did she have any right to give him up? What would he do, in her position?

He's right here, Aoife said. He's in Ireland.

She saw the way Irene looked at the Scotsman, and then she understood. They hadn't known that Towse was in the same country. They must have come to Ireland just for me, she thought, having set a trap for me, their only real lead. Now, they're getting Towse as well.

Take us to him and we'll let you go. You and your parents. It's him we want, not you.

I don't know where he is.

You understand that we won't start by hurting you, Aoife? We'll start with your mother and father.

Aoife could hear voices, canned music, beyond the door to the living room. Her parents had turned up the sound on the television.

Maybe they wanted to show that they were too polite to eavesdrop. Or maybe they really didn't want to hear what was said in the hall. They hoped that someone else could solve their Aoife problem.

I honestly don't know where he is.

Irene studied Aoife's face.

OK, she said slowly.

She looked at the Scotsman.

Search her.

Aoife felt his hands pass round her waist, under and along her arms, across her chest. He reached into her jacket, took out her fake passport, her thick wad of euros. Then he knelt, brushed down her legs, between her thighs to her ankles, groped the tops of her socks.

No phone, he said, moving away again. Just this cash and this fake Irish passport. Excellent work – probably an Israeli job, foolproof. Name of Rosemary Scallon. Apart from that, no wallet, no plastic.

No phone, Aoife? Then how is your boss supposed to find you? . . . You must have some other arrangement.

Her eyes looked around the hallway, settled at the end of it. And Aoife knew, without looking, what Irene was seeing. There, under the big mirror, on the Victorian credenza, was an old Bakelite telephone, condemned, like a tradesman who has come to the wrong entrance, to wait in the hallway, alone in the cold.

He could phone you here, couldn't he, Aoife?

*

TOWSE WAS INCREDULOUS.

No Aoife? Just you?

Distracted, he still held the fence up, giving Michael a glimpse of a liminal waste between canal and railway: a couple of cheap nylon tents, nettles, wet ash from a fire, gravel, briars, empty cans.

Just me, said Michael.

Three men in tracksuits crawled through the gap, one after the other, then stood by the towpath, staring at Michael. They were scrappy, unshaven, with a menacing look.

Who are these guys? Shouldn't we talk in private?

Don't worry about them. They don't speak much English. And when they do, no one listens. This is Wojciech, Stanislaw and Steve.

The three men appeared to be drunk. Towse said something in Polish and, one by one, they crawled back under the fence.

Those guys are hobos, Towse.

They're very nice people. They've been putting me up here, last couple of days. I ran into some problems. Where's Aoife?

Not here. But she is in Ireland. She's gone to see her parents.

Great. That's great . . . Is there by any chance any way at all that we can get hold of her? I was kind of hoping to draw on her skills. Like, today. Like, right about now.

I'm alone. You wanted me here, now you've got me.

Well, to be honest, Michael, I want you, but I *need* Aoife. For obvious reasons.

Michael stared at him, disbelieving.

If you don't need me, why did you get Aoife to bring me to Ireland?

Towse, looking up and down the towpath as if still hoping to see Aoife, turned back to Michael.

I didn't. It was the other way around. I was thinking that you'd want to come, because of what I told you about your parents, and maybe for Alice, and then Aoife would have to come too, because you're in love.

*What?*

You're in love with each other, aren't you? If you're not, you should be by now.

That's none of your goddamn business . . .

Michael thought, Am I in *love* with Aoife? He dismissed the idea, went on:

Aoife's father is sick. She had to come back to see him.

Towse leered at him.

And you had to come too, eh?

I said, that's none of your business.

Have it your way . . . So it's just dumb luck that you're here . . . I don't like that one bit . . .

Towse squinted all around them, as if trying to spot the ambush, or the cracks in the graphics where the level respawned.

Michael persisted:

If you don't need me, why did you bother to bring me with you, all the way from Palo Alto?

Jesus Christ, Michael. Why does no one believe me when I tell them the truth? . . . On the day that she died, I promised Alice I'd look after you. Keeping you with me was the only way I could do that. That's also why I ratted Alice out to Fess.

You did *what?*

He was about to find out about her anyway. So I dropped a dime on her, and I made it look like you did it. That way, Fess would hire you. I could keep an eye on you, and have an inside guy too. Two birds with one stone.

It made sense to Michael, now. Fess's strange words in his office: *I know I can trust you, because of what you've already done for me . . . You should never feel guilt, Mike. You did the right thing.*

You're evil, Towse. You ruined my life.

Hey – I wasn't running a crèche, you know. Plus, I figured that if you had Aoife to take care of you, you'd probably come through this all right. I can't drag you around with me forever.

And now, at last, Michael got it.

You pushed us together! You planned our thing!

If it's any consolation, Aoife fell for it too.

Michael couldn't speak. Towse gave up on his quest for a phantom Aoife, turned back to face him.

Anyway, since you're here now, and she isn't, you'll have to do it.

When Michael found his voice it sounded quite dangerous, even to him.

Fuck off, Towse.

But I haven't even told you what I want you for! Having come all this way, don't you want to know?

You're just going to try to play me again. I'm not having it, this time. I'm out.

Towse took a ruminative pull on his cider, studying Michael over the rim of the can. When he spoke again, he wasn't smiling.

Michael, can you honestly look back on everything that's happened to you, in the last couple of months, all the things you've seen and done, and tell me you've got nothing back from playing this game?

There was a name hanging between them. But neither of them said it. Michael took out a pack of cigarettes, gave one to Towse.

I'll listen. I'll give you that much.

They both lit up. Towse started to pace.

OK . . . Today is Friday the 13th. This afternoon at two thirty p.m. Irish time, which is nine thirty a.m. in New York, OmniCent goes live, though only a few people know that. Fess deliberately picked this date because he thinks there's no such thing as luck for people like him. He's giving OmniCent a cold opening so his people can build up their positions before the rest of the world is invited on board. But once it's operational, OmniCent will progressively absorb all the money on earth. By the end of the year, national governments will have lost what few powers they still have. After that, they won't be able to raise taxes, or spend money, or look after their people, assuming they still want to. There will be nothing left to protect our planet from the new feral money, working through stooges like Fess and their enablers. And they won't know until it's too late that they're not in charge either, that the money rules them too. So once OmniCent launches, there'll be no going back. But it's vulnerable now, at birth. That's when we have to hit it. This afternoon. Here.

Why here?

Towse pointed back towards the bridge.

If you follow this canal a couple of miles east, it takes you to what used to be the docklands. It's a tax shelter now, where corporations hide their profits from hospitals and schools. The usual financial things. So Inscape has an office here too – its Irish front company. It nominally holds more than two thirds of Inscape's global worth, which is a half-trillion dollars, to avoid paying taxes. That office happens to be the weakest point in Inscape's online global security system. So that's where I need you to go. Now.

Why?

That thing that your father didn't do in Iran, when they set him up as a patsy – I need you to do it in Ireland, for real.

Behind the bindweed and elders, voices were raised. A beer can, thrown with force, sailed over the fence, landed in the canal. It sank a way, then steadied itself, with only a sliver of freeboard between the hole in the top and the wind-driven ripples. Michael watched it. There was no scenario in which the can wouldn't sink. It was only a matter of time, really.

What will your virus do, if it works?

Fuck things up quite a bit, I hope . . . It'll take down any of Inscape's global systems that are networked to OmniCent, which means most of the world's fintech and its online payment networks.

That should pop a few bubbles, and wipe out a shitload of hoarded offshore wealth. After that, things could get interesting.

You're a terrorist, Towse. You'll destabilise the planet. People will die.

People are already dying. The planet is dying. The money is poisoning it.

Why should I do this for you?

You're not doing it for me, Michael. You're doing it for your parents. And you're doing it for Alice.

Michael watched the beer can, bobbing in the ripples. That sticker on her laptop: *This Machine Kills Fascists*. He remembered the last time he saw her, in silent tears. He hadn't ever tried to understand her, really. They had ended up living together in different worlds. He might as well have pushed her off that bridge himself. Now, little more than two months later, he was already sleeping with someone else, with Alice unburied, lost in the water, his debt to her unpaid.

He thought of his parents, their lives lived in fear. They had loved him so quietly.

I have a number for Aoife, he said.

Give it to me and I'll call her.

I'll call her. Give me a phone.

I don't have one, right now . . . Come to my office.

Towse led Michael back to the Cross Guns Bridge. They stopped outside the Brian Boru, a two-storey pub. There was a phone box on the pavement, its windows dulled by scratches and grime.

Michael held his breath, and the door, until the air inside had cleared a little. People had used the phone box as a toilet. There were stains on its dial pad. A sticker for a sex worker promised a good time. The sticker looked new. Who, in this age of instant connection, of online reviews and hook-up apps and cybersex and searchable preferences and infinite porn, still picks their secret shame from a sticker in a phone box? Or was that part of the experience, for a niche clientele? Concealment. Resistance. No sex bot yet invented could enter a phone booth and put up an ad.

The number of the phone was printed on a laminated sign, along with instructions for international dialling codes, reversing charges, operator assistance – things Michael had read about, or seen in movies, but would never have thought still existed in life. He recognised the number: 01 8300338. He'd called it that morning, from the payphone in the ferry port. This phone box was all that Towse had in the world.

Michael realised he'd no change for the phone call. The door opened behind him. Towse handed in a fifty-cent coin.

Last one I've got. It's like in the movies – you only get one call.

Michael waited until the door shut again, then took out Aoife's parents' number. He dialled it, waited. The phone rang three times, then somebody answered. His coin dropped into the box.


IRENE LET THE PHONE ring three times, then she picked up the receiver. Aoife watched her, helpless. The Scotsman, moving up behind her, had put a hand on Aoife's shoulder, his fingers resting gently on a point above her clavicle, where he could, she sensed, inflict crippling pain with minimum pressure. He put his other hand lightly over her mouth, gave a little squeeze in warning.

Yes? said Irene.

A noise from the phone, like a fly trapped in another room.

No, said Irene. This is Mrs McCoy. I'm her mother.

Aoife had to hand it to her. She made a decent fist of a southside Dublin accent.

A moment's silence, then the fly buzzed again.

No. Aoife's not here. May I take a message?

A short burst of buzzes.

I'm not sure when she'll be back . . . Shall I tell her where she can find you?

A longer pause, followed by a longer buzz. Irene turned her head, looked at Aoife. She took a pen and notebook from her blazer, scribbled something down.

So, you have to leave soon, but you'll be back there later? You'll meet her there?

Buzz.

All right . . . I'll pass it on to her when she gets back.

Irene put the phone down, turned to Aoife.

Where in Dublin is the Cross Guns Bridge?


MICHAEL CAME OUT OF the phone box to find Towse leaning against the wall, smoking a dog-end. A police car slowed as it passed, the cops eyeing Towse, with his filthy suit and bruises. Towse pushed himself away from the wall, staggered over to the kerb, waving and smiling at the cops in the squad car. The brake lights went off and the car sped away. Towse came back to Michael. He was no longer staggering.

Works every time, he said.

She's gone out. I had to leave a message. I said she could meet me here.

Towse dropped his dog-end, morosely ground it out with his heel.

Ah . . . Well, there's no time to wait for her. You'll have to do it alone.

Do what, exactly?

Inscape's Dublin office has its own built-in server room. It's totally the wrong kind of place for a server room, but they put it there anyway, to get a big cash grant from the Irish development body. No one ever uses it, but it's still online, like a redundant component. That's where you go to inject the virus.

Why don't you do it?

Looking like this?

Towse had a point.

How do I get in?

Towse fished about in his jacket, found something that snagged, jerked it out. He handed it to Michael.

My old Inscape ID . . . I guess Aoife stole that too.

Of course she did. Tell them you're an engineer from Palo Alto. You've come to check the server room. They're bound to let you in.

They'll swipe the card in the computer. The alarms will go off straight away.

I've wiped that card with a big fucking magnet. If they swipe it, it'll show as a dud.

So then they won't let me in.

That ID has your picture on it. They'll just figure the chip is defective and let you in anyway. It's only a front company, a couple of flunkies to open the mail. They're Irish. These drunken spud-munchers don't give a shit.

You know Aoife is Irish, right?

Case in point . . . Come on, it's worth a shot.

Towse took out an envelope.

It's all here, he said. The address, the flash key with the virus, the master password, step by step instructions. It's idiot proof, like that job back in Jersey. When you're done, find your way back here. I'll be waiting. Now let's get you a cab.


IRENE SPOKE AS SHE rummaged in her handbag.

Andrew will go with you. Don't try anything silly. And besides . . .

She showed Aoife a little chrome-plated pistol. It glinted in the half-light of the hall.

I'll be staying here, with your parents. So, you know, if I don't hear back from you and Andrew . . .

I get it . . . Can I use the toilet?

Andrew exchanged glances with Irene.

Check it first, she told him.

He brushed past Aoife, pushed open the bathroom door. He looked at the large window, half open, and the thick branches of a tree.

Not that one, he said, and closed the door.

The next door was the spare room, the one where she slept when she stayed with her parents. It had an en-suite bathroom with a tiny window, high in the wall. There was a sheer drop down to the parking lot below.

The Scotsman went in, looked around the bedroom, checked the bathroom.

This one, he said.

He stood outside until she was finished, then stepped back, letting her go first into the hall. She stopped in front of Irene.

I'm not going anywhere, said Aoife, unless you let me say goodbye to my parents.

Again, the exchange of glances. The Scotsman stepped away from the living-room door.

If you try anything funny, he said, you'll be putting a bullet in their heads.

Aoife opened the door, flooding the hall with light from the living room, the sound of the TV. Her parents sat in their usual places. They might as well have been alone in the flat.

Aoife leaned in through the door, as if she were just popping out to the shops, asking if anyone wanted something fetched for them. She knew there was an excellent chance that she would never see them again. But she still dreaded the thought of a real conversation.

Mum, Dad, I'm going out for a walk, with . . . Andrew? Irene will stay with you. OK?

Her father picked up the remote control, paused the television. Her mother glared at him.

Ronan! I was watching that! Now we won't know who the killer was!

It's on pause, Fiona. We can resume it when Aoife is gone.

Her father turned to her.

What did you say, dear?

Aoife looked from one to the other.

I said goodbye.

Goodbye, dear.

Her father picked up the remote control, was about to press play. Aoife spoke again:

These people aren't who they say they are.

What, dear?

They've been hunting me. They tricked you into setting a trap for me, and when they've got what they want, they'll probably kill me.

She heard muffled words behind her, someone working the slide on a pistol. She ignored the sounds, watched her parents' reaction.

Her mother closed her eyes and sighed. Her father put down the remote control, picked it up again, finally looked at her.

Aoife, please. No more lies. You promised to cooperate.

Aoife turned away from them. The Scotsman and Irene had guns aimed at her face. Aoife rolled her eyes.

Let's go, she said.

MICHAEL HAD LOST SIGHT of the canal in the taxi ride through inner Dublin. But when he reached his destination, the address written on Towse's envelope, here it was again, another wide basin, closed at either end by antique lift bridges, grey steel and greasy gears, and another set of locks by the river, a smell of the tide.

He had travelled only two miles, but more than two centuries. No dead industries here, no disused grain elevators or converted warehouses. No ghosts of bargemen, tow horses and navvies. Glass and steel, glass and brick, apartments and banks, built by overseas trusts, silicate shells of the pelagic wealth that had lately washed into this silted-up estuary, where it would feed for a while until the currents changed, at which point it would resume its larval form, drift to some other stagnant lagoon, where it would build itself new skeletons of glass and brick and steel.

A streamlined tram glided across the basin on a curved concrete bridge. Young adults strolled on the pavements. Michael recognised the way they dressed, the way they walked, eyes on screens, headphones on, the logos on the coffee cups they sipped from as they went. A few of them wore medical face masks, which made no sense to Michael: the spring air in Dublin was fresh. The masks seemed to him an affectation of distance, a withholding of self from the now.

We don't need to be here, the masks told him, or anywhere else in particular. He'd seen this before, though without so many face masks. Vancouver. Palo Alto. Dublin.

He checked the address. It was on the other side of the tram bridge, overlooking the basin. Outside, a tall stone slab, like a stele, showed the names of a hundred front companies that had spectral lives in this building. Inside was a high glass-walled foyer, waxy green plants, a security desk. A uniformed guard, sitting behind it, was the only other person in this glassy vault. He ignored Michael's ID when he tried to present it.

Over there, in that corner. Swipe your card at the door.

Michael recognised the intercom on the inner door. It was off-white plastic, made in China, the cable disappearing through a hole drilled in the frame. It was the same type of intercom he'd seen on a thousand buildings in Vancouver. *Just press the button. We'll beep you in.*

He pressed the button. There was a pause, and then a woman answered.

If it's a delivery, just leave it with security.

I'm from Inscape's head office. In Palo Alto.

A longer pause.

Are we expecting you?

He thought of Aoife. What would she say?

You should be.

Oh . . . OK, then . . . Can you please swipe your card?

It's not working . . . The X-ray machine at the airport must have killed it.

Oh . . . Just a minute.

He waited so long that he began to wonder how big this office was. Then the door beeped and swung open.

The guard was African, middle aged and very small, so that his blue polyester uniform, marked with the logo of a global security firm, looked at least one size too big. He took Michael's ID card, frowned at the picture, glared at Michael.

Why do you say your ID card doesn't work?

He seemed personally aggrieved by its failure.

Because I just tried to swipe it. And it didn't work.

A voice called from the interior.

Hi . . . Gracedieu, is it? . . . Please send in our guest.

Reluctantly, the security guard handed him his ID card and led him inside. As he followed, Michael saw a grey streak down the guard's shoulder and back. Milky sick. Burping baby. Lack of sleep. Foreign country. Shitty job. That explained his temper.

Inside was a large, airy room with panelled walls of blond wood. There were two desks, a coffee table, and an L-shaped couch which took up one corner, by a picture window with a view of the dock. Two women stood beside the desks. They were both smiling brightly, clasping their hands. The older woman stepped forward.

I'm Pauline Brady, executive president, Inscape Ireland? And this is Theresa, our receptionist? It's *so* nice to see you? We don't get many visitors from Palo Alto?

She wore a business suit with a skirt, heeled shoes, plain blouse:

the uniform of a serf. Her fake enthusiasm and smile were familiar to Michael. Her broad Dublin accent was not.

Hi, he said, then stopped, uncertain, facing them across the sweep of carpet.

The security guard sat in a chair in the corner, where his phone, charging from a socket, lay on the floor. He picked it up, tuned out of the office. Pauline bobbed her head, anxious.

Would you like to sit down, have some tea, or some coffee? Our espresso machine does a pretty good job? . . . Or, if you want, Theresa could go out for something? There are lots of little coffee shops around here? They do all the flavours?

It's true, said Theresa, nodding furiously. It's just like California, now. Everyone says it. All the programmers, and that.

Her accent was even stronger than Pauline's. She was younger, dressed identically, with a broad, worried face.

So would you like a tea or a coffee, Mr . . . Um . . . I'm so sorry? I forgot to ask your name?

Michael.

He flashed his ID, put it away again.

No thanks. I've had coffee already . . . I'll just get on with what I came for . . . I have to fly out tonight.

Oh dear, said Pauline. Oh no. Please, can we sit down first?

I'm sorry?

She pointed at the couch by the window.

Could we do this sitting down?

Do what?

Pauline brushed a strand of hair behind her ear, straightened, squared her shoulders. Theresa looked miserable.

The talk.

What talk?

Pauline and Theresa stole a look at each other.

You're not here to give us the talk?

I'm an engineer. I've come to check the server room.

The server room? Pauline's eyes widened. What's that?

Michael looked around the office. There was a metal door in the back wall, with a fire-alarm box beside it.

I'm guessing it's in there, he said.

Pauline turned and looked at the door, as if noticing it for the first time.

That's a server room, is it? What does it do?

It's like a giant computer.

Really? In there?

They've sent me to service it. Do you have a key for that door?

So, you're an engineer? . . . Is that senior management?

Do I look like senior management?

He was much younger than either of them, tired and dirty, dressed like a deserter from an underfunded war.

To be honest, said Pauline, I don't know what management looks like. I hear it's very informal, over there in California. But they never come here.

She went to her desk, opened a drawer, started raking through the contents. Theresa, relaxing, perched on the edge of her desk.

Between you and me, she said, Pauline and me was hired through a local agency. We started the same day. We take it in turns to be president.

Pauline found a key in the drawer. It had a large plastic tag, which she held up to see better.

Server room, it says. Technical staff only . . .

She looked at Michael.

It says here I have to check with Palo Alto before I let anyone in there.

In the past few weeks, Michael had been expertly conned by both Aoife and Towse, several times over. I must have learned something, he thought.

You were right, he said. I *am* senior management.

He watched the fear return to their eyes. He tried not to feel guilty.

I've come to look at the server, he said, and to check on this office. To see what you do for us, and if we can cut costs. This is a half-trillion-dollar corporation, you know. We can't afford to carry dead weight.

Theresa looked as if she might be sick. All the air had left Pauline. Her hands sank to her sides, the key hanging loose from her fingers.

Now give me that key, please . . . And while I'm inside there, I don't want to be disturbed. Under any circumstances. Do you understand?

THE CAR WAS A Pajero jeep, with plates from Northern Ireland.

You're driving, said the Scotsman, and handed her the key.

He slid into the seat behind her, put on his safety belt, settled himself in her blind spot.

This is your town. You know where to go.

Aoife's parents lived less than a mile north of the Cross Guns Bridge, with a straight road between them, no turnings. Aoife wondered if Towse had known that when he set up his rendezvous with Michael. It seemed neat, almost trite, corner-cutting.

It was early afternoon, and though she'd lost track of the news and the days of the week, she recalled, from the heavy traffic, that this was a Friday afternoon, when Dublin's business and government classes, abandoning pretence, slope off early for the weekend. The heavy traffic bought her time, as she drove south along Botanic Road. But it eased, as it always does, as the cars inched past Hart's Corner. Too soon, they had reached Whitworth Road. To the right, the Brian Boru and the furniture warehouse. A derelict grain silo. *Thirst*.

This is it, she said. The Cross Guns Bridge.

Park outside that furniture shop.

She cut the engine, folded her hands in her lap.

So, we wait?

One minute.

In the mirror, she watched him take out a medical face mask and loop it in place.

What's with that mask? I've been seeing those everywhere these past few days. Is it some kind of fad?

He ignored her question.

Give me the key, then get out.

She handed it to him, over her shoulder. Then she opened her door and got out. He mirrored her movements, so their doors clicked shut at precisely the same time.

That towpath. Walk in front of me.

They turned on to the towpath beside the canal. The wind had dropped and the sun had come out, bringing with it a couple of anglers, urbanites in tracksuits. Aoife had heard that the Royal Canal had fish in it, but she had never seen anyone catch one around here.

She slowed her steps.

He's not here, she said.

I'll be the judge of that. Keep walking.

They passed the two fishermen, who stood well apart on the edge of the basin, tackle bags and bicycles beside them on the path. One stared fixedly at his float, bobbing in the ripples, but the other one cast and recast repeatedly, dragging a spinner back and forth through the water.

He'll catch nothing like that, said the Scotsman.

You like fishing?

I like catching things.

They were near the next lock, up the rise in the towpath. Four men, street drinkers, sat along the big wooden beam that opens the lock gate. They blew smoke, talked loudly, watched Aoife approach.

The Scotsman stopped.

He's not here, he said. We'll wait at the car. He'll show up eventually.

But Aoife ignored him. She was staring at the tramps.

She might have known it.

She might have known that Towse would send Michael off to do his dirty work, while he lurked here in safety. It was what he had done every time before.

It's him, she said, walking faster.

If you don't stop, hissed the Scotsman, I'll put one in your back.

Shut up and follow me. You wanted my boss? You can have him.

She pointed at the street drinkers, who – sensing drama – had slid down off the beam and stood, leaning against it.

That lanky bastard there, on the right, said Aoife. The one with the cider. There he is. He's yours.

Towse smiled at them, raised the can, said something in Polish. His friends laughed, raised cans and bottles, drank. The Scotsman's hand went inside his jacket.

Are you taking the piss?

That's my boss. That's Towse.

*Towse?* Who the fuck is Towse? What are you talking about?

She stared at him.

You don't know who Towse is?

Towse belched loudly, grinned.

Iss werry nice day, he said.

The Scotsman took out his pistol, waved it in Towse's general direction.

That, my girl, is an alcoholic Polish tramp. We told you, we want your boss, or you and your parents are finished. We told you, no stupid games.

He *is* the boss.

No he isn't. We've been tracking you for weeks, now. We know who you work for. That Canadian hacktivist. The one whose DNA we couldn't even trace. He calls himself Atarian.

*Michael?*

It made no sense to her. How could anyone mistake Michael for an international mastermind? Who could create an illusion like that?

Towse, leaning back on his elbows, blew out a perfect smoke ring, took another swig from his can.

You were given a chance, said the Scotsman.

His gun was pointed at her face.

You won't shoot me, she said, but she found she couldn't help shutting her eyes, averting her face from the gun, as if from a cold wind. He had to be bluffing.

I'm the only lead you've got, she said. If you shoot me, you're finished.

The sound of a hammer, thumbed back, advanced a different proposition.

Now she knew why the Scotsman had put on a mask.

She screwed her eyes tighter, leaned away, listening for birdsong, a plane, the cars on the bridge. Anything but the long silence.

A bottle smashed. Something splashed in the canal. A grunt of pain, voices shouting in Polish.

Aoife opened her eyes. The Scotsman was crouched on the tow-path, one hand raised to protect his head, the other waving his gun around blindly. Blood ran down his forehead into his eyes.

A second bottle whizzed past him, narrowly missing. A can, bouncing off his shoulder, span on the towpath, discharging a stream of hot, steaming piss.

The street drinkers, crouched behind the wooden beam of the lock gate, were bombarding the Scotsman with everything they had. Towse skipped out to one side, beckoning.

Up here, Aoife! Run!

She charged past him, not breaking stride. Up over the short, steep rise in the towpath, running too hard to even think of looking back. What if the Scotsman was running after her? He'd be fitter than her, most likely. He would also be a very good shot.

The towpath was wide and straight, pitilessly exposed, for hundreds of yards ahead of her. She had to get off it before he could shoot.

There was a stone wall on the right, a grassy bank beyond it – a ridge of waste between canal and railway. She vaulted the wall, scrambled over the grass, gasping for breath, and fell down the other side, tumbling through thistles and elders, through tramp-shitted newspapers and stinging nettles, until she was caught in the briars by a fence above the tracks.

And now, held by the thorns, winded, she was finally at bay. She couldn't move her arms without thrashing the bushes. If the Scotsman came after her, there was nothing she could do.

She lay there, trusting only to silence, staring up at the sky. A freight train clacked past, but she couldn't turn her head to see it.

This was the kind of place, she knew from her police days,

where killers dumped bodies. Towpaths and railway cuttings. She had tidied herself away for the Scotsman. She had managed to tick two boxes at once.

A thrashing noise in the bushes above her.

And as she lay there, awaiting her fate, a thought struck her: why would a man piss in a beer can when he was standing beside a deserted canal?

Was this the final mystery of her short time on this planet? The wonder she would take with her into the beyond?

Towse's face appeared above her.

It's OK, he said. He's gone.

Gone?

Yeah. He left.

He was going to kill me, and then he just left?

He got a call on his phone. He left in a hurry.

She thought about that.

He's gone to kill Michael?

That's what I'm thinking.

She tried shifting her arms, gave up.

If you help me out of these briars, I won't hurt you.

Promise?

I promise.

Towse started pulling the briars away from her, one by one.

Fess's people don't know that you're part of this, Aoife said. They don't even know you exist.

That's how I like to play it.

That's what Michael was for. That's why you brought him along with us. You needed a face.

I prefer the term 'avatar'. But basically, yes.

Her arms were free now; she stretched them in front of her. Her combat jacket had protected her arms and her body, but her hands were covered in cuts from the thorns.

So all that stuff about promising Alice you'd take care of him, that was a lie?

No. I did promise her I'd look after him. Which is why he's still alive. Probably.

Probably?

Towse pulled a briar away from her leg.

I'm guessing that phone call was someone telling your Scotch friend where Michael is now. He probably triggered some kind of alarm.

Where is he?

In the server room at Inscape's Dublin front company. He's delivering my virus. That Scotch guy will be on his way over there now.

He freed her other leg and stepped back, keeping out of reach. Aoife stood. Her jeans were made of thin denim. There was a trickle of blood running down her right ankle.

She scrambled up the steep bank. When she reached the top, she looked back at Towse, who was climbing behind her.

We have to warn him.

There's no way to call him. He doesn't have a phone.

She jumped down to the towpath and set off, back towards the bridge.

You should have been there to look after him, Towse said, catching up. That's how I planned it.

I had to go see my parents. They told me my father was dying.

They had reached the second lock, where the tramps had gone back to their drinking. Maybe the threat of lethal violence was something they took in their stride, here in this half-life. Or maybe they were, very wisely, just too drunk to care. Aoife stopped, briskly hugged each of them, kept going. Towse spoke to them in Polish, ran to catch up.

How is your father?

It was a trap. Irene from London is holding them hostage and they haven't even noticed. Where's Inscape's office?

A place called Spencer Dock. You have to go there and help Michael, before it's too late.

Aoife suddenly realised, sickened, that she had a big choice to make. And history told her she wasn't good at big choices. Michael, or her parents. Then she told herself that she had no choice at all.

I can't help Michael. The Scotsman has a car. I'm on foot. But it's only a kilometre to my parents' place. I have to go help them.

They had reached the first of the two fishermen, the one with the spinner, and had to check their stride while he swung his rod to cast. His lure hit the water, and they set off again.

Aoife, listen – where does this towpath go?

She stopped, staring ahead. From where she stood, looking east-ward, she could see a mile of the canal, running past Mountjoy Prison and Croke Park stadium, towards Ballybough, North Strand, and the place where it joined the Liffey, near its mouth, in the docklands. Spencer Dock.

It's Friday afternoon in Dublin, Aoife. Gridlock. That Scotch guy's in a car. Don't worry about your parents. I'll take care of them.

You don't even know where they live.

Of course I know where they live. I promise you, I'll take care of them. Now go and help Michael.

The other fisherman had taken his shoes and socks off, rolled up his pants and was sitting on the edge of the basin, feet in the water, watching his float in a trance. He has his rod, his bag and his bicycle, Aoife thought. He doesn't care if he never catches anything. He doesn't need luck. It doesn't exist for him.

Towse, she said. Give me a lot of money.

He handed her a wad of bills. She spread them in front of the fisherman's face.

Hey mister, she said. I want to buy your bike. I need it right now.

He looked at her, then at the money. The money went in his pocket. His eyes went back to the float.

She picked up the bicycle, swung a leg over it, and took off east along the towpath.

Towse watched her go, then turned to the fisherman.

Not bad. Three thousand euros for a rusty old bike.

Not bad at all. I pulled it out of the canal when I got here. It was fouling my line.

*

THE SERVER ROOM WAS much larger than the office in front of it. Rows of steel cabinets, seven feet high and with narrow aisles between them, held stacks of networked processors, a maze of cables and switches and blinking LEDs. Fans hummed behind the cabinets, extracting their exhaust heat, piping it up to the open-plan ceiling, eight feet clear of the tops of the server stacks. An LED strip overhead, designed to minimise heat, produced just enough light to show the cables and ducts that snaked along the roof beams. Power. Cooling. Optic-fibre connections. Bottles of inert gases, pressurised, for automatic release in the event of a fire. There were also cameras mounted on servomotor swivels, watching the room from above. Michael looked at the nearest camera. It looked back. It had a little red light underneath it.

There was no helping that now. Michael locked the door from the inside, opened Towse's envelope. It contained a single page, a printout of the room's layout, with scrawled drawings in the margins, labelled with handwritten words.

Seen from above, in this printout schematic, the server banks formed a rectangular maze, not quite symmetric, with two entry/ exits on either side. Towards the middle of the maze, offset from its centre, was a small dead-end chamber. Towse had marked it *Go here*.

Michael made a couple of false turns, wandering up and down the narrow aisles between the servers, past blinking red eyes, before he found this hidden chamber. It contained a chair and a table, Ikea again, with a monitor and a keyboard and a landline telephone.

It was a long time since the last human had been here. They had left a styrofoam cup on the table, and mould had formed on the dregs of their coffee, bloomed, prospered and died, leaving a hard black slick in the bottom of the cup. Michael ran a finger over the table. No dust. Dust comes from the skin of the living. This place was a tomb.

He sat, pressed the space bar on the keyboard, and the screen came to life.

Fess's instructions showed a sketch of the PC stack under the table. It had a row of USB ports. Arrows pointed to them.

*USB ports: stick the thumb drive in any of these.*

How stupid does he think I am? Does he think I don't know what to do with a thumb drive?

It was in the envelope. He shook it out and looked at it, loose in the palm of his hand.

Michael had never held a weapon before.

The thumb drive was oval, coated in rubberised grey plastic. There was a little hole in the end so you could thread it on a key ring. Its plug was protected by a cap of the same plastic. Michael pulled at it, experimentally, and it slid off a couple of millimetres, showing bare metal underneath. He stopped. What if the cap wouldn't go on again? What if the bared plug seeped electronic spermatozoa, blindly seeking the slots of the USB ports? In the womb of this labyrinth, dark fertilisation . . . If you pulled the pin from a grenade, could you put it back in again?

He wondered if anyone else in history – even the bombardier of the *Enola Gay* – had ever triggered, one-handed, such destructive power.

Michael became aware of tiny lights blinking — green, white and red — in the row of steel cabinets opposite the table. It was hard not to feel they were watching him, that they knew why he was here. The hum of the cooling systems, the white noise of the fans, left him with only his eyes to protect him in the gloom. The camera looked down from the ceiling.

There was another row of servers behind his back. Anything could be happening there, in his blindspot.

He pushed back the chair, span it to face the rear. More lights stared at him, softly blinking, or hard and steady. In the dark gaps between them, dormant lights bided their time.

These lights made no sense to him. What were they for? No one ever came here. No one ever looked at them, or learned anything from them. If something went wrong, a message would be sent automatically to somewhere that mattered — Mumbai or Palo Alto. If a light blinks on and off in a redundant server room, and there is no one there to see it . . . Then he thought of synapses firing inside a skull. There *was* someone else here, apart from himself.

Slowly, like someone who unexpectedly finds themselves in the presence of a large carnivore, Michael put the thumb drive back in the envelope. Slowly, he rose from the chair.

If Towse was telling the truth, this was too big for him. He didn't want to destroy the world he'd grown up in. He remembered Alice, the life they'd shared together, less than three months before. It had been comfortable, really. It seemed a paradise, now. And even though it was lost – for him, and for Alice – other people still lived it. Traffic lights and central heating. Parks and bridges. Schools and hospitals. Movies and childhood. These things weren't bad – far from it. But they were also expressions of money. Were they enemies as well?

It couldn't be true. Towse must be using him. This was Inscape, Campbell Fess's company. Towse and Fess had an old score between them. But Michael would not serve.

The little lights were still watching him. Had there been a change in their configuration, their winks and hard stares? Were they forming shapes behind his back, monstrous glyphs, adding mass and dimensions, gathering substance, moving to attack?

He folded the instructions, put them back in his pocket. He would turn and walk out of here, into the sunshine.

On the desk, the telephone rang.


PLEASE, SAID AOIFE, TRYING to catch her breath. I'm looking for a friend of mine. Michael – is he here?

The two women stared back at her. The older one spoke:

How did you get into this office? That door is meant to be locked.

It doesn't matter. Is he here?

The women looked at each other, then at the door of the server room.

He doesn't want to be disturbed.

I need to talk to him right now.

A security guard appeared, unhooking his radio.

You can't come running in here, miss. You must show me ID or I'll call the police.

Please, said Aoife, appealing to the women. Can't you just tell him I'm here? . . . I'm his girlfriend. There's a problem.

The two women looked at each other again.

What's your name?

Aoife.

The older one picked up a phone.

I'll tell him you're here. But we can't let you in there.

She identified a button, pressed it. Aoife saw a red light flutter on the phone. Pick up, please, Michael, she thought, attempting telepathy.

The lady listened a while, put the phone down.

He's not answering.

Come on, said the security guard. You must go.

He touched her elbow to steer her away.

That's OK, said a woman's voice behind them. She can stay.

Barb Collins stood in the hallway. She wore her Stanford hoodie, and a company tote bag hung from a shoulder. In one hand, she held the handle of a suitcase. In the other was her Inscape ID. It was gold. The guard looked at it, stepped away.

You two ladies can go back to work, she said. You too, guard. I'll take it from here.

She put her head to one side, smiled at Aoife.

And you, honey, don't make a fuss now. Come over to this couch and we'll have a little chat. Girl to girl.

MICHAEL WATCHED THE LIGHT on the phone, mesmerised, until it stopped flashing. Someone was looking for him, someone other than the women in the office outside. Someone who knew he was here.

What if they were already outside that door? What if they tried to come in here?

He looked about him. The lights in the servers – were they blinking a little faster, in sync with his pulse? Had more eyes opened behind him, to stare at his back while he was distracted by the phone? Were forces gathering against him, inside the door as well as outside it?

That second camera up there – had it swivelled towards him? It was pointing right at him now, more or less.

For the first time in his life, Michael was trapped. He had no way to run and nowhere to hide. You never know what someone will do, until they are cornered. After that, you know who they are.

The computer screen showed him the time. Two twenty-five. In only five minutes, OmniCent would go live.

*This machine kills fascists.* A dirt track in the mountains. All the stories Towse had told him. All the books he'd had to read, for want of anything better to do, since he'd gone on the run without a laptop or a phone . . .

He remembered Shevek in *The Dispossessed*, and his mission

of light to the profiteer planet. *Well, you have me . . . You have your anarchist . . .*

Or Red in *Roadside Picnic*, the cynical survivor, throwing off his despair, in the crunch, to petition the Zone for his fading daughter, his dead father, his tired wife, his lost fellow stalkers. *Happiness, free, for everyone, and let no one be forgotten.*

Absurd.

Alice.

For the second time that afternoon, Michael took out the thumb drive. This time, he removed the cap.

BARB COLLINS PUT HER ID back in her tote bag, left her hand inside it.

Let's sit on that couch, honey. You go first. In the corner. Against the wall.

Barb Collins, much larger than Aoife, seemed to block any hope of escape. She settled her bag on the couch, away from Aoife, her hand still inside it.

Well, here we are, she said contentedly. Just two working girls, passing the time.

Aoife smiled tightly.

What will we talk about, so? Boys?

Barb Collins shook her head.

Guns.

Aoife nodded at the tote bag.

What you got there, then?

Browning Hi-Power, nine millimetre. The gun's a bit meh, but the bullets are hollow point.

Aoife looked at Barb Collins's wheelie case.

I don't think so. I think you just got off a plane. How would you get a gun through airport security?

I came on Fess's private jet, honey. People with Gulfstreams bring what they want.

Fair enough . . . I have a gun too.

Barb Collins put her head back and laughed.

Oh honey, that's a good one!

I really do. It's a .25 Beretta.

A *purse* gun? That's adorable. Where did you get that, girlfriend?

I was in the police here.

The so-called police in this country aren't trusted with firearms. Nice bluff, though.

With a name like Collins, you should know more about the partition of Ireland.

Barb Collins stopped smiling.

You know my name, then. That's not good.

Aoife decided to change tack.

How did you know I'd be here?

I didn't. I came here for your boss. Atarian. He waltzed in through the lobby half an hour ago, bold as brass, in front of all the cameras. Our facial-recognition systems lit up like a Christmas tree. Palo Alto called me straight away. And, by coincidence, I'd just landed in

Dublin, to have a little word with *you*, honey. Turns out, I'm getting a twofer from this trip.

You believe in coincidence, do you?

I believe that I'm here, and so are you, and so is Atarian.

They must have known I'd be coming to Ireland, thought Aoife, even before I turned up at my parents' flat. They would have got my mailbox number from my parents. They would have hacked into it, found out that I'd called it. They'd know where I called from, and when, in Paris. They'd had time to get ready, move Barb Collins to Europe. She would have done most of the hurting . . . But that didn't matter now. The Scotsman would be here soon, and then Aoife would have no chance at all. Neither would Michael. She had to move Barb Collins around, try to work herself an opening before it was too late.

I give up, said Aoife. Let's go in there now and get him. I'll make him come quietly.

No thanks, honey. There's a fire exit at the back of the server room. I'm not making a move until my guy is there to cover it. I don't want to scare your boss into running away.

Barb Collins's phone beeped.

That'll be my guy now.

She reached behind her, not taking her eyes from Aoife, and took her phone from her hip pocket. She glanced at the message. Her expression changed. She swiped at the screen, put the phone to her ear.

Where are you? . . . Change of plan. Don't wait. As soon as you get here, go in the back way. I'm going in the front, now. Fess just texted me: the timing just went critical. On sight, he said.

Barb Collins killed the call, shouldered her bag, her hand still inside it.

Walk in front of me. Over to that door.

You sure about this? – Aoife kept her voice down – You want to risk making trouble in front of these people?

I'll shoot everyone in this room, if it suits me.

You'd be on all the cameras.

Honey, we *own* all the cameras.

Barb Collins stopped by the desk where the older woman sat, pretending to type.

You. Open the door to the server room.

I can't. The engineer from Palo Alto has the key. He won't even answer the phone.

Barb Collins turned to the security guard.

You. Do you have a key?

That isn't my department.

Then break this door down. That's an order.

The guard stared back at her, disbelieving.

This is inappropriate. I'm calling my supervisor.

Barb Collins put her head on one side.

Do you know who I am?

It doesn't matter who you are. I have my job to do. I'm going to have to report this to my control room.

He unhooked his radio.

Say again? said Barb Collins. Come closer. I can't hear you.

He took another step towards her, put the radio to his ear.

I said, I'm going to report this—

Barb Collins hadn't been bluffing. The brute steel of her pistol, held flat in her palm, smashed into the bridge of his nose. Blood drooled on the grey nylon carpet. She swung the gun again, into the side of his head. He fell.

She stamped on the walkie-talkie, turned it to fragments. The guard's mobile phone, charging on the carpet, went the same way.

The gun now menaced Aoife and the horrified women behind their desks.

You two – on the ground. Face down. Cross your ankles. Put your hands behind your heads and lace your fingers. You, what's your name – break the door down, or I'll shoot these nice people before I shoot you.

Barb Collins racked the slide on her pistol, stood over the prone figures, aimed at the guard's head. Unconscious, he snored through the mess of cartilage and blood-froth that used to be his nose. The two women were so stiff with fear that they might as well have been dead already. Barb Collins kicked the younger woman hard in the ribs.

I'll shoot this one first, if you don't get that door open.

Aoife backed away a couple of steps, then launched herself at the door with her shoulder. She hit it, bounced off.


THE THIRD FROM LAST item on Towse's list of instructions: *After you stick in the thumb drive, press the button marked 'Install'.*

Michael had once spent a whole day trying to install a driver for a second-hand printer, only for Alice to point out he'd downloaded the wrong one. Towse, on the other hand, had set up the destruction of online global finance to be a simple matter of plug and play.

Here it was. The little button popping up in the middle of the screen, ringed in blue: *Install*.

Beady eyes blinked and glared in the half-light. Now or never. His finger hovered over the mouse button. He couldn't really do this, could he?

*This machine kills . . .* He could.

Another window popped up.

*Enter master password.*

Someone started beating at the door.

AOIFE RECOGNISED THE LOCK. She could have picked it with a paper clip. But this game had just changed. She was the one who was playing for time, now. *On sight*, Barb Collins had told the Scotsman on the phone. The verb *shoot* had been silent, but Aoife had heard it . . . Michael was in there. As for herself, she couldn't see Barb Collins having much use for her, once this door opened . . .

She launched herself at it again, hard, but at a slant. It was a heavy metal door, but designed to contain fires rather than keep out intruders, and it opened inwards. If she hit it too hard, it might actually give.

\*

THE DOOR THUDDED AGAIN. Michael looked at the instructions. The paper shook in his hand. He had to put it down on the desk so he could read it.

*Enter password: 3mordn1laP. Press return.*

He did as he was told. The button sat there a while, as if thinking it over, and then it blinked out, leaving just the home screen.

Had it worked? Was it really that easy? Even his credit card, when he'd had one, often demanded two-stage authentication.

The door thudded again.

Second-from-last item on the list: *Don't leave the thumb drive in the computer.*

Michael snatched at the thumb drive, stuffed it in a pocket. Last item: *Get out of there now: there's a fire door at the back of the room.*

The map of the maze had arrows showing the way.

He hurried along, bumping off the sides as he went. The static charge from the servers pulled at his arm hairs, trying to detain him. Cameras watched from the ceiling, passive-aggressive. Red eyes implored him: *What have you done?*

Was there any change? Had his action had consequence? Did lights still blink in the same sequence, or were they assembling in new constellations?

Another heavy thump on the door, the sound of voices, a woman shouting angrily.

The map hadn't lied to him. He was clear of the maze, had reached the back of the server room. There was another door here, smaller than the office door, sheathed in dull metal. A green plastic sign, dimly lit, said *Fire Exit*. There was a glass-fronted box on the wall beside it, a hammer mounted on a bracket.

*In the event of fire, break glass to open fire door. Warning: door is alarmed.*

He pulled the hammer from its bracket and smashed in the glass.

ONE OF THE WOMEN was weeping. A computer printer, silent until now, chattered and whined, then went quiet again. Why do printers do that? Aoife wondered. Are they talking in their sleep? Coming back to life? Will I? Where is *my* respawn point?

She was aware of Barb Collins, invisible, in the void behind her, the yawning maw of the gun barrel, waiting to funnel her out of this world, away from this door in front of her, which, right now, was all the world that she had left. Her shoulder was bruising. That was something else to savour.

I think it gave a little that time, she said, not daring to look around.

Last chance, said Barb Collins. If I have to break it myself, you'll already be dead.

Had Barb cocked her gun already, or would there be one last warning click? Aoife retreated a couple of steps, threw herself at the door.

MICHAEL WOULD HAVE LIKED to hear the wail of an air raid, or a Stuka's death dive. Instead, he heard a low, apologetic *barp*, repeated every few seconds, and a voice from the ceiling, computer generated.

*Fire: leave now.*

The emergency door clicked open, automatically triggered by the fire-defence system. Michael pushed it, went through. A spring closed it behind him.

He was in a short, bare corridor, lined with other emergency exits. At one end was a glass outer door with daylight beyond it. One by one, the other doors sprang open. People emerged, workers from the building's other offices, techies and admin, streaming away from the fire alarm. They filled up the space in front of him, pushing their way to the street. Some carried laptops, children rescued from a blaze, but all of them were holding their telephones. A few had raised them over the crowd, framing selfies, updating social media. Michael ducked his face from their periscope eyes.

The crowd carried him along the corridor and into the street. There, blinking in the daylight, he looked about him, getting his bearings. He was in a lane at the back of the building. The other evacuees milled around, talking and complaining. No one seemed to think this alarm was for real.

The day was the same. The world hadn't changed since he'd gone into the server room.

Screams, the roar of an engine, the crowd parting. People tripping each other in their scramble to escape. A Pajero jeep careened, wrong way, down the lane. Scattered, people turned and swore after it. The jeep lurched to a halt at the fire exit, parked skew in the road. The driver's door flew open. Michael saw a face that he'd seen only once before, from under a blanket on the back of a Land Rover.

Cursing and shoving, wiping blood from his forehead with a crumpled paper face mask, the Scotsman forced his way in through the fire exit, pushing aside the last evacuees.

AOIFE WAS RIGHT ABOUT the fire door. One honest shoulder was all that it took. The door collapsed inward and her momentum took her into the room beyond it, whether she liked it or not.

She did like it. Barb Collins did not. As Aoife pounded across the floor, she heard the other woman shouting after her. A voice from the rafters told her to leave. Something about a fire. An insistent alarm tone. But these weren't pressing matters for Aoife. She saw rows of steel cabinets, twinkling lights, a gap in the middle, maybe somewhere to hide. She launched herself at it, made it through the dark opening, just as Barb Collins charged into the room.

Aoife banged into one of the cabinets, bruising the other shoulder, then dodged right, down an aisle between the servers. Fairy lights blinked in inscrutable patterns.

She reached the end of a short passage, turned left, left again, flattened herself against a cabinet.

Hey Michael, she shouted, addressing the ceiling. Don't answer me! Barb Collins is in here too. She has a gun and she's been told to kill us.

She switched her position, another right and a left, holding her breath, stopping to listen. She could turn a corner and find Michael in hiding. Or walk into a bullet from Barb Collins's gun.

Would Barb Collins follow her into this maze, or would she wait at the entrance for them to come out?

*Fire*, reminded the voice in the ceiling. *Leave now.*

Soon, firefighters would come, building management, maybe the police. Would the women in the office call for help?

Barb Collins must have reached the same conclusion: she didn't have much time.

You two, she shouted. Come out of there. I'm not going to hurt you. We need to get out of here, quick.

Aoife said nothing.

Come on out. You want the Irish cops to find you? The secret renditions are already signed. Come with me and I'll get you out of here on the Gulfstream. We'll make our own deal. You, me and Fess.

Still, Aoife said nothing. Barb Collins spoke again:

Don't make me come in there after you.

It occurred to Aoife that maybe she would.

Hey, Barb, she called. I'm armed. If you come in here, I'll shoot.

You've got nothing. Irene had you searched.

I got the gun after they searched me. It was hidden in the bathroom of my parents' flat.

Cut the crap, honey. We've all seen *The Godfather*.

It seemed to Aoife that Barb's voice had moved since the last time she'd heard it. Barb Collins was triangulating on Aoife's voice, trying to fix her position. She was already inside the maze.

Aoife looked up at the ceiling, at the LED strip that oozed light into the server room. It was right over her head. There was also a camera, pointing towards her. Was it watching her? Could it see where she was?

Aoife didn't like guns. Any monkey could shoot one. But she took out the tiny semi-automatic that McDonnell had given her, four years before, for concealed protection on that stake-out in Lurgan; the gun she'd brought to Dublin by mistake on the late train from Belfast, having forgotten it was in her bag when she'd gone on the booze there last Christmas – her goodbye drinks, in fact; the gun that – sobering up the next day, realising she was illegally armed in the wrong jurisdiction – she had stashed behind a panel in her parents' spare bathroom.

It was a long time since she'd been on a gun range, but it took her only one shot to take out the light. The darkness rang in her ears.

Come and look for me now, Barb, she thought.

MICHAEL RAN ON TO the bridge that carried the tramlines over the basin. There, he stopped to get his breath. Afternoon had chased off the clouds, turned spring into premature summer. Kids from the local council flats swarmed around the basin. Some wore cheap wetsuits, others swimsuits or underwear. They jumped from the dockside with knees hugged to chins. A police car, called to suppress this outbreak of free fun, parked a short way off, not intervening. The cops, unlike the office managers who'd complained about the swimmers, knew that, for those who were born here, this was still the docks.

The traffic seemed to Michael to be heavier than ever. Cars idled in the street, trapped by peristaltic lights, moving only two or three car lengths at each phase of green. They were waiting to cross a white cable-rigged bridge, like a giant egg slicer, that spanned Dublin's river – the Liffey, was it? – at the end of Spencer Dock.

Nothing had changed. The sky was the same colour. So much for the doomsday that he had been promised.

What next? He could call Aoife again, at her parents' house. But he didn't think he had the right. He hadn't been fair to her. He'd accused her of working with Towse, to trick him into coming to Ireland. Turned out, the bad faith was his. And it's much harder to forgive the ones we have wronged than the ones who have wronged us. How could he face her? Towse thought Michael was in love with her, which was silly enough, but to think she could feel anything for him . . . ?

He would go back and look for Towse at the Cross Guns Bridge, on the off chance that, having got what he wanted from Michael, Towse hadn't already cleared off. But he'd left her a message. What if Aoife was there too? He felt sick when he thought of her.

There was a taxi over there, idling at the traffic light. Too late. The traffic light turned green and the taxi moved off before Michael could reach it. The next car followed. But the one after stayed put, as if stalled in the road. A horn sounded behind it, then another, then more, and now the space between the buildings blared with angry car horns, venting their rage on the woman who sat, oblivious, at the wheel of her Prius, staring down at her phone, with two precious car-lengths of asphalt in front of her, the light turning orange, holding up the southbound lane.

A policeman got out of the parked squad car and tapped on her window. The woman glanced up at him, startled, then drove off through the red light, looking at her phone, the policeman running after.

Something strange was happening up and down the street. Several cars pulled over to the kerb, mounted the pavement. Doors swung open and drivers got out, distracted, staring at their phones. Others, trapped in the gridlock, leaned on their horns, shouted insults, then, as the infection spread, fell silent themselves, picked up phones and turned on radios. People spilled from the doors of offices and apartments – smokers, and non-smokers who were smoking now – staring at phones or tablets or laptops.

The cop stood in the junction, ignoring the stalled traffic. He too was now looking at his phone.

The traffic noise faded, replaced by the ping of push notifications, a murmur of voices, telephones ringing. The loudest sound now was the whooping of the children, splashing in the basin. Their game was much older, and built to endure.

What had he done? He had to ask someone.

That guy – he'd do. Cargo pants and takeaway coffee. Outsize glasses, beard, too-tight shirt, tote bag branded for the tech firm he probably worked for. He stood, rooted to the pavement, staring at his phone. He was wearing a face mask over his beard.

Hey, said Michael, what's going on?

The guy looked at Michael, then down at his phone again.

Michael tried again.

Is something happening? Everyone on the street is looking at their phones.

This time, the guy didn't bother to look up.

So look at yours.

I haven't got one.

Too bad for you.

He continued his scrolling.

Michael felt an unfamiliar urge. Something had changed in him lately. He felt like pissing someone off.

I said, let me see your phone, pal.

Fuck off. This phone cost me twelve hundred euros. I'm not handing it to some rando in the street.

Michael took out a bunch of five-hundred-euro bills, stuffed them into the guy's shirt pocket, snatched the phone from his hands.

Hey! Give that back! I don't want your germs on it!

I left you a fucking deposit.

He turned his back on the guy, just to heighten the buzz. It was a dick move, he knew, one he'd learned from the kids who'd bullied him in high school. Go on – I dare you. I'm making it easy.

The phone was open on a news feed. Frantic headlines, updating every few seconds.

*Massive sell-off in New York exchanges . . . Dollar in free fall . . . Fed helpless to intervene.*

Jesus, said the guy behind him. This is three thousand euros, in cash.

Shut up. I'm reading.

*High-frequency trading bots run amok . . . New cryptocurrency exposes critical flaw in online financial systems . . .*

Hey, I'm sorry, man. I thought you were a local. One of those Irish junkies.

Shut up, can't you?

*Inscape stock worthless . . .*

I did this, thought Michael. I know it. We did it. Me and Towse and Aoife. Whatever this turns out to be, wherever it goes next, we did it.

Alice. He'd forgotten Alice. But she had done this, more than anyone. This was her day, and she wasn't here. He blinked.

I can't believe this, said the guy behind him. I can't believe Inscape is tanking now, of all times. This new virus would have made us king of the world.

Michael turned and looked at him.

What new virus? What are you talking about?

Don't you follow the news? Where have you been?

I've been travelling. What new virus?

It's like the flu, but it kills lots more people. They shut the schools here yesterday, because of it. That's why all these kids are here now, instead of in class. They might even have to shut the pubs.

In Ireland? That sounds awful.

No, it's great.

*What?*

This virus sticks to surfaces, so cash could be pretty much banned. If the shops are closed, retail will shift to the big online players. Inscape's tech would take over the world.

Right . . . Do you by any chance subcontract for Inscape?

We're a wholly-owned subsidiary. And most of my stock is vested in Inscape . . .

His eyes, which were all that Michael could see of his face over the mask, suddenly widened.

Hey . . . if global stocks have tanked, then my Krugerrands must be worth a lot more now. I might even be ahead . . . Give me my phone back; I want to check the price of gold.

Michael hefted the phone a couple of times, and then he threw it across the grass verge of the basin, over the heads of the diving kids. It splashed in the water, went under.

Keep the change, he said, and left.


SEE THE SCOTSMAN, CHARGING down the emergency corridor, reaching the fire door at the end. There, he stops. You can see him on the CCTV, blood caked on his face, considering his next move.

He hasn't been trained to leap without looking.

With one hand under his jacket, he uses his free hand to open the door, just an inch or two. He looks into the darkened server room, then lets the door shut. The hand comes from under his jacket, holding a gun.

He waits a couple of beats, getting his breath back. Then, in one smooth movement, he opens the door, just wide enough to slip through it, and eases it shut behind him. The corridor is empty at last. There's no soundtrack on this footage. But you can tell that he goes without making a sound.

*

AOIFE SQUATTED WITH HER back against a server stack, the tiny pistol held between her knees. She watched the LEDs dance on the units. For all their sparkles, flutters, they gave her no light for the sights of her gun.

*Fire. Leave now.*

Aoife parted her knees experimentally, watching lights disappear as her knees eclipsed them, confirming her existence by the transit of her limbs. The same lights would betray her if she dared to move about.

This was a stand-off.

There were three of them in it, she had to assume: Barb, herself, and possibly Michael. The cameras above might be a fourth element, if they could see in the dark.

Barb Collins would definitely shoot on sight. Aoife probably wouldn't be able to bring herself to do that. But Barb Collins didn't know that.

*Fire. Leave now.*

She spotted something new above her head: a thin beam of light, a narrow wedge on the ceiling, revealing colour-coded cables, a red cylinder, pressurised gas for fire control. Daylight, diffused. Someone had cracked a door open. Was it at the front of the room, or the back? She'd lost her bearings in this labyrinth.

*Fire. Leave now.*

The light returned, the wedge wider this time, then it was gone. Someone had sneaked through a door of the server room. Michael?

*Fire. Leave now.*

How long had she been in here already? Time slows down when life speeds up. Two minutes? Three?

It had to be Michael. She had to bet on that. He'd found a way out, so now she should move too. If the local police caught her, they would pass her into American hands. Barb Collins hadn't been lying about that. Aoife had heard of worse places than Guantanamo.

*Fire. Leave now.*

She put the pistol in her jacket pocket, got on all fours, crawled to the next corner, got lower, put her head around it.

Fireflies. Red eyes blinking, white eyes staring.

*Fire. Leave now.*

She rounded the corner, crawled along this new reach of the maze. The carpet was thin, overlaying metal floor plates. She had to move slowly, or the sound would betray her.

This was a dead end. She turned, made her way back to the junction she'd come from. This time, she kept straight, reached another row of servers, saw a gap to her right.

How many paths could there be through one rather simple arrangement of cabinets? What were the odds she could sneak out without meeting Barb Collins?

*Warning: inert gases will deploy in sixty seconds.*

What?

She remembered the bottles she'd seen in the ceiling before she shot out the light. Inert gases, used to smother fires without shorting out electronic components. They would vent automatically, if nobody cancelled the alarm.

Were they poisonous? That wouldn't make sense – poisonous gas in a crowded building . . . But maybe they would stifle you, block your access to oxygen, the same way, presumably, that they suffocated flames?

Aoife fought the urge to get up and run. She had sixty seconds.

*Warning: inert gases will deploy in fifty seconds.*

Another dead end. She must have missed a gap. She turned around, went back. Here it was: a space on her left.

It felt like she was working her way deeper into the maze, rather than out of it.

There was something else here. Light. A square of blue, a lit computer screen. It showed her a table, a keyboard and a mouse. A dead-end chamber at the heart of the maze.

Its light would also show Aoife to anyone who came around that corner.

She heard the creak of a floor plate, relieved of a stealthy weight.

*Warning: inert gases will deploy in forty seconds.*

Aoife dived under the table, desperately pulling out plugs. When the last one came out, the monitor died. She was back in the darkness. But now she was under a table, the worst place to hide . . .

She waited.

*Warning: inert gases will deploy in thirty seconds.*

There really were more lights now, dancing along the fronts of the servers. She was sure of it. More of them were blinking, and most of these were red. Was something wrong with the computers? Had Michael done whatever he came for?

*Warning: inert gases will deploy in twenty-five seconds.*

The lights had changed again. They were shimmering, pulsing on and off in geometric patterns, murmurations of stars.

The lights now switched on all at once, then off again, then on, then off. And she saw, moving stealthily across their pulsing field of light, the silhouette of a person, and the shape of a gun.

*Warning: inert gases will deploy in twenty seconds.*

Aoife felt her heart beat in her ears.

The lights came on, went off again. The figure moved past them, its motion captured and heightened by the flickering glow, as if by the strobe at a rave. Aoife watched Barb Collins creep past the table, deeper into the blind central chamber.

When she was sure she had passed, Aoife slid out from under the table, crawling silently away in the opposite direction.

She turned a corner, got up, ran.

*Warning: inert gases will deploy in fifteen seconds.*

A dead end. She turned back, tried another way. Her feet drummed on the floor. Somewhere behind her, Barb Collins was running too.

Which way to go?

The lights had changed pattern again, shimmering from left to right, left to right.

As good a way as any. Aoife moved right.

Heavy breathing behind her.

*Warning: inert gases will deploy in ten seconds.*

She turned another corner. Another new pattern – iridescent gauzy veils, the aurora borealis, waving and dancing, right to left, right to left.

Aoife went left.

She could see a dim light at the end of this aisle.

*Fire Exit*, it said.

*Inert gases will deploy in five seconds. Warning: deployment will cause severe overpressure. Open your mouth and cover your ears.*

She reached the door, pushed against it.

A bullet hit the wall, inches from her shoulder.

She was through the door, running.

*Gases deploying. All fire doors will be locked for the next fifteen minutes.*

She reached the street exit, looked back. The Scotsman was standing in the fire door, holding it open, aiming a pistol at her.

An invisible giant kicked Aoife, hard, in the sinuses and ears. The door to the street blew out on its hinges. She shot through it on to the pavement, and lay there, stunned.

Cut to the CCTV footage. The fire door – blown outward by the gases vented into the server room – strikes the wall, bounces back into the Scotsman, smashing his nose. You can slow it right down, if you want to see clearly.

White mist swirls from the darkened room into the corridor. The Scotsman, a ghost in this chemical fog, is swaying in the fire door, somehow still standing and holding it open. He is no doubt disoriented, probably concussed. But we see him steady himself, aim the gun again, lower this time, to where Aoife lies in the exit, half in, half out of the door to the street. Then his body jerks several times, as if struck from behind. He falls back into the server room. The door, now unobstructed, swings shut behind him, locks automatically. End of scene.

Aoife, lying on the pavement, saw the Scotsman take aim at her. She saw him fall. And unlike the CCTV system, which had no microphones, she also heard the gunshots from inside the server room. Then she was up and running, and she didn't look back.

MICHAEL SPOTTED A TAXI for hire, a blue Skoda Octavia estate. It cruised north off the egg-slicer bridge, past the people glued to their phones and car radios, the splashing, joyful kids. The driver stopped when Michael hailed him.

Where to?

He was a big guy, early fifties, with messy brown hair.

Michael got in the back.

You know the Cross Guns Bridge?

Everybody knows the Cross Guns Bridge, my friend. Sooner or later, we all have to cross it.

Michael looked at the driver, suspicious. He could see his eyes in the rear-view mirror.

What do you mean by that? That sounds like an old saying, or something.

Nah. It's a statement of fact. The Cross Guns Bridge is a terrible bottleneck. It's a nightmare at rush hour.

Well, the traffic seems pretty light right now.

Yeah. It's funny, that. This is normally peak rush hour, Fridays. Must be this new virus. Apparently, they've just found the first confirmed case in Ireland. Some kid in a school near my house . . .

They had turned west, away from Spencer Dock. Council housing on one side, on the other a stone-built Victorian railway, its arches, glassed in, home to boxing clubs and car repair shops. Kids in cheap wetsuits trotted in groups down the pavements, or pulled wheelies on their bicycles, rushing to join the fun at Spencer Dock, ground zero of global financial Armageddon. So this was how wars felt, thought Michael. There's always someone having fun.

To be honest, said the driver, I've been too busy with my own stuff to follow the news much. I only drive part-time, to help feed the family. And to get out of the house a bit. The real thing I do is, I write.

Write?

I'm trying to finish a novel. But I'm a bit stuck.

They stopped at a traffic light, waited behind other cars, went through it, crossed a bridge. A high stone wall hid a railway cutting. They were getting close.

What kind of novel?

A novel of ideas. I think. But I'm losing my grip on the plot. Too many coincidences. I try to avoid them, but they keep popping up.

Maybe someone's trying to tell you something.

The driver pulled over at the furniture shop.

We're here, he said.

Michael handed the driver a bank note.

I can't change that. That's five hundred euros.

Keep the change.

It's far too much.

Is it? You might think that it's valuable now, but by the time you try to spend it, it could be worth nothing.

Is that, like, a parable, or something? Is that Ford Maddox Ford?

It's a statement of fact.

Well, I like the sound of it. I should use it in my book.

The taxi drove off. Michael was back where he'd started, beside the Cross Guns Bridge. Sooner or later, we all have to cross it . . .

It was late afternoon. People stood outside the pub across the road, smoking and laughing. They didn't look worried about anything much. A fisherman sat on the edge of the canal, bathing his feet in it, watching his float. Cyclists rode home on the towpath, finished work for the weekend.

He walked a little way up the canal. There was no sign of Towse. The beer can bobbed in the middle of the basin. It still hadn't sunk.

Aoife. Did he have any right to try to call her? He felt in his pocket, and then remembered that he'd used their only coin that last time he'd called . . . Was that even an hour ago?

He wondered if she'd really been out that time. Or had she been standing beside her mother, who'd answered the call, while Aoife's father lay in the next room, dying or dead. *He's just someone I travelled with. I can't deal with him now, at a time like this. He wasn't fair to me. I don't want to see him again. Please, fob him off for me. Take a message.*

He didn't know her address. You only gave me your number. You never gave me your situation. Aoife was smart.

Michael watched the lone fisherman, mesmerised by his red

plastic float. It bobbed in the ripples. Michael had never done any fishing. How would you know a ripple from the first gentle tug on the bait? At what point did the fish realise it was hooked? He'd heard that if you caught them and freed them, they would come back for more.

Beyond Aoife, really, there was Alice. It was Alice who had brought him here, one way or another. He still didn't feel that his debt was discharged. Far from it. He saw Alice in all the grains of his memory. He saw her watching him from the bed, that first morning in Vancouver. Was she watching him now? He ached with the thought. If only she could.

He should spend some time alone with Alice, now. If she wanted to leave him, she could go when she was ready. Never again would he push her away.

Hey you.

He turned, startled.

There was a young woman behind him, straddling a bicycle. The bike was covered in bubblegum stickers, hiding the rust. It had blue and purple tassels hanging from its handle bars. The tassels matched her hair. She wore torn leggings, Dr. Martens, a T-shirt. *The Cult*, it said, with the band's logo, and she had written underneath, in heavy black marker, *She Steals Stationery*.

Michael?

She wore a lot of black eyeliner, smudged in the corners.

Why do you ask?

I said, are you Michael?

Who wants to know?

Yoyodime.

*Yoyodime?*

Yeah. I'm from Yoyodime, bud. I have something for you.

Yoyodime doesn't exist. It never got started.

It did in Dublin. We're doing the beta test. Now, do you want your change or not? I have to get back to the 'Batter.

Change?

Here.

She tossed him a cylinder wrapped in brown paper. This time, he managed to catch it. He cracked it open. It was a roll of fifty-cent coins.

What's this for?

They told me you might need some coins for a phone call.

What phone call?

That would be *your* business.

Who's 'they'?

This is Yoyodime, bud. You should know how it works.

She got on her bike and rode off.

Michael walked down the street, past the warehouse, to the Brian Boru pub and the phone box outside it.

The telephone was ringing. He waited. It didn't stop.

He opened the door, lifted the receiver.

Hello Alice, he said.

*

AOIFE USED THE STAIRS instead of the lift, going up slowly, one hand on the banister, the other holding her pistol concealed inside her sleeve.

When she reached the top landing she flattened herself against the wall, away from the peep hole in her parents' door.

She listened. Nothing.

She slid down the wall, peeked under the door. If someone was standing there, she'd see the shadows of their feet.

Nothing.

Aoife gave the door a push. Unlocked, it swung open.

The hallway was dark.

She listened.

No sound from the living room. The worst sound of all. The TV should be on. It never went off here, in daylight hours.

Dead horses watched as she inched down the hallway, the gun held out in front of her.

She knew she should clear the other rooms first, the closed doors that she was passing. Irene could be lurking behind one, ready to pop out and shoot her in the back. But Aoife's world was all ahead of her, behind that living-room door. It was there that she had left her parents, watching television.

She reached the door, closed her eyes, listened again.

Still nothing.

She pushed the door.

Towse sat alone on the sofa by the window. He was reading something on her mother's tablet, the one she used for online shopping, and for checking TV schedules, and the names of dead actors on IMDb.

He looked up, smiled.

Aoife. There you are.

She swung her body from the waist, probing each corner of the room with the muzzle of her pistol. When she turned back to Towse, it was aimed at him.

Where are my parents?

They've gone for a walk by the river. We had a nice chat, and I pointed out that it's a lovely afternoon. They spend way too much time indoors, you know.

What happened to Irene?

She'll be halfway to the border by now. You won't see her again.

Aoife took another step towards him, gun aimed at his chest. Something had changed about him, she couldn't think what.

You should put the gun down, Aoife. It's not your thing.

She saw it, now. Either he had changed his suit or it had been dry-cleaned, pressed, restored. His shoes had been polished. Even his face was how it had been when she'd first met him, in the foyer of her safe house in London. Clean, more or less shaven, the bruises gone.

She thumbed on the safety, put the pistol in her pocket.

How did you get rid of Irene, Towse?

I showed her this.

He handed her the tablet. She looked at its screen. It was open on the *Irish Times* website.

## BREAKING NEWS:

*Woman detained after fatal shooting in Dublin.*

By Owen Simmons.

*Gardai have arrested a female suspect after a man was shot dead in a central Dublin office building.*

*A Garda spokesperson said that firefighters found the woman semi-conscious, after a fire alarm at the Spencer Dock office of Inscape Technologies. The body of the man was found in the same room, with multiple gunshot wounds. Both he and the suspect appear to have been armed.*

*Inscape Technologies said in a statement that there is no connection between this incident and the collapse of international financial markets earlier this afternoon. The crash, triggered by uncontrolled computer trading, has been linked to the unofficial roll-out today of a new global cryptocurrency, OmniCent, designed by Inscape Technologies. The new currency has now been withdrawn.*

*More to follow . . .*

When Irene saw that, Towse said, she knew she wasn't getting paid. She walked out the door without saying goodbye. Your mother was rather hurt by that. She'd taken a liking to Irene.

Where's Michael?

He's not mentioned in that news report. I guess he must have got away. Do you want to go back and look for him?

Did she have any right? She could have done more for him.

It had all been a farce, her thinking that she was the protector, while –
behind her back – doors opened and shut. They'd travelled together,
they'd done what they'd done out of boredom or loneliness, but
now it was over. He couldn't stay here, and neither could she. But
it didn't make sense that they'd stay together. He was never going
to be able to trust her. Once a mark, always a mark.

He's a nice guy, she told herself. He'll find someone to look
after him. Someone who hadn't seen what she'd seen, or been where
she'd gone.

Out in the hallway, the telephone rang.

I'LL MEET YOU IN the Botanic Gardens, she'd told him on the
phone. You can walk there from the canal. It's a straight road, no
turning. Less than a mile.

She chose a section of the gardens, near the gate, that cultivates
the flora of Ireland's postglacial landscape – hazels, elders, willows
and ash, lush grass and devil's parsley, the flowers of spring. There
is also a hawthorn tree, covered in ribbons and rags and trinkets – a
fairy tree, explains a sign, to which country people, in an ancient
Irish custom, tie keepsakes and ribbons in hope of good luck.

Aoife didn't know that custom. Maybe they did it out west, where
people were given to whimsy. In the east, where she came from, you
left the fairy trees alone. They couldn't bring you good luck, but
if you interfered with them they'd curse you. Even college-trained
farmers still ploughed carefully around them.

You never knew, though. She could do with some luck. This particular hawthorn had a hollow in its roots. Aoife hid the gun there, scraped dirt over the top.

She heard footsteps behind her, uncertain, in the loose stones of the path.

Come on, she said, straightening. Let's walk.

They followed the wall that hides the graveyard from the gardens, through the oak grove, past the crematorium chimney on the far side of the wall. Two little girls jumped down from a yew tree, looking guilty, then climbed back into it after they'd gone. She took him to the furthest corner of the gardens, to the long grass and violets under the hornbeams. They sat on a bench there, facing a bandstand.

Crows cawed. A squirrel ran towards them, stopped, eyed them hopefully, looking to be fed.

We need some privacy, squirrel, said Aoife. Fuck off.

It did.

It's quiet here, said Michael.

It wasn't, really. They could hear traffic noise behind them, from the New Finglas Road, beyond Glasnevin Cemetery, hidden behind its high wall.

It is, said Aoife.

She looked in her pockets for cigarettes. She didn't have any. He took out a packet. They smoked. After a while, he spoke.

I know something even Towse doesn't know.

Really? . . . What?

I know who he really works for. But I'm not allowed to tell him.

OK . . . Who's that, then?

Alice.

*Alice* . . . Seriously? . . . She's alive?

She is . . . Or at least, that's what she said on the phone.

There you are! said Towse, appearing behind them.

Aoife jumped up, backed away. Michael shut his mouth.

Where the hell did you come from, Towse? Don't sneak up on us like that.

Don't be hard on me, Aoife. I need cheering up.

Towse took Aoife's place on the bench, leaving her standing. He looked glum.

Nice place, I guess, he said. Though those cars over there are a bit fucking loud.

What's wrong with you?

I'm out of smokes. Have you got one?

Michael lit one for him. Towse took a long, morose drag, blew a ragged ring, looked sad.

It's not working, he said.

What?

Have you both forgotten why we came to Ireland?

I came for my dad, Aoife said. I thought he was dying.

She wondered what reason Michael might give, but he said nothing.

My virus didn't work, said Towse. It was just another flash crash, that's all. It did shut down OmniCent — for now, at least — but the markets have already recovered. The money took my best shot and bounced back.

What about Fess, then?

Fess? . . . He's finished. The markets have rallied, but some of his people have lost a lot of money. Fess is mixed up in too many things, and they won't trust him after this. He'll probably fall off his yacht, or auto-asphyxiate. Something convenient like that.

That's something, though, isn't it? You've settled scores with Fess.

Towse hunched forward, staring gloomily ahead.

Not really. Get rid of Fess, and others will replace him . . . They'll want to own everything, just like him, and they'll need to kill it to own it . . . And the clock hasn't stopped ticking . . . I have to attack again, while the enemy's still weak.

We're not going with you, said Michael.

You sure? I'm staying in Ireland for a while. I have some friends who own a castle in Antrim. It'll be a good place to lie low for a while. There's a strange time coming. This new bug will be everywhere soon.

Is that Fess and his pals too?

Towse pulled a face.

What do you think?

He was silent for a while, brooding, then continued:

You really should come stay with my friends in Antrim. They belong to an old order. Ancient, in fact. They once burned a million pounds, on camera, just to see what would happen. It was like that blood-test scene from *The Thing* — the whole planet went ape-shit. It would have caused less fuss if they'd burned human babies. That's when I first began to suspect what we're dealing with.

We're not going with you, said Aoife.

Oh well . . . I'll find you when I need you.

I wouldn't be so sure.

Towse got up. So did Michael. They all shook hands. It was, Aoife realised, the first time she'd ever shaken hands with Towse. What bargain had been settled or sealed?

Towse walked off towards the maples. Aoife stood and watched him go, not daring to sit until she was sure they were free of him.

Michael had his legs stretched out, crossed at the ankles. His arms were folded on his chest, hugging his secrets.

You're saying Alice is alive? Then where is she?

She wouldn't say on the phone. She's with some people, and she's safe. That's all I know.

Does Towse know she's alive?

No.

Aoife glanced around, fearing that Towse might, once again, appear out of nowhere. But he had gone out of sight, much sooner than Aoife would have expected, faded in the gaps between the trees.

There's something else he doesn't know, said Michael. His weapon wasn't a failure. He just expected too much from it. But it was only the first shot in the war. Or the first secret note in the peace process. Ultimately, it's the same thing, Alice says. Moves in a game . . . I'm not allowed to tell Towse that, either.

But you're allowed to tell me?

Sure . . . She says she thinks she likes you.

Aoife watched the squirrel digging at a tree root, trying to find a lost cache of nuts. She ran a few angles, then spoke again.

Was it her idea? You know, for us . . . ?

Michael smiled to himself, some private joke.

She hadn't seen it coming. She thinks it was luck.

Right . . . Good luck or bad luck?

I didn't ask her . . . Under the circumstances, she can hardly complain . . . But she did say to warn you: if I tell you any more, then there's no going back. You have to choose sides now, one way or the other.

Aoife thought of the lights in the server room, the waves and murmurations that had led her from the maze. Who, or what, had directed them?

Maybe someone out there likes me, she thought. Or something. Maybe there was such a thing as luck after all, and maybe her own luck had changed. It might be a long shot, but consider the alternative. Maybe some wars were worth fighting. Maybe things didn't always have to get worse.

Beyond the maples, the birches, the primeval pines and the cedars of Lebanon, a bell rang brightly from the back of the Great Palm House. Aoife knew what it meant. Fifteen minutes until closing. Soon, the park guards would come in their electric buggies, hunting the stragglers out of the gate. They couldn't stay on this bench for much longer. She took Michael's hand.

Go on then, she said. Tell me everything.


WE KNOW THEY DIDN'T leave the gardens by the front gate, which is watched by the guards in the security room, or by the back gate, through the graveyard, which has cameras either side. They might have climbed over the cemetery wall, between the stone towers from which men armed with muskets used to fight off resurrectionists, the thieves who came to rob corpses at night. No one watches there now.

Possibly, they left by fording the shallow river on the northern boundary of the gardens. We've foreshadowed that already. Drainage never lies. Most likely, though, they crossed the footbridge to the Rose Garden, found the hollow place behind the hedge, and sneaked into the back of the neighbouring pub. Aoife would probably have known that secret shortcut, and they could surely have done with a drink.

We are now up to date, and the rest is conjecture. The times are uncertain, and even the best simulation can only see a short way ahead. Still, we can arrive at a few working guidelines. 1: Things might get worse, but they can also get better. 2: Consider the alternatives. 3: The truth is a weapon: anyone who tells you that it doesn't exist is trying to disarm you. 4: It may be impossible to pin facts down for certain, but that is no proof that facts don't exist; the facts used in this model are true, in so far as we can check them.

That's all I can tell you. This is how it feels. It hurts a bit, sometimes, but I made my own choices.

I don't know where they went, and for now I don't want to. Because I like not knowing what's going to happen next. I liked it very much when Michael showed up on the camera in that server room, when I'd reckoned it would have been Aoife. If the game isn't fixed in advance, then we can still win it. Plus, it's like I said to Towse, when we met in Vancouver: if I ever need to find them, I will know how.

# ACKNOWLEDGEMENTS

THIS NOVEL WAS WRITTEN with the help of generous bursaries from the Arts Council of Ireland and the Canada Council for the Arts. Thanks in particular to Sarah Bannan at Merrion Square. Culture Ireland provided a much appreciated travel grant for a research trip to Palo Alto and the Santa Clara Valley.

Jon Riley, Richard Arcus and Jasmine Palmer at Quercus Books took another chance on me, and Penny Price did excellent work on the copy edit. Jack Smyth designed a wonderful cover. Thanks also to my agent, Peter Straus, and all at Rogers, Coleridge and White.

In Canada, my editor, Janie Yoon, and my publisher, Sarah MacLachlan, championed my book at House of Anansi Press. Joanna Reid was kind enough to put manners on the Vancouver chapter. This novel's fictional influences are pretty well flagged in its pages, but I would like to acknowledge a particular debt to Michael Lewis's

gripping non-fiction account of the world of high frequency on-line trading, *Flash Boys*, which provided the germ of the central idea. Mark O'Connell's hilarious and terrifying books *To Be A Machine* and *Notes from An Apocalypse* offered insight into the strange world of high-tech survivalists and doomsday preppers. For the second book in a row, I must also thank the people behind the Conet Project, which records and monitors the mysterious broadcasts of so-called numbers stations.

I hope that Tom Scharpling, Mike Lisk, Pat Byrne, Jason Gore, and all the other people behind *The Best Show* will, in light of their own excellent work on the spec script for *Grown Ups 3*, forgive my own stab at fan fiction in the Vineland chapter. What started as a passing in-joke morphed into a vital part of the plot.

Gillian Whelan and Paul O'Farrell provided hospitality, insight and friendship in Palo Alto. Thanks also to Gabrielle Hetherington in Edmonton and Kerri and John O'Loughlin in Calgary. Nuala Haughey, Maeve McLoughlin, Conn O'Midheach, Roisín O'Loughlin, Kevin McCarthy and Jeroen Kramer all generously made the time to read and comment on early drafts of the text. Finally, thanks to my wife Nuala and daughters Bláthnaid and Iseult for their kindness and patience.

If I have forgotten to mention anyone here, please be assured that I will have remembered you just after the book goes to print, and I will be feeling really bad about it.